MARTIN BECK MYSTERIES

THE MARTIN BECK MYSTERY SERIES

by

MAJ SJÖWALL and

PER WAHLÖÖ

Roseanna
The Man Who Went Up in Smoke
The Man on the Balcony
The Laughing Policeman
The Fire Engine That Disappeared
Murder at the Savoy
The Abominable Man
The Locked Room
Cop Killer
The Terrorists

MARTIN BECK MYSTERIES:

ROSEANNA

THE MAN WHO WENT UP IN SMOKE

by

MAJ SJÖWALL AND PER WAHLÖÖ

Mystery Guild
GARDEN CITY, NEW YORK

CONTENTS

ROSEANNA

INTRODUCTION

I read *Roseanna* almost as soon as it came out, back in 1965.
Now, as I'm reading the novel again, I realize that my first reading took place forty years ago and I was only seventeen at the time. Right now that seems to me incomprehensible. How many books have I read since then? And why is it that I remember *Roseanna* so well? I have a strong and indisputable memory that back then I thought of the novel as straightforward and clear, a convincing story presented in an equally convincing form. Today, as I reread the novel, I see that my first impression still holds true. The book has hardly aged at all. Even the language seems energetic and alive. But what *has* changed is the world, and I have too. Back then everybody smoked all the time, and there were no mobile phones; public telephones were in use. Everyone went to cafés for lunch, no one had tiny tape recorders in their pockets, and computers were still practically unknown. Sweden was still a society with closer ties to the past than to the future. The huge waves of immigrants hadn't yet begun. Workers arrived to take jobs in certain major industries, but as yet there was no steady influx of refugees. And everyone showed their passports at the border, even those traveling only to Norway or Denmark.

Per Wahlöö has now been dead for many years, while Maj Sjöwall has grown older along with me and all the readers they reached a generation ago. Now I'm rereading the novel *Roseanna* on a December day forty years after its first publication. I've forgotten a great deal, of course, but the novel still stands strong. It's well thought-out, well structured. It's evident that Sjöwall and Wahlöö had carefully laid the groundwork for their plan to write ten books about the National Homicide Bureau—in fictional form but based on reality.

The aim is quite clear. From the very first pages of the novel, for instance, the authors present a thorough examination of the joint decision-making process of various agencies as they organize the dredging of a sludge-filled area of the Göta Canal. This desire to be as thorough as possible continues throughout the entire novel. The intent of the authors is evident—they build up a trust in their readers by presenting meticulous and credible descriptions of various institutions and structures within Swedish society, as it was in the mid-1960s. A country in which Tage Erlander was the prime minister, and cars still drove on the left-hand side of the road.

There is one small detail on the second page of the novel that fascinates me when I see it again. The story begins in early July, with the date clearly specified. A dredging boat has arrived at the canal in Östergötland. The authors write: "The vessel . . . moored at Borenshult as the neighborhood children and a Vietnamese tourist looked on." A Vietnamese tourist! In Sweden in 1965! That may have happened once, at most. But here the authors are giving a nod to the major event of my generation, the Vietnam War. It was the period in Sweden's postwar history when the world had begun to open up. This is worth pointing out, since the authors had a radical purpose in mind for the books they were planning about the National Homicide Bureau. They wanted to use crime and criminal investigations as a mirror of Swedish society—and later on include the rest of the world. Their intent was never to write crime stories as a form of entertainment. They were influenced and inspired by the American writer Ed McBain. They realized that there was a huge unexplored territory in which crime novels could form the framework for stories containing social criticism.

I can't even count how many times I've been asked what Sjöwall and Wahlöö's books have meant to me. I think that anyone who writes about crime as a reflection of society has been inspired to some extent by what they wrote. They broke with the previous trends in crime fiction. In Sweden Stieg Trenter dominated the market in the 1950s, along with Maria Lang and H. K. Rönnblom. They wrote detective stories in which solving the mystery was the main concern. In Trenter's books, the streets, pubs, and food are all described in great detail, but the setting is merely the setting—there is never any direct, real-life connection between the crime and the place where it occurred. The British-style detective novel was the dominant form until the publication of *Roseanna*. Of particular importance was the fact that Sjöwall and Wahlöö broke with the hopelessly stereotyped character descriptions that were so prevalent. They showed people evolving right before the reader's eyes.

Before 1965 I had read several of Per Wahlöö's novels. I recall especially *The Lorry*, which was set in fascist Spain. He wrote well, using a straightforward and simple language that gave his story a certain force. I liked what I read. But the publication of *Roseanna* signaled something different. I don't know exactly what it meant for Maj Sjöwall to become his collaborator, except that she must have been a source of great inspiration. I have a clear memory that I went back and reread *Roseanna* after a couple of weeks. I can't remember ever having done that before.

Per Wahlöö and Maj Sjöwall have said that they did find inspiration for their work in the United States. I've already mentioned Ed McBain. But I suspect that they most likely sought inspiration farther back in time, at least as far back as Edgar Allan Poe in the nineteenth century. Many consider Poe's stories from the mid-1800s to be the basis for modern crime fiction. I don't agree. This seems to indicate a serious lack of understanding even today, because the roots of crime fiction go back much farther. Read the classic Greek dramas! What are they about? People and society tangled up in hostilities which lead to violence, crime, and punishment. And there is also an element of crime writing mirrored in the works of Shakespeare. Of course there aren't any police, but there are investigations, analyses, and attempts to understand who and what lie behind certain brutal crimes. We are continuing traditions, whether we're conscious of doing so or not.

In many ways *Roseanna* is an incredibly fascinating book. I don't intend to discuss the plot or the resolution of the crime, but let me say that it's probably one of the first crime novels in which *time* clearly plays a major role. There are long periods during which nothing happens, when the investigation into who murdered Roseanna and threw her in the Göta Canal seems to be standing still; then it may move a few centimeters before coming to a halt again. It's quite clear that for Martin Beck and his colleagues, the passage of time is both frustrating and a necessary evil. Homicide investigators who have no patience lack a key tool. It takes six months before the crime is solved. By then we, as readers, know that it could just as well have taken five years, but the police would not have given up. The book describes the fundamental virtue of the police: patience.

I haven't counted how many times Martin Beck feels sick in *Roseanna*, but it happens a lot. He can't eat breakfast because he doesn't feel good. Cigarettes and train rides make him sick. His personal life also makes him ill. In *Roseanna* the homicide investigators emerge as ordinary human beings. There is nothing at all heroic about them. They do their job, and they get sick. I no longer remember how I reacted forty years ago, but I think it was a revelation to see such real people as police officers in *Roseanna*.

And the book still holds up today. It's lively, stylistically taut, and the unfolding of the story is skillfully planned.

Of course it's a modern classic. It was the first one in the series of ten books that Maj Sjöwall and Per Wahlöö had planned. And even with their very first book, they hit the mark.

—*Henning Mankell*

1

They found the corpse on the eighth of July just after three o'clock in the afternoon. It was fairly well intact and couldn't have been lying in the water very long.

Actually, it was mere chance that they found the body at all. And finding it so quickly should have aided the police investigation.

Below the locks at Borenshult there is a breakwater which protects the entrance to the lake from the east wind. When the canal opened for traffic that spring, the channel had begun to clog up. The boats had a hard time maneuvering and their propellers churned up thick clouds of yellowish mud from the bottom. It wasn't hard to see that something had to be done. As early as May, the Canal Company requisitioned a dredging machine from the Civil Engineering Board. The papers were passed from one perplexed civil servant to another and finally remitted to the Swedish National Shipping and Navigation Administration. The Shipping and Navigation Administration thought that the work should be done by one of the Civil Engineering Board's bucket dredging machines. But the Civil Engineering Board found that the Shipping and Navigation Administration had control over bucket dredging machines and in desperation made an appeal to the Harbor Commission in Norrköping, which immediately returned the papers to the Shipping and Navigation Administration, which remitted them to the Civil Engineering Board, at which point someone picked up the telephone and dialed an engineer who knew all about bucket dredging machines. He knew that of the five existing bucket dredgers, there was only one that could pass through the locks. The vessel was called *The Pig* and happened just then to be lying in the fishing harbor at Gravarne. On the morning of July 5 *The Pig* arrived and moored at Borenshult as the neighborhood children and a Vietnamese tourist looked on.

One hour later a representative of the Canal Company went on board to discuss the project. That took the whole afternoon. The next day was a Saturday and the vessel remained by the breakwater while the men went home for the weekend. The crew consisted of a dredging foreman, who was also the officer in command with the authority to take the vessel to sea, an excavating engineer, and a deck man. The latter two men were from Gothenburg and took the night train from Motala. The skipper lived in Nacka and his wife came to get him in their car. At seven o'clock on Monday morning all three were on board again and one hour later they began to dredge. By eleven o'clock the hold was full and the dredger went out into the lake to dump. On the way back they had to lay off and wait while a white steamboat approached the Boren locks in a westerly direction. Foreign tourists crowded along the vessel's railing and waved excitedly at the working crew on the dredger. The passenger boat was elevated slowly up the locks toward Motala and Lake Vättern and by lunch time its top pennant had disappeared in back of the uppermost sluice gate. At one-thirty the men began to dredge again.

The situation was this: the weather was warm and beautiful with mild temperate winds and idly moving summer clouds. There were some people on the breakwater and on the edge of the canal. Most of them were sunning themselves, a few were fishing, and two or three were watching the dredging activity. The dredger's bucket had just gobbled up a new mouthful of Boren's bottom slime and was on its way up out of the water. The excavating engineer was operating the familiar handgrips in his cabin. The dredging foreman was having a cup of coffee in the galley, and the deck man stood with his elbows on the railing and spit in the water. The bucket was still on the way up.

As it broke through the surface of the water, a man on the pier took a few steps toward the boat. He waved his arms and shouted something. The deck man looked up to hear better.

"There's someone in the bucket! Stop! Someone's lying in the bucket!"

The confused deck man looked first at the man and then

at the bucket which slowly swung in over the hold to spit out its contents. Filthy gray water streamed out of the bucket as it hung over the hold. Then the deck man saw what the man on the breakwater had seen. A white, naked arm stuck out of the bucket's jaw.

The next ten minutes seemed endless and chaotic. Someone stood on the pier and said, over and over again: "Don't do anything; don't touch anything; leave everything alone until the police come . . ."

The excavating engineer came out to see what was going on. He stared, then hurried back to the relative security of his seat behind the levers. As he let the crane swing and the bucket open, the dredging foreman and the deck man took out the body.

It was a woman. They laid her on her back on a folded tarpaulin out on the breakwater. A group of amazed people gathered around and stared at her. Some of them were children and shouldn't have been there but no one thought to send them away. But all of them had one thing in common: they would never forget how she looked.

The deck man had thrown three buckets of water over her. Long afterwards, when the police inquiry was bogged down, there were people who criticized him for this.

She was naked and had no jewelry on. The lines of her tan made it apparent that she had sunbathed in a bikini. Her hips were broad and she had heavy thighs. Her pubic hair was black and wet and thick. Her breasts were small and slack with large, dark nipples. A red scratch ran from her waist to her hipbone. The rest of her skin was smooth without spots or scars. She had small hands and feet and her nails were not polished. Her face was swollen and it was hard to imagine how she had actually looked alive. She had thick, dark eyebrows and her mouth seemed wide. Her medium-length hair was dark and lay flat on her head. A coil of hair lay across her throat.

2

Motala is a medium-sized Swedish city in the province of Östergötland at the northern end of Lake Vättern. It has a population of 27,000. Its highest police authority is a Commissioner of Police who is also the Public Prosecutor. He has a Police Superintendent under him who is the chief executive of both the regular police constabulary and the criminal police. His staff also includes a First Detective Inspector in the ninth salary grade, six policemen and one policewoman. One of the policemen is a trained photographer and when medical examinations are needed they usually fall back on one of the city's doctors.

One hour after the first alarm, several of these people had gathered on the pier at Borenshult, several yards from the harbor light. It was rather crowded around the corpse and the men on the dredger could no longer see what was happening. They were still on board in spite of the fact that the vessel was prepared to make way with its port bow against the breakwater.

The number of people behind the police barricade on the abutment had increased tenfold. On the other side of the canal there were several cars, four of which belonged to the police, and a white-painted ambulance with red crosses on the back doors. Two men in white overalls leaned against a fender smoking. They seemed to be the only people who weren't interested in the group out by the harbor light.

On the breakwater the doctor began to gather his things together. He chatted with the Superintendent who was a tall, gray-haired man named Larsson.

"There isn't much I can say about it now," said the doctor.

"Does she have to remain lying here?" Larsson asked.

"Isn't that more your business," replied the doctor.

"This is hardly the scene of the crime."

"Okay," the doctor agreed, "See that they drive her to the mortuary. I'll telephone ahead."

He shut his bag and left.

The Superintendent turned and called, "Ahlberg, You're going to keep the area blocked off, aren't you?"

"Yes, damn it."

The Commissioner of Police hadn't said anything out by the harbor light. He didn't usually enter investigations in the early stages. But on the way in to town, he said: "You'll keep me informed."

Larsson didn't even bother to nod.

"You'll keep Ahlberg on it?"

"Ahlberg's a good man," said the Superintendent.

"Yes, of course."

The conversation ended. They arrived, left the car and went into their separate offices. The Commissioner placed a telephone call to the County Authority in Linköping who merely said: "I'll be waiting to hear from you."

The Superintendent had a short conversation with Ahlberg. "We have to find out who she is."

"Yes," said Ahlberg.

He went into his office, called the Fire Department and requisitioned two frogmen. Then he read through a report on a burglary in the harbor. That one would be cleared up soon. Ahlberg got up and went to the officer on duty.

"Is there anyone reported missing?"

"No."

"No notification of missing persons?"

"None that fit."

He went back to his office and waited.

The call came after fifteen minutes.

"We have to ask for an autopsy," said the doctor.

"Was she strangled?"

"I think so."

"Raped?"

"I think so."

The doctor paused a second. Then he said: "And pretty methodically, too."

Ahlberg bit on his index fingernail. He thought of his

vacation which was to begin on Friday and how happy his wife was about it.

The doctor misinterpreted the silence.

"Are you surprised?"

"No," said Ahlberg.

He hung up and went into Larsson's office. Then they went to the Commissioner's office together.

Ten minutes later the Commissioner asked for a medico-legal post-mortem examination from the County Administrator who contacted the Government Institute for Forensic Medicine. The autopsy was conducted by a seventy year old professor. He came on the night train from Stockholm and seemed bright and cheerful. He conducted the autopsy in eight hours, almost without a break.

Then he left a preliminary report with the following wording: "Death by strangulation in conjunction with gross sexual assault. Severe inner bleeding."

By that time the records of the inquiry and reports had already begun to accumulate on Ahlberg's desk. They could be summed up in one sentence: a dead woman had been found in the lock chamber at Borenshult.

No one had been reported missing in the city or in neighboring police districts. There was no description of any such missing person.

3

It was a quarter after five in the morning and it was raining. Martin Beck took more time brushing his teeth than usual to get rid of the taste of lead in his mouth.

He buttoned his collar, tied his tie and looked listlessly at his face in the mirror. He shrugged his shoulders and went out into the hall, continued on through the living room, glanced longingly at the half-finished model of the training ship *Danmark*, on which he had worked until the late hours the night before, and went into the kitchen.

He moved quietly and softly, partly from habit and partly not to wake the children.

He sat down at the kitchen table.

"Hasn't the newspaper come yet?" he said.

"It never comes before six," his wife answered.

It was completely light outside but overcast. The daylight in the kitchen was gray and soupy. His wife hadn't turned on the lights. She called that saving.

He opened his mouth but closed it again without saying anything. There would only be an argument and this wasn't the moment for it. Instead he drummed slowly with his fingers on the formica table top. He looked at the empty cup with its blue rose pattern and a chip in the rim and a brown crack down from the notch. That cup had hung on for almost the duration of their marriage. More than ten years. She rarely broke anything, in any case not irreparably. The odd part of it was that the children were the same.

Could such qualities be inherited? He didn't know.

She took the coffee pot from the stove and filled his cup. He stopped drumming on the table.

"Don't you want a sandwich?" she asked.

He drank carefully with small gulps. He was sitting slightly round-shouldered at the end of the table.

"You really ought to eat something," she insisted.

"You know I can't eat in the morning."

"You ought to in any case," she said. "Especially you, with your stomach."

He rubbed his fingers over his cheek and felt some places he'd missed with his razor. He drank some coffee.

"I can make some toast," she suggested.

Five minutes later he placed his cup on the saucer, moved it away without a sound, and looked up at his wife.

She had on a fluffy red bathrobe over a nylon nightgown and she sat with her elbows on the table, supporting her chin with her hands. She was blond, with fair skin and round, slightly popping eyes. She usually darkened her eyebrows but they had paled during the summer and were now nearly as light as her hair. She was a few years older than he and in spite of the fact that she had gained a good deal of weight in the last few years, the skin on her throat was beginning to sag a little.

She had given up her job in an architect's office when their daughter was born twelve years ago and since then had not thought about working again. When the boy started school, Martin Beck had suggested she look for some part-time work, but she had figured it would hardly pay. Besides, she was comfortable with her own nature and pleased with her role as a housewife.

"Oh, yes," thought Martin Beck and got up. He placed the blue-painted stool under the table quietly and stood by the window looking out at the drizzle.

Down below the parking place and lawn, the highway lay smooth and empty. Not many windows were lighted in the apartments on the hill in back of the subway station. A few seagulls circled under the low, gray sky. Otherwise there was not another living thing to be seen.

"Where are you going?" she said.

"Motala."

"Will you be gone long?"

"I don't know."

"Is it that girl?"

"Yes."

"Do you *think* you'll be gone long?"

"I don't know any more about it than you do. Only what I've seen in the newspapers."

"Why do you have to take the train?"

"The others took off yesterday. I wasn't supposed to go along."

"They'll drive with you, of course, as usual?"

He took a patient breath and gazed outside. The rain was letting up.

"Where will you stay?"

"The City Hotel."

"Who will be with you?"

"Kollberg and Melander. They went yesterday."

"By car?"

"Yes."

"And you have to sit and get shaken up on the train?"

"Yes."

Behind him he heard her washing the cup with the chip in the rim and the blue roses.

"I have to pay the electric bill and also Little One's riding lessons this week."

"Don't you have enough money for that?"

"I don't want to take it out of the bank, you know that."

"No, of course not."

He took his wallet out of his inner pocket and looked into it. Took out a 50 crown note, looked at it, put it back and placed the wallet back in his pocket.

"I hate to draw out money," she said. "It's the beginning of the end when you start that."

He took the bill out again, folded it, turned around and laid it on the kitchen table.

"I've packed your bag, Martin."

"Thanks."

"Take care of your throat. This is a treacherous time of the year, particularly the evenings."

"Yes."

"Are you going to take that awful pistol with you?"

"Yes, no. Yes, no. What's the difference?" Martin Beck thought to himself.

"What are you laughing at?" she asked.

"Nothing."

He went into the living room, unlocked a drawer in the secretary and took out the pistol. He put it in his suitcase and locked the drawer again.

The pistol was an ordinary 7.6 millimeter Walther, licensed in Sweden. It was useless in most situations and he was a pretty poor shot anyway.

He went out into the hall, put on his trenchcoat, and stood with his dark hat in his hands.

"Aren't you going to say goodbye to Rolf and the Little One?"

"It's ridiculous to call a twelve year old girl 'Little One.'"

"I think it's sweet."

"It's a shame to wake them. And anyway, they know that I am going."

He put his hat on.

"So long. I'll call you."

"Bye bye, and be careful."

He stood on the platform and waited for the subway and thought that he really didn't mind leaving home in spite of the half-finished planking on the model of the training ship *Danmark*.

Martin Beck wasn't chief of the Homicide Squad and had no such ambitions. Sometimes he doubted if he would ever make superintendent although the only things that could actually stand in his way were death or some very serious error in his duties. He was a First Detective Inspector with the National Police and had been with the Homicide Bureau for eight years. There were people who thought that he was the country's most capable examining officer.

He had been on the police force half of his life. At the age of twenty-one he had begun at Jakob Police Station and after six years as a patrol officer in different districts in central Stockholm, he was sent to the National Police College. He was one of the best in his class and when the course was finished he was appointed a Detective Inspector. He was twenty-eight years old at the time.

His father had died that year and he moved from his furnished room in the middle of the city back to the family home in southern Stockholm to take care of his mother. That summer he met his wife. She had rented a cottage with a friend out in the archipelago where he happened to be with his sailing canoe. He fell very much in love. Then, in the autumn, when they were expecting a child, they got married at City Hall and moved to her small apartment back in the city.

One year after the birth of their daughter, there wasn't much left of the happy and lively girl he had fallen in love with and their marriage had slipped into a fairly dull routine.

Martin Beck sat on the green bench in the subway car and looked out through the rain-blurred window. He thought about his marriage apathetically, but when he realized that he was sitting there feeling sorry for himself, he took his newspaper out of his trenchcoat pocket and tried to concentrate on the editorial page.

He looked tired and his sunburned skin seemed yellowish in the gray light. His face was lean with a broad forehead and a strong jaw. His mouth, under his short, straight nose, was thin and wide with two deep lines near the corners. When he smiled, you could see his healthy, white teeth. His dark hair was combed straight back from the even hairline and had not yet begun to gray. The look in his soft blue eyes was clear and calm. He was thin but not especially tall and somewhat round-shouldered. Some women would say he was good looking but most of them would see him as quite ordinary. He dressed in a way that would draw no attention. If anything, his clothes were a little too discreet.

The air in the train was close and stuffy and he felt slightly uncomfortable as he usually did when he was on the subway. When they arrived at Central Station, he was the first one at the door with his suitcase in his hand.

He disliked the subway. But since he cared even less for bumper-to-bumper automobile traffic, and that 'dream apartment' in the center of the city was still only a dream, he had no choice at the moment.

The express to Gothenburg left the station at 7:30 p.m. Martin Beck thumbed through his newspaper but didn't see a line about the murder. He turned back to the cultural pages and began to read an article on the anthroposophist Rudolf Steiner but fell asleep in a few minutes.

He awoke in good time to change trains at Hallsberg. The lead taste in his mouth had come back and stayed with him despite the three glasses of water that he drank.

He arrived in Motala at 10:30 p.m. and by then the rain

had stopped. Since it was his first visit there, he asked at the kiosk in the station the way to the City Hotel and bought a pack of cigarettes and the Motala newspaper.

The hotel was on the main square only a few blocks from the railroad station. The short walk stimulated him. Up in his room he washed his hands, unpacked, and drank a bottle of mineral water which he got from the porter. He stood by the window for a moment and looked out over the square. It had a statue in the center which he guessed was of Baltzar von Platen. Then he left the room to go to the police station. Since he knew it was right across the street, he left his trenchcoat in the room.

He told the officer on duty who he was and was immediately shown to an office on the second floor. The name Ahlberg was on the door.

The man sitting behind the desk was broad and thick-set and slightly bald. His jacket was on the back of his chair and he was drinking coffee out of a container. A cigarette was burning on the corner of an ash tray which was already filled with butts.

Martin Beck had a way of slinking through a door which irritated a number of people. Someone once said that he was able to slip into a room and close the door behind him so quickly that it seemed as if he were still knocking on the outside.

The man behind the desk seemed slightly surprised. He pushed his coffee container away and got up.

"My name is Ahlberg," he said.

There was something expectant in his manner. Martin Beck had seen the same thing before and knew what this sprang from. He was the expert from Stockholm and the man behind the desk was a country policeman who had come to a standstill on an investigation. The next few minutes would be decisive for their cooperation.

"What's your first name?" said Martin Beck.

"Gunnar."

"What are Kollberg and Melander doing?"

"I have no idea. Something I've forgotten, I suspect."

"Did they have that we'll-settle-this-thing-in-a-flash look?"

The local policeman ran his fingers through his thin blond hair. Then he smiled wryly and took to his familiar chair.

"Just about," he said.

Martin Beck sat down opposite him, drew out a pack of cigarettes and laid it on the edge of the desk.

"You look tired," Martin Beck stated.

"My vacation got shot to hell."

Ahlberg emptied the container of coffee, crumpled it and threw it into the wastebasket under the desk.

The disorder on his desk was remarkable. Martin Beck thought about his own desk in Stockholm. It was usually quite neat.

"Well," he said. "How goes it?"

"Not at all," said Ahlberg. "After more than a week we don't know anything more than what the doctor has told us."

Out of habit he went on to the routine procedures.

"Put to death by strangulation in conjunction with sexual assault. The culprit was brutal. Signs of perverse tendencies."

Martin Beck smiled. Ahlberg looked at him questioningly.

"You said 'put to death.' I say it myself sometimes. We've written too many reports."

"Yeah, isn't it hell?"

Ahlberg sighed and ran his fingers through his hair.

"We brought her up eight days ago," he said. "We haven't learned a thing since then. We don't know who she is, we don't know the scene of the crime, and we have no suspects. We haven't found a single thing that could have any real connection with her."

4

"Death by strangulation," thought Martin Beck.

He sat and thumbed through a bunch of photographs which Ahlberg had dug out of a basket on his desk. The pictures showed the locks, the dredger, its bucket in the foreground, the body lying on the embankment, and in the mortuary.

Martin Beck placed a photo in front of Ahlberg and said:

"We can have this picture cropped and retouched so that she looks presentable. Then we can begin knocking on doors. If she comes from around here someone ought to recognize her. How many men can you put on the job?"

"Three at most," said Ahlberg. "We're short of men right now. Three of the boys are on vacation and one of them is in the hospital with a broken leg. Other than the Superintendent, Larsson and myself, there are only eight men at the station."

He counted on his fingers.

"Yes, and one of them is a woman. Then too, someone has to take care of the other work."

"We'll have to help if worst comes to worst. It's going to take a hell of a lot of time. Have you had any trouble with sex criminals lately by the way?"

Ahlberg tapped his pen against his front teeth while he was thinking. Then he reached into his desk drawer and dug up a paper.

"We had one in for examination. From Västra Ny, a rapist. He was caught in Linköping the day before yesterday but he had an alibi for the entire week, according to this report from Blomgren. He's checking out the institutions."

Ahlberg placed the paper in a green file which lay on his desk.

They sat quietly for a minute. Martin Beck was hungry. He thought about his wife and her chatter about regular meals. He hadn't eaten for twenty-four hours.

The air in the room was thick with cigarette smoke. Ahlberg got up and opened the window. They could hear a time signal from a radio somewhere in the vicinity.

"It's one o'clock," he said. "If you're hungry I can send out for something. I'm as hungry as a bear."

Martin Beck nodded and Ahlberg picked up the telephone. After a while there was a knock at the door and a girl in a blue dress and a red apron came in with a basket.

After Martin Beck had eaten a ham sandwich and had a few swallows of coffee, he said:

"How do you think she got there?"

"I don't know. During the day there are always a lot of people at the locks so it could hardly have happened then. He could have thrown her in from the pier or the embankment and then later the backwash from the boats' propellers might have moved her further out. Or maybe she was thrown overboard from some vessel."

"What kind of boats go through the locks? Small boats and pleasure craft?"

"Some. Not so terribly many. Most of them are freighters. And then there are the canal boats, of course, the *Diana*, the *Juno* and the *Wilhelm Tham*."

"Can we drive down there and take a look?" asked Martin Beck.

Ahlberg got up, took the photograph that Martin Beck had chosen, and said: "We can get going right away. I'll leave this at the lab on the way out."

It was almost three o'clock when they returned from Borenshult. The traffic in the locks was lively and Martin Beck had wanted to stay there among the vacationers and the fishermen on the pier to watch the boats.

He had spoken with the crew of the dredger, been out on the embankment and looked at the system of locks. He had seen a sailing canoe cruising in the fresh breeze far out in the water and had begun to long for his own canoe which he had sold several years ago. During the trip back to town he sat thinking about sailing in the archipelago in summers past.

There were eight, fresh copies of the picture from the photo laboratory lying on Ahlberg's desk when they returned. One of the policemen, who was also a photographer, had re-touched the picture and the girl's face looked almost as if she had been photographed alive.

Ahlberg looked through them, laid four of the copies in the green folder and said:

"Fine. I'll pass these out to the boys so that they can get started immediately."

When he came back after a few minutes Martin Beck was standing next to the desk rubbing his nose.

"I'd like to make a few telephone calls," he said.

"Use the office farthest down the corridor."

The room was larger than Ahlberg's and had windows on two walls. It was furnished with two desks, five chairs, a filing cabinet and a typewriter table with a disgracefully old Remington.

Martin Beck sat down, placed his cigarettes and matches on the table, put down the green folder and began to go through the reports. They didn't tell him much more than he had already learned from Ahlberg.

An hour and a half later he ran out of cigarettes. He had placed a few telephone calls without result and had talked to the Commissioner and to Superintendent Larsson who seemed tired and pressed. Just as he had crumpled the empty cigarette package, Kollberg called.

Ten minutes later they met at the hotel.

"God, you look dismal," Kollberg said. "Do you want a cig-arette?"

"No thank you. What have you been doing?"

"I've been talking to a guy from the *Motala Times*. A local ed-itor in Borensberg. He thought he had found something. A girl from Linköping was to have started a new job in Borensborg ten days ago but she never arrived. She was thought to have left Linköping the day before and since then, no one has heard from her. No one thought to report her missing since she was generally unreliable. This newspaperman knew her employer and started making his own inquiries but never bothered to get a description of her. But I did. And it isn't the same girl. This one was fat and blond. She's still missing. It took me the entire day."

He leaned back in his chair and picked his teeth with a match.

"What do we do now?"

"Ahlberg has sent out a few of his boys to knock on doors. You ought to give them a hand. When Melander gets here we'll have a run through with the Commissioner and Larsson. Go over to Ahlberg and he'll tell you what to do."

Kollberg straightened his chair and got up.

"Are you coming too?" he asked.

"No, not now. Tell Ahlberg that I'm in my room if he wants anything."

When he got to his room Martin Beck took off his jacket, shoes, and tie and sat down on the edge of the bed.

The weather had cleared and white puffs of cloud moved across the sky. The afternoon sun shone into the room.

Martin Beck got up, opened the window a little, and closed the thin, yellow drapes. Then he lay down on the bed with his hands folded under his head.

He thought about the girl who had been pulled out of Boren's bottom mud.

When he closed his eyes he saw her before him as she looked in the picture, naked and abandoned, with narrow shoulders and her dark hair in a coil across her throat.

Who was she? What had she thought? How had she lived? Whom had she met?

She was young and he was sure that she had been pretty. She must have had someone who loved her. Someone close to her who was wondering what had happened to her. She must have had friends, colleagues, parents, maybe sisters and brothers. No human being, particularly a young, attractive woman, is so alone that there is no one to miss her when she disappears.

Martin Beck thought about this for a long time. No one had inquired about her. He felt sorry for the girl whom no one missed. He couldn't understand why. Maybe she had said that she was going away? If so, it might be a long time before someone wondered where she was.

The question was: how long?

5

It was eleven-thirty in the morning and Martin Beck's third day in Motala. He had gotten up early but accomplished nothing by it. Now he was sitting at the small desk thumbing through his notebook. He had reached for the telephone a few times, thinking that he really ought to call home, but nothing had come of the idea.

Just like so many other things.

He put on his hat, locked the door to his room, and walked down the stairs. The easy chairs in the hotel lobby were occupied by several journalists and two camera cases with folded tripods, bound by straps, lay on the floor. One of the press photographers stood leaning against the wall near the entrance smoking a cigarette. He was a very young man and he moved his cigarette to the corner of his mouth and raised his Leica to look through the viewer.

When Martin Beck went past the group he drew his hat down over his face, ducked his head against his shoulder and walked straight ahead. This was merely a reflex action but it always seemed to irritate someone because one of the reporters said, surprisingly sourly:

"Say, will there be a dinner with the leaders of the search this evening?"

Martin Beck mumbled something without even knowing what he had said himself and continued toward the door. The second before he had opened the door, he heard the little click which indicated that the photographer had taken a picture.

He walked quickly down the street, but only until he thought he was out of the range of the camera. Then he stopped and stood there indecisively for about ten seconds. He threw a half-smoked cigarette into the gutter, shrugged his shoulders and walked over to a taxi stand. He slumped into the back seat, rubbed the tip of his nose with his right index finger, and peered over toward the hotel. From under his hat brim he saw the man who had spoken to him in the lobby. The journalist stood directly in front of the hotel and stared after the taxi. But only for a moment. Then he, too, shrugged his shoulders and went back into the hotel.

Press people and personnel from the Homicide Division of the National Police often stayed at the same hotel. After a speedy and successful solution to a crime, they often spent the last evening eating and drinking together. Over the years this had become a custom. Martin Beck didn't like it but several of his colleagues thought otherwise.

Even though he hadn't been on his own very much, he had still learned a little about Motala during the forty-eight hours he had been there. At least he knew the names of the streets. He watched the street signs as the taxi drove by them. He told the driver to stop at the bridge, paid him, and stepped out. He stood with his hands on the railing and looked along the canal. While he stood there he realized that he had forgotten to ask the driver to give him a receipt for the fare and that there would probably be some kind of idiotic nonsense back at the office if he were to make one out himself. It would be best to type out the information, it would give more substance to his request.

He was still thinking about that as he walked along the path on the north side of the canal.

During the morning hours there had been a few rain showers and the air was fresh and light. He stopped, right in the middle of the path, and felt how fresh it was. He drank in the cool, clean odor of wild flowers and wet grass. It reminded him of his childhood, but that was before tobacco smoke, gasoline odors and mucus had robbed his senses of their sharpness. Nowadays it wasn't often he had this pleasure.

Martin Beck had passed the five locks and continued along the sea wall. Several small boats were moored near the locks and by the breakwater, and a few small sailboats could be seen out in the open water. One hundred and fifty feet beyond the jetty, the dredger's bucket clanged and clattered under the watchful eye of some seagulls who were flying in wide, low circles. Their heads moved from one side to the other as they waited for whatever the bucket might bring up from the bottom. Their powers of observation and their patience were admirable, as was their staying power and optimism. They reminded Martin Beck of Kollberg and Melander.

He walked to the end of the breakwater and stood there for a while. She had been lying here, or more accurately, her violated body had been lying here, on a crumpled tarpaulin practically on view to anyone for public inspection. After a few hours it had been carried away by two businesslike, uniformed men with a stretcher and, in time, an elderly gentleman whose profession it was to do so, had opened it up, examined it in detail, and then sewed it together again before it was sent to the mortuary. He hadn't seen it himself. There was always something to be thankful for.

Martin Beck became conscious of the fact that he was standing with his hands clasped behind his back as he shifted his weight from the sole of one foot to another, a habit from his years as a patrolman which was totally unconscious and almost unbreakable. He was standing and staring at a gray and uninteresting piece of ground from where the chalk marks from the first, routine investigation had long since been washed away by the rain. He must have occupied himself with this for a long time because the surroundings had gone through a number of changes. When he looked up he observed a small, white passenger boat entering one of the locks at a good speed. When it passed the dredger, some twenty cameras pointed at it, and, as if to underscore the situation, the dredging foreman climbed out of his cabin and also photographed the passenger boat. Martin Beck followed the boat with his eyes as it passed the jetty and noted certain ugly details. The hull had clean lines but the mast was cut off and the original smokestack, which had surely been high and straight and beautiful, had been replaced by a strange, streamlined little tin hood. From inside the ship growled something that must have been a diesel engine. The deck was full of tourists. Nearly all of them seemed to be elderly or middle-aged and several of them wore straw hats with flowered bands.

The boat was named *Juno*. He remembered that Ahlberg had mentioned this name the first time they had met.

There were a lot of people on the breakwater and along the edge of the canal now. Some of them fished and others sunbathed, but most of them were chiefly occupied with watching the boat. For the first time in several hours Martin Beck found a reason to say something.

"Does the boat always pass here at this time of day?"

"Yes, if it comes from Stockholm. Twelve-thirty. Right. The one that goes in the other direction comes by later, just after four. They meet at Vadstena. They tie up there."

"There are a lot of people here, on shore, I mean."

"They come down to see the boat."

"Are there always so many?"

"Usually."

The man he was talking to took the pipe from his mouth and spat in the water.

"Some pleasure," he said. "To stand and stare at a bunch of tourists."

When Martin Beck walked back along the brink of the canal he passed the little passenger boat again. It was now about halfway up, peacefully rising in the third lock. A number of passengers had gone on land. Several of them were photographing the boat, others crowded around the kiosk on shore where they were buying postcards and plastic souvenirs which, without doubt, were made in Hong Kong.

Martin Beck couldn't really say that he was short of time so with his innate respect for government budgets he took the bus back to town instead of a taxi.

There were no newspapermen in the hotel lobby and no messages for him at the desk. He went up to his room, sat down at the table and looked out over the Square. Actually he should have gone over to the police station but he had already been there twice before lunch.

A half hour later he telephoned Ahlberg.

"Hi. I'm glad you called. The Public Prosecutor is here."

"And?"

"He's going to hold a press conference at six o'clock. He seems worried."

"Oh."

"He would like you to be there."

"I'll be there."

"Will you bring Kollberg with you. I haven't had time to tell him yet."

"Where is Melander?"

"Out with one of my boys following up a lead."

"Did it sound as if it could be anything important?"

"Hell, no."

"And otherwise?"

"Nothing. The Prosecutor is worried about the press. The other telephone is ringing now."

"So long. See you later."

He remained seated at the table and listlessly smoked all his cigarettes. Then he looked at the clock, got up, and went out into the corridor. He stopped three doors down the hall, knocked and walked in, quietly and very quickly, in his usual manner.

Kollberg lay on the bed reading an evening paper. He had taken off his shoes and jacket and opened his shirt. His service pistol lay on the night table, wrapped up in his tie.

"We've fallen back to page twelve today," he said. "The poor devils, they don't have an easy time of it."

"Who?"

"Those reporters. 'The mystery tightens around the bestial murder of the woman in Motala. Not only the local police but even the Homicide Division of the National Police are fumbling around hopelessly in the dark.' I wonder where they get all that?"

Kollberg was fat and had a nonchalant and jovial manner which caused many people to make fateful mistakes in judging him.

" 'The case seemed to be a routine one in the beginning but has become more and more complicated. The leaders of the search are uncommunicative but are working along several different lines. The naked beauty in Boren . . .' oh, crap!"

He looked through the rest of the article and threw the newspaper on the floor.

"Yes, she was some beauty! A completely ordinary bow-legged woman with a big rear end and very small breasts."

"She had a big crotch, of course," said Kollberg. "And that was her misfortune," he added philosophically.

"Have you seen her?" Martin Beck asked.

"Of course, haven't you?"

"Only her pictures."

"Well I've seen her," said Kollberg.

"What have you been doing this afternoon?"

"What do you think? Reports from knocking on doors. What garbage! It's insane to send out fifteen different guys all over the place. Everybody expresses themselves differently and sees things differently. Some of them write four pages about seeing a one-eyed cat and saying that the kids in a house are snot-nosed, and others write up finding three bodies and a time bomb in a few paragraphs. They even ask totally different questions."

Martin Beck said nothing. Kollberg sighed.

"They should have a formula," he said. "They would save four-fifths of the time."

"Yes."

Martin Beck searched in his pockets.

"As you know I don't smoke," said Kollberg jokingly.

"The Public Prosecutor is holding a press conference in a half an hour. He would like us to be there."

"Oh. That ought to be lively."

He pointed to the newspaper and said:

"If *we* questioned the reporters for once. For four days in a row that guy has written that an arrest can be expected before the end of the afternoon. And the girl looks a little bit like Anita Ekberg and a little bit like Sophia Loren."

He sat up in bed, buttoned his shirt and began to lace his shoes.

Martin Beck walked over to the window.

"It's going to rain any minute," he said.

"Oh damn," Kollberg said and yawned.

"Are you tired?"

"I slept two hours last night. We were out in the woods in the moonlight searching for that type from St. Sigfrid's."

"Yes, of course."

"Yes, of course! And after we had wandered around for seven hours in this damn tourist place someone got around to telling us that the boys back at Klara station in Stockholm got the guy in Berzelii Park the night before last."

Kollberg finished dressing and put his pistol in place. He took a quick look at Martin Beck and said: "You look depressed. What is it?"

"Nothing special."

"Okay, let's go. The world press is waiting."

There were about twenty journalists in the room in which the press conference was to be held. In addition, the Public Prosecutor, the Superintendent of Police, Larsson, and a TV photographer with two spotlights were there. Ahlberg wasn't there. The Prosecutor sat behind a table and was looking thoughtfully through a folder. Several of the others were standing. There weren't enough chairs for everyone. It was noisy and everyone was talking at once. The room was crowded and the air was already unpleasant. Martin Beck, who disliked crowds, took several steps away from the others and stood with his back to the wall in the space between those who would ask the questions and those who would answer them.

After several minutes the Public Prosecutor turned to the Chief of Police and asked, loudly enough to cut through all the other noise in the room:

"Where the devil is Ahlberg?"

Larsson grabbed the telephone and forty seconds later Ahlberg entered the room. He was red-eyed and perspiring and still in the process of getting into his jacket.

The Public Prosecutor stood up and knocked lightly on the table with his fountain pen. He was tall and well built and quite correctly dressed, but almost too elegant.

"Gentlemen, I am pleased to see that so many of you have come to this impromptu press conference. I see representatives of all branches of media, the press, radio and television."

He bowed slightly toward the TV photographer, who was obviously the only press person present in the room whom he could definitely identify.

"I am also pleased to be able to say that from the outset your manner of handling this tragic and . . . sensitive matter has been, for the most part, correct and responsible. Unfortunately, there have been a few exceptions. Sensationalism and loose speculations do not help in such a . . . sensitive case as . . ."

Kollberg yawned and didn't even bother to put his hand in front of his mouth.

"As you all know this case has . . . and I certainly do not need to point it out again, special . . . sensitive aspects and . . ."

From the opposite side of the room Ahlberg looked at Martin Beck, his pale blue eyes filled with gloomy recognition and understanding.

". . . and just these . . . sensitive aspects call for a particularly careful way of treating them."

The Public Prosecutor continued to speak. Martin Beck looked over the shoulder of the reporter who sat in front of him and saw a drawing of a star on his notebook. The TV man was leaning against his tripod.

". . . and naturally I want to, no, more properly said, we neither want to nor can we hide our gratefulness for all the help in this . . . sensitive case. In short, we need the support of what we often call that great detective, the Public."

Kollberg yawned again. Ahlberg looked desperately unhappy.

Martin Beck finally ventured a look at the people in the room. He knew three of the journalists, they were older and came from Stockholm. He also recognized a few others. Most of them seemed very young.

"In addition, gentlemen, the collected information that we do have is at your disposal," said the Public Prosecutor and sat down.

With that he had clearly said his piece. In the beginning Larsson answered the questions. Most of them were asked by three young reporters who followed each other's questions in rapid order. Martin Beck noted that a number of newspapermen sat quietly and didn't take any notes. Their attitude toward the lack of real leads in the case seemed to show compassion and understanding. The photographers yawned. The room was already thick with cigarette smoke.

QUESTION: Why hasn't there been a real press conference before this one?

ANSWER: There haven't been many leads in this case. In addition, there are certain important facts in this case that could not be made public without hindering its solution.

QUESTION: Is an arrest immediately forthcoming?

ANSWER: It is conceivable, but from the present standpoint we cannot give you a definite answer, unfortunately.

QUESTION: Do you have any real clues in this case?

ANSWER: All we can say is that our investigations are following certain distinct lines.

(After this amazing series of half truths the Chief of Police threw a sorrowful look at the Public Prosecutor who stubbornly examined his cuticles.)

QUESTION: Criticism has been directed toward several of my colleagues. Is it the opinion of those in charge of the case that these colleagues have more or less intentionally twisted the facts?

(This question was asked by the notoriously well-known reporter whose article had made such a deep impression on Kollberg.)

ANSWER: Yes, unfortunately.

QUESTION: Isn't it more a case of the police leaving us reporters out in the cold and not giving us useful information? And deliberately leaving us to our own devices to find out whatever we can in the field?

ANSWER: Humn.

(Several of the less talkative journalists began to show signs of displeasure.)

QUESTION: Have you identified the corpse?

(Superintendent Larsson, with a quick glance, threw the ball over to Ahlberg, sat down, and demonstratively took a cigar out of his breast pocket.)

ANSWER: No.

QUESTION: Is it possible that she is from this city or somewhere around here?

ANSWER: It doesn't seem likely.

QUESTION: Why not?

ANSWER: If that were the case we would have been able to identify her.

QUESTION: Is that your only reason for suspecting that she comes from another part of the country?

(Ahlberg looked dismally at the Chief of Police who was devoting all his attention to his cigar.)

ANSWER: Yes.

QUESTION: Has the search of the bottom near the breakwater produced any results?

ANSWER: We have found a number of things.

QUESTION: Do these things have anything to do with the crime?

ANSWER: That is not easy to answer.

QUESTION: How old was she?

ANSWER: Presumably between twenty-five and thirty.

QUESTION: Exactly how long had she been dead when she was found?

ANSWER: That isn't easy to answer, either. Between three and four days.

QUESTION: The information that has been given to the public is very vague. Isn't it possible to tell us something more exact, information which really says something?

ANSWER: That's what we are trying to do here. We have also retouched a picture of her face which you are welcome to, if you want to have it.

(Ahlberg reached for a group of papers on the desk and started to hand them out. The air in the room was heavy and humid.)

QUESTION: Did she have any particular marks on her body?

ANSWER: Not as far as we know.

QUESTION: What does that mean?

ANSWER: Simply, that she had no marks at all.

QUESTION: Has a dental examination given any special clues?

ANSWER: She had good teeth.

(A long and pressing pause followed. Martin Beck noted that the reporter in front of him was still doodling with the star he had drawn.)

QUESTION: Is it possible that the body was thrown into the water at some other place and that it was brought to the breakwater by the current?

ANSWER: It doesn't seem likely.

QUESTION: Have you learned anything by knocking on doors?

ANSWER: We are still working on that.

QUESTION: To sum up, isn't it so that the police have a complete mystery on their hands?

It was the Public Prosecutor that answered:

"Most crimes are a mystery in the beginning."

With that, the press conference ended.

On the way out, one of the older reporters stopped Martin Beck, laid his hand on his arm and said: "Don't you know anything at all?" Martin Beck shook his head.

In Ahlberg's office two men were going through all the material they had gathered from the operation of knocking on doors.

Kollberg walked over to the desk, looked at several of the papers, and shrugged his shoulders.

Ahlberg came in. He took off his jacket and hung it over the back of his chair. Then he turned to Martin Beck and said:

"The Public Prosecutor wants to talk to you. He is still in the other room."

The Prosecutor and the Police Superintendent were still sitting behind the table.

"Beck," said the Prosecutor, "I don't see that your presence is necessary here any longer. There simply is not any work for the three of you."

"That's true."

"In general I think that a lot of what is left to do can be done conveniently some other place."

"That is possible."

"To put it simply, I don't want to detain you here, especially if your presence is more motivated in another direction."

"That is also my point of view," the Chief of Police added.

"Mine also," said Martin Beck.

They shook hands.

In Ahlberg's office it was still very quiet. Martin Beck did not break that silence.

After a while Melander came in. He hung up his hat and nodded to the others. Then he went over to the desk, sat down at Ahlberg's typewriter, put some paper in it and knocked out a few lines. He pulled the paper out of the typewriter, signed it, and placed it in the folder on the desk.

"Was that anything?" asked Ahlberg.

"No," said Melander.

He hadn't changed his manner since he had come in.

"We are going home tomorrow," Martin Beck said.

"Great," said Kollberg and yawned.

Martin Beck took a step toward the door and then turned and looked at the man at the typewriter.

"Are you coming along to the hotel?" he asked.

Ahlberg put his head back and looked at the ceiling. Then he got up and began to straighten his tie.

In the hotel lobby they separated from Melander.

"I've already eaten," he said. "Good night."

Melander was a clean living man. In addition he was economical with his expense account and subsisted mainly on hot dogs and soft drinks when he was out on a job.

The other three went into the dining room and sat down.

"A gin and tonic," said Kollberg. "Schweppes."

The others ordered beef, aquavit and beer. Kollberg took

his drink and finished it in three swallows. Martin Beck took out a copy of the material which had been given to the reporters and read through it.

"Will you do me a favor," said Martin Beck looking at Kollberg.

"Always ready to," answered Kollberg.

"I want you to write a new description, write it for me personally. Not a report but a real description. Not a description of a corpse but of a human being. Details. How she might have looked when she was alive. There's no hurry about it."

Kollberg sat quietly for a while.

"I understand what you mean," he said. "By the way, our friend Ahlberg supplied the world press with an untruth today. She actually did have a birthmark, on the inside of her left thigh. Brown. It looked like a pig."

"We didn't see it," said Ahlberg.

"I saw it," Kollberg said.

Before he left he said:

"Don't worry about it. No one can see everything. Anyway, it's your murder now. Forget that you've seen me. It was only an illusion. So long."

"So long," said Ahlberg.

They ate and drank silently. A lot later and without looking up from his drink, Ahlberg said:

"Are you planning to let this one go now?"

"No," replied Martin Beck.

"I'm not either," said Ahlberg. "Never."

A half hour later they separated.

When Martin Beck went up to his room he found some folded papers under his door. He opened them and immediately recognized Kollberg's orderly, easy to read, handwriting. Because he had known Kollberg well for a long time he wasn't at all surprised.

He undressed, washed the top of his body in cold water and put on his pajamas. Then he put his shoes out in the corridor, laid his trousers under the mattress, turned on the night table lamp, turned off the ceiling light and got into bed.

Kollberg had written:

"The following can be said about the woman who is occupying your thoughts:

1) She was (as you already know) 5 feet, 6½ inches tall, had gray-blue eyes and dark brown hair. Her teeth were good and she had no scars from operations or other marks on her body with the exception of a birthmark, high up on the inside of her left thigh about an inch and a half from her groin. It was brown and about as large as a dime, but uneven and looked like a little pig. She was, according to the man who performed the autopsy (and I had to press him to tell me this on the telephone), twenty-seven or twenty-eight years old. She weighed about one hundred and twenty-three pounds.

2) She was built in the following manner: Small shoulders and a very small waist, broad hips and a well developed rear end. Her measurements ought to have been approximately: 32-23-37. Thighs: heavy and long. Legs: muscular with relatively heavy calves but not fat. Her feet were in good condition with long, straight toes. No corns but heavy calluses on the soles of her feet, as if she had gone barefoot a lot and worn sandals or rubber boots a great deal of the time. She had a lot of hair on her legs, and must have been bare-legged most of the time. Condition of her legs: some defects. She was somewhat knock-kneed and seems to have walked with her toes pointed outward. She had a good deal of flesh on her body but was not fat. Slender arms. Small hands but long fingers. Shoe size was seven.

3) The suntan on her body showed: she had sunbathed in a two-piece bathing suit and worn sunglasses. She had worn thong sandals on her feet.

4) Her sex organ was well developed with a heavy growth of dark hair. Her breasts were small and slack. The nipples were large and dark brown.

5) Rather short neck. Strong features. A large mouth with full lips. Straight, thick, dark eyebrows and lighter eyelashes. Not long. Straight, short nose which was rather broad. No traces of cosmetics on her face. Fingernails and toenails hard, and clipped short. No traces of nail polish.

6) In the record of the autopsy (which you have read) I place special attention on the following: She had not had a child and never had an abortion. The murder had not been committed in connection with any conventional act (no trace of sperm). She had eaten three to five hours before she died: meat, potatoes, strawberries and milk. No traces of sickness or any organic changes. She did not smoke.

I've left a call to be awakened at six o'clock. So long."

Martin Beck read through Kollberg's observations twice before he folded the papers and laid them on his night table. Then he turned off the light and rolled over toward the wall.

It had begun to get light before he fell asleep.

6

The heat was already trembling over the asphalt when they drove away from Motala. It was early in the morning and the road lay flat and empty ahead of them. Kollberg and Melander sat in the front and Martin Beck sat in the back seat with the window down and let the breeze blow on his face. He didn't feel well and it was probably due to the coffee that he had gulped down while he was getting dressed.

"Kollberg was driving, poorly and unevenly," Martin Beck thought, but for once he remained silent. Melander looked blankly out the window and bit hard on the stem of his pipe.

After they had driven silently for about three-quarters of an hour Kollberg nodded his head to the left where a lake could be seen between the trees.

"Lake Roxen," he said. "Boren, Roxen and Glan. Believe it or not that's one of the few things I remember from school."

The others said nothing.

They stopped at a coffee house in Linköping. Martin Beck still didn't feel well and remained in the car while the others had something to eat.

The food had put Melander in a better mood and the two men in the front seat exchanged remarks during the rest of the trip. Martin Beck still remained silent. He didn't want to talk.

When they reached Stockholm he went directly home. His wife was sitting on the balcony sunbathing. She had shorts on and when she heard the front door open she took her brassiere from the balcony railing and got up.

"Hi," she said. "How are you?"

"Terrible. Where are the children?"

"They took their bikes and went off to swim. You look pale. You haven't eaten properly of course. I'll fix some breakfast for you."

"I'm tired," said Martin Beck. "I don't want anything to eat."

"But it will be ready in a second. Sit down and . . ."

"I don't *want* any breakfast. I think I'll sleep for a while. Wake me up in an hour."

It was a quarter after ten.

He went into the bedroom and closed the door after him.

When she awakened him he thought he had only slept for a few minutes.

The clock showed that it was a quarter of one.

"I told you one hour."

"You looked so tired. Commissioner Hammar is on the telephone."

"Oh, damn."

An hour later he was sitting in his chief's office.

"Didn't you get anywhere?"

"No. We don't know a thing. We don't know who she was, where she was murdered, and least of all by whom. We know approximately how and where but that's all."

Hammar sat with the palms of his hands on the top of the desk, and studied his fingernails and wrinkled his forehead. He was a good man to work for, calm, almost a little slow, and they always got along well together.

Commissioner Hammar folded his hands and looked up at Martin Beck.

"Keep in contact with Motala. You are most probably right. The girl was on vacation, thought to be away, maybe even out of the country. It might take two weeks at least before anyone misses her. If we count on a three week vacation. But I would like to see your report as soon as possible."

"You'll get it this afternoon."

Martin Beck went into his office, took the cover off his typewriter, thumbed through the papers he had received from Ahlberg, and began to type.

At five-thirty the telephone rang.

"Are you coming home to dinner?"

"It doesn't seem so."

"Aren't there any other policemen but you?" said his wife.

"Do you have to do everything? When do they think you'll see your family? The children are asking for you."

"I'll try to get home by six-thirty."

An hour and a half later his report was finished.

"Go home and get some sleep," said Hammar. "You look tired."

Martin Beck was tired. He took a taxi home, ate dinner and went to bed.

He fell asleep immediately.

At one-thirty in the morning the telephone awakened him.

"Were you asleep? I'm sorry that I woke you up. I only wanted to tell you that the case has been solved. He turned himself in."

"Who?"

"Holm, the neighbor. Her husband. He collapsed, totally. It was jealousy. Funny, isn't it?"

"Whose neighbor? Who are you talking about?"

"The dame in Storängen, naturally. I only wanted to tell you so that you wouldn't lie awake and think about it unnecessarily. . . . Oh, God, have I made a mistake?"

"Yes."

"Damn it, of course. You weren't there. It was Stenström. I'm sorry. I'll see you in the morning."

"Nice of you to call," said Martin Beck.

He went back to bed but he couldn't sleep. He lay there looking at the ceiling and listening to his wife's mild snoring. He felt empty and depressed.

When the sun began to shine into the room he turned over on his side and thought: "Tomorrow I'll telephone Ahlberg."

He called Ahlberg the next day and then four or five times a week during the following month but neither of them had anything special to say. The girl's origins remained a mystery. The newspapers had stopped writing about the case and Hammar had stopped asking how it was going. There was still no report of a missing person that matched in any way. Sometimes it seemed as if she had never existed. Everyone except Martin Beck and Ahlberg seemed to have forgotten that they had ever seen her.

In the beginning of August, Martin Beck took one week's vacation and went out to the archipelago with his family.

When he got back he continued to work on the routine jobs which came to his desk. He was depressed and slept poorly.

One night, at the end of August, he lay in his bed and looked out in the dark.

Ahlberg had called rather late that evening. He had been at the City Hotel and sounded a little drunk. They had talked for a while about the murder and before Ahlberg had hung up, he had said: "Whoever he is and wherever he is, we'll get him."

Martin Beck got up and walked barefooted into the living room. He turned on the light over his desk and looked at the model of the training ship *Danmark*. He still had the rigging to finish.

He sat down at the desk and took a folder out of a cubby-hole. Kollberg's description of the girl was in the folder together with copies of the pictures that the police photographer in Motala had taken nearly two months ago. In spite of the fact that he practically knew the description by heart he read it again, slowly and carefully. Then he placed the photographs in front of him and studied them for a long time.

When he put the papers back in the folder and turned off the light, he thought: "Whoever she was, and wherever she came from, I'm going to find out."

7

"Interpol, the devil with them," said Kollberg.

Martin Beck said nothing. Kollberg looked over his shoulder.

"Do those louses write in French too?"

"Yes. This is from the police in Toulouse. They have a missing person."

"French police," said Kollberg. "I made a search with them through Interpol last year. A little gal from Djursholm section. We didn't hear a word for three months and then got a long letter from the police in Paris. I didn't understand a word of it and turned it in to be translated. The next day I read in the newspaper that a Swedish tourist had found her. Found her, hell. She was sitting in that world-famous cafe where all the Swedish beatniks sit . . ."

"Le Dôme."

"Yes, that one. She was sitting there with some Arab that she was living with and she had been sitting there every day for nearly six months. That afternoon I got the translation. The letter stated that she hadn't been seen in France for at least three months and absolutely was not there now. In any case, not alive. 'Normal' disappearances were always cleared up within two weeks, they wrote, and in this case, unfortunately, one would have to assume some kind of crime."

Martin Beck folded the letter and placed it in one of his desk drawers.

"What did they write?" asked Kollberg.

"About the girl in Toulouse? The Spanish police found her in Mallorca a week ago."

"Why the devil do they need so many official stamps and so many strange words to say so little."

"You're right," said Martin Beck.

"Anyway, your girl must be Swedish. As everyone thought from the beginning. Strange."

"What's strange?"

"That no one has missed her, whoever she is. I sometimes think about her too."

Kollberg's tone changed gradually.

"It irritates me," he said. "It irritates me a lot. How many blanks have you drawn now?"

"Twenty-seven with this one."

"That's a lot."

"You're right."

"Don't think too much about the mess."

"No."

"Well meant advice is easier to give than to take," thought Martin Beck. He got up and walked over to the window.

"I'd better be getting back to my murderer," said Kollberg. "He just grins and gnashes his teeth. What behavior! First he drinks a bottle of soda water and then he kills his wife and children with an axe. Then he tries to set fire to the house and cuts his throat with a saw. On top of everything else he runs to the police crying and complains about the food. I'm sending him to the nut house this afternoon.

"God, life is strange," he added and slammed the door after him as he left the room.

The trees between the police station and Kristineberg's Hotel had begun to turn and to lose some of their leaves. The sky lay low and gray with trailing rain curtains and storm-torn clouds. It was the twenty-ninth of September and autumn was definitely on the way. Martin Beck looked distastefully at his half-smoked cigarette and thought about his sensitivity to temperature change and of the six months of winter's formidable colds which would soon strike him.

"Poor little friend, whoever you are," he said to himself.

He was conscious of the fact that their chances were reduced each day that passed. Maybe they would never even find out who she was, not to speak of getting the person who was guilty, unless the same man repeated the crime. The woman who had lain out there on the breakwater in the sun at least had a face and a body and a nameless grave. The murderer was nothing, totally without contours, a dim figure, if that. But dim figures have no desires and no sharp pointed weapons. No strangler's hands.

Martin Beck straightened up. "Remember that you have three of the most important virtues a policeman can have," he thought. "You are stubborn and logical, and completely calm. You don't allow yourself to lose your composure and you act only professionally on a case, whatever it is. Words like repulsive, horrible, and bestial belong in the newspapers, not in your thinking. A murderer is a regular human being, only more unfortunate and maladjusted."

He hadn't seen Ahlberg since that last evening at the City Hotel in Motala but they had talked on the telephone often. He had spoken to him last week and he remembered Ahlberg's final comment: "Vacation? Not before this thing is solved. I'll have all the material collected soon but I'm going to continue even if I have to drag all of Boren myself."

These days Ahlberg wasn't much more than merely stubborn, Martin Beck thought.

"Damn, damn, damn," he mumbled and rapped his forehead with his fist.

Then he went back to his desk and sat down, swung his chair a quarter turn to the left and stared listlessly at the paper in the typewriter. He tried to remember what it was he wanted to write before Kollberg had come in with the letter from Interpol.

Six hours later, at two minutes before five he had put on his hat and coat and already begun to hate the crowded subway train to the south. It was still raining and he could already perceive both the musty odor of wet clothing and the frightening feeling of having to stand hemmed in by a compact mass of strange bodies.

One minute before five, Stenström arrived. He opened the door without knocking as usual. It was irritating but endurable in comparison with Melander's woodpecker signals and Kollberg's deafening pounding.

"Here's a message for the department of missing girls. You'd better send a thank you letter to the American Embassy. They sent it up."

He studied the light red telegram sheet.

"Lincoln, Nebraska. What was it the last time?"

"Astoria, New York."

"Was that when they sent three pages of information but forgot to say that she was a Negro?"

"Yes," said Martin Beck.

Stenström gave him the telegram and said:

"Here's the number of some guy at the embassy. You ought to call him."

With guilty pleasure at every excuse to postpone the subway torture, he went back to his desk but it was too late. The embassy staff had gone home.

The next day was a Wednesday and the weather was worse than ever. The morning paper had a late listing of a missing twenty-five year old housemaid from a place called Räng which seemed to be in the south of Sweden. She had not returned after her vacation.

During the morning registered copies of Kollberg's description and the retouched photographs were sent to the police in southern Sweden and to a certain Detective Lieutenant Elmer B. Kafka, Homicide Squad, Lincoln, Nebraska, U.S.A.

After lunch Martin Beck felt that the lymph glands in his neck were beginning to swell and by the time he got home that evening it was hard for him to swallow.

"Tomorrow the National Police can manage without you, I've decided," said his wife.

He opened his mouth to answer her but looked at the children and closed it again without saying anything.

It didn't take her long to take advantage of her triumph.

"Your nose is completely stopped up. You're gasping for breath like a fish out of water."

He put down his knife and fork, mumbled "thanks for dinner," and absorbed himself with his rigging problem. Gradually, this activity calmed him completely. He worked slowly and methodically on the model ship and had no unpleasant thoughts. If he actually heard the noise from the television in the next room, it didn't register. After a while his daughter stood on the threshold with a sullen look and traces of bubblegum on her chin.

"Some guy's on the phone. Wouldn't you know, right in the middle of Perry Mason."

Damn it, he would have to have the telephone moved.

Damn it, he would have to start getting involved in his children's upbringing. Damn it, what does one say to a child who is thirteen years old and loves the Beatles and is already developed?

He walked into the living room as if he had to excuse his existence and cast a sheepish look at the great defense lawyer's worn out dogface which filled the television screen. He picked up the telephone and took it out into the hall with him.

"Hi," said Ahlberg. "I think I've found something."

"Yes?"

"Do you remember that we spoke about the canal boats which pass here in the summer at twelve-thirty and at four o'clock during the day?"

"Yes."

"I have tried to check up on the small boats and the freight traffic this week. It's almost impossible to do with all the boats that go by. But an hour ago one of the boys on the regular police staff suddenly said that he saw a passenger boat go past Platen's moat in a westerly direction in the middle of the night sometime last summer. He didn't know when and he hadn't thought about it until now, when I asked him. He had been doing some special duty in that area for several nights. It seems completely unbelievable but he swore that it was true. He went on vacation the next day and after that he forgot about it."

"Did he recognize the boat?"

"No, but wait. I called Gothenburg and spoke to a few men in the shipping office. One of them said that it certainly could be true. He thought the boat was named *Diana* and gave me the captain's address."

A short pause followed. Martin Beck could hear that Ahlberg had struck a match.

"I got hold of the captain. He said he certainly did remember although he would rather have forgotten it. First they had to stop at Hävringe for three hours because of heavy fog and then a steam pipe in the motor had broken . . ."

"Engine."

"What did you say?"

"In the engine. Not the motor."

"Oh yes, but in any case they had to stay over more than eight hours in Söderköping for repairs. That means that they were nearly twelve hours late and passed Borenshult after midnight. They didn't stop either in Motala or Vadstena but went directly on to Gothenburg."

"When did this happen? Which day?"

"The second trip after midsummer, the captain said. In other words, the night before the fifth."

Neither of them said anything for at least ten seconds. Then Ahlberg said:

"Four days before we found her. I called the shipping office guy again and checked out the time. He wondered what it was all about and I asked him if everyone on board had reached Gothenburg in good order. He said, 'Why shouldn't they have,' and I answered that I didn't really know. He must have thought that I was out of my mind."

It was quiet again.

"Do you think it means anything?" Ahlberg said finally.

"I don't know," answered Martin Beck. "Maybe. You've done a fine job in any event."

"If everyone who went on board arrived in Gothenburg, then it doesn't mean very much."

His voice was a strange mixture of disappointment and modest triumph.

"We have to check out all the information," Ahlberg said.

"Naturally."

"So long."

"So long. I'll call you."

Martin Beck remained standing a while with his hand on the telephone. Then he wrinkled his forehead and went through the living room like a sleepwalker. He closed the door behind him carefully and sat down in front of the model ship, lifted his right hand to make an adjustment on the mast, but dropped it immediately.

He sat there for another hour until his wife came in and made him go to bed.

8

"No one could say that you look particularly well," said Kollberg.

Martin Beck felt anything but well. He had a cold, and a sore throat, his ears hurt him and his chest felt miserable. The cold had, according to schedule, entered its worst phase. Even so, he had deliberately defied both the cold and the home front by spending the day in his office. First of all he had fled from the suffocating care which would have enveloped him had he remained in bed. Since the children had begun to grow up, Martin Beck's wife had adopted the role of home nurse with bubbling eagerness and almost manic determination. For her, his repeated bouts of colds and flu were on a par with birthdays and major holidays.

In addition, for some reason he didn't have the conscience to stay home.

"Why are you hanging around here if you aren't well?" said Kollberg.

"There's nothing the matter with me."

"Don't think so much about that case. It isn't the first time we have failed. It won't be the last either. You know that just as well as I do. We won't be any the better or the worse for it."

"It isn't just the case that I'm thinking about."

"Don't brood. It isn't good for the morale."

"The morale?"

"Yes, think what a lot of nonsense one can figure out with plenty of time. Brooding is the mother of ineffectiveness."

After saying this Kollberg left.

It had been an uneventful and dreary day, full of sneezing and spitting and dull routine. He had called Motala twice, mostly to cheer up Ahlberg, who in the light of day, had decided that his discovery wasn't worth very much as long as it couldn't be connected with the corpse at the locks.

"I suspect that it is easy to overestimate certain things when you've been working like a dog for so long without results."

Ahlberg had sounded crushed and regretful. It was almost heartbreaking.

The girl who had disappeared from Räng was still missing. That didn't worry him. She was 5 feet, 1 inch tall, had blond hair and a Bardot hair style.

At five o'clock he took a taxi home but got out at the subway station and walked the last bit in order to avoid the devastating economic argument which undoubtedly would have followed if his wife had happened to see him get out of a taxi.

He couldn't eat anything but drank a cup of camomile tea. "For safety's sake, so that he'd get a stomach ache too," Martin Beck thought. Then he went and lay down and fell asleep immediately.

The next morning he felt a little better. He ate a biscuit and drank with stoic calm the cup of scalding hot honey water which his wife had placed in front of him. The discussion about his health and the unreasonable demands that the government placed on its employees dragged on and by the time he arrived at his office at Kristineberg, it was already a quarter after ten.

There was a cable on his desk.

One minute later Martin Beck entered his chief's office without knocking even though the "Don't Disturb" red light was on. This was the first time in eight years he had ever done this.

The ever-present Kollberg and Commissioner Hammar were leaning against the edge of the desk studying a blueprint of an apartment. They both looked at him with amazement.

"I got a cable from Kafka."

"That's a hell of a way to start a work day," said Kollberg.

"That's his name. The detective in Lincoln, in America. He's identified the woman in Motala."

"Can he do that by cable?" asked Hammar.

"It seems so."

He put the cable on the desk. All three of them read the text.

THAT'S OUR GIRL ALL RIGHT. ROSEANNA MCGRAW, 27, LI-
BRARIAN. EXCHANGE OF FURTHER INFORMATION NECES-
SARY AS SOON AS POSSIBLE.

KAFKA, HOMICIDE

"Roseanna McGraw," said Hammar. "Librarian. That's one you never thought of."

"I had another theory," said Kollberg. "I thought she was from Mjölby. Where's Lincoln?"

"In Nebraska, someplace in the middle of the country," said Martin Beck. "I think."

Hammar read through the cable one more time.

"We had better get going again then," he said. "This doesn't say particularly much."

"Quite enough for us," said Kollberg. "We aren't spoiled."

"Well," said Hammar calmly. "You and I ought to clear up what we're working on first."

Martin Beck went back to his office, sat down a moment and massaged his hairline with his fingertips. The first surprised feeling of progress had somehow disappeared. It had taken three months to come up with information that in ninety-nine cases out of a hundred you had free from the beginning. All the real work remained to be done.

The embassy people and the County Police Superintendent could wait. He picked up the telephone and dialed the area code for Motala.

"Yes," said Ahlberg.

"She's been identified."

"For sure?"

"It seems so."

Ahlberg said nothing.

"She was an American. From a place called Lincoln in Nebraska. Are you writing it down?"

"Hell, yes."

"Her name was Roseanna McGraw. I'll spell it: R for Rudolf, O for Olof, S for Sigurd, E for Erik, A for Adam, N for Niklas, again N for Niklas, A for Adam. New word: capital M for Martin, C for Cesar, capital G for Gustav, R for Rudolf, A for Adam, W for Wilhelm. Have you got that?"

"Sure I've got it."

"She was twenty-seven years old and a librarian. That's all I know at the moment."

"How did you manage that?"

"Only routine. They began to look for her after a while. Not through Interpol. Via the embassy."

"The boat?" said Ahlberg.

"What did you say?"

"The boat. Where would an American tourist be coming from if not from a boat? Maybe not from my boat but from some pleasure yacht. Quite a few go through here."

"We don't know if she was a tourist."

"That's right. I'll get going immediately. If she knew anyone here or lived in town, I'll know about it in twenty-four hours."

"Fine. I'll call you as soon as I know more."

Martin Beck ended the conversation by sneezing in Ahlberg's ear. By the time he tried to apologize, the other had already hung up.

In spite of his headache and his clogged up ears he felt better than he had for a long time. He felt like a long-distance runner one second before the starting gun. There were only two things that worried him: the murderer had jumped the gun and was three months ahead of him, and he didn't know in which direction to run.

Somewhere under this surface of disquieting perspective and speculations of unknown worth his policeman's brain had already begun to plan the routine searches of the next forty-eight hours, which, he knew in advance, would obtain certain results. This was as sure as the fact that sand will run down in an hour glass.

For three months he hadn't really thought about anything but this. The moment when the investigation would really begin. It had been like trying to get out of a swamp in coal-black darkness and now he was feeling the first solid piece of ground under his feet. The next one would not be as far away.

He wasn't expecting any quick results. If Ahlberg found out that the woman from Lincoln had worked in Motala, or had been visiting friends in that city, or had even been there, he would be more surprised than if the murderer walked through the door and placed the evidence of the murder on his desk.

On the other hand he was waiting for the supplementary material from the U.S.A. without feeling particularly impatient. He thought about all the different statements that would gradually be sent on from the man in America and about Ahlberg's stubborn contention, which was actually totally groundless, that the woman had come by boat. It was more logical to think that the body had been brought down to the water by car.

Immediately afterwards he began thinking about Detective Lieutenant Kafka, how he looked, and if the police station where he worked resembled the ones people saw on television.

He wondered what time it was right now in Lincoln and where the woman had lived. He wondered if her apartment was empty, with white sheets covering the furniture, if the air in it was close and heavy, and filled with dust.

It struck him that his knowledge of the geography of North America was rather poor. He didn't know where Lincoln was at all and the name Nebraska was just another name to him.

After lunch he went to the library and took a look at a world atlas. He soon found Lincoln. The city certainly was inland, in fact as far in the middle of the United States as any city could be. It seemed to be a rather large city but he couldn't find any books containing information on North American cities. With the help of his pocket almanac he studied the time difference and figured it to be seven hours. It was now two-thirty in the afternoon in Stockholm and it was seven-thirty in the morning in Lincoln. Presumably Kafka was still in bed, reading his morning newspaper.

He studied the map for several minutes, then placing his finger on the pin-sized point in the southeast corner of the state of Nebraska, which was nearly one hundred longitude degrees west of Greenwich, he said to himself: "Roseanna McGraw."

He repeated the name several more times almost as if to nail it down in his consciousness.

When he got back to the police station Kollberg was sitting at the typewriter.

The telephone rang before either of them had time to say anything. It was the switchboard.

"The Central Telephone Office has advised us that there is a phone call coming from the United States. It is coming in about thirty minutes. Can you take it?"

Detective Lieutenant Kafka was not lying in bed reading the newspaper! Once again he had drawn too hasty a conclusion.

"From America. Well I'll be damned," said Kollberg.

The call came after three-quarters of an hour. At first there were only confused noises and then a lot of telephone operators all talking at once, and then a voice came through, amazingly clear and distinct.

"Yeah, Kafka speaking. That you Mr. Beck?"

"Yes."

"You got my wire?"

"Yes. Thank you."

"It's all clear, isn't it?"

"Is there not any doubt about that it is the right woman?" asked Martin Beck.

"You sound like a native," said Kollberg.

"Nope, sir, that's Roseanna all right. I got her identified in less than one hour—thanks to your excellent description. I even double-checked it. Gave it to her girlfriend and that ex-boyfriend of hers down in Omaha. Both were quite sure. All the same, I've mailed photographs and some other stuff for you."

"When did she leave home?"

"Beginning of May. Her idea was to spend about two months in Europe. It was her first trip abroad. As far as I know she was traveling alone."

"Do you know anything about her plans?"

"Not very much. In fact no one here does. I can give you one clue. She wrote a postcard from Norway to her girlfriend, saying that she was to stay one week in Sweden, then proceed to Copenhagen."

"Did she not write anything more?"

"Well, she said something about boarding a Swedish ship. For some sort of lake cruise through the country or something like that. That point was not very clear."

Martin Beck held his breath.

"Mr. Beck, are you still there?"

"Yes."

The connection was getting worse rather quickly.

"I understand she was murdered," shouted Kafka. "Did you get the guy?"

"Not yet."

"I can't hear you."

"In a short time, I hope, not yet," said Martin Beck.

"You shot him?"

"I did what? No, no, not shot . . ."

"Yeah, I hear, you shot the bastard," screamed the man on the other side of the Atlantic. "That's great. I'll give that to the papers here."

"You are misunderstanding," Martin Beck roared.

He heard Kafka's final reply like a weak whisper through ethereal noise.

"Yeah, I understand perfectly well. I've got your name all right. So long. You'll be hearing from me. Well done, Martin."

Martin Beck put down the receiver. He had been standing up during the entire conversation. He was panting and perspiration had broken out all over his face.

"What are you doing?" asked Kollberg. "Do you think that they have speaking-tubes to Nebraska?"

"We couldn't hear very well toward the end. He thought that I had shot the murderer. He said he was going to tell that to the newspapers."

"Great. Tomorrow you'll be the hero of the day over there. The day after, they'll make you an honorary citizen and at Christmas time they'll send you the key to the city. A gilded one. 'Shoot-em-up-Martin, The avenger from south Stockholm.' The boys are going to have a good time with this one."

Martin Beck blew his nose and wiped the perspiration from his face.

"Well, what did he actually say? Or did he only go on about how clever you are?"

"It was mostly you that was praised. For your description. 'Excellent description,' he said."

"Was he positive of the identification?"

"Yes, definitely. He had checked with her friend and with some sort of former beau."

"What else?"

"She left home in the middle of May. She was to spend two months in Europe. It was her first trip out of the country. She sent a postcard from Norway to her girlfriend and wrote that she would be here for a week and then continue on to Copenhagen. He said that he had mailed some pictures of her and some other things."

"Was that all?"

Martin Beck went over to the window and gazed out. He bit on his thumbnail.

"She wrote on the postcard that she was going to take a boat trip. Some sort of cruise through Sweden on the lakes and inland waterways . . ."

He turned around and looked at his colleague. Kollberg was no longer smiling and the teasing look had left his eyes. After a while he said, very slowly:

"So she did come with the canal boat. Our friend in Motala was right."

"It seems so," said Martin Beck.

9

Martin Beck took a deep breath when he came out of the subway station. The trip, with its crowded subway cars, had made him feel slightly ill as usual.

The air was clear and light and a fresh breeze swept in over the city from the Baltic. He crossed the street and bought a pack of cigarettes in a tobacco store. He walked on toward Skepps Bridge and stopped, lit a cigarette and stood with his elbows on the bridge railing. A cruise ship bearing an English flag was anchored at a pier in the distance. He couldn't make out the name but guessed that it was the *Devonia*. A group of seagulls screeched as they fought over some garbage which had been thrown overboard. He stood for a while looking at the ship and then continued on toward the pier.

Two dismal looking men sat on a pile of wood. The first one tried to light a cigarette butt in a wooden holder and when he didn't succeed the other one, whose hands shook less, tried to help him. Martin Beck looked at his wristwatch. Five minutes to nine. "They must be broke," he thought, "otherwise they would be waiting by the door of the liquor store at this time of day."

He passed the *Bore II* which was tied up at the pier loading freight and stood on the curb directly across from the Hotel Reisen. It took a few minutes before he managed to break through the unending line of automobiles and get across the street.

The passenger list for the *Diana*'s trip on July 3 was not in the canal boat's shipping office. It was in the Gothenburg office but they had promised to send it as soon as possible. However, a list of the crew and other personnel was given to him immediately. When he left, he took a few brochures with him which he read on the way back to the office.

Melander was already sitting in his visitor's chair when he arrived.

"Hi there," Martin Beck said.

"Good morning," said Melander.

"That pipe smells dreadful. But by all means sit here and poison the air. You are most welcome. Or was there something special you wanted?"

"You don't get cancer as quickly if you smoke a pipe. Your brand of cigarettes are said to be the most dangerous, by the way. At least that's what I've heard. Otherwise, I'm on duty."

"Check with American Express, the Post Office, banks, the telephone company, other contacts, you understand, don't you?"

"I believe so. What was the woman's name again?"

Martin Beck wrote the name on a piece of paper, ROSEANNA MCGRAW, and gave it to Melander.

"How do you pronounce it?"

He left and Martin Beck opened the window. It was chilly and the wind blew through the tree tops and swept up the leaves on the ground. After a while he shut the window again, hung his jacket over the back of his chair and sat down.

He picked up the telephone and dialed the number of the National Office for Aliens. If she had registered at a hotel she ought to be on file there. Some record of her ought to be there in any event. He had to wait a long time before anyone answered and then it took ten minutes before the girl came back to the phone. She had found the card. Roseanna McGraw had stayed at the Hotel Gillet in Stockholm from June 30 until July 2.

"Please send me a photocopy," said Martin Beck.

He pressed down the buttons on the telephone and waited for the disconnected signal with the receiver still in his hand. Then he telephoned for a taxi and put on his jacket. Ten minutes later he got out of the taxi, paid the driver, and entered the hotel through its glass doors.

In front of the reception desk stood a group of six men. They had name tags on their lapels and were all talking at the same time. The desk clerk looked unhappy and threw up his arms in a complaining gesture. It looked as if the discussion would take some time, so Martin Beck sat down in one of the armchairs in the lobby.

He waited until the discussion was over and let the group disappear into the elevator before he went up to the desk.

The desk clerk looked stoically through the register until he found the name. He turned the book toward Martin Beck so that he could read it. She had printed with attractive, even letters. Place of Birth: Denver, Col. USA. Home Address: Lincoln, Nebr. Last Place Visited: Nebr. USA.

Martin Beck checked the guests who had registered on June 30 and the days immediately preceding and following. Above Roseanna McGraw's name were the names of no less than eight Americans. All except the two names on top of the list had given some place in the U.S.A. as their last place visited. The first one had written Phyllis with the rest of the name illegible. She had written North Cape, Sweden, as the last place visited. The person who had registered just beneath her had written North Cape, Norway, in the same column.

"Was it a group tour?" asked Martin Beck.

"Let's see," said the desk clerk and turned his head to look. "No, I don't really remember, but it is very likely. We sometimes have American groups here. They arrive with the 'dollar train' from Narvik."

Martin Beck showed the man a photograph but he shook his head in reply.

"No, I'm sorry, we have so many guests here . . ."

No one had recognized her but the trip to the hotel had some results. Now he knew where she had stayed, he had seen her name in the register and had even looked at the room she had stayed in. She had left the hotel on July 2.

"And then? Where did you go?" he said quietly to himself.

His temples were throbbing and his throat hurt. He wondered how much fever he had, and went back to the office.

She could have traveled with the canal boat and gone on board the night before it left Stockholm. He had read in the brochure from the shipping office that passengers could go on board the night before the boat left. He was more and more convinced that she had been on the *Diana* in spite of the fact that there was still no evidence of it.

He wondered where Melander was and reached for the

telephone. Just as he was about to dial the number he heard a distinct pecking at the door.

Melander stood in the doorway.

"No," he said. "Neither American Express nor any other such place knows anything about her. I'll go and get something to eat now if you don't mind."

He had no objection and Melander disappeared.

He telephoned Motala but Ahlberg wasn't in.

His headache was getting worse. After looking for some headache pills for a while he went up to Kollberg's office to borrow a few. Just inside the door he started coughing so badly that he couldn't say anything for a long time.

Kollberg cocked his head and looked at him worriedly.

"You sound worse than eighteen Ladies of the Camelias. Come here and let the doctor look at you."

He looked at Martin Beck through his magnifying glass.

"If you don't listen to the doctor you won't have much time left. Go home and creep into bed and drink a real large glass of toddy. Preferably three of them. Rum toddies. That's the only thing that will help. Then go to sleep and you'll wake up like new."

"What do you think it is? And, by the way, I don't like rum," said Martin Beck.

"Take cognac then. Don't worry about Kafka. If he calls, I'll take care of him. My English is excellent."

"He won't call. Do you have any headache pills?"

"No, but you can have a chocolate praline."

Martin Beck returned to his office. The air in the room was thick and smoky but he didn't want to open the window and let the cold air in.

Ahlberg still wasn't there when he telephoned a half hour later. He took out the list of the *Diana*'s crew. It contained eighteen names and addresses from different parts of the country. Six of them were in Stockholm and there were two names without an address. Two of them lived in Motala.

At four-thirty he decided to take Kollberg's advice. He cleaned off his desk and put his hat and coat on.

On the way home he stopped at a pharmacy and bought a box of pills.

He found a drop of cognac in the pantry, poured it into a cup of bouillon, and took the cup with him into the bedroom.

By the time his wife had come in with a heat lamp he was already asleep.

He awoke early the next morning but stayed in bed until a quarter to eight. Then he got up and got dressed. He felt a great deal better and his headache had disappeared.

On the dot of nine he opened the door to his office. An envelope with a red special delivery sticker lay on his desk. He opened it up with his index finger without taking the time to take off his overcoat.

The envelope contained a passenger list.

His eyes caught her name immediately.

McGraw, R., Miss, USA: Single cabin A 7.

10

"I knew that I was right," Ahlberg said. "I had a feeling. How many passengers were there on the boat?"

"According to the list there were sixty-eight," said Martin Beck and filled in the number on the paper in front of him with a pen.

"Are their addresses listed?"

"No, only nationalities. It's going to be one hell of a job to find all these people. We can cross off some of them, of course. Children and old women, for example. Then too, we have the crew and other personnel to get hold of. That makes eighteen more but I have their addresses."

"You said that Kafka thought that she was traveling alone. What do you think?"

"It doesn't seem as if she was with anyone. She had a single cabin. According to the deck plan it was the one farthest back toward the stern on the middle deck."

"I must admit that it doesn't tell me very much," said Ahlberg. "In spite of the fact that I see that boat several times a week every summer I don't really know what it looks like. I've never been on board any of them. All three seem alike to me."

"Actually, they are not really alike. I think we ought to try and get a look at the *Diana*. I'll find out where she is," said Martin Beck.

He told Ahlberg about his visit to the Hotel Gillet, gave him the address of the pilot and chief engineer both of whom lived in Motala, and promised to call again when he found out where the *Diana* was now.

After he had finished the conversation with Ahlberg, he went into his chief's office with the passenger list.

Hammar congratulated him on the progress and asked him to go and have a look at the boat as soon as possible. Kollberg and Melander would have to worry about the passenger list for the time being.

Melander didn't seem very enthusiastic about the task of locating the addresses of sixty-seven unknown people spread out over the entire globe. He sat in Martin Beck's office with a copy of the passenger list in his hand and made a fast tabulation:

"Fifteen Swedes, of which five are named Andersson, three named Johansson, and three named Petersson. That sounds promising! Twenty-one Americans, minus one, of course. Twelve Germans, four Danes, four Englishmen, one Scot, two Frenchmen, two South Africans—we can look for them with tom-tom drums—five Dutchmen and two Turks."

He tapped his pipe against the wastepaper basket and put the list into his pocket.

"Turks. On the Göta Canal," he mumbled and left the room.

Martin Beck telephoned the canal boat office. The *Diana* was at Bohus for the winter, a community on the Göta River about twelve miles from Gothenburg. A man from the Gothenburg office would meet them there and show them the boat.

He called Ahlberg and informed him that he would take the afternoon train to Motala. They agreed that they would leave Motala at seven o'clock the following morning in order to be in Bohus around ten o'clock.

For once he missed the rush hour going home and the subway car was almost empty.

His wife had begun to understand how important this case was to him and only ventured a mild protest when he told her that he was leaving. She packed his suitcase in sullen silence but Martin Beck pretended not to notice her demonstrable sulkiness. He kissed her absentmindedly on the cheek and left home a full hour before train time.

"I didn't bother to reserve a room for you at the hotel," said Ahlberg, who was waiting with his car in front of the railroad station in Motala. "We have a formidable sofa you can sleep on."

They sat up late and talked that evening and when the alarm

clock rang the next morning they felt anything but rested.
Ahlberg telephoned the S.K.A.* and they promised to send two
men to Bohus. Then they went down to the car.

The morning was cold and gray and after they had driven
a while it began to rain lightly.

"Did you get hold of the pilot and the chief engineer?"
Martin Beck asked, when they had left the city behind them.

"Only the chief engineer," said Ahlberg. "He was a tough
guy. I had to drag every word out of him. In any case he had
very little to do with the passengers. And on this particular trip
he was obviously fully occupied due to the trouble with the
motor . . . sorry, the engine. He was in a bad mood the minute
I mentioned that trip. But he said that there had been two boys
helping him and that as far as he knew, they had signed on a
boat which was going to England and Germany right after the
Diana's last trip."

"Oh, well." Martin Beck replied. "We'll get hold of them.
We'll have to go through all the shipping company lists."

The rain increased and by the time they reached Bohus the
water was pouring over the windshield. They didn't see very
much of the town because the heavy rain blocked their view
but it looked rather small with a few factories and a large building which stretched out along the river. They found their way
to the edge of the river and after they had driven slowly for a
while, they caught sight of the boats. They looked deserted and
spooky and the men couldn't make out the names of the boats
until they were almost on top of the pier.

They remained in the car and watched for the man from
the shipping office. There was no one in sight but another car
was parked not too far from them. When they drove over to it,
they saw a man sitting behind the wheel, looking in their direction.

They pulled up and parked their car next to the other
one. The man rolled down his side window and shouted something. Through the noise of the rain they could make out their
names and Martin Beck nodded 'yes' while he opened his
window.

The man introduced himself and suggested that they go
on board immediately in spite of the heavy rain.

He was short and heavy and when he hurried off ahead of

* Statens Kriminal Teknista Anstalt—the federal criminal technical bureau.

them toward the *Diana,* he almost seemed to be rolling forward. With a certain amount of trouble, he got over the railing and waited while Martin Beck and Ahlberg climbed after him.

The little man unlocked a door on the starboard side and they walked into some kind of a coatroom. On the other side there was a similar door which led out to the port promenade deck.

On the right there were two glass doors leading into the dining room and between the doors was a large mirror. Directly in front of the mirror a flight of stairs led to a lower deck. They followed them and then went down still another flight of stairs which led to four large cabins and a large lounge with lace-covered sofas. The little man showed them how the sofas could be hidden by a curtain.

"When we have deck passengers they can usually sleep here," he said.

They climbed back up the stairs to the next deck where there were cabins for passengers and crew, toilets and bathrooms. The dining room was on the middle deck. There were six round tables which could each accommodate six persons, a buffet toward the stern, a reading and writing room where one could look out through a large window, and a small serving room, with a dumbwaiter, leading to the galley below.

When they went out on the promenade deck again the rain had nearly stopped. They walked toward the stern. On the starboard side there were three doors, the first one led to the serving room and the other two to cabins. On the other side there was a ladder going to the upper deck and on up to the bridge. Next to the ladder was Roseanna McGraw's cabin.

The door to that cabin opened directly toward the stern. The cabin was small, no more than twelve feet long, and lacked ventilation. The back rest on the bed could be lifted up and turned into a top bunk. There was also a wash basin with a mahogany cover which, when down, provided some counter space. On the bulkhead over the wash basin was a mirror with a holder for a glass and toilet articles. The cabin floor was covered with a rug which was tacked down and there was a place for luggage under the bunk. At the end of the bed there was an empty space with some clothing hooks on the bulkhead.

There was hardly room for three people in there which was soon obvious to the man from the shipping office. He went out and sat on a box containing life jackets and looked anxiously at his soaking wet shoes which dangled a good bit above the deck.

Martin Beck and Ahlberg examined the small cabin. They hadn't hoped to find any traces of Roseanna since they knew that the cabin had been cleaned a good number of times since she had occupied it. Ahlberg lay down on the bed carefully and stated that there was hardly enough room in it for an adult person.

They left the cabin door open and went out and sat down beside the man on the life jacket box.

After they had been sitting quietly for a while, looking into the cabin, a large, black car drove up. It was the men from the S.K.A. They carried a large, black case between them and it didn't take long before they had begun to work.

Ahlberg poked Martin Beck in the ribs and nodded his head toward the ladder. They climbed up to the upper deck. There were two lifeboats there, one on each side of the smoke-stack, and several large containers for deck chairs and blankets, but otherwise the deck was quite empty. Up on the bridge deck were two passenger cabins, a storeroom, and the captain's cabin which was behind the pilot room.

At the foot of the ladder Martin Beck stopped and took out the deck plans which he had received from the canal boat office. Following this, they went through the boat one more time. When they returned to the stern of the middle deck, the little man was still sitting on the box, looking sorrowfully at the men from the S.K.A. who were on their knees in the cabin pulling tacks out of the rug.

It was two o'clock by the time the large, black police car drove off toward the Gothenburg road with a shower of mud spraying from its wheels. The technicians had taken everything that was loose in the cabin with them, although it wasn't very much. They didn't think it would take long for them to have the results of their analysis finished.

Martin Beck and Ahlberg thanked the man from the shipping office and he shook their hands with exaggerated enthusiasm, clearly grateful to be finally getting away from there.

When his car had disappeared round the first bend in the road, Ahlberg said: "I am tired and rather hungry. Let's drive down to Gothenburg and spend the night there. Okay?"

About a half hour later they parked outside of a hotel on Post Street. They took single rooms, rested for an hour, and then went out to eat dinner.

While they were eating Martin Beck talked about boats and Ahlberg talked about a trip he had taken to the Faroe Islands.

Neither of them mentioned Roseanna McGraw.

11

To get from Gothenburg to Motala one takes Route 40 eastward via Borås and Ulricehamn to Jönköping. There, one turns northward onto the European Route 3 and continues on to Ödeshög, and follows Route 50 from there past Tåkern and Vadstena into Motala. It is a distance of approximately 165 miles and on this particular morning it took Ahlberg only about three and a half hours to cover it.

They had started at five-thirty in the morning, just at daybreak, while the garbage trucks were loading and newspaper women and one or two policemen were the only people to be seen on the rain-cleaned streets. A good many flat, gray miles disappeared behind the car before Ahlberg and Martin Beck broke the silence. After they had passed Hindås, Ahlberg cleared his throat and said:

"Do you really think it happened there? Inside that crowded cabin?"

"Where else?"

"With other people only a few inches away, behind the wall in the next cabin?"

"Bulkhead."

"What did you say?"

"Behind the bulkhead, not the wall."

"Oh," said Ahlberg.

Six miles later Martin Beck said:

"With others so close by, he would have to keep her from screaming."

"But how could he stop her? He must have . . . been at it rather long?"

Martin Beck did not answer. Each of them was thinking about the small cabin with its few Spartan conveniences. Neither of them could keep their imagination from entering the picture. Both of them were experiencing the same feeling of helpless, creeping unpleasantness. They reached in their pockets for cigarettes and smoked in silence.

When they drove into Ulricehamn, he said: "She could have received some of the injuries after she was already dead, or at least, unconscious. There are things in the autopsy statement that suggest it could have happened that way."

Ahlberg nodded. Without having to talk about it they both knew that such a thought made them feel better.

In Jönköping they stopped at a cafeteria and got some coffee. It didn't sit well with Martin Beck as usual, but at the same time it perked him up a little.

At Gränna, Ahlberg said what they had both been thinking for the last few hours:

"We don't know her."

"No," replied Martin Beck without taking his eyes from the hazy but pretty view.

"We don't know who she was. I mean . . ."

He was silent.

"I know what you mean."

"You do, don't you? How she lived. How she acted. What kind of people she went around with. That kind of thing."

"Yes."

All that was true. The woman on the breakwater had received a name, an address and an occupation. But nothing more. . . .

"Do you think that the technical boys will find something?"

"We can always hope."

Ahlberg gave him a quick look. No, they didn't need fancy phrases. The only thing they could conceivably hope for from the technical report was that it would, at least, not contradict their assumption that cabin A 7 was the scene of the crime. The *Diana* had made twenty-four trips on the canal since the woman from Lincoln had been on board. That would mean that the cabin had been well cleaned at least as many times; that the bedclothes, towels and other paraphernalia which had been there had been washed over and over again and were hopelessly mixed together by now. It also meant that between thirty and forty people had occupied the cabin after Roseanna McGraw. All of them had naturally left their traces.

"We still haven't heard the records of witnesses' examinations," said Ahlberg.

"Yes."

Eighty-five people, one of whom was presumably guilty, and the rest of whom were possible witnesses, each had their small pieces that might fit into the great jig-saw puzzle. Eighty-five people, spread over four different continents. Just to locate them was a Herculean task. He didn't dare think about the process of getting testimony from all of them and collecting the reports and going through them.

"And Roseanna McGraw," said Ahlberg.

"Yes," said Martin Beck.

And after a while:

"I can only see one way."

"The guy in America?"

"Yes."

"What's his name?"

"Kafka."

"That's a strange name. Does he seem competent?"

Martin Beck thought about the absurd telephone conversation a few days earlier and produced the first smile of that dismal day.

"Hard to say," he replied.

Halfway between Vadstena and Motala Martin Beck said, more or less to himself:

"Suitcases. Clothing. Toilet articles, the toothbrush. Souvenirs she had bought. Her passport, money, traveler's checks."

Ahlberg's hands gripped the wheel harder.

"I'll comb the canal carefully," he said. "First between Borenshult and the harbor. Then east of Boren. The locks have already been covered, but . . ."

"Lake Vättern?"

"Yes. We have almost no chance there and maybe not even in Boren if the dredger has buried everything there by now. Sometimes I dream about that damned apparatus and wake up in the middle of the night swearing. My wife thinks that I've gone mad. Poor thing," he said and drove to a stop in front of the police station.

Martin Beck looked at him with a quick, passing feeling of envy, disbelief, and respect.

Ten minutes later Ahlberg was sitting at his desk in his shirtsleeves as usual, talking to the lab. While he was talking, Larsson entered the room, shook hands with Martin Beck and raised his eyebrow questioningly. Ahlberg hung up the receiver.

"There were some traces of blood on the mattress and the rug. Fourteen counting carefully. They are analyzing them."

If these traces of blood had not been found, the theory of cabin number A 7 as the scene of the crime would not have been likely.

The Superintendent didn't seem to notice their relief. Their wordless communication was carried on wave-lengths that were unfamiliar to him. He raised his eyebrow again and said: "Was that all?"

"A few old fingerprints," said Ahlberg. "Not particularly many. They must have cleaned pretty well."

"The Public Prosecutor is on his way here," said Larsson.

"He's most welcome, of course," Ahlberg responded.

Martin Beck left on a 5:20 p.m. train via Mjölby. The trip took four and a half hours and he worked on a letter to America the entire time. When he got to Stockholm, the draft was finished. He wasn't completely satisfied with it but it would have to do. To save time he took a taxi to Nikolai Station, borrowed an examining room, and typed up the letter. While he was reading the finished copy, he heard brawling and swearing nearby and heard a constable say: "Take it easy boys, take it easy."

For the first time in a long while he remembered his own days as a patrolman and how deeply he had disliked the results of Saturday nights.

At a quarter of eleven he stood in front of the mailbox on Vasa Street. The metal top closed with a bang.

He walked southward in the light rain, past the Hotel Continental and the new, tall department stores. On the escalator down to the subway, he thought about Kafka and wondered if this man, whom he didn't know, would understand what he meant.

Martin Beck was tired and fell asleep soon after he got into the subway, safe in the knowledge that he wouldn't be getting off before the end of the line.

12

Ten days later Martin Beck received a reply from America. He saw it on his desk when he arrived in the morning, even before he had shut the door behind him. While he hung up his coat he glanced at his face in the mirror. He was pale and looked sallow and he had dark circles under his eyes. This was no longer due to the flu but to the fact that he had gone without much sleep. He tore open the large brown envelope and took out two transcripts of examinations, a typewritten letter and a card with biographical data. He thumbed through the papers with curiosity but thwarted his impulse to begin reading them immediately. Instead, he went in to the administrative office and asked for a rapid translation with three copies.

Afterwards he walked up one flight of stairs, opened a door, and walked into Kollberg's and Melander's office. They sat at their desks working, with their backs to one another.

"Have you changed the furniture?"

"It's the only way we can manage," said Kollberg.

He was pale and red-eyed just like Martin Beck. The imperturbable Melander looked no different than usual.

A copy of a report on thin, yellow paper lay in front of Kollberg. He was following each line with his index finger and said:

"Mrs. Lise-Lotte Jensen, sixty-one years old, has told the police in Vejle, Denmark, that it was a wonderful trip. That the smörgåsbord was wonderful, that it rained one whole day and one whole night and that the boat was delayed and that she was seasick the night it rained out in the lake, which was the second night. In spite of all that, the trip was wonderful and all the other passengers were *so* nice. She can't remember the nice girl in the picture. In any case they didn't sit at the same table. But the captain was charming and her husband said that it wasn't possible to eat all that good food so it certainly could have been possible that not everyone went to all the meals. The weather was wonderful except when it rained. They had no idea that Sweden could be so nice! Damn it, I had no idea it could be either," continued Kollberg. "They mostly played bridge with that charming gentleman from South Africa and his wife, Mrs. Hoyt, who came from Durban. Of course the cabins were rather small and the second night—here's something—there was a big, hairy arachnida on the bed. Her husband had a great deal of trouble getting it out of the cabin. Well, does arachnida mean a sex maniac?"

"A spider," said Melander without taking his pipe out of his mouth.

"I love the Danes," Kollberg continued. "They have neither seen nor heard anything unusual and, 'finally,' writes the policeman named Toft in Vejle who conducted the examination, 'there is obviously nothing in the testimony of this delightful, elderly couple which can spread any light on the case.' His art of deduction is crushing."

"Let's see, let's see," Melander grumbled to himself.

"Here's to our Danish brothers," said Kollberg.

Martin Beck leaned over the desk and leafed through the papers. He mumbled something which was inaudible. After ten days of work they had managed to locate two-thirds of the people who had been on board the *Diana.* By one means or another they had contacted more than forty persons and in twenty-three cases, they had regular examination transcripts at their disposal. The results were meager. Of those who had thus far been examined there was no one who could remember anything about Roseanna McGraw other than that they thought they had seen her on board some time during the trip.

Melander took his pipe out of his mouth and said: "Karl-Åke Eriksson, one of the crew. Have we found him?"

Kollberg checked one of his lists.

"A stoker. No, but we know a little about him. He shipped out from the Seamen's House in Gothenburg three weeks ago. On a Finnish freighter."

"Uhum," said Melander. "And he is twenty-two years old?"

"Yes, and what do you mean with that uhum?"

"His name reminded me of something. You ought to remember it too. But he didn't call himself by the same name then."

"Whatever you remember must certainly be right," said Kollberg with resignation.

"That devil has a memory like a circus elephant," he said to Martin Beck. "It's like sharing an office with a computer."

"I know."

"One who smokes the world's worst tobacco," said Kollberg.

"I'll have it in a minute," said Melander.

"Sure, I know. Damn it I'm tired," answered Kollberg.

"You don't get enough sleep," said Melander.

"Yes."

"You ought to see to it that you get plenty of sleep. I sleep eight hours every night. Fall asleep the minute I put my head on the pillow."

"What does your wife say about that?"

"Nothing. She goes to sleep even faster. Sometimes we don't even get to turn out the light."

"Nonsense. No, in any case, I don't get enough sleep these days."

"Why not?"

"I don't know. I just can't sleep."

"What do you do then?"

"Just lie there and think about how dreadful you are."

Kollberg grabbed his letter basket. Melander knocked the ashes out of his pipe and gazed at the ceiling. Martin Beck, who knew him, realized that he had just fed new material into that priceless memory where he stored everything he had ever seen, read, or heard.

A half hour after lunch one of the girls from the administrative office came in with the translations.

Martin Beck took off his jacket, locked his door and began to read.

First the letter. It read:

Dear Martin:

I think I understand what you mean. The transcripts of examinations which I am enclosing have been typed directly from the tapes. I haven't made any changes or shortened them in any way. You can judge the material for yourself. If you would like me to, I can dig up a few more people who knew her but I think that these two are the best. I hope to God that you get the devil that did it. If you get the guy, don't forget to give it to him for me too. I am enclosing a collection of all the biographical data I could get hold of and a commentary on the transcripts.

Sincerely,
Elmer

He laid the letter aside and took out the transcripts. The first one contained the heading:

"Examination of Edgar M. Mulvaney at the office of the District Attorney, Omaha, Nebraska, October 11, 1964. Examining Officer: Detective Lieutenant Kafka. Witness to the Examination: Sergeant Romney.

KAFKA: You are Edgar Moncure Mulvaney, thirty-three years old, living at 12 East Street here in town. You are an engineer and have been employed for one year as an Assistant Department Head at the Northern Electric Company in Omaha. Is that correct?

MULVANEY: Yes, that's right.

K: You are not under oath and your testimony will not be registered with a notary public. Some of the questions that I am going to ask you have to do with intimate details of your private life and you may find them unpleasant. You are being examined for information and none of the things that you say will be made public or will be used against you. I cannot force you to answer but I want to state the following: by answering all the questions fully and truthfully and as explicitly as possible, you can make a contribution which will help to see that the person or persons responsible for the murder of Roseanna McGraw are captured and punished.

M: I'll do my best.

K: You were living in Lincoln until eleven months ago. You also worked there.

M: Yes, as an engineer with the Department of Public Works, the section that took care of street lighting.

K: Where did you live?

M: In a building at 83 Greenrock Road. I shared an apartment with a colleague. We were both bachelors then.

K: When did you get to know Roseanna McGraw?

M: It was nearly two years ago.

K: In other words the autumn of 1962?

M: Yes, in November.

K: Under what circumstances did you meet?

M: We met at the house of one of my colleagues, Johnny Matson.

K: At a party?

M: Yes.

K: Did that Matson go around with Roseanna McGraw?

M: Hardly. It was an open house party where a lot of people came and went. Johnny knew her slightly from the library where she worked. He had invited all kinds of people. Lord knows where he got hold of all of them.

K: How did you meet Roseanna McGraw?

M: I don't know. We simply met there.

K: Had you gone to the party specifically looking for female company?

     (Pause)

K: Will you kindly answer the question.

M: I'm trying to remember. It's possible. I didn't have a particular girl I was going with at that time. But more likely I went there because I didn't have anything better to do.

K: And what happened?

M: Roseanna and I met by sheer chance, so to speak. We talked for a while. Then we danced.

K: How many dances?

M: The first two. The party had hardly begun.

K: Then you met right away?

M: Yes, we must have.

K: And?

M: I suggested that we leave.

K: After only two dances?

M: More exactly, during the second dance.

K: And what did Miss McGraw answer?

M: She said: 'Yes, let's go.'

K: Without any other comment?

M: Yes.

K: How did you presume to make such a suggestion?

M: Do I have to answer questions like that?

K: If you don't, this conversation is meaningless.

M: Okay, I noticed that she was getting excited while we were dancing.

K: Excited? In what way? Sexually?

M: Yes, naturally.

K: How did you know?

M: I can't (pause) exactly explain. In any case it was obvious. It was her behavior. I can't really be more precise.

K: And you? Were you sexually excited?

M: Yes.

K: Had you had anything to drink?

M: One martini, at most.

K: And Miss McGraw?

M: Roseanna never drank liquor.

K: So you left the party together? What happened then?

M: Neither of us had driven there. We took a taxi to the house that she was living in, 116 Second South Street. She still lives there. Lived, I mean.

K: She let you go with her—just like that?

M: Oh, we made some conversation. The usual stuff, you know. I don't remember the words. Actually, they seemed to bore her.

K: Did you get close to one another in the taxi?

M: We kissed.

K: Did she object?

M: Not at all. Anyway, I said we kissed.
   (Pause)

K: Who paid the taxi driver?

M: Roseanna. I didn't have time to stop her.

K: And then?

M: We went into the apartment. It was very nice. I remember that I was surprised. She had a lot of books.

K: What did you do?

M: Aw . . .

K: Did you have intercourse?

M: Yes.

K: When?

M: Almost immediately.

K: Will you please give an account, as carefully as possible, of what happened.

M: Say, what the hell are you doing? Is this some kind of private Kinsey Report?

K: I'm sorry. I want to remind you of what I said at the beginning of our conversation. This can be important.
   (Pause)

K: Are you having difficulty remembering?

M: God, no.

(Pause)

M: It feels strange to sit here and talk about a person who hasn't done any harm and who is dead anyway.

K: I understand your feelings. If I keep on insisting it's only because we need your help.

M: Okay, ask.

K: You came into the apartment together. What happened?

M: She took off her shoes.

K: And then?

M: We kissed.

K: And then?

M: She went into the bedroom.

K: And you?

M: I followed her. Do you want the details?

K: Yes.

M: She undressed and lay down.

K: On the bed?

M: No, *in* the bed. Under the sheets and blankets.

K: Was she totally undressed?

M: Yes.

K: Did she seem shy?

M: Not at all.

K: Did she turn out the lights?

M: No.

K: And you?

M: What do you think?

K: Did you have sexual intercourse then?

M: What in hell do you think we did? Crack nuts? Yes, I'm sorry but . . .

K: How long did you stay?

M: I don't know exactly, until one or two. Then I went home.

K: And this was the first time that you saw Miss McGraw?

M: Yes, it was the first time.

K: What did you think of her when you left there? And the next day?

(Pause)

M: I thought . . . first I thought that she was just an ordinary, cheap tramp although she had not given that impression at all in the beginning. Then I thought that she was a nympho-maniac. One idea was crazier than the other. Now, here, especially since she is dead, it seems absurd that I ever could have thought either of those things.

(Pause)

K: Listen to me, my friend. I assure you that it is just as painful for me to ask these questions as it is for you to answer them. I would never have done this if there hadn't been a purpose. The worst part of it is that we are not through yet. Not by a longshot.

M: I'm sorry that I got upset just now. It's just that I'm not accustomed to the situation and the surroundings. It seems so crazy to sit here and say things about Roseanna, things I have never said to anyone, with detectives running around outside the room and while the tape recorder turns and turns and the sergeant just sits over there and stares. Unfortunately, I'm not exactly a cynic, particularly when it has to do with . . .

K: Jack, close the Venetian blinds over there. Then wait outside.

(Pause)

ROMNEY: Goodbye.

M: I'm sorry.

K: You have nothing to be sorry about. What actually happened between you and Miss McGraw? After your first meeting?

M: I telephoned her two days later. She didn't want to see me then, she said so quite directly. But she said to call again if I wanted to. The next time I called her—it must have been about a week later—she invited me up.

K: And you . . .

M: Yes, we slept together. Then it continued like that. Sometimes once a week, sometimes twice. We always met at her apartment. Often on Saturdays, then we were together on Sundays if we were both free.

K: How long did this go on?

M: For eight months.

K: Why did it break up?

M: I fell in love with her.

K: I am afraid that I don't really understand.

M: Actually it's quite simple. To tell the truth I had been in love with her for a long time. I really loved her. But we never talked about love, so I said nothing.

K: Why not?

M: Because I wanted to hold her. Then when I told her . . . Well, then it was all over.

K: How did it happen?

M: You have to understand that Roseanna was the most up-right person I have ever met. She liked me a lot and above all, she liked to sleep with me. But she didn't want to live with me. She never made any secret of that. Both she and I knew precisely why we would meet.

K: How did she react when you told her that you loved her?

M: She was sad. Then she said: 'We'll sleep together one more time and tomorrow you'll leave here and that's the end. We are not going to hurt one another.'

K: Did you accept that?

M: Yes. If you had known her as well as I had you would have understood that there wasn't anything else to do.

K: When did this happen?

M: On July 3 last year.

K: And that was the end of all contact between you?

M: Yes.

K: Did she see other men during the period you were going together?

M: Yes and no.

K: In other words, did you have the impression that she was together with other men from time to time?

M: It wasn't a question of impressions. I know. In March I attended a four-week course in Philadelphia. Even before I left, she told me that I couldn't count on her being . . . faithful for such a long time. When I came back I asked her and she said that she had done it once, after three weeks.

K: Had sexual intercourse?

M: Yes. Boy, that's a hell of an expression. I asked her with whom, stupidly enough.

K: What did she answer?

M: That it was none of my business. And it wasn't either, especially from her point of view.

K: During the eight months that you saw her did you have intimate . . . sleep together regularly? Do I understand you correctly?

M: Yes.

K: But what about the evenings and nights that you weren't together? What did she do then?

M: She was alone. She liked being alone. She read a great deal and, anyway, she sometimes worked evenings. She wrote some, too, but I don't know what. She never mentioned it to me. You understand, Roseanna was very independent. Then too, we really didn't have the same interests. Except for one thing. But we got along well together and that's the truth.

K: How can you be sure that she was alone when you weren't there?

M: I . . . I was jealous sometimes. Once in a while when she wouldn't see me I went there and stood outside her apartment house watching. Twice I even stood there from the time she came home until the time that she left in the morning.

K: Did you give her money?

M: Never.

K: Why not?

M: She didn't need my money, she told me so from the very beginning. If and when we went out, she always paid for herself.

K: And when you stopped seeing each other? What did she do then?

M: I don't know. I never saw her again. It wasn't too long before I got a new job and moved here.

K: How would you describe her character?

M: She was very independent, as I said earlier. Honest. Completely natural, in every way. For example, she never wore make-up or jewelry. She seemed calm and relaxed for the most part, but once she said that she didn't want to see me too often because she knew that if she did I would get on her nerves. She said everyone did and that in our case it was unnecessary.

K: I am going to ask you some rather intimate questions now.

M: Go ahead. I'll answer anything now.

K: Have you any idea of how many times you were together?

M: Yes. Forty-eight times.

K: Are you sure? Exactly?

M: Yes. I can even tell you why. Every time we met and slept together I drew a small, red ring around the date on my office calendar. Just before I threw it away I counted the days.

K: Would you say that her sexual behavior patterns were normal?

M: She was very sexual.

K: Had you had enough experience to judge that?

M: I was thirty-one years old when we met. A certain amount had happened before that time.

K: Did she usually have an orgasm when you had sexual intercourse?

M: Yes, always.

K: Did you usually have intercourse several times in an evening?

M: No. Never. It wasn't necessary.

K: Did you use contraceptives?

M: Roseanna had some kind of pills. She took one every morning.

K: Did you usually discuss sexual matters?

M: No, never. We knew what we needed to know.

K: Did she often speak about her previous affairs?

M: Never.

K: And you?

M: Only once. She seemed totally uninterested and I never talked about it again.

K: What did you speak about?

M: Anything and everything. Mostly everyday things.

K: Whom did she see, other than you?

M: No one. She had a friend, a girl at the library, but they rarely saw one another outside of work. Roseanna liked to be alone, as I said.

K: But she went to that party where you met?

M: Yes, in order to meet someone to sleep with. She had been . . . abstaining for a long time then.

K: How long?

M: For more than six weeks.

K: How do you know that?

M: She said so.

K: Was she difficult to satisfy?

M: Not for me, in any case.

K: Was she demanding?

M: She wanted what all normal women want. That a man would take her until she didn't have anything left, if I understand you correctly.

K: Did she have any particular habits?

M: In bed?

K: Yes.

M: Harrison's Law isn't valid in Nebraska, is it?

K: No, you don't have to worry about that.

M: It doesn't really matter. She had only one habit which could possibly be called special. She scratched.

K: When?

M: Generally speaking, all the time. Especially when she had an orgasm.

K: How?

M: How?

K: Yes, how did she scratch?

M: I understand. Well, with both hands and all her fingers. Like a claw. From the hips, over the back and all the way up to the neck. I still have marks. It looks like they'll never go away.

K: Did she show much variety in her sexual exertions?

M: What unbelievable expressions you use! No, not at all. She always lay in the same way. On her back with a pillow under her hips and her legs spread wide apart and raised high. She was completely natural and direct and open in this as in everything else. She wanted to do it, she wanted a lot and at one time, without digression or deviations and in the only way that was natural for her.

K: I understand.

M: You ought to understand at this point.

(Pause)

K: Just one more thing. From what you've said I have the impressions that during your time together it was you who took the initiative, that it was always you who contacted her. You telephoned and she answered, either that you should come up, or that she didn't care to see you then and that you should call another day. It was always she who decided if and when you would meet?

M: I believe so.

K: Did she ever call you and ask you to come over?

M: Yes, four or five times.

(Pause)

K: Was it hard for you when you broke up?

M: Yes.

K: You have been very helpful. And very honest. Thank you.

M: I hope you understand that this conversation must be confidential. I met a girl here last Christmas and we got married in February.

K: Naturally. I said that in the beginning.

M: Okay, now maybe you can turn off the tape recorder.

K: Of course."

Martin Beck put down the bound report and thoughtfully dried the perspiration from his forehead and palms with a crumpled handkerchief. Before he began to read again he went out to the toilet, washed his face and drank a glass of water.

13

The second report from Kafka was not as long as the first. It also had a rather different tone.

"Examination of Mary Jane Peterson held at Police Headquarters, Lincoln, Nebraska, October 10, 1964. Examining Officer: Detective Lieutenant Kafka. Witness to the Examination: Sergeant Romney.

ROMNEY: This is Mary Jane Peterson. She is single, twenty-eight years old, and lives at 62 South Street. Employed at the Community Library here in Lincoln.

KAFKA: Have a seat, Miss Peterson.

PETERSON: Thank you. What's this all about?

K: Just a few questions.

P: About Roseanna McGraw?

K: That's right.

P: I don't know any more than what I've already said. I received a postcard from her. That's all. Have you brought me here from my work just to hear me say it again?

K: Were you and Miss McGraw friends?

P: Yes, of course.

K: Did you live together before Miss McGraw took her own apartment?

P: Yes, for fourteen months. She came here from Denver and had no place to go. I let her live with me.

K: Did you share the expenses for the apartment?

P: Naturally.

K: When did you separate?

P: More than two years ago. It was sometime during the spring of 1962.

K: But you continued to see one another?

P: We met every day at the library.

K: Did you also see each other in the evening?

P: Not very often. We saw enough of each other during working hours.

K: What did you think of Miss McGraw's character?

P: *De mortuis nihil nisi bene.*

K: Jack, take over here. I'll be right back.

R: Lieutenant Kafka asked you what you thought of Miss McGraw's character?

P: I heard him and I answered: *De mortuis nihil nisi bene.* That's Latin and means 'One shouldn't speak ill of the dead.'

R: The question was this: what was her character like?

P: You can ask someone else about that. May I go now?

R: Just try and you'll see.

P: You're a dope. Has anyone ever told you that?

R: If I were in your shoes, God forbid, I'd be pretty careful about talking like that.

P: Why?

R: Maybe because I don't like it.

P: Ha!

R: What was her character like?

P: I think you had better ask someone else about that, you idiot.

K: That's fine, Jack. Now, Miss Peterson?

P: Yes, what is it?

K: Why did you and Miss McGraw separate?

P: We were crowded. Anyway, I can't see that it's any business of yours.

K: You were good friends, weren't you?

P: Yes, of course.

K: I have a report from the police in the third district from the record on April 8, 1962. At ten past two in the morning several tenants in the building at 62 South Street complained of screaming, loud arguments and continuous noise from an apartment on the fourth floor. When police officers Flynn and Richardson got there ten minutes later they were not let into the apartment and had to get the superintendent to open the door with a pass key. You and Miss McGraw were found in the apartment. Miss McGraw had on bathrobe, and you were dressed in high-heeled shoes and what Flynn described as a white cocktail dress. Miss McGraw was bleeding from a scratch on her forehead. The room was disorderly. Neither of you would make a complaint, and order was restored—at least that's what it says here—and the policemen left the apartment.

P: What do you mean by bringing that thing up?

K: The next day Miss McGraw moved to a hotel, and one week later found her own apartment a few blocks up the same street.

P: I'm asking you again. What do you mean by bringing up that old scandal story? As if I haven't had enough unpleasantness already.

K: I am trying to convince you of the necessity of answering our questions. It's also a good idea to tell the truth.

P: Okay, I threw her out. Why not? It was my apartment.

K: Why did you throw her out, as you put it?

P: What difference does that make today? Who would be interested in a three year old fight between two girlfriends?

K: Anything that has to do with Roseanna McGraw is of interest just now. It seems—as you see in the papers—that there's not much to write about her.

P: Do you mean to say that you can blow up this story for the newspapers if you want to?

K: This report is a public document.

P: In that case isn't it odd that they haven't already gotten hold of it.

K: That's partly because Sergeant Romney got hold of it first. The minute he sends it back to the central archives anyone is free to take any part of it.

P: And if he doesn't send it back?

K: Then it's a different story.

P: Will the record of this examination also be available to the public?

K: No.

P: Can I depend on that?

K: Yes.

P: Okay, what do you want to know? Hurry up, though, so I can get out of here before I become hysterical.

K: Why did you force Miss McGraw to leave your apartment?

P: Because she embarrassed me.

K: In what way?

P: Roseanna was trash. She was in heat like a bitch. And I said it to her face.

K: What did she answer to that?

P: My dear Lieutenant, Roseanna didn't answer such commonplace statements. She held herself above them. Just lay naked on the bed as usual and read some philosopher. And then she would look at me. Large-eyed, uncomprehending and indulgent.

K: Was she very temperamental?

P: She had no temperament at all.

K: What was the direct cause of your sudden breakup?

P: You can try to figure that one out yourself. Even you ought to have enough imagination for that.

K: A man?

P: A slob she wanted to sleep with while I sat and waited for him in some hole about thirty miles from here. He had misunderstood in some way—he was pretty dumb too—and thought that he was to pick me up at home. When he got there I'd already left. Roseanna was home, naturally. She was always home. And so whatever happened, happened. Thank God that slob had left by the time I got back. Otherwise I would have been behind bars in Sioux City at this point.

K: How did you find out what had happened?

P: Roseanna. She always told the truth. I asked her why she had done it. She said, 'Now, Mary Jane, I *wanted* to do it.' And besides she was logical: 'Now, Mary Jane, it only shows that he isn't worth putting stock in.'

K: Would you still state that you and Miss McGraw were friends?

P: Yes, oddly enough. If Roseanna ever had a friend it was I. It was better after she had moved and we didn't have to see each other day in and day out. When she first came here—from college—she was always alone. Her parents had just died in Denver at almost the same time. She didn't have any brothers or sisters or any other relatives or any friends. She was also short of money. There was something muddled about her inheritance and year after year went by without it being settled. Eventually she got the money, right after she took that apartment.

K: What was her character like?

P: I think that she suffered some kind of independence complex which had some unusual expressions. One of her attitudes was to dress sloppily. She took a certain pride in looking horrible. At best she went around in slacks and a large, baggy sweater. It was hard for her to force herself to put on a dress to go to work. She had a lot of strange ideas. She almost never wore a bra and she needed to more than most of us. She hated to wear shoes. In general, she said she didn't like clothing. When she was at home she often ran around naked the entire day. She never wore a nightgown or pajamas. That irritated me terribly.

K: Was she messy?

P: Only with her appearance, but I am sure that was put on. She pretended that she never realized there were such things as cosmetics, hairdressers or nylon stockings. But with other things she was almost meticulous, above all with her books

K: What kind of interests did she have?

P: She read a lot. Wrote a bit, but don't ask me what because I don't know. In the summer she was often out for hours. She said that she liked to walk. And then men. But she didn't have a lot of interests.

K: Was Miss McGraw an attractive woman?

P: Not at all. You ought to have understood that from what I've said. But she was man crazy and that goes a long way.

K: Did she have any steady man in her life?

P: When she moved out she did go around now and then with a man who worked for the Highway Department for a half a year. I met him a few times. Lord knows how often she cheated on *him*, probably hundreds.

K: While you were living together, did she often bring men to the apartment?

P: Yes.

K: What do you mean by often?

P: What do *you* mean?

K: Did it happen several times a week?

P: Oh, no, there had to be some moderation.

K: How often did it happen? Answer!

P: Don't use that tone of voice.

K: I'll use any tone of voice I want to. How often did she bring men home to the apartment?

P: Once or twice a month.

K: Was it always different men?

P: I don't know. I didn't always see them. As a matter of fact I usually didn't see them. At times she kept pretty much to herself. Often she had people here when I was out dancing or someplace.

K: Didn't Miss McGraw go out with you?

P: Never. I don't even know if she could dance.

K: Can you give me the names of any of the men she went around with?

P: There was a German student whom we met at the library. I introduced them. I remember his name was Mildenberger. Uli Mildenberger. She brought him home three or four times.

K: During how long a period?

P: A month, possibly five weeks. But he telephoned her every day, and between times they certainly met somewhere else. He lived here in Lincoln for several years but went back to Europe last spring.

K: What did he look like?

P: Handsome. Tall, blond and broad-shouldered.

K: Did you have intimate relations with this Mildenberger?

P: What the hell business is that of yours?

K: How many different men do you think she brought home during the time you lived together?

P: Oh, six or seven.

K: Was Miss McGraw attracted to a certain type of man?

P: In this instance she was perfectly normal. She wanted to have good looking guys. The kind that at least looked like men.

K: What do you know about her trip?

P: Only that she had been planning it for a long time. She wanted to take the boat over and then travel around Europe for a month and see as much as possible. Then she thought she might stay in one place for the rest of the time, in Paris or Rome or someplace. Why are you asking about all this anyway? The police over there shot the man that murdered her.

K: That information was unfortunately incorrect. Due to a misunderstanding.

P: May I finally go now? _I_ actually have work to do.

K: How did you react when you learned what had happened to Miss McGraw?

P: At first it was a real shock but I wasn't terribly surprised.

K: Why not?

P: And you ask that? After you know how she lived?

K: That will be all now. Goodbye Miss Peterson.

P: And you won't forget what you've promised?

K: I haven't promised anything. You can shut off the tape recorder now, Jack."

Martin Beck swung back in his chair, put his left hand to his mouth and bit on the knuckle of his index finger. Then he took the last remaining paper that he had received from Lincoln, Nebraska, and read through Kafka's explanation absentmindedly.

"Roseanna Beatrice McGraw. Born, May 18, 1937 in Denver, Colorado. Father, small-scale farmer. The farm was about twenty miles from Denver. Education: college in Denver and three years at the University of Colorado. Both parents died in the fall of 1960. Inheritance, about $20,000, paid out in July, 1962. Miss McGraw has not left a will and as far as one knows has no heirs.

"As far as the reliability of the witnesses: my impression was that in some way Mary Jane Peterson altered reality and that she held back certain details, obviously ones that might be disadvantageous to her. I have had a chance to check out Mulvaney's testimony on several points. The statement that R. McG. had only met one other man during the period from November 1962 to July 1963 seems to be correct. I got this from some kind of diary that I found in her apartment. The date was March 22 and the man's initials are U. M. (Uli Mildenberger?) She always made a note of her relationships in the same way, a sort of code with the date and the initials. I have not been able to find any untruths or direct lies in Mulvaney's story.

"Regarding the witnesses: Mulvaney is about 6 feet 2 inches tall, quite strong, blue eyed and has dark blond hair. Seems straightforward but a little naive. Mary Jane Peterson is quite a girl, attractive, stylishly dressed, strikingly slender and well developed. Neither of them have a police record, other than the ridiculous story about the trouble in the girls' apartment in 1962.

(signed)"

Martin Beck put on his jacket and set the lock on the door. Then he went back to his desk. He spread Kafka's papers out in front of him and sat completely still with his elbows on the desk and his forehead in his hands.

14

Martin Beck looked up from the records of the examinations when Melander opened the door to his office. This was something that didn't happen very often.

"Karl-Åke Eriksson-Stolt," said Melander. "Do you remember him?"

Martin Beck thought for a moment.

"Do you mean the fireman on the *Diana*? Was that his name?"

"He calls himself Eriksson now. Two and a half years ago he was called Eriksson-Stolt. That's when he was sentenced to a year in prison because he had seduced a girl who was not yet thirteen years old. Don't you remember? A tough, long-haired, fresh guy."

"Yes, I think I remember. Are you sure it's the same fellow?"

"I checked with the Seamen's Association. It's the same guy."

"I don't remember very well how it happened. Didn't he live in Sundyberg?"

"No, in Hagalund, with his mother. It happened one day when his mother was at work. He didn't go to work. He took the janitor's daughter home with him. She wasn't quite thirteen and it was later proven that she was a bit retarded. He managed to get her to drink alcohol, I think it was aquavit mixed with juice and when she was drunk enough, he slept with her."

"Was it her parents who reported him?"

"Yes, and I went out to get him. During the examination

he tried to play tough and stated that he had thought that the girl was of age and that she wanted to. She really didn't look a day over eleven and even then she seemed young for her age. The doctor who examined her said that she may have gone through shock, but I don't know. In any case, Eriksson was sentenced to a year of hard labor."

Martin Beck had a chill when he realized that this man had been on board the *Diana* at the same time as Roseanna.

"Where is he now?" he asked.

"On a Finnish freighter. It's called the *Kalajoki*. I'll find out where she is. Notice that I said *she*."

The same minute that Melander closed the door behind him, Martin Beck picked up the telephone and called Ahlberg.

"We've got to get hold of him," said Ahlberg. "Call me as soon as you have talked to the shipping line. I want him here, even if I have to swim after him myself. The other fireman has also shipped out on another boat, but I'll find out where soon. In addition, I ought to talk with the chief engineer again. He's left the sea and is now working for Electrolux."

They hung up. Martin Beck sat unoccupied for a few minutes while he wondered what he should do. Suddenly, he became nervous, left his office, and walked upstairs.

Melander had just finished a telephone conversation when he entered the room. Kollberg wasn't there.

"That boat, the *Kalajoki*. It's just leaving Holmsund. It's tied up at Söderhamn for the night. The shipping line has confirmed the fact that he's on board."

Martin Beck returned to his office and called Ahlberg again.

"I'll take one of my boys with me and drive up and get him," said Ahlberg. "I'll call you when we have got him."

They were silent for a moment. Then Ahlberg said: "Do you think it was he?"

"I don't know. It could be a possibility of course. I have only seen him once, and that was more than two years ago, just before he was sentenced. A pretty twisted type."

Martin Beck spent the rest of the afternoon in his office. He wasn't in the mood to work but he managed to get a number of routine things done. He kept thinking about the Finnish freighter that was on its way to Söderhamn. And about Roseanna McGraw.

When he went home he tried to work on his model ship

but after a while he merely sat there with his elbows on the table and his hands clasped in front of him. He could hardly expect to hear anything from Ahlberg before the next morning and finally he went to bed. He slept fitfully and awakened at five o'clock in the morning.

By the time the morning newspaper hit the floor with a thump he was already shaved and dressed. He had read through the sports pages by the time Ahlberg called.

"We have him here now. He's playing hard-boiled. Not saying anything. I can't exactly say that I like him. By the way, I've spoken to the Prosecutor. He says that we need an expert examiner and that I should ask you to come down. I think it's necessary."

Martin Beck looked at his wristwatch. By now he knew the time-table by heart.

"Okay. I can make the seven-thirty train. See you. So long."

He asked the taxi to drive past Kristineberg where he stopped for his file containing the examination records. At twenty-five minutes after seven he was sitting on the train.

Karl-Åke Eriksson-Stolt was born in Katarina parish twenty-two years ago. His father died when he was six years old and the following year his mother had moved to Hagalund. He was an only child. His mother, who was a seamstress, had supported him until he had finished school. The only teacher who had remembered him said that he had been of average intelligence, noisy and insubordinate. After he left school, he had held several different jobs, mostly as a messenger boy or a construction worker. When he was eighteen years old he went to sea, first as an ordinary seaman and then as a fireman. The Seamen's Association had nothing particular to say about him. One year later he moved back to his mother's and let her support him for a year until the State took over that detail. A year and a half ago he was released from the penitentiary.

Martin Beck had studied this record the day before but read through it carefully one more time. There was also a statement from the examining psychiatrist in the folder. It was rather short and mainly spoke about libido, lethargy and frigidity. In addition it stated that Karl-Åke Eriksson-Stolt had psychopathic tendencies and a strongly developed sex drive, a combination that could lead to abnormal expressions.

Martin Beck went directly to the police station from the railroad station and knocked on Ahlberg's door at ten minutes to eleven. Superintendent Larsson was in Ahlberg's office. They looked tired and worried and seemed relieved to pass the ball to someone else. Neither of them had succeeded in getting a word out of Eriksson with the exception of a number of swear words.

Ahlberg looked through the file quickly. When he closed it Martin Beck said: "Did you get hold of the other fireman?"

"Yes, in a way. He's working on a German boat that is in the Hook of Holland right now. I telephoned Amsterdam this morning and spoke with the police superintendent there who knew a little German. You ought to hear my German. If I understood him correctly there is someone in the Hague who speaks Danish who could take care of the official examination. Now if he understood *me* correctly, we ought to hear something from there tomorrow."

Ahlberg sent out for coffee and after Martin Beck had two cups, he said: "Okay. We might as well start now. Where shall we work?"

"In the next room. There's a tape recorder and whatever else you need there."

Eriksson looked just about the way Martin Beck had remembered him. About five feet, eleven inches tall, thin and gangly. A long, thin face with close-set blue eyes under long, curly eyelashes and straight, heavy eyebrows. A straight nose, a small mouth with thin lips and a weak chin. Long whiskers and a little dark mustache which Martin Beck could not remember having seen before. He had bad posture and was round-shouldered. He was dressed in a pair of old blue-jeans, a blue workshirt, black leather vest and black shoes with pointed toes.

"Sit down," said Martin Beck and nodded toward a chair on the other side of the desk. "Cigarette?"

Eriksson took the cigarette, lit it and sat down. He placed the cigarette in the corner of his mouth, slunk down in his chair and raised his right foot on his left knee. Then he put his thumbs inside his belt and tapped his left foot while he looked at the wall above Martin Beck's head.

Martin Beck looked at him for a moment, turned on the tape recorder which was placed on a low table beside him, and began to read some of the papers in his file.

"Eriksson, Karl-Åke. Born November 23, 1941. Seaman, currently employed on the Finnish freighter *Kalajoki*. Home address, Hagalund, Solna. Is that right?"

Eriksson made a small motion with his head.

"I asked you a question. Is that right? Is the information correct? Answer. Yes or no."

E: Yes, damn it.

B: When did you sign on the *Kalajoki?*

E: Three or four weeks ago.

B: What did you do before that?

E: Nothing particular.

B: Where did you do nothing particular?

E: What?

B: Where were you living before you signed on the Finnish boat?

E: With a friend in Gothenburg.

B: How long did you stay in Gothenburg?

E: A few days. Maybe a week.

B: And before that?

E: At my old lady's, my mother's.

B: Were you working then?

E: No, I was sick.

B: What was wrong with you?

E: I was just sick. Felt bad and had a fever.

B: Where did you work before you were sick?

E: On a boat.

B: What was the name of the boat?

E: The *Diana.*

B: What kind of a job did you have on the *Diana?*

E: Fireman.

B: How long were you on the *Diana?*

E: The whole summer.

B: From . . . ?

E: From the first of July until the middle of September. Then they lay off. They put the boat up, too. They only run in the summer. Back and forth with a bunch of corny tourists. Damn dull. I wanted to sign off the tub but my buddy wanted to stay on, and anyway, I needed the cash.

After that strain on his oratorical powers, Eriksson seemed completely exhausted and sank even further down in his chair.

B: What's your buddy's name? What was his job on the *Diana?*

E: Fireman. There were three of us at the engine. Me, my buddy and the engineer.

B: Did you know any of the other crew members?

Eriksson bent forward and put out his cigarette in the ash
tray. "What the hell kind of an examination is this," he said,
and threw himself back in his chair. "I haven't done anything.
Here I've gone and gotten a job and some damn cops come
and . . ."

B: You will answer my questions. Did you know any of the
other crew members?

E: Not when I started. I only knew my buddy then. But you
get to meet the others later. There was a guy who worked on
the deck that was kind of fun.

B: Did you meet any girls on the trips?

E: There was only one gal who was anything at all but she
went around with the cook. The rest of them were old
bags.

B: The passengers then?

E: We didn't see much of them. I really didn't meet any girls.

B: Did you work in shifts, the three of you in the engine
room?

E: Yes.

B: Do you remember if anything unusual happened at any
time during the summer?

E: No, what do you mean, unusual?

B: If any one trip was different from the rest. Didn't the engine break down at some point?

E: Yes, that's right. A steampipe broke. We had to go into
Söderköping for repairs. It took a hell of a long time. But that
wasn't my fault.

B: Do you remember when it happened?

E: Just after we'd passed Stegeborg.

B: Yes, but which day did it happen?

E: Who the hell knows. What kind of damn nonsense is
this? It wasn't my fault that the engine broke down. Anyway, I
wasn't working then. It wasn't my shift.

B: But when you left Söderköping? Was it your shift then?

E: Yes, and before that too. All three of us had to work like
hell to get the barge going again. We worked all night and
then we worked the next day, the engineer and I.

B: What time did you go off the shift during the day?

E: The day after Söderköping? Quite late in the afternoon,
I think.

B: Then what did you do when you were free?

Eriksson looked emptily at Martin Beck and didn't answer.

B: What did you do when you had finished working that day?

E: Nothing.

B: You must have done something? What did you do?

(The same empty look.)

B: Where was the boat when you were free?

E: I don't know. At Roxen, I think.

B: What did you do when you got off your shift?

E: Nothing, I told you.

B: You must have done *something*. Did you meet anyone?

Eriksson looked bored and stroked his neck.

B: Think about it. What did you do?

E: What a lot of garbage. What do you think anyone can do on that damned tub? Play football? The boat was right out in the middle of the water. Now listen, the only things you could do on that tub were eat and sleep.

B: Did you meet anyone that day?

E: Sure, I met Brigitte Bardot. How the hell can I know if I met anyone. It was a few years ago.

B: Okay. We'll start over. Last summer, when you were working on the *Diana*, did you meet anyone or any of the passengers?

E: I didn't meet any passengers. We didn't get to meet the passengers anyway. And even if we had, I wasn't interested. A bunch of snotty tourists. The hell with them.

B: What's the name of your buddy who also worked on the *Diana*?

E: Why? What's this all about anyway? We didn't do anything.

B: What's his name?

E: Roffe.

B: First name and last name.

E: Roffe Sjöberg.

B: Where is he now?

E: He's on some German boat. I don't know where the hell he is. Maybe he's in Kuala Lampur. I don't know.

Martin Beck gave up. He turned off the tape recorder and got up. Eriksson began to stretch slowly to get out of his chair.

"Sit down," roared Martin Beck. "Sit there until I tell you to get up."

He called in to Ahlberg who stood in the doorway five seconds later.

"Get up," said Martin Beck, and went out of the room ahead of him.

When Ahlberg came back to his office Martin Beck was sitting beside his desk. He looked up at him and shrugged his shoulders.

"Let's go and eat now," he said. "I'll try again later."

15

At nine-thirty the next morning Martin Beck sent for Eriksson for the third time. The examination continued for two hours and brought equally poor results.

When Eriksson slouched out of the room escorted by a young constable, Martin Beck put the tape recorder on rewind and went to get Ahlberg. They listened to the tape mostly in silence which was broken only now and then by Martin Beck's short comments.

A few hours later they were sitting in Ahlberg's office.

"Well, what do you think?"

"It wasn't he," said Martin Beck. "I'm almost sure of it. In the first place he isn't intelligent enough to keep up the mask. He simply doesn't understand what it's all about. He's not faking."

"Maybe you're right," said Ahlberg.

"In the second place, and this is only instinct, but I'm convinced of it in any case. We know a little about Roseanna McGraw, don't we?"

Ahlberg nodded.

"So it's very hard for me to believe that she would willingly go to bed with Karl-Åke Eriksson."

"No, that's right. She was willing, but not with just anyone. But who said that she did willingly?"

"Yes. It must have been that way. She met someone that she thought she would like to go to bed with and by the time it had gone far enough for her to discover her mistake, it was too late. But it wasn't Karl-Åke Eriksson."

"It could have happened some other way," said Ahlberg doubtfully.

"How? In that tiny cabin? Someone forced open the door and threw himself on her? She would have fought and screamed like mad and people on board would have heard her."

"He could have threatened her. With a knife or maybe a pistol."

Martin Beck shook his head slowly. Then he got up quickly and walked over to the window. Ahlberg followed him with his eyes.

"What should we do with him?" asked Ahlberg. "I can't hold him much longer."

"I'd like to talk with him one more time. I don't think he really knows why he is here. I am going to tell him now."

Ahlberg got up and put on his jacket. Then he went out.

Martin Beck remained seated for a while, thinking. After that he sent for Eriksson, took his briefcase and went into the examining room next door.

"What the hell is all this about?" asked Eriksson. "I haven't done anything. You can't keep me here when I haven't done anything. God damn it. . . ."

"Be quiet until I tell you you can talk. You are here to answer my questions," said Martin Beck.

He took out the retouched photograph of Roseanna Mc-Graw and held it up in front of Eriksson.

"Do you recognize this woman?" he asked.

"No," Eriksson answered. "Who is she?"

"Look carefully at the picture and then answer. Have you ever seen the woman in this photograph?"

"No."

"Are you sure?"

Eriksson placed one elbow on the back of his chair and rubbed his nose with his index finger.

"Yes. I've never laid eyes on the dame."

"Roseanna McGraw. Does that name mean anything to you?"

"What a hell of a name. Is this a joke?"

"Have you heard the name Roseanna McGraw before?"

"No."

"Then I'm going to tell you something. The woman in the photograph is Roseanna McGraw. She was an American and a passenger on the *Diana*'s first trip out of Stockholm on July 3. The *Diana* was delayed on that trip by twelve hours, first due to fog south of Oxelösund and then due to an engine breakdown. You have already said that you were on that trip. When the vessel arrived in Gothenburg ten hours off schedule Roseanna McGraw wasn't on it. She was killed during the night between July 4–5 and was found three days later in the lock chamber at Borenshult."

Eriksson sat straight up in his chair. He grabbed the arm rests and chewed on the left corner of his mouth.

"Is that why . . . ? Do you think that . . . ?"

He pressed the palms of his hands together, placed his hands tightly between his knees and bent forward so that his chin nearly rested on the desk. Martin Beck saw how the skin on the bridge of his nose had paled.

"I haven't murdered anyone! I've never seen that dame! I swear!"

Martin Beck said nothing. He kept looking directly at the man's face and saw the fear grow in his enlarged eyes.

When he spoke his voice was dry and toneless.

"Where were you and what were you doing on the night of July 4–5?"

"In my cabin. I swear! I was in my cabin sleeping! I haven't done anything! I've never seen that dame! It isn't true!"

His voice rose to a falsetto and he threw himself back in his chair. His right hand went up to his mouth and he began to bite on his thumb while he stared at the photograph in front of him. Then his eyes narrowed and his voice became thin and hysterical.

"You're trying to trick me. You think you can frighten me, don't you? All that about the girl is fake. You've talked with Roffe and that devil said it was me. He's squealed. He did it, not me. I haven't done anything. That's the truth. I haven't done anything. Roffe said it was me, didn't he? He said it."

Martin Beck didn't take his eyes away from the man's face.

"That bastard. He fixed the lock and he stole the money."

He bent forward and his voice became eager. The words poured out of him.

"He forced me to go along with it. He had worked in that damn building. It was his idea all along. I didn't want to. I said so. I refused. I didn't want to have anything to do with such a thing. But he forced me, that damned louse. He squealed, that ass. . . ."

"Okay," said Martin Beck. "Roffe squealed. You'd better tell me everything now."

One hour later he played back the tape for Larsson and Ahlberg. There was a complete confession of a burglary which Karl-Åke Eriksson and Roffe Sjöberg had committed in a garage in Gothenburg one month earlier.

When Larsson had left to telephone to the Gothenburg police, Ahlberg said: "In any case we know where we have him for the time being."

He sat quietly for a while and drummed on the desk.

"Now there are about fifty possible suspects left," said Ahlberg. "If we go on the premise that the murderer was among the passengers."

Martin Beck remained silent and looked at Ahlberg who sat with his head down and seemed to be examining his fingernails. He looked just as depressed as Martin Beck had felt when he realized that the examination of Eriksson wasn't leading anywhere.

"Are you disappointed?" he asked.

"Yes, I'll have to admit it. For a while I really thought we were there and now it seems that we have just as far to go."

"We've made some progress in any case. Thanks to Kafka."

The telephone rang and Ahlberg answered it. He sat listening for a long while with the receiver pressed against his ear. Then he cried suddenly:

"*Ja, ja, ich bin hier.* Ahlberg *hier.*"

"Amsterdam," he said to Martin Beck who left the room discreetly.

While he was washing his hands he thought '*an, auf, hinter, in, neben, über, unter, vor, zwischen,*' and he was reminded of the first sticky odor of a room many years ago and of a round table with a baize cloth and an elderly teacher with a thin German grammar book between her fat fingers. When he went back Ahlberg had just put down the phone.

"What a language," he said. "Roffe Sjöberg wasn't on the boat. He had signed on in Gothenburg but he never went on board. Well, that will be Gothenburg's headache now."

Martin Beck slept on the train. He didn't wake up before it arrived in Stockholm. He really only woke up when he got into his own bed at home.

16

At ten minutes after five Melander tapped at the door. He waited about five seconds before he showed his long, thin face in the door opening and said: "I thought I'd leave now. Is that all right?"

He had no official reason for asking but he went through the same process every day. On the other hand, he never bothered to announce his arrival in the morning.

"Certainly," said Martin Beck. "So long."

After a moment he added, "Thanks for your help today."

Martin Beck remained and listened to the work day die away. The telephones were the first to become silent, then the typewriters, and then the sound of voices stopped until finally even the footsteps in the corridors could no longer be heard.

At five-thirty he called home.

"Shall we wait for dinner?"

"No, go ahead and eat."

"Will you be late?"

"I don't know. It's possible."

"You haven't seen the children for ages."

Without doubt he had both seen and heard them less than nine hours ago, but she knew that just as well as he.

"Martin?"

"Yes."

"You don't sound well. Is it anything special?"

"No, not at all. We have a lot to do."

"Is that all?"

"Yes, of course."

Now she sounded like herself again. The moment had passed. A few of her standard phrases and the discussion was over. He had held the receiver to his ear and heard the click when she put hers down. A click, and empty silence and it was as if she were a thousand miles away. Years had passed since they had really talked.

He wrinkled his forehead and sighed and looked at the papers on his desk. Each one of them had something to say about Roseanna McGraw and the last days of her life. He was sure of that. And still, they didn't tell him anything.

It seemed meaningless to read through all of them once again but he probably should do it anyway, and do it now. He would start soon.

He stretched out his hand to get a cigarette but the package was empty. He threw it into the wastepaper basket and reached in the pocket of his jacket for another pack. During the past few weeks he had smoked twice as much as he usually did and he felt it, both in his wallet and in his throat. It seemed that he had used up his reserve pack because the only thing he found in his pockets was something that he did not immediately recognize.

It was a postcard, bought at a tobacco shop in Motala. It showed the lock chamber at Borenshult seen from above. The lake and the breakwater were in the background and two men were in the process of opening the sluice gates for a passenger boat rising in the foreground. The picture was obviously quite old because the ship on the photograph no longer existed. Her name was *Astrea* and she had long since succumbed to the wreckers and the blowtorches.

But then, at the time when the photograph was taken, it had been summer and suddenly he remembered the fresh odor of flowers and wet shrubbery.

Martin Beck opened a drawer and took out his magnifying glass. It was shaped like a scoop and there was an electric battery in the handle. When he pressed the button, the object under study was illuminated with a small bulb. It was a good photograph and he could quite clearly make out the skipper on the port side of the bridge and several of the passengers who were hanging on the railing. The forward deck of the ship was loaded with cargo, still another sign that the picture was far from new.

He had just moved his glance slightly to the right when Kollberg walloped on the door with his fists and walked in.

"Hi, were you frightened?"

"Frightened to death," answered Martin Beck and felt his heart skip a beat.

"Haven't you gone home yet?"

"Sure. I'm sitting three stories up in my apartment and eating chicken."

"By the way, when do we get paid?"

"Tomorrow, I hope."

Kollberg collapsed in the visitor's chair.

They sat quietly for a while. Finally Kollberg said: "That was a flop, wasn't it? Examining that tough guy you went down and mangled?"

"He didn't do it."

"Are you absolutely sure?"

"No."

"Do you *feel* sure?"

"Yes."

"That's good enough for me. When you get right down to it there is a difference between seducing a twelve year old girl and killing a full grown woman."

"Yes."

"And anyway, she would never have gone for a type like that. Not if I've read my Kafka right."

"No," Martin Beck agreed with conviction. "She wouldn't have."

"What did the guy in Motala think? Was he disappointed?"

"Ahlberg? Yes, somewhat. But he's stubborn. What did Melander say, by the way?"

"Nothing. I've known that fellow since our training days and the only thing that has ever depressed him was tobacco rationing."

Kollberg took out a notebook with a black cover and thumbed through it thoughtfully.

"While you were away I went through everything again. I tried to make up a summary."

"Yes?"

"I asked myself, for example, the question that Hammar is going to ask us tomorrow: What do we know?"

"And what did you answer?"

"Wait a minute. It's better if you answer. What do we know about Roseanna McGraw?"

"A little. Thanks to Kafka."

"That's right. I would even venture to say that we know all the important factors about her. Further: what do we know about the actual murder?"

"We have the scene of the crime. We also know approximately how and when it happened."

"Do we actually know where it happened?"

Martin Beck drummed his fingers on the top of the desk. Then he said:

"Yes. In cabin A 7 on board the *Diana*."

"According to the blood-type that's right. But that would never hold as evidence."

"No, but *we* know it," said Martin Beck quickly.

"Okay. We'll pretend that we know it. When?"

"On the night of July 4. After dark. In any event sometime after dinner which ended at eight o'clock. Presumably sometime between nine o'clock and midnight."

"How? Yes, on that point we have the autopsy report. We can also guess that she undressed herself, of her own free will. Or possibly under threat for her life. But that doesn't seem likely."

"No."

"And so, last but not least, what do we know about the culprit?"

Kollberg answered his own question in twenty seconds: "That the person in question is a sadist and sexually twisted."

"That the person in question is a man," Martin Beck added.

"Yes, most likely. And pretty strong. Roseanna McGraw was clearly not dropped off a wagon."

"We know that he was on board the *Diana*."

"Yes, if we assume that our earlier theory was correct."

"And that he must belong in one of two categories: passengers or the crew."

"Do we really know that?"

It was silent in the room. Martin Beck massaged his hairline with the tips of his fingers. Finally he said: "It must be so."

"Must it?"

"Yes."

"All right, we'll say it is. But on the other hand, we don't have any idea what the murderer looks like or of his nationality. We have no fingerprints and nothing that can tie him to the crime. We don't know if he knew Roseanna McGraw earlier. We don't know where he came from, or where he went or where we could find him today."

Kollberg was very serious now.

"We know damned little, Martin," he said. "Are we even absolutely sure that Roseanna McGraw *didn't* step off the boat in Gothenburg safe and sound? That someone didn't kill her afterwards? Someone who knew where she had come from and who might have transported her body back to Motala and then thrown it in?"

"I've thought of it. But it's too absurd. Things don't happen that way."

"Since we haven't yet received the menu from the boat for those days, it is still theoretically possible. Even if it stretches the imagination. And even if we manage to prove, really prove, that she never got to Gothenburg, there is still another possibility: she could have gone ashore while the boat was in the lock chamber at Borenshult and met some nut who was wandering around in the bushes."

"In that case we ought to have found something."

"Yes, but 'ought to' is a weak concept. There are things in this case that almost drive me crazy. How in hell could she disappear during half the trip without anyone noticing it, not even the room steward or the waiter in the dining room?"

"The person who killed her must have stayed on board. He arranged the cabin to make it look normal and used. It was only a question of one night."

"Where did the sheets go? And the blankets? They must have had blood on them. He couldn't very well just sit down and start doing laundry. And if he had thrown everything in the water, where did he get fresh things from?"

"There wasn't that much blood, the autopsy didn't say so. And if the person who killed her was familiar with the vessel, he could have gotten fresh bedding from the supply closet."

"Would a passenger be that much at home on the boat? And wouldn't someone notice?"

"It isn't so hard. Have you ever been on a passenger ship at night?"

"No."

"Everyone goes to sleep. It's completely quiet and empty. Almost all the closets and cupboards are unlocked. When this boat passed Lake Vättern, during the night watch, there were only three people who were definitely awake. Those on watch, two on the bridge and one in the engine room."

"Shouldn't someone have noticed that she didn't get off in Gothenburg?"

"There is no set procedure for getting off when the boat lands there. They tie up at Lilla Bommen and the passengers grab their things and rush down the gangway. On this particular trip, most people were in a hurry because the ship had been delayed. In addition, contrary to usual, it was dark when they got in."

Martin Beck stopped speaking and gazed at the wall for a while.

"What irritates me most is that the passengers in the next cabin didn't notice anything," he said.

"I can explain that, I found out just two hours ago that a Dutch couple had cabin A 3. Both were over seventy and nearly stone deaf."

Kollberg turned the page and scratched his head.

"Our so called theory of how, when and where the crime took place is mainly built on principles of probability, logical assumptions and the application of some psychology. It certainly is weak on evidence. We have to hold to it in any case because it's all we have to go on. But we must also appraise the statistics in the same way, right?"

Martin Beck leaned back in his chair and crossed his arms over his chest.

"Let's hear it," he said.

"We know the names of eighty-six people who were on board. Sixty-eight passengers plus the eighteen that made up the crew. Thus far we have located, or in some way been in contact with all of them, with the exception of eleven. But we know the nationalities, sexes, and—with three exceptions—the ages of all of them. Now, let's use a process of elimination. First of all we have to eliminate Roseanna McGraw. That leaves eighty-five. After that, all the women, eight in the crew and thirty-seven among the passengers. That leaves forty. Among these there are four boys under ten and seven men over seventy. That leaves twenty-nine. Furthermore, there was the captain and the helmsman. They were on watch between eight o'clock and midnight, giving each other alibis. They hardly had time to murder anyone. It's a bit less clear with the people in the engine room. Deduct those two and we have a grand total of twenty-seven. We have, however, the names of twenty-seven male persons between the ages of fourteen and sixty-eight. Twelve are Swedish, seven of whom were crew members, five Americans, three Germans, one Dane, one South African, an Englishman, a Frenchman, a Scot, a Turk and a Dutchman. The geographic spread is equally terrifying. One of the Americans lives in Texas, another in Oregon. The Englishman lives in Nassau in the Bahamas, the South African in Durban, and the Turk in Ankara. It's going to be one hell of a trip for whoever examines them. In addition, there are four out of this twenty-seven whom we haven't been able to locate. One Dane, and three Swedes. We haven't been able to show that any of these passengers have traveled with the canal boats earlier, in spite of the fact that Melander has plowed through passenger lists for the past twenty-five years. My own theory is that none of the passengers could have done it. Only four of them were traveling in single cabins. The others ought to have been more or less observed by their spouses or whomever they shared a cabin with. None of them really knew their way around the boat well enough or the routine on board to have done it. That leaves the eight men in the crew, the helmsman, the two firemen, a cook, and three deck boys. We have already eliminated the chief engineer, he fell by the wayside because of his age. My theory is that none of them could have done it either. They were under too much observance by each other and the possibilities of fraternizing with the passengers were quite limited. So my theory says that no one murdered Roseanna McGraw. And it must be wrong. My theories are always wrong. Oh, the perils of thought."

It was quiet for thirty seconds. Then Kollberg said:

"Now if it wasn't that creature Eriksson. . . . Damn, but it was good luck that you got him arrested anyway. . . . By the way, are you listening? Have you heard what I said?"

"Yes, of course," said Martin Beck absentmindedly. "Yes, I'm listening."

It was true. Martin Beck had been listening. But Kollberg's voice had sounded more and more distant during the last ten minutes. Two totally different ideas had suddenly occurred to him. One was an association with something he had heard someone say, and it had immediately penetrated the bottom of his unfulfilled and forgotten thoughts. The other was more tangible, a new plan of attack that could well be worked out.

"She must have met someone on board," he said to himself.

"Unless it was suicide," said Kollberg with a measure of irony.

"Someone who didn't plan to kill her, at least in the beginning, and who also had no reason to keep himself hidden. . . ."

"Sure, that's what we think, but what difference does it make when we don't . . ."

Martin Beck saw clearly a scene from his last July day in Motala. The ugly vessel, *Juno,* as she rounded the dredger and nosed in toward the harbor chamber.

He straightened up, took out the old postcard, and stared at it.

"Lennart," he said to Kollberg. "How many cameras were used during those days? At least twenty-five, more likely thirty, maybe even forty. At each lock, people went on shore to take pictures of the boat and of each other. There must be pictures from that trip pasted into twenty or thirty family albums. All kinds of pictures. The first ones were probably taken right at the pier in Stockholm, and the last ones in Gothenburg. Let's say that twenty people took thirty pictures each during those three days. That's about one roll per person, and some might have taken more. Lennart, that means there must be at least six hundred photographs. . . . Do you understand. . . . six hundred photographs. Maybe even a thousand."

"Yes," said Kollberg slowly. "I understand, what you mean."

17

"It will be a terrible job, of course," said Martin Beck.

"No worse than what we're already doing," answered Kollberg.

"Maybe it's only a wild idea. I could be completely wrong."

This was a game that they had played many times before, Martin Beck doubting and needing support. He knew in advance what the answer would be and he also knew that Kollberg knew he knew. Even so, they stuck to their ritual.

"It will have to give us something," said Kollberg stubbornly.

And after a few seconds he added: "Anyway, we have a head start. We already know where they are, with a few exceptions, and we've already had contact with most of them."

It was easy for Kollberg to sound convinced. That was one of his specialties.

After a while Martin Beck asked: "What time is it?"

"Ten minutes after seven."

"Is there anyone on the list who lives in the vicinity?"

Kollberg studied his notebook.

"Nearer than you think," he said. "On North Mälarstrand. A retired colonel and his wife."

"Who's been there? You?"

"No, Melander. Nice people," he said.

"Was that all?"

"Yes."

* * *

The street was wet and slippery and Kollberg swore bitterly when his back wheels skidded. Three minutes later they were there.

The colonel's wife opened the door.

"Axel, there are two gentlemen from the police here," she called in towards the living room in a very loud voice.

"Ask them to come in," roared the colonel. "Or would you rather I came out and stood in the hall?"

Martin Beck shook the rain off his hat and walked in. Kollberg wiped his feet energetically.

"We are having maneuver weather," bellowed the colonel. "Please excuse me, gentlemen, for not getting up."

On the low table in front of him was a half-played game of dominoes, a cognac glass, and a bottle of Rémy Martin. Nearby, the television was blaring away deafeningly.

"Maneuver weather, as I said. Would you gentlemen like to have some cognac? That's the only thing that helps."

"I'm driving," shouted Kollberg as he looked seriously at the bottle.

It took ten seconds before Martin Beck's feelings of solidarity won out. He shook his head.

"You do the talking," he said to Kollberg.

"What was that?" the colonel screamed.

Martin Beck managed a smile and made a nonchalant gesture. He was convinced that the least attempt to enter into the discussion would ruin his voice for a whole week. The conversation continued.

"Photographs? No, we never take pictures any more. I see so poorly and Axel always forgets to wind the film after he's taken a picture. That nice young man who was here two weeks ago asked the same thing. He was such a nice boy."

Martin Beck and Kollberg exchanged a quick look, not only in astonishment, over the remarkable statement about Melander.

"But strangely enough," thundered the colonel, "Major Jentsch. . . . But of course, naturally you don't know who he is. We sat with him and his wife during the trip. A procurement officer, a most pleasant man. As a matter of fact we were commissioned the same year but the unfortunate end of the campaign against the Bolsheviks put an end to his career. You know, the promotions came quickly as long as the war continued, but after 1945, that was that. Well, it wasn't so serious for Jentsch. He was a procurement officer and they were worth their weight in gold right after the war. I remember he received a Director's position with a food company in Osnabrück. Yes, we had some things in common, a lot to talk about, and the time passed quickly. A great deal, as I said. For nine months, maybe it was eleven as a matter of fact, well, in any case he had been the liaison officer with the Blue Division. You know about the Blue Division? The Spanish élite troops that Franco put in against the opposition. And I must say, we often tear apart the Italians and Greeks and Spaniards and others here at home . . . yes, we rip them up pretty well, but I must say, as I have said, that these boys, in the Blue Division, in other words, they really could . . ."

Martin Beck turned his head and looked with despair at the television screen which was now showing a program that must have been at least one month old about picking beets in southern Sweden. The colonel's wife was watching the program attentively and seemed unconscious of her surroundings.

"I understand," Kollberg screamed.

Then he took a deep breath and with admirable strength of voice and direction continued:

"What was it you began to say about photographs?"

"What? Oh yes, I was saying that strangely enough Major Jentsch was an expert in handling a camera, in spite of the fact that he doesn't hear or see any better than we do. He took a lot of photographs on the trip and just a few days ago we received a whole envelope full of them from him. I think that was very thoughtful of him. It must have been expensive for him to have them printed for us. They are very good photographs. Pleasant memories no matter what."

Martin Beck moved toward the television and lowered the volume a little. It had happened instinctively, in self-protection, without his really having been conscious of what he had done. The colonel's wife looked at him uncomprehendingly.

"What? Yes, naturally. Missan, will you get the photographs we received from Germany. I would like to show them to these gentlemen."

Martin Beck watched the woman who was called Missan from under knotted eyebrows as she got out of her TV chair.

The pictures were in color and about 3 by 4 inches in size. There were about fifteen of them in the envelope and the man in the easy chair held them between his thumb and his index finger. Martin Beck and Kollberg stood bent forward, one on either side of him.

"This is us and here is Major Jentsch's wife, oh yes, and you can see my wife here . . . yes, and here am I. This photograph was taken from the command bridge. That was the first day out. I'm talking to the captain, as you probably can see. And here . . . unfortunately I don't see too well either . . . will you give me the magnifying glass, darling . . . ?"

The colonel wiped off the magnifying glass slowly and carefully before he continued.

"Yes, here we are. Now you can see Major Jentsch himself, and then me and my wife. . . . Major Jentsch's wife must have taken this photograph. It looks a bit dimmer than the rest. And here we are again, in the same place but from a slightly different angle, it seems to me. And . . . let me see . . . the lady that I am talking to here was a Frau Liebeneiner, she was German too. She ate at our table, too, a very charming and fine woman, but, unfortunately, a bit elderly. She lost her husband at El Alamein."

Martin Beck paid closer attention and saw a very old woman in a flowered dress with a pink hat. She stood next to one of the lifeboats with a cup of coffee in one hand and a piece of pastry in the other.

The inspection continued. The shots were all the same. Martin Beck began to get a pain in his back. He knew now, without doubt, just how Major Jentsch's wife looked.

The last picture lay on the mahogany table in front of the colonel. It was one of those which Martin Beck had already spoken of. The *Diana* seen directly from the stern, tied up at the pier in Stockholm, with the City Hall in the background and two taxis right up at the gangway.

The picture must have been taken just before the boat sailed because there were a lot of people already on board. To the stern of the port lifeboat on the shelter deck, Major Jentsch's wife from Osnabrück could be seen. Directly below her stood Roseanna McGraw. She was bending forward with her arms resting on the railing and her feet spread apart. She had sandals on, and sunglasses. She wore a full yellow dress with shoulder straps. Martin Beck bent as far over as he could and tried to make out the people standing next to her. At the same time he heard Kollberg whistle through his teeth.

"Oh yes, oh yes," said the colonel undisturbed. "This is the ship, here at Riddarholm. There is the City Hall tower. And there is Hildegard Jentsch. That was before we met. And, yes, that was strange. This young girl also sat at our table a few times. She was English or Dutch, I think. They must have moved her to another table later so that we old folks could have a little more room for our elbows."

A strong, wrinkled index finger, with a lot of white hairs enlarged under the magnifying glass, rested on the girl in the sandals and the loose, yellow dress.

Martin Beck took a breath in order to say something, but Kollberg was quicker.

"What?" asked the colonel. "Am I certain? Of course I am certain. She sat at the same table as we did at least four or five times. She never said anything though, if I remember correctly."

"But . . ."

"Yes, of course your colleague showed me her portrait, but you understand, it wasn't her face that I recognize. It's the dress, or more correctly, not exactly the dress, either."

He turned to the left and placed his powerful index finger on Martin Beck's chest.

"It was the décolleté," he said in a thundering whisper.

18

It was a quarter past eleven and they were still sitting in the office at Kristineberg. The breeze was blowing freshly and small drops of rain splashed against the windows.

Twenty photographs were spread out on the table in front of Martin Beck. He had pushed nineteen of them aside and was studying the picture of Roseanna McGraw in the magnifying glass's circle of light for, perhaps, the fiftieth time. She looked just exactly as he had imagined her. Her glance seemed to be directed upward, probably in the direction of Riddarholm's tower. She looked healthy and alert and totally unconscious of the fact that she had only about thirty-six hours left to live. On her left was cabin number A 7. The door was open but the picture didn't show enough for anyone to see how it looked inside.

"Do you realize that we were lucky today," said Kollberg. "It's the first time, too, since we started on this damned case. One usually has some luck, sooner or later. This time though, it was a lot later."

"We've had some bad luck also."

"You mean because she was sitting at a table with two deaf old men and three half-blind women? That's not bad luck. That's just the law of averages. Let's go home and go to bed now. I'll drop you off. Or would you rather take that great gift to humanity, the subway?"

"We have to get a telegram off to Kafka first. We can send the rest of it by letter tomorrow."

They were finished a half hour later. Kollberg drove

quickly and carelessly through the rain but Martin Beck didn't seem nervous, in spite of the fact that driving usually put him in a bad mood. They didn't speak at all during the trip. When they pulled up in front of the house where Martin Beck lived, Kollberg finally said: "Now you can go to bed and think about all this. So long."

It was quiet and dark in the apartment but when Martin Beck went past his daughter's room, he heard the sound of radio music. She was probably lying in bed with the transistor radio under her pillow. When he was a boy he had read sea adventure novels with a flashlight under the blankets.

There was some bread and butter and cheese on the kitchen table. He made a sandwich for himself and looked for a bottle of beer in the ice-box. There wasn't any. He stood at the sink, ate his frugal supper, and washed it down with half a glass of milk.

Then he went into the bedroom and got into bed, very carefully. His wife turned toward him, half asleep, and tried to say something. He lay quietly on his back and held his breath. After a few minutes her breath was even and unconscious again. He relaxed, closed his eyes and began to think.

Roseanna McGraw had been in one of the earliest photographs. In addition, these photographs had clearly identified five other people, two retired military couples and the widow Liebeneiner. He could easily expect to receive between twenty-five and thirty more sets of pictures, most of them with more photographs than this one. Each negative would be rooted out, every picture would be studied carefully to find out whom he, or she, knew in each picture. It had to work. Eventually, they could map out Roseanna McGraw's final trip. They should be able to see it in front of them like a film.

A great deal depended on Kafka and what he could obtain from eight households spread across the continent of North America. Americans were wasteful with film. Weren't they known for that? And then, if anyone other than the murderer had been in contact with the woman from Lincoln, wouldn't it very likely have been one of her own countrymen? Maybe they should look for the murderer mainly among the Americans on board. Maybe, one of these days, he would have the telephone pressed against his ear and hear Kafka say: "Yeah, I shot the bastard."

In the middle of this thought Martin Beck fell asleep, suddenly, and without trying.

It rained the next day, too, and it was gray and sprinkling. The last yellow leaves of fall stuck sadly to the walls of the house and to the windowpanes.

Almost as if Martin Beck's night-time thoughts had reached him, Kafka sent a laconic telegram:

SEND AS MUCH MATERIAL AS POSSIBLE.

Two days later, Melander, who never forgot anything, took his pipe out of his mouth and said, tranquilly: "Uli Mildenberger is in Hamburg. He was there all summer. Would you like to have him examined?"

Martin Beck thought about it for about five seconds. "No."

He was on the point of adding: "Make a note of his address," but stopped himself at the last minute, shrugged his shoulders and went on with his business.

During these days, he often had very little to do. The case had reached a point where it was going on its own pretty much at the same time as it was spreading itself out all over the globe. There was an open "hot line" between himself and Ahlberg in Motala. After that, it was spread like the rays of the sun all over the map from the North Cape in the north to Durban in the south and Ankara in the east. By far, the most important line of contact led to Kafka's office in Lincoln, nearly six thousand miles to the west. From there it branched out to a handful of geographically separated places on the American continent.

With so many widespread informants at their disposal, couldn't they ensnare and catch a murderer? The logical answer, unfortunately, was, No. Martin Beck had painful memories from a case involving another sex murder. It had taken place in a cellar in one of the Stockholm suburbs. The body had been found almost immediately and the police had arrived on the scene less than an hour later. Several persons had seen the murderer and gave lengthy descriptions of him. The man had left his footprints, cigarette butts, matches, and even several other objects. In addition, he had handled the body with a particularly idiosyncratic perversity. But they had never been able to get him. Their optimism had slowly turned into frustration at their impotence. All the clues had led to nothing. Seven years later, the man was discovered in the act of attempted rape, and arrested. During the examination that followed, he suddenly broke down and admitted the earlier murder.

That crime and its solution seven years later had been only a small incident on the side for Martin Beck. But it had been of the utmost importance to one of his older colleagues. He remembered so well how that man had sat month after month, year after year, in his office late into the night, going through all the papers and rechecking the testimony for the five hundredth, or possibly the thousandth time. He had met that man many times in unexpected places and in surprising circumstances when the man should have been off duty or on vacation but was, instead, always looking for new angles in the case which had become the tragedy of his life. In time, he had become sick and was given his pension early, but even then, he hadn't given up the search. And then, finally, the case was cleared up when someone who had never been arrested or even suspected of a crime, suddenly burst into tears before an astonished policeman down in Halland and confessed to the seven year old crime of strangulation. Martin Beck sometimes wondered if that solution, which came so late, had really given the old detective any peace.

It could happen that way. But that woman in the cellar had been all the things that Roseanna McGraw wasn't, a rootless, wandering person who was hardly a member of society and whose asociability was as indisputable as the contents of her handbag.

Martin Beck thought a great deal about this while he waited for something to happen.

Meanwhile, in Motala, Ahlberg was occupied in annoying the authorities by insisting that every square inch of the bottom of the canal should be dragged and gone over by frogmen. He rarely got in touch with Martin Beck himself but was constantly waiting for the telephone to ring.

After a week, a new telegram arrived from Kafka. The message was cryptic and surprising:

YOU WILL HAVE A BREAK ANY MINUTE NOW.

Martin Beck telephoned Ahlberg.
"He says that there will be a break for us any time now."
"He probably knows that we need one," said Ahlberg.

Kollberg added his dissenting opinion: "The man is near-sighted. He's suffering from the disease we call intuition."

Melander didn't say anything at all.

In ten more days, they had received about fifty pictures and had about three times as many negatives printed. Many of the pictures were of poor quality and they could find Roseanna McGraw in only two of them. Both were taken at the Riddarholm pier and she was still standing alone in the stern of A deck, not very far from her cabin. One of the pictures showed her bending over and scratching her right ankle, but that was all. Otherwise they identified twenty-three more passengers, bringing the total identified up to twenty-eight.

Melander was in charge of scrutinizing the pictures and after he was through with them, he sent them to Kollberg who tried to place them in some kind of chronological order. Martin Beck studied all of them, hour after hour, but said nothing.

The next few days brought a few dozen more pictures but Roseanna McGraw wasn't to be seen on any of them.

On the other hand a letter arrived from Ankara, at last. It was on Martin Beck's desk the morning of the thirteenth day, but it took two more days before the Turkish Embassy presented them with a translation. Contrary to all expectations the contents of that letter seemed to represent the most progress in a long time.

One of the Turkish passengers, a twenty-two year old medical student named Günes Fratt said that he recognized the woman in the picture but he didn't know her name or her nationality. After a "forceful examination" conducted by a high level police officer with a very long name which seemed made up of only the letters ö, ü, and z, the witness had admitted that he had found the woman attractive and had made two "verbal overtures" to her in English during the first day of the trip, but that he had not been encouraged. The woman had not replied. Somewhat later on the trip, he thought he had seen her with a man and had drawn the conclusion that she was married and that she had only happened to appear alone. The only thing the witness could say about the man's appearance was that he was "presumably tall." During the latter part of the trip, the witness had not seen the woman. Günes Fratt's uncle, who was examined "informally" by the official with that impossible name, stated that he had kept a watchful eye on his nephew during the entire trip and that the boy had not been left alone for more than ten minutes at a time.

The embassy added the comment that both the travelers belonged to wealthy and highly respected families.

The letter did not particularly surprise Martin Beck. He had known all along that a letter containing that kind of information would appear sooner or later. Now they had moved a step forward and while he was getting the information together to send to Motala, he was mostly thinking about how it would feel to be "forcefully examined" by a high official of the Turkish police.

One flight up, Kollberg took the news in his stride.

"The Turks? Yes, I've heard about their methods."

He looked through his lists.

"Picture number 23, 38, 102, 109 . . ."

"That's enough."

Martin Beck looked through the pile of pictures until he found one which showed both of the men very clearly. He looked for a moment at the uncle's white mustache and then moved his eyes to Günes Fratt who was short, elegantly dressed, and had a small, dark mustache and even features. He didn't look so unattractive.

Unfortunately, Roseanna McGraw had thought differently.

This was the fifteenth day since they had thought of collecting photographs. By now they had definitely identified forty-one passengers who had appeared in one or another of the pictures. In addition, two more pictures of the woman from Lincoln had been added to the collection. Both of them had been taken while the boat was in the Södertälje canal. Roseanna McGraw was in the background of one of them, out of focus and with her back turned toward the camera. But in the other, she was seen in profile by the railing with a railroad bridge behind her. She was three hours nearer her death, and had taken off her sunglasses and was squinting up at the sun. The wind had blown her dark hair and her mouth was half-open, as if she were on the verge of saying something or had just yawned. Martin Beck looked at her for a long time through the magnifying glass. Finally he said:

"Who took this picture?"

"One of the Danes," answered Melander. "Vibeke Amdal from Copenhagen. She was traveling alone in a single cabin."

"Find out whatever you can about her."

A half hour later the bomb exploded.

"There's a cable from the United States," said the woman on the other end of the telephone. "Shall I read it to you?

"STRUCK A GOLD MINE YESTERDAY. TEN ROLLS EIGHT MIL-LIMETER COLOR FILM AND 150 STILLS. YOU WILL SEE A LOT OF ROSEANNA MCGRAW. SOME UNKNOWN CHARACTER SEEMS TO BE WITH HER. PAN AMERICAN GUARANTEES DELIVERY STOCKHOLM THURSDAY.

KAFKA.

"Shall I try to translate it?"

"No thank you. That's okay for now."

Martin Beck fell into his chair. He rubbed his hairline and looked at his desk calendar. It was Wednesday, November 25.

Outside, it was raining, and it was chilly. It would soon begin to snow.

19

They showed the film at a studio right across the street from the North Station. It was crowded in the screening room and even at that moment Martin Beck had difficulty in getting over his aversion to groups of people.

His chief was there and so were the County Police Superintendent, the Public Prosecutor, Superintendent Larsson and Ahlberg. They had driven up from Motala. In addition, Kollberg, Stenström and Melander were there.

Even Hammar, who had seen more crime in his day than all the others put together, seemed quiet and tense and alert.

The lights were turned out.

The projector started to whirl.

"Oh, yes, yes . . . ah."

As usual it was hard for Kollberg to keep quiet.

The film started with a shot of the king's guard in Stockholm. They passed Gustaf Adolf's Square. Swung in toward the North Bridge. The camera panned toward the Opera House.

"No style," said Kollberg. "They look like military police."

The County Police Superintendent whispered "shush."

Then came shots of pretty Swedish girls with turned up noses sitting in the sun on the steps of the Concert Hall. The tall buildings in the center of the city. A tourist poster in front of a Laplander's tent at Skansen's Park. Gripsholm Castle with a group of folk dancers in the foreground. Some middle-aged Americans with violet lips and sunglasses. The Hotel Reisen, Skepps Bridge, the stern of the *Svea Jarl*, shots from a boat trip to Djurgården and of a large passenger ship anchored in Stockholm seen from a sightseeing boat.

"Which boat is that?" asked the County Police Superintendent.

"Moore-McCormack's *Brazil,*" said Martin Beck. "It comes here every summer."

"What building is that?" asked the County Police Superintendent a little later.

"It's an old people's home," said Kollberg. "Haile Selassie saluted it once when he was here before the war. He thought it was the Royal Palace."

Seagulls, gracefully flapping their wings. Shots from the suburb Farsta, lines of people getting onto a bus with a plexiglass roof. Fishermen, sinisterly staring into the camera.

"Who took the pictures?" asked the County Police Superintendent.

"Wilfred S. Bellamy, Jr. from Klamath Falls, Oregon," said Martin Beck.

"Never heard of it," said the County Superintendent.

Svartmans Street, the pump of Brunkeberg Street, underexposed.

"Now," said the County Police Superintendent.

The *Diana* at Riddarholm's pier. Directly from the stern. Roseanna McGraw in a recognizable pose with her eyes looking straight up.

"There she is," said the County Superintendent.

"Oh God," said Kollberg.

The woman with the violet lips moved in from the left, with a toothy smile. Everything except for the shipping company's flag and the City Hall tower could be seen. White dots. Flickerings. Red-brown shadows. Darkness.

The lights were turned on and the man in the white coat glanced at the door.

"Just one second. There's a little trouble with the projector."

Ahlberg turned around and looked at Martin Beck.

"Now it caught fire and burned up," said First Detective Assistant Lennart Kollberg, who was a mind reader.

At the same moment the lights went out.

"Let's get it in focus, now, boys," said the County Superintendent.

Some more shots of the city, the backs of tourists, West

Bridge, a pan shot of the bridge. Whitecaps on the water, the Swedish flag, some sailboats in a race. A long sequence of Mrs. Bellamy with her eyes closed sunning herself in a deck chair.

"Watch the background," said the County Police Superintendent.

Martin Beck recognized several of the people on the film: none of them were Roseanna McGraw.

The Södertälje locks, a road bridge, a railroad bridge. The mast seen from below with the shipping line's flag blowing lightly in the breeze against a blue sky. A motor sailer coming toward them with fish piled up on its deck, someone waving. The same motor sailer seen from the stern, Mrs. Bellamy's wrinkled profile to the right in the picture.

Oxelösund, from the water, its modern church tower against the sky, the steel mill with billowing chimneys. The film rose and fell with the boat's slow, soft rolling and had a diffuse, gray-green tone.

"The weather is worse now," said the County Superintendent.

The entire screen looked light gray, a quick turn of the camera, a bit of the bridge deck which was empty. The City of Gothenburg's flag, wet and slack, on the bow ahead in the distance. The helmsman in the picture, balancing a tray on the way down a ladder.

"What now?" asked the County Police Superintendent.

"They're outside of Hävringe," said Martin Beck. "Sometime around five or six o'clock. They've stopped because of the fog."

A shot from the stern of the shelter deck, deserted deck chairs, light gray, damp. No people.

The camera to the right, then with a light turn, back again. Roseanna McGraw on the ladder-way leading up from A deck, still bare-legged and in sandals but with a thin, plastic raincoat over her dress and a scarf drawn over her hair. Past the lifeboat, right into the camera, a quick, indifferent look at the photographer, her face calm and relaxed, out of the picture to the right. A quick turn. Roseanna McGraw from the back, with her elbows on the railing, the weight of her body resting on her right foot, on her toes, scratching her left ankle with her right hand.

Just about twenty-four hours from her death. Martin Beck held his breath. No one in the room said anything. The woman from Lincoln faded away while white spots streamed over the screen. The film had come to an end.

The fog had disappeared. A strained, violet-lipped smile. Shots of an elderly couple in deck chairs with blankets over their knees. There was no sunshine but it was not raining either.

"Who are they?" asked the County Superintendent.

"Two other Americans," said Kollberg. "Their name is Anderson."

The boat in a lock. A picture from the bridge over the forward deck, a lot of backs. A member of the crew on land, bent forward, pushing the wheel for the lock chamber's gates. The camera flew on, the lock gates opened. Mrs. Bellamy's wrinkled, double chin seen from below with the bridge and the name of the ship in the background.

Another shot from the bridge. A new lock. The forward deck full of people. A change of scene to a man talking busily and wearing a straw hat.

"Cornfield, an American. He traveled alone," said Kollberg.

Martin Beck wondered if he had been the only one to see Roseanna McGraw in the scene that had just passed. She had been standing by the starboard railing, leaning on her elbows as usual, dressed in slacks and a dark sweater.

Shots of the locks continued but she was not in any of them.

"Where would that be?" asked the County Superintendent.

"Karlsborg," answered Ahlberg. "Not at Lake Vättern though. This is a bit west of Söderköping. They left Söderköping at a quarter to ten. This ought to have been around eleven o'clock."

A new lock. Another view of the forward deck. There she was again. Her sweater was black and had a turtleneck collar. A lot of people stood near her. She turned her face toward the camera and seemed to laugh. A fast change of scene. A shot of the water. A long sequence with Mrs. Bellamy and the Andersons. At one point the colonel from North Mälarstrand walked by, between the subject and the eye of the camera.

Martin Beck's neck was perspiring. Ten hours left. Had she laughed?

A short shot of the forward deck with only three or four persons on it. The boat was out on a lake. White spots. End of that roll.

The County Police Superintendent turned around.

"Roxen?"

"No, Asplången," said Ahlberg.

A drawbridge. Buildings on the shore. People on shore, waving and staring.

"Norsholm," said Ahlberg. "It's a quarter after three now."

The camera stayed stubbornly on the shore. Trees, cows, houses. A little girl, seven or eight years old, walked on the path along the edge of the canal. A blue cotton summer dress, two pigtails and wooden shoes. Someone on board threw a coin on the path. She picked it up, curtsied shyly, and looked confused. More coins were thrown. The child picked them up. She ran a few steps to keep up. A woman's hand with a shining half-dollar between two sinewy fingers with crimson colored fingernails. The camera came back again. Mrs. Bellamy with an exalted expression, throwing coins. The girl on the shore with her entire right hand full of money, totally confused, with her astonished blue eyes.

Martin Beck didn't see it. He heard Ahlberg take a deep breath, and Kollberg move in his chair.

In back of the do-gooding woman from Klamath Falls, Oregon, Roseanna McGraw had crossed the shelter deck from left to right. She had not been alone. At her left, and pressed closely to her, there had been another person. A man in a sport cap. He was a head taller than she and his profile could be seen during a brief tenth of a second against the light background.

Everyone had seen him.

"Stop the film," said the County Police Superintendent.

"No, no," said Ahlberg.

The camera did not return to the boat. A number of green shores glided past. Meadows, trees, tall grass blowing in the breeze, until the summer countryside faded away behind a lot of white spots.

Martin Beck took his handkerchief out of his breast pocket, crumpled it in his hands, and dried his neck.

The picture that covered the screen was new and surprising. The canal lay before and below them; it curved through a long, soft distance between tree-covered shores. Along the left side ran a path, and far off to the left some horses were grazing behind a fence. A group of people were walking along the path.

Ahlberg spoke before the County Superintendent had a chance to.

"This is west of Roxen now. The boat has passed Berg's locks. The photographer must have gone ahead to Ljungsbro during that time. There is the last lock before the one at Borensberg. It's about seven o'clock in the evening now."

The white bow with the Gothenburg flag appeared in the foreground far ahead. The people on the path came nearer.

"Thank God," said Ahlberg.

Only Martin Beck knew what he meant. The man who took the movie had an alternative. He could have gotten off the boat and gone with a guide who showed people around a monastery in Vreta during the time the boat was in the lock chamber.

Now there was a shot of the entire boat, moving slowly along the canal, inertly, with a gray-white plume of smoke which was reflected against the evening light.

But no one in the projection room looked at the boat any longer. The group of passengers on the path had come so close that separate individuals could be discerned. Martin Beck immediately identified Günes Fratt, the twenty-two year old medical student from Ankara. He walked ahead of the others, waving to the person who was following him.

Then he saw her.

About forty-five feet behind the main group there were two figures. One of them was Roseanna McGraw, still wearing light slacks and a dark sweater. Beside her, taking long steps, walked the man in the sport cap.

They were still quite far away.

"Let there be enough film," thought Martin Beck.

They came nearer. The position of the camera did not change.

Could they make out the faces?

He saw the tall man take her by the arm, as if to help her past a puddle of water in the path.

Saw them stop and look at the boat, which passed by and began to hide them from view. They were gone. But Mr. Bellamy from Klamath Falls was more stubborn than ever and held the position of his camera. Roseanna McGraw passed the boat, could be seen completely and clearly down on the path. She stopped walking and nodded her head, stretched out her right arm toward the person who was still hidden, but who then appeared. There.

The change of scene came as a shock. The sluice gate in the foreground, around and about, on the periphery, observers' legs. He thought he saw a pair of light trousers, feet in sandals and a pair of low shoes right beside them.

The picture was gone. It flickered slightly. Several people sighed. Martin Beck twisted his handkerchief between his fingers.

But it wasn't over yet. A somewhat underexposed shot of a face with violet lips and sunglasses filled the screen, and then disappeared to the right. Along the port side of A deck a waitress in a white blouse banged on a gong. Roseanna McGraw stepped out from behind her coming from the door to the dining room, wrinkled her forehead, looked up at the sky, laughed, and turned toward someone who was hidden. Not completely. They could see an arm in speckled tweed, a bit of a shoulder. Then came the white spots, and then the film faded and ended in gray, gray, gray.

She had laughed. He was certain of it. At seven o'clock on the evening of the fourth of July. Ten minutes later she had eaten beefsteak, fresh potatoes, strawberries and milk, while a Swedish colonel and a German major had exchanged viewpoints on the siege of Stalingrad.

The screen was flooded with light. More locks. A blue sky with floating clouds. The captain with his hand on the telegraph machine.

"Sjötorp," said Ahlberg. "Twelve o'clock the next day. Soon they'll be out in Lake Vänern."

Martin Beck remembered all the details. One hour later it had stopped raining. Roseanna McGraw was dead. Her body had been lying naked and violated in the mud near the breakwater at Borenshult for nearly twelve hours.

On the canal boat's deck people were stretched out in deck chairs, talking, laughing, and looking up at the sun. A wrinkled, upper class woman from Klamath Falls, Oregon, smiled violetly toward the camera.

Now they were in Lake Vänern. People moved about here and there. The repulsive young man from the examination room in Motala emptied a sack of ashes into the lake. His face was sooty and he looked angrily at the photographer.

No woman in a dark sweater and light pants and sandals.

No tall man in a tweed jacket and a sport cap.

Roll after roll of film went by. Vänersborg in the evening sun. The *Diana* tied up there at the pier. A shot of a deck boy going on land. The Tröllhatten canal.

"There's a motor bike on the forward deck," said Ahlberg.

The boat lay tied up at Lilla Bomen in Gothenburg in the clear morning sun, at the stern of the full rigger, the *Viking*. A shot of the forward deck, people going down the gangway. The motor bike was no longer there.

Another shot, the woman with the violet lips sitting stiffly in one of Gothenburg's sightseeing boats, a pan over the Garden Association's flowers, white spots running vertically over the screen.

Fade-out. The end. The lights turned on.

After fifteen seconds of total silence Commissioner Hammar got out of his chair, looked from the County Police Superintendent to the Public Prosecutor and over at Larsson.

"Lunchtime, gentlemen. You are guests of the government."

He looked blandly at the others and said: "I guess that you will want to remain here for a little while."

Stenström left too. He was actually working on a different case.

Kollberg looked questioningly at Melander.

"No, I've never seen that man before."

Ahlberg held his right hand in front of his face.

"A deck passenger," he said.

He turned around and looked at Martin Beck.

"Do you remember the man that showed us around the boat in Bohus? The draperies that could be drawn if any of the deck passengers wanted to sleep on one of the sofas?"

Martin Beck nodded.

"The motor bike wasn't there in the beginning. The first time I saw it was in the locks after Söderköping," said Melander.

He took his pipe out of his mouth and emptied it.

"The guy in the sport cap could be seen there too," he said. "Once, from the back."

When they ran the film the next time, they saw that he was right.

20

The first snow of winter had begun to fall. It flew against the windows in large, white flakes which melted immediately and ran down the window panes in broad rills. It murmured in the rain gutters and heavy drops splashed against the metal window sills.

In spite of the fact that it was twelve noon, it was so dark in the room that Martin Beck had to turn on his reading light. It spread a pleasant light over his desk and the open file in front of him. The rest of the room lay in darkness.

Martin Beck put out his last cigarette, lifted up the ash tray and blew the ashes from the top of his desk.

He felt hungry and regretted that he had not gone to the cafeteria with Kollberg and Melander.

Ten days had passed since they had seen Kafka's film and they were still waiting for something to happen. Just as everything else in this case had, the new clue had disappeared in a jungle of question marks and doubtful testimony. Examination of witnesses had been conducted almost completely by Ahlberg and his staff, very carefully and with a great deal of energy. But the results had been meager. The most positive thing that could be said was that they had not heard anything to negate their theory that a deck passenger had come on board the boat in Mem, Söderköping or Norsholm, and had stayed on the boat all the way to Gothenburg. Nor was there anything to contradict their assumption that this deck passenger had been a man of average build, somewhat above average height, and that he had been wearing a sport cap, a gray speckled tweed jacket, gray gabardine trousers, and brownish shoes. Or, in addition, that he had a blue Monark motor bike.

The first mate, whose testimony was the most helpful, thought that he had sold a ticket to someone who reminded him of the man in the pictures. He did not know when. He wasn't even sure if it had been this past summer. It could have been one of the previous summers. He did have a weak recollection, however, that the man, if indeed it was the same one that they meant, could have had a bicycle or a motor bike with him and, in addition, some fishing equipment and other stuff which could point to the fact that he was a sport fisherman.

Ahlberg had heard this testimony himself and had pushed the witness to the boundary of the conceivable. A copy of the record was in Martin Beck's file.

AHLBERG: Is it usual to carry deck passengers on a cruise?
WITNESS: It was more usual in past years but there are always a few.
A: Where do they usually get on?
W: Wherever the boat stops, or at the locks.
A: What is the most natural stretch for deck passengers to stay on board?
W: Any part of the trip. A lot of people on bicycles or hikers get on in Motala or Vadstena to get across Lake Vättern.
A: And others?
W: Yes, what shall I say. We used to take vacationers from Stockholm to Oxelösund, and from Lidköping to Vänersborg, but we stopped that.
A: Why?
W: It got too crowded. The regular passengers have paid a good price. They shouldn't have to be crowded out by a bunch of old women and young people running around with their thermoses and lunch baskets.
A: Is there anything to contradict the fact that a deck passenger could have come on board at Söderköping?
W: Not at all. He could have come on board anyplace. At any lock, too. There are sixty-five locks on the way. In addition, we tie up at several different places.
A: How many deck passengers could you take on board?
W: At one time? Nowadays, seldom more than ten. Most of the time only two or three. Sometimes none at all.
A: What kind of people are they? Are they usually Swedish?

W: No, not at all. They are often foreigners. They can be anyone at all, although most of them are the kind that like boats
and take the trouble to find out what the time-table is.

A: And their names are not placed on the passenger lists?

W: No.

A: Do the deck passengers have a chance to eat meals on
board?

W: Yes, they can eat like the others if they want to. Often, in
an extra sitting after the others have finished. There are fixed
prices for the cost of the meal. À la carte, so to speak.

A: You said earlier that you haven't the slightest recollection of the woman on this photograph, and now you say that
you think you recognize this man. There was no purser on
board and as the first mate, didn't you have the responsibility
to take care of the passengers?

W: I take their tickets when they come on board and I welcome them. After that they are left in peace. The idea of this
trip isn't to shout out a lot of tourist information. They get
enough of that in other places.

A: Isn't it odd that you don't recognize these people? You
spent nearly three days with them.

W: All the passengers look alike to me. Remember, I see two
thousand of them every summer. In ten years that makes
twenty thousand. And while I'm working I am on the bridge.
There are only two of us who can take watches. That makes
twelve hours a day.

A: This trip was a special one, anyway, with unusual events.

W: I still had a watch on the bridge for twelve hours in any
case. And, anyway, I had my wife with me on that trip.

A: Her name isn't on the passenger list.

W: No, why should it be? Members of the crew have the
right to take their dependents along on some of the trips.

A: Then the information that there were eighty-six people
on board for this trip is not reliable. With deck passengers
and dependents it could just as well have been one hundred?

W: Yes, of course.

A: Well, the man with the motor bike, the man on this picture, when did he leave the boat?

W: If I'm not even sure that I've ever seen him, how the devil should I know when he got off? A number of people who
were in a hurry to catch trains, or planes, or other boats de-
barked at three o'clock in the morning as soon as we got to

Lilla Bommen. Others stayed on and slept through the night and waited to debark in the morning.

A: Where did your wife get on board?

W: Here in Motala. We live here.

A: In Motala? In the middle of the night?

W: No, on the way up to Stockholm five days earlier. Then she left the boat on the next trip up, the eighth of July at four o'clock in the afternoon. Are you satisfied now?

A: How do you react when you think about what happened on that trip?

W: I don't believe that it happened as you say it did.

A: Why not?

W: Someone would have noticed it. Think about it, one hundred people on a small boat which is ninety feet long and fifteen feet wide. In a cabin which is as big as a rat trap.

A: Have you ever had anything other than a professional relationship with the passengers?

W: Yes, with my wife.

Martin Beck took the three photographs out of his inner pocket. Two of them had been made directly from the movie film, one was a partial blow-up of a black and white amateur picture from a group that Kafka had sent. They had two things in common: they depicted a tall man in a sport cap and a tweed jacket and they were both of very poor quality.

At this juncture hundreds of policemen in Stockholm, Gothenburg, Söderköping and Linköping had received copies of these pictures. In addition they had been sent to every public prosecutor's office and almost every police station from one end of the country to the other, and to several places in other countries.

They were poor photographs but anyone who was really acquainted with the man ought to have recognized him.

Maybe. But at their last meeting Hammar had said: "I think it looks like Melander."

He had also said: "This is no case. It is a guessing contest. Have we any reason to believe that the man is a Swede?"

"The motor bike."

"Which we are not sure was his."

"Yes."

"Is that all?"

"Yes."

Martin Beck put the pictures back in his inner pocket. He took Ahlberg's record of the hearing and looked back through several answers until he found the one he was looking for:

W: Yes, they can eat like the others, if they want to. Often, in an extra sitting after the others have finished. . . .

He thumbed through the papers and took out a list of the canal boats' personnel for the last five years. He read through the list, took his pen from the desk holder and placed a mark next to one of the names. It read:

Göta Isaksson, waitress, Polhems Street 7, Stockholm. Employed at the SHT Restaurant from October 15, 1964. The *Diana*, 1959–1961, the *Juno*, 1962, the *Diana*, 1963, the *Juno*, 1964.

There was no notation that either Melander or Kollberg had examined her.

Both telephone numbers for the taxi companies were busy and after he had dismissed the thought of getting hold of a radio car, he put on his hat and coat, turned up his collar and walked through the slush to the subway.

The headwaiter at the SHT Restaurant seemed harassed and irritated, but showed him to one of Miss Göta's tables right next to the swinging doors which led to the kitchen. Martin Beck sat down on the banquette and picked up the menu. While he was reading it, he looked out over the restaurant.

Almost all the tables were taken and only a few of the patrons were women. At several tables there were men sitting alone, most of them in late middle age. To judge by their familiar manner with the waitresses, most of them ate there quite often.

Martin Beck watched the waitresses who rushed in and out through the swinging doors. He wondered which of them was Miss Göta and it took almost twenty minutes before he found out.

She had a round, friendly face, large teeth, short rumpled hair, the color of which Martin Beck described as "hair color."

He ordered small sandwiches, meatballs and an Amstel beer and ate slowly while he waited for the lunchtime rush to ebb away. When he had finished eating and had downed four cups of coffee, Miss Göta's other tables were empty and she came over to his.

He told her why he had come and showed her the photograph. She looked at it for a while, laid it down on the table, and took a breath before answering.

"Yes," she said. "I recognize him. I don't have any idea of who he is but he has traveled with the boats several times. Both the *Juno* and the *Diana*, I believe."

Martin Beck took the picture and held it up before her.

"Are you certain?" he asked. "The picture isn't very clear, it could be someone else."

"Yes, I'm certain. He was always dressed like that, by the way. I recognize the jacket and that cap."

"Do you remember if you saw him this past summer? You were on the *Juno* then, weren't you?"

"Yes. Let me think. I don't really think so. I see so many people. But the summer before last, I know that I saw him several times. Twice, in any case. I was on the *Diana* then and the girl I worked with, the other waitress, knew him. I remember that they used to talk to each other. He wasn't a regular passenger. I think he only went part of the way. He was a deck passenger. In any event he used to eat at the second or third sitting and he didn't come to all of the meals. But I think he usually got off in Gothenburg."

"Where does your friend live?"

"I wouldn't exactly call her my friend, we only worked together. I don't know where she lives, but she usually went to Växjö at the end of the season."

Miss Göta shifted her weight to the other foot and crossed her hands over her stomach as she looked up at the ceiling.

"Yes, that's right. Växjö. I think she lives there."

"Do you know how well she knew this man?"

"No, I really don't. I think she was a bit taken with him. She used to meet him sometimes when we were off duty although we weren't actually supposed to mix with the passengers. He looked quite pleasant. Attractive in a way. . . ."

"Can you describe him? I mean hair color, the color of his eyes, height, age, and so forth."

"Well, he was pretty tall. Taller than you are, I think. Not thin, not fat, but stockily built, one could say. He had rather broad shoulders, and I think he had blue eyes. I'm not sure about that, of course. Light hair, the kind called ash blond, a little lighter than mine. I didn't see his hair very much because he usually had that cap on. And he had nice teeth, I do remember that. His eyes were round . . . I mean I think he was a little popeyed. But he was definitely good looking. He could be between thirty-five and forty."

Martin Beck asked a few more questions but didn't get much more information. When he got back to his office he looked through the list again and soon found the name he was looking for. There was no address given, only a notation that she had worked on the *Diana* from 1960 until 1963.

It took him only a few minutes to find her name in the Växjö telephone book but he had to wait a long time before she answered the telephone. She seemed very unwilling to meet him but she couldn't really refuse.

Martin Beck took the night train and arrived in Växjö at 6:30 a.m. It was still dark and the air was mild and hazy. He walked through the streets and watched the city awaken. At a quarter of eight he was back at the railroad station. He had forgotten his galoshes and the dampness had begun to penetrate the thin soles of his shoes. He bought a newspaper at the kiosk and read it, sitting on a bench in the waiting room with his feet up against a radiator. After a while he went out, looked for a cafe which was open, drank some coffee and waited.

At nine o'clock he got up and paid his check. Four minutes later he was standing in front of the woman's door. The name Larsson was on a metal plate and above it was a calling card with the name Siv Svensson printed in an ornate style.

The door was opened by a large woman in a light blue bathrobe.

"Miss Larsson?" said Martin Beck.

The woman tittered and disappeared. From inside the apartment he heard her voice: "Karin, there's a man at the door asking for you."

He didn't hear an answer but the large woman came back and asked him to come in. Then she disappeared.

He stood in the small, dark hall with his hat in his hand. It was several minutes before a pair of drapes were pushed aside and a voice said to him, "Come in."

"I wasn't expecting you this early," said the woman who was standing inside.

She had gray streaks in her dark hair which was swept up sloppily from her neck. Her face was thin and seemed small in relation to her body. Her features were even and pretty but her skin was sallow and she had not had time to put on any make-up. There were still traces of mascara around her eyes, which were brown and slightly slanted. Her green jersey dress was tight across her breasts and her broad hips.

"I work late every night so I usually sleep late in the morning," she said with some annoyance.

"I beg your pardon," said Martin Beck. "I have come to ask your help in a matter which has a connection with your employment on the *Diana*. Did you work there last summer too?"

"No, last summer I was on a boat that went to Leningrad," answered the woman.

She was still standing up and looked at Martin Beck cautiously. He sat down in one of the flowery easy chairs. Then he gave her the picture. She took it and looked at it. A nearly imperceptible change crossed her face, her eyes widened for a fraction of a second, but when she handed the picture back to him her face was stiff and dismissing.

"Yes?"

"You know this man, don't you?"

"No," she answered, without the slightest hesitation.

She walked across the room and took a cigarette out of a glass box which lay on the tile table in front of the window. She lit the cigarette and sat down on the sofa across from Martin Beck.

"What do you mean? I've never seen him. Why are you asking?"

Her voice was calm. Martin Beck looked at her for a while. Then he said:

"I know that you know him. You met him on the *Diana* the summer before last."

"No, I've never seen him. You had better go now. I have to get some sleep."

"Why are you lying?"

"You have no right to come here and be impertinent. You had better leave now, as I said."

"Miss Larsson. Why won't you admit that you know who he is? I know that you are not telling the truth. If you don't tell the truth now, it could be unpleasant for you later on."

"I don't know him."

"Since I can prove that you have been seen with this man several times, it would be better to tell the truth. I want to know who the man on the photograph is and you can tell me. Be reasonable."

"This is a mistake. You must be wrong. I don't know who he is. Please leave me alone."

During the conversation Martin Beck looked steadily at the woman. She was sitting on the edge of the sofa and constantly tapping her index finger against her cigarette although there wasn't any ash to knock off. Her face was tense and he saw how her jawbones moved under her skin.

She was frightened.

He stayed in the flowery chair and tried to get her to talk. But now, she said nothing at all, only sat stiffly on the sofa and peeled pieces of orange colored nail polish off her fingernails. Finally, she got up and walked back and forth across the room. After a while Martin Beck also got up, took his hat, and said goodbye. She didn't answer. She stood there stiff and dismissing with her back turned toward him.

"You will hear from me again," he said.

Before he left he laid his card on the table.

It was evening before he got back to Stockholm. He went directly to the subway and went home.

The next morning he telephoned Göta Isaksson. She wasn't going to work until the afternoon shift so that he was welcome to stop by whenever he wanted. One hour later he sat in her small apartment. She made some coffee in the kitchenette and when she had poured it and sat down opposite him, he said:

"I went down to Växjö yesterday and talked with your colleague. She denied that she had known the man. And she seemed frightened. Do *you* know why she won't admit that she knew him?"

"I have no idea. I actually know very little about her. She wasn't particularly talkative. We did work together for three summers but she seldom said anything about herself."

"Do you remember if she used to talk about men during the time you were together?"

"Only one. I remember that she said she had met a nice man on the boat. That must have been the second summer we worked together."

She cocked her head and counted to herself.

"Yes, it must have been the summer of '61."

"Did she speak about him often?"

"She mentioned him from time to time. It seemed as if she was seeing him too now and then. He must have been on several trips or else have met her in Stockholm or Gothenburg. Maybe he was a passenger. Maybe he was there because of her. What do I know?"

"You never saw him?"

"No. I've really never thought about it until now when you started asking questions. It *could* have been the same man as the one in the picture although it seemed as if she hadn't met him until two summers ago. And then she never said anything."

"What did she say about him the first summer? 1961?"

"Oh, nothing special. That he was nice. I think that she said that he was refined in some way. I suspect that she meant that he was well mannered and polite and so forth, as if ordinary people weren't good enough for her. But then she stopped talking about him. I think it was over or else something happened between them because she seemed rather depressed toward the end of that summer."

"The following summer, did you see each other then?"

"No, she was still on the *Diana* then and I was working on the *Juno*. We saw each other a few times in Vadstena, I think. The boats meet there, but we never spoke. Won't you have some more coffee?"

Martin Beck could feel his stomach reacting but he couldn't bring himself to say No.

"Has she done anything? I mean, you're asking so many questions."

"No," said Martin Beck. "She hasn't done anything but we want to get hold of the man in the photograph. Do you remember if she said or did anything the summer before last which could have any connection with the man in this picture?"

"No, not that I remember. We shared a cabin and she was sometimes out at night. I suspect that she was meeting some man, but I'm not the type that meddles in other people's business. But I know that she wasn't particularly happy. I mean that if she was in love with someone, she should have seemed happy. But she wasn't. To the contrary, she was nervous and sad. Almost a bit strange. But that could have been because she was sick. She quit before the end of the season, a month early, I think. She just didn't show up one morning and I had to work alone the whole day before they found a replacement. They said that she had gone to the hospital, but no one knew what was wrong with her. She didn't come back that summer in any event. I haven't seen her since."

She poured some more coffee and offered Martin Beck some cookies, while she continued to talk, freely and a great deal, about her work routine, her fellow employees, and some passengers she remembered. It was another full hour before he left there.

The weather had gotten better. The streets were nearly dry and the sun shone down from a clear sky. Martin Beck didn't feel too well, due to the coffee, and he walked back to his office at Kristineberg. While he walked along the water at North Mälarstrand he thought about what he had learned of the two waitresses.

He hadn't learned anything at all from Karin Larsson but the visit to Växjö had convinced him that she knew the man but didn't dare talk about it.

From Göta Isaksson he had learned that:

Karin Larsson had met a man on board the *Diana* during the summer of 1961. Probably a deck passenger, who had possibly traveled with the boat several times that summer.

That two summers later, the summer of 1963, she had met a man, probably a deck passenger, who traveled with the boat now and then. The man could well have been identical to the one on the photograph, according to Göta Isaksson.

That she had seemed depressed and nervous that summer and had quit her job before the end of the season sometime at the beginning of August, and had gone into the hospital.

He didn't know why. Nor did he know which hospital she had gone to and how long she had stayed. The only chance seemed to be to ask her directly.

He dialed the number in Växjö as soon as he got back to his office but didn't get any answer. He suspected that she was asleep or else was working on an early shift.

During the course of the afternoon he called again several times and also a few times during the evening.

On his seventh attempt at two o'clock in the afternoon the following day, a voice which he thought belonged to the large woman in the blue bathrobe answered.

"No, she's away."

"When?"

"She left last night. Who's calling?"

"A good friend. Where did she go?"

"She didn't say. But I heard her call and ask about the trains to Gothenburg."

"Did you hear anything else?"

"It sounded as if she was thinking about working on some boat."

"When did she decide to go?"

"She must have decided awfully quickly. There was some man here yesterday morning and right after that she made up her mind to leave. She seemed changed."

"Do you know which boat she was going to begin working on?"

"No, I didn't hear."

"Will she be gone long?"

"She didn't say. Can I give her any message if I hear from her?"

"No, thank you."

She had gone away, in a great hurry. He was sure that she was already on some boat going far out of reach. And now he was certain of what had before been only a guess.

She was frightened to death of someone or something and he had to find out why.

21

The office at the Växjö hospital was quick in getting the information.

"Larsson, Karin Elisabeth, yes, that's right, someone by that name did enter the women's clinic on August 9 and stayed until October 1 last year. For what? You will have to talk to the doctor about that."

The doctor at the women's clinic said: "Yes, it's quite possible that I remember. I'll call you back after I've looked at the records."

While Martin Beck waited he looked at the photographs and read through the description which they had made up after his conversation with Göta Isaksson. It was imperfect but a great deal better than the one they had a few hours earlier.

Height: approximately 6' 1". Body build: normal. Hair color: ash blond. Eyes: presumably blue (green or gray), round, slightly protrudent. Teeth: white, healthy.

The phone call came an hour later. The doctor had located the records.

"Yes, it was just as I thought. She came here on her own the evening of August 9. I remember that I was just going to go home when they called me to take a look at her. They had taken her into the examining room and she was bleeding pretty heavily from her genitals. She had obviously been bleeding heavily for quite a while because she had lost a lot of blood and was in pretty bad shape. No direct danger of course. When I asked her what had happened, she refused to answer. It is not unusual in my department that the patient won't discuss the reason for their bleeding. You can figure the reason out your-self and anyway, it usually comes out sooner or later. But this one didn't say anything at all in the beginning and later on she lied. Do you want me to read directly from the record for you? Otherwise I can tell you in layman's language."

"Yes, please do," said Martin Beck. "My Latin isn't very good."

"Mine neither," said the doctor.

He came from southern Sweden and spoke calmly, evenly and methodically.

"As I said, she bled profusely and had pain, so we gave her an injection. The bleeding came partially from the mouth of the uterus and partly from a wound in the vagina. At the mouth of the uterus and on the back part of the walls of the vagina were wounds which must have been made by a hard, sharp object. Around the muscles at the opening of the vagina there were splits which showed that the instrument must also have been terribly coarse. It isn't unusual for a woman who has un-dergone a careless or badly performed abortion, or has tried to do the abortion herself, to end up with bad wounds. But I can state that I have never seen anything like her condition in connection with an abortion. It seems totally impossible that she could have made such an attack on herself."

"Did she say that she had, that she had done it herself?"

"Yes, that's what she claimed when she finally said some-thing. I tried to get her to tell me how it had happened but she kept on saying that she had done it herself. I didn't be-lieve her and she knew that I didn't believe her and finally she didn't even try to convince me but just kept repeating what she had already said; 'I did it myself, I did it myself,' like a broken phonograph record. The strange part of it was that she hadn't even been pregnant. The uterus was damaged but if she had been pregnant it must have been in such an early stage that she couldn't possibly have known it herself."

"What do you think had happened?"

"Some perverse maniac. It sounds crazy to say it right out but I am almost sure she was trying to protect someone. I was worried about her so we kept her here until October 1 al-though we could well have let her go earlier. In addition, I hadn't given up hope that she might speak up and tell us about it. But she kept on denying everything else and finally we had to let her go home. There was nothing more I could do. I did speak about it to some acquaintances in the police force here, and they must have done something, but never came up with anything."

Martin Beck said nothing.

"As I told you I don't know exactly what happened," said the doctor. "But it was some kind of a weapon, it's not easy to say what. Maybe a bottle. Has something happened to her?"

"No, I only wanted to talk with her."

"That isn't going to be particularly easy."

"No," said Martin Beck. "Thank you for the help."

He put his pen back in his pocket without having made a single note.

Martin Beck rubbed his hairline with the tips of his fingers while he looked at the picture of the man in the sport cap.

He thought about the woman in Växjö whose fear had caused her to hide the truth so stubbornly and carefully and had now driven her to flee from all questions. He stared at the photograph and mumbled, "Why?" But he knew already that there was only one answer to that question.

The telephone rang. It was the doctor.

"I forgot something that might be of interest to you. The patient in question had been in the hospital earlier, at the end of December 1962, to be exact. I forgot it, partly because I was on vacation then, partly because she was in another section of the hospital. But I read about it in her record when I took care of her. That time she had broken two fingers, the index finger and the middle finger on her left hand. That time, too, she refused to say how it had happened. Someone asked her if she had fallen down some stairs and at first she had replied that it had happened that way. But according to the doctor who took care of her at the time, that wasn't likely. The fingers had been broken backwards, toward the back side of her hand, but otherwise there were no other wounds at all. I don't know much more than that. She was treated as usual with gypsum and the like and she healed normally."

Martin Beck thanked him and hung up the receiver. He picked it up immediately again and dialed the number of the SHT Restaurant. He heard a lot of noise from the kitchen and someone calling out "Three beef à la Lindström!" right next to the receiver. A few minutes later Göta Isaksson answered.

"It's so noisy here," she said. "Where were we when she got sick? Yes, I do remember that. We were in Gothenburg then.

She wasn't there when the boat left in the morning and then they didn't get a replacement for her until we got into Töreboda."

"Where did you stay in Gothenburg?"

"I used to stay at the Salvation Army Hotel on Post Street but I don't know where she stayed. Presumably on board or at some other hotel. I'm sorry but I have to go now. The customers are waiting."

Martin Beck called Motala and Ahlberg listened silently.

"She must have gone to the hospital in Växjö directly from Gothenburg," he said, finally. "We had better find out where she stayed on the night of the eighth and ninth of August. It must have happened then."

"She was in pretty bad shape," said Martin Beck. "It's strange that she could get herself to Växjö in that condition."

"Maybe the man that did it lived in Gothenburg. In that case it must have happened in his house."

He was silent for a moment. Then he said:

"If he does it one more time, we'll get him. Even though she wouldn't say who he was, she knew his name."

"She's frightened," said Martin Beck. "Frightened to death as a matter of fact."

"Do you think it's too late to get hold of her?"

"Yes," replied Martin Beck. "She knew what she was doing when she ran off. As far as we are concerned she can be out of reach for years. We also know what she did."

"What did she do?" asked Ahlberg.

"She fled for her life," said Martin Beck.

22

The trampled, dirty snow was packed on the streets. Melting snow fell from the rooftops and dropped from the large, yellow star which hung between the buildings on either side of Regering Street. The star had been hanging there for a few weeks in spite of the fact that Christmas was still almost a month away.

Hurried people crowded the sidewalks and a steady stream of traffic filled the streets. Now and then a car would increase its speed and sneak into an opening in the line of cars, spraying muddy snow with its wheels.

Patrolman Lundberg seemed to be the only person who was not in a hurry. With his hands behind his back he walked down Regering Street toward the south staying close to the rows of Christmas decorated windows. Melting snow from the rooftops fell in heavy drops on his patrolman's hat and the slush squeaked under his galoshes. Near NK, he turned off onto Småland Street where the crowds and the traffic weren't as heavy. He walked carefully down the hill and outside of the house where the Jakob Police Station once stood. He stopped and shook the water from his hat. He was young and new to the police force and didn't remember the old police station which had been torn down several years ago and whose district is now part of the Klara Police Station.

Constable Lundberg belonged to the Klara police force and had an errand on Småland Street. At the corner of Norrland Street was a cafe. He entered it. He had been told to collect an envelope from one of the waitresses there.

While he waited, he leaned against the counter and looked around. It was ten o'clock in the morning and only three or four tables were occupied. Directly across from him, a man was sitting with a cup of coffee. Lundberg thought that his face looked familiar and searched his memory. The man began to reach for money in his trouser pocket, and while he was doing so he looked away from the constable.

Lundberg felt the hair on his neck stiffen.

The man on the Göta Canal!

He was almost sure that it was he. He had seen the photograph up at the station house several times and his picture was etched in his memory. In his eagerness he almost forgot the envelope, which was given to him the same second as the man got up and left a few coins on the table. The man was bare-headed and wasn't wearing an overcoat. He moved toward the door and Lundberg established that he was the same height and had the same build and hair coloring as the description.

Through the glass doors he could see the man turn to the right and, with a quick tip of his hat to the waitress, he hurried after him. About thirty feet up the street the man went into a driveway door and Lundberg reached it just in time to see the door close after the man. There was a sign on the door which said: J. A. ERIKSSON MOVING COMPANY./OFFICE. In the upper part of the door there was a glass window. Lundberg went up to the doorway slowly. He tried to look into the glass window as he went by but was only able to make out another glass window at a right angle to the door. Inside were two trucks with J. A. ERIKSSON MOVING COMPANY painted on their doors.

He passed the office door again, more slowly this time. With his neck outstretched, he looked in more carefully. Inside the glass windows were two or three partitions with doors leading to a corridor. On the nearest door which led to the smallest partitioned area and had a window in the glass, he could read the word CASHIER. On the next door there was a sign saying OFFICE—Mr. F. Bengtsson.

The tall man was standing there behind the counter, talking on the telephone. He stood turned toward the window with his back to Lundberg. He had changed from his jacket into a thin, black office coat and was standing with one hand in his pocket. A man in a windbreaker and a fur cap came in through the door farthest back on the short side of the corridor. He had some papers in his hands. When he opened the office door he looked toward the outer door and saw Lundberg who continued calmly out the doorway.

He had done his first shadowing.

"Now damn it," said Kollberg. "We can begin."

"Presumably he has his lunch hour at twelve o'clock," said Martin Beck. "If you hurry, you can get there. Clever boy, that Lundberg, if he's right. Call in when you can this afternoon so that Stenström can relieve you."

"I think I can manage myself today. Stenström can jump in this evening. So long."

At a quarter of twelve Kollberg was at his place. There was a bar right across the street from the moving company and he sat down there by the window. On the table in front of him was a cup of coffee and a small, red vase with a tired tulip in it, a twig of evergreen, and a dusty, plastic Santa Claus. He drank his coffee slowly and never took his eyes off the driveway across the street. He guessed that the five windows to the left of the driveway door belonged to the moving company, but he couldn't distinguish anything behind the glass due to the fact that the bottom halves of the windows were painted white.

When a truck with the moving company's name on the doors came out of the driveway, Kollberg looked at the clock. Three minutes to twelve. Two minutes later the office door opened and a tall man in a dark gray coat and a black hat came out. Kollberg put the money for his coffee on the table, got up, took his hat as he followed the man with his eyes. The man stepped off the curb, and crossed the street past the bar. When Kollberg came out on to the street he saw the man turn the corner onto Norrland Street. He followed him but didn't have to go far. There was a cafeteria about sixty feet from the corner which the man entered.

There was a line in front of the counter where the man waited patiently. When he got there he took a tray, grabbed a small container of milk, some bread and butter, ordered something at the window, paid, and sat down at an empty table with his back to Kollberg.

When the girl at the window shouted "One salmon!" he

got up and went to get his plate. He ate slowly and with concentration and only looked up when he drank his milk. Kollberg had gotten a cup of coffee and placed himself so that he could see the man's face. After a while he was even more convinced that this really was the man on the film.

He neither drank coffee nor smoked after his meal. He wiped his mouth carefully, took his hat and coat and left. Kollberg followed him down to Hamn Street where he crossed over to the King's Gardens. He walked rather quickly and Kollberg stayed about sixty feet behind through the East Allé. At Mollin's fountain he turned to the right, passed the fountain which was half filled with dirty, gray snow, and continued up on the West Allé. Kollberg followed him past the "Victoria and Blanche" cafe, across the street to NK, down Hamn Street to Småland Street, where he crossed the street and disappeared into the driveway door.

"Oh yes," thought Kollberg, "that was certainly exciting."

He looked at his watch. Lunch and the walk had taken exactly three-quarters of an hour.

Nothing particular happened during the afternoon. The trucks returned, still empty. People went in and out of doors. A station wagon drove out and came back. Both trucks went out again and when one of them came back it almost collided with the station wagon which was on its way out.

Five minutes before five one of the truck drivers came out of the driveway door with a heavy, gray-haired woman. At five o'clock the other driver came out. The third had still not come back with his truck. Three more men followed him out and crossed the street. They entered the bar and loudly ordered their beers which they received and drank in silence.

Five minutes after five, the tall man came out. He stood in front of the door, took out a key ring from his pocket, and locked the door. Then he placed the key ring back in his pocket, checked to see if the door was properly locked, and walked out onto the street.

While Kollberg was putting his coat on he heard one of the beer drinkers say: "Folke's going home now."

And one of the others: "What does he have to do at home when he isn't hooked. He doesn't know how good he has it. You should have heard my old lady when I came home last night. . . . What a time just because a man goes and has a few beers before he goes home after work. I swear. . . ."

Kollberg didn't hear any more. The tall man who, without a doubt, was named Folke Bengtsson had disappeared out of sight. Kollberg caught up with him on Norrland Street again. The man was walking through the crowds toward Hamn Street and he continued on to the bus stop right across the street from NK.

By the time Kollberg got there four people were in line behind Bengtsson. He hoped that the bus wouldn't be too full to take them both. Bengtsson looked straight ahead of him the entire time and seemed to be looking at the Christmas decorations in NK's windows. When the bus arrived he hopped up on the step and Kollberg just managed to get on himself before the doors closed.

The man got off at St. Erik's Square. The traffic was tight and it took him a few minutes to get by all the traffic lights and cross to the other side of the square. On Rörstand Street he walked into a supermarket.

He continued along Rörstand Street, passed Birk Street, slunk across the street and went through a door. After a while Kollberg followed him and read the names on the mailboxes. There were two entrances to the house, one from the street and the other from the garden. Kollberg congratulated himself and his luck when he saw that Bengtsson lived in an apartment facing the street, two flights up.

He stationed himself in a doorway across the street and looked up at the third floor. In four of the windows there were frilly tulle curtains and a number of potted plants. Thanks to the man in the bar, Kollberg knew that Bengtsson was a bachelor and doubted that these windows belonged to his apartment. He concentrated his attention on the other two windows. One of them was open and while he was watching it, a light was turned on in the second one, which he presumed was the kitchen window. He saw the ceiling and the upper part of the walls which were white. A few times he could see someone moving about inside but not quite clearly enough to be sure it was Bengtsson.

After twenty minutes it was dark in the kitchen and a light was turned on in the other room. A little later Bengtsson appeared in the window. He opened it wide and leaned out. Then he closed it again, and closed the Venetian blinds. They were yellow and let light come through and Kollberg saw Bengtsson's silhouette disappear inside the room. The

windows were without drapes because on both sides of the
blinds broad streams of light appeared.

Kollberg went and telephoned to Stenström.

"He's home now. If I don't call you back before nine
come and take over."

Eight minutes after nine, Stenström arrived. Nothing had
happened except that the light had been turned off at eight
o'clock and after that there had been only a weak, cold blue
stream of light from between the blinds.

Stenström had an evening paper in his pocket and an-
nounced that the man was probably looking at a long, American film on the television.

"That's fine," said Kollberg. "I saw it ten or fifteen years
ago. It has a wonderful ending. Everyone dies except the girl.
I'll run along now and maybe I'll get to see some of it. If you
call me before six I'll come over here."

It was a cold and clear morning. Ten hours later Stenström
hurried off toward St. Erik's Square. Since the light had been
turned off at ten-thirty in the room on the third floor, nothing had happened.

"Be careful that you don't freeze," Stenström had said
before he left. When the door opened and the tall man came
out, Kollberg was thankful for a chance to move.

Bengtsson had on the same overcoat as he had the day
before but he had changed his hat to a gray Crimea cap. He
walked quickly and the breath from his mouth looked like
white smoke. At St. Erik's Square he took a bus to Hamn Street
and a few minutes before eight Kollberg saw him disappear behind the door to the moving company.

A few hours later he came out again, walked the few steps
to the cafe in the house next door, drank a cup of coffee and
ate two sandwiches. At twelve o'clock he went to the cafeteria
and when he had eaten, he took his walk through the city and
went back to his office. At a few minutes after five he locked
the door behind him, took the bus to St. Erik's Square, bought
some bread in a bakery, and went home.

At twenty minutes after seven he came out of his front
door again. At St. Erik's Square he walked to the right, and
continued over the bridge and finally swung in to Kungsholm Street where he disappeared into a doorway. Kollberg
stood for a while outside the door where the word BOWLING

shone in large, red letters. Then he opened the door and went in.

The bowling hall had seven lanes and in back of a railing was a bar with small, round tables and some chairs. Echoes of voices and laughter filled the room. Now and then he heard the sound of rolling balls and the bang that followed.

Kollberg couldn't see Bengtsson anywhere. On the other hand he immediately spotted two of the three men from the bar the previous day. They sat at a table in the bar and Kollberg drew back toward a door in order not to be recognized. After a while the third man came toward the table together with Bengtsson. When they had begun to bowl, Kollberg left.

After a few hours the four bowlers came out. They separated at the trolley stop at St. Erik's Square and Bengtsson walked back the way he had come, alone.

At eleven o'clock it got dark in Bengtsson's apartment but by that time Kollberg was already home and in bed, while his bundled up colleague paced back and forth on Birk Street. Stenström had a cold.

The next day was a Wednesday and it went by pretty much as the earlier days. Stenström nursed his cold and spent the major part of the day in the cafe on Småland Street.

That evening Bengtsson went to the movies. Five rows in back of him Kollberg watched while a blond, half naked Mr. America struggled with an ancient monster in cinemascope.

The next two days were similar. Stenström and Kollberg took turns following the man's uneventful and highly regimented life. Kollberg visited the bowling alley again and found out that Bengtsson played well and that for years he had played every Tuesday with his three friends from work.

The seventh day was a Sunday and according to Stenström the only interesting thing that happened during the entire day was a hockey match between Sweden and Czechoslovakia which, together with Bengtsson and ten thousand others, he attended.

Kollberg found a new door to stand in on Sunday night.

When, for the second Saturday in a row, he saw Bengtsson come out of his office, lock the door at two minutes after twelve and begin to walk toward Regering Street, he thought: "Now we'll go to the Löwenbräu and have a beer." When

Bengtsson opened the door to the Löwenbräu, Kollberg stood at the corner of Drottning Street and hated him.

That evening he went up to his office at Kristineberg and looked at some pictures from the film. He didn't know how many times he had looked at them.

He looked at each picture for a long time and very carefully, but in spite of the fact that it was hard to believe, he still saw the man whose quiet life he had witnessed for two weeks.

23

"It must be the wrong guy," said Kollberg.

"Are you getting tired?"

"Don't misunderstand me. I have nothing against standing and sleeping in a doorway on Birk Street night after night, but . . ."

"But what?"

"For ten out of fourteen days this is exactly what has happened: at seven o'clock he opens the blinds. At one minute after seven he opens the window. At twenty-five minutes to eight he shuts the window. At twenty minutes to eight he walks out of his front door, walks over to St. Erik's Square and takes the number 56 bus to the corner of Regering Street and Hamn Street, walks to the moving company and unlocks the door at one half minute before eight. At ten o'clock he goes down to the City Cafe, drinks two cups of coffee and eats a cheese sandwich. At one minute after twelve he goes to either one of two cafeterias. He eats. . . ."

"What does he eat?" asked Martin Beck.

"Fish or fried meat. He is finished at twenty minutes past twelve, takes a quick walk through the middle of town, and goes back to work. At five minutes past five he locks up and goes home. If the weather is terrible he takes the number 56 bus. Otherwise he walks up Regering Street, King Street, Queen Street, Barnhus Street, Uppland Street, Observatory Street, through Vasa Park, across St. Erik's Square, past Birk Street and home. On the way he sometimes shops in some supermarket where there aren't too many people. He buys milk and cake every day and every few days he gets bread, butter, cheese and marmalade. He has stayed home and looked at the boob tube eight evenings out of the fourteen. On Wednesdays he has gone to the seven o'clock show at the movies. Fanciful nonsense films, both times. I was the one that had to sit through them. On the way home he stuffs a frankfurter into himself, with both mustard and catsup. Two Sundays in a row he has taken the subway to the stadium to see the ice hockey games. Stenström got to see those. Two Tuesdays in a row he has gone bowling with three men from his company. On Saturdays he works until twelve. Then he goes to the Löwenbräu and drinks a stein of beer. In addition, he eats a portion of frankfurter salad. Then he goes home. He doesn't look at the girls on the street. Sometimes he stops and looks at the posters in front of the movie houses or in the shop windows, mostly sporting goods and hardware stores. He doesn't buy any newspapers and doesn't subscribe to any either. On the other hand he does buy two magazines, *Rekord-Magasinet* and some kind of fishing magazine. I've forgotten what it is called. Garbage! There is no blue Monark motor bike in the cellar of the apartment house he lives in but there is a red one made by Svalen. It's his. He rarely gets any mail. He doesn't mix with his neighbors but does greet them on the stairs."

"What is he like?"

"How the devil should I know?" Kollberg said.

"Seriously."

"He seems healthy, calm, strong and dull. He keeps his window open every night. Moves naturally and without trouble, dresses well, doesn't seem nervous. He never seems to be in a hurry but doesn't drag. He ought to smoke a pipe. But doesn't."

"Has he noticed you?"

"I don't think so. Not me, in any case."

They sat quietly for a while watching the snow which came down in large, wet flakes.

"You understand," Kollberg said, "I have a feeling that we could keep on like this right up until he has his vacation next summer. It is a fascinating act, but can the country afford to keep two supposedly capable detectives . . ."

He stopped in the middle of the sentence.

"Capable, yes, by the way, last night there was a drunk who

said "boo" to me while I stood there and watched the apartment. I almost got a heart attack."

"*Is* it the right guy?"

"He sure looks like it judging from the film."

Martin Beck rocked in his chair.

"Okay, We'll bring him in."

"Now?"

"Yes."

"Who?"

"You. After work. So that he doesn't neglect anything. Take him up to your office and get the personal information. When you've got that, call me."

"Soft line?"

"Definitely."

It was nine-thirty on December 14. Martin Beck had suffered through the National Police's Christmas party with doughy cake and two glasses of almost alcohol free glögg.

He called the Public Prosecutor in Linköping and Ahlberg in Motala and was surprised to hear them both say: "I'm coming."

They arrived around three o'clock. The Public Prosecutor had come up via Motala. He exchanged a few words with Martin Beck and then went into Hammar's office.

Ahlberg sat in Martin Beck's visitor's chair for two hours but they only exchanged a few remarks of interest. Ahlberg said:

"Do you think it was he?"

"I don't know."

"It must be."

"Yes."

At five minutes after five they heard a knock on the door. It was the Public Prosecutor and Hammar.

"I am convinced that you are right," said the Prosecutor. "Use whatever method you like."

Martin Beck nodded.

"Hi," said Kollberg. "Have you time to come up? Folke Bengtsson, who I've mentioned to you, is here."

Martin Beck put down the receiver and got up. When he got to the doorway he turned around and looked at Ahlberg. Neither of them said anything.

He walked slowly up the stairs. In spite of the thousands of examinations he had conducted, he had a funny, bad feeling in his stomach and in the left part of his chest.

Kollberg had taken off his jacket and stood with his elbows on the desk, calm and jovial. Melander sat with his back to them, tranquilly occupied with his papers.

"This is Folke Bengtsson," said Kollberg, and stood up.

"Beck."

"Bengtsson."

They shook hands. Kollberg put his jacket on.

"I'll run along now. So long."

"So long."

Martin Beck sat down. There was a sheet of paper in Kollberg's typewriter. He pulled it up a bit and read: "Folke Lennart Bengtsson, Office Manager, Born 6/8/1926 in Gustaf Vasa's parish, Stockholm. Unmarried."

He looked at the man. Blue eyes, a rather ordinary face. A few streaks of gray in his hair. No nervousness. In general, nothing special.

"Do you know why we have asked you to come here?"

"As a matter of fact, no."

"It is possible that you can help us with something."

"What would that be?"

Martin Beck looked toward the window and said:

"It's beginning to snow heavily now."

"Yes, it is."

"Where were you during the first week of July last summer? Do you remember?"

"I ought to. I was on vacation then. The company that I am with closes down for four weeks right after midsummer."

"Yes?"

"I was in several different places, two weeks on the West Coast, among others. I usually go fishing when I'm off. At least one week in the winter too."

"How did you get there? By car?"

The man smiled.

"No, I don't have a car. Not even a driver's license. I went on my motor bike."

Martin Beck sat quietly for a second.

"There are worse ways to travel. I had a motor bike too for a few years. What kind do you have?"

"I had a Monark then, but I got a new one this past fall."

"Do you remember how you spent your vacation?"

"Yes, of course. I spent the first week at Mem, that's on the Östgöta coast, right where the Göta Canal begins. Then I went on to Bohuslän."

Martin Beck got up and went over to the water pitcher which stood on top of a file near the door. He looked at Melander. Walked back. He lifted the hood off the tape recorder and plugged in the microphone. The man looked at the apparatus.

"Did you go by boat between Mem and Gothenburg?"

"No, from Söderköping."

"What was the name of the boat?"

"The *Diana*."

"Which day did you travel?"

"I don't remember exactly. One of the first days in July."

"Did anything special happen during the trip?"

"No, not that I can remember."

"Are you sure? Think about it."

"Yes, that's right. The boat had some engine trouble. But that was before I went on board. It had been delayed. Otherwise I wouldn't have made it."

"What did you do when you got to Gothenburg?"

"The boat got in very early in the morning. I went up to a place called Hamburgsund. I had reserved a room there."

"How long did you stay?"

"Two weeks."

"What did you do during those two weeks?"

"Fished as often as I could. The weather was poor."

Martin Beck opened Kollberg's desk drawer and took out the three photographs of Roseanna McGraw.

"Do you recognize this woman?"

The man looked at the pictures, one after the other. His expression didn't change in the slightest.

"Her face looks familiar in some way," he said. "Who is she?"

"She was on board the *Diana*."

"Yes, I think I remember," the man said indifferently.

He looked at the pictures again.

"But I'm not sure. What was her name?"

"Roseanna McGraw. She was an American."

"Now I remember. Yes, that's right. She was on board. I talked with her a few times. As well as I could."

"You haven't seen or heard her name since then?"

"No, actually not. That is to say, not before now."

Martin Beck caught the man's eyes and held them. They were cold and calm and questioning.

"Don't you know that Roseanna McGraw was murdered during that trip?"

A slight shift of expression crossed the man's face.

"No," he said, finally. "No . . . I really didn't know that."

He wrinkled his forehead.

"Is it true?" he said suddenly.

"It seems very strange that you haven't heard anything about it. To be blunt, I don't believe you."

Martin Beck got the feeling that the man had stopped listening.

"Naturally, now I understand why you have brought me here."

"Did you hear what I just said? It seems very strange that you haven't heard anything about it in spite of everything that's been written about this case. I simply don't believe you."

"If I had known anything about it I certainly would have come involuntarily."

"Come in voluntarily?"

"Yes, as a witness."

"To what?"

"To say that I had met her. Where was she killed? In Gothenburg?"

"No, on board the boat, in her cabin. While you were on board."

"That doesn't seem possible."

"Why not?"

"Someone must have noticed it. Every cabin was fully occupied."

"It seems even more impossible that you never heard anything about it. I find that hard to believe."

"Wait, I can explain that. I never read the newspapers."

"There was a lot about this case on the radio, too, and on the television news programs. This photograph was shown on Aktuellt. Several times. Don't you have a television?"

"Yes, of course. But I only look at nature programs and at movies."

Martin Beck sat quietly and stared at the man. After a minute he said:

"Why don't you read the papers?"

"They don't contain anything that interests me. Only politics and . . . yes, things like you just mentioned, murders and accidents and other miseries."

"Don't you ever read anything?"

"Yes, of course. I read several magazines, about sports, fishing, outdoor life, maybe even a few adventure stories sometimes."

"Which magazines?"

"*The Sportsman,* just about every issue. *All-Sport* and *Rekord-Magazine,* I usually buy them, and *Lektyr.* I've read that one since I was little. Sometimes I buy some American magazines about sport fishing."

"Do you usually talk about the events of the day with your fellow workers?"

"No, they know me and know that I'm not interested. They talk about things with each other, of course, but I seldom listen. That's actually true."

Martin Beck said nothing.

"I realize that this sounds strange, but I can only repeat that it's true. You have to believe me."

"Are you religious?"

"No, why do you ask?"

Martin Beck took out a cigarette and offered the man one.

"No thank you. I don't smoke."

"Do you drink?"

"I like beer. I usually take a glass or two on Saturdays after work. Never anything stronger."

Martin Beck looked at him steadily. The man made no attempt to avoid his glance.

"Well, we found you finally, anyway. That's the main thing."

"Yes. How did you do that, figure out that I was on board, I mean?"

"Oh, it was accidental. Someone recognized you. It's like this: so far you are the only person we have been in contact with who has spoken to this woman. How did you meet her?"

"I think that . . . now I remember. She happened to be standing next to me and asked me something."

"And?"

"I answered. As well as I could. My English isn't that good."

"But you often read American magazines?"

"Yes, and that's why I usually take an opportunity to talk

with Englishmen and Americans. To practice. It doesn't happen very often. Once a week I usually go to see an American film, it doesn't matter which. And I often look at detective films on the television, although the subject doesn't interest me."

"You spoke with Roseanna McGraw. What did you talk about?"

"Well . . ."

"Try to remember. It could be important."

"She talked a bit about herself."

"What, for example?"

"Where she lived, but I don't remember what she said."

"Could it have been New York?"

"No, she named some state in America. Maybe Nevada. I actually don't remember."

"What else?"

"She said that she worked in a library. I remember that very well. And that she had been to the North Cape and in Lapland. That she had seen the midnight sun. She also asked about a number of things."

"Were you together a lot?"

"No, I couldn't say that. I spoke with her three or four times."

"When? During which part of the trip?"

The man didn't answer immediately.

"It must have been the first day. I actually remember that we were together between Berg and Ljungsbro, where the passengers usually get off the boat while the boat is in the locks."

"Do you know the canal area well?"

"Yes, rather well."

"Have you been on it before?"

"Yes, several times. I usually plan to ride part of the way on the boats when it fits in with my vacation plans. There aren't too many of those old boats left and it really is a fine trip."

"How many times?"

"I can't exactly say right away. Maybe if I think about it, but it must have been at least ten times over the years. Different stretches. I only rode the whole way once, from Gothenburg to Stockholm."

"As a deck passenger?"

"Yes, the cabins are booked well in advance. In addition, it's rather expensive to go as a cruise passenger."

"Doesn't it get uncomfortable without a cabin?"

"No, not at all. You can sleep on a sofa in the salon under the deck if you want to. I am actually not terribly fussy about those things."

"So, you met Roseanna McGraw. You remember that you were with her at Ljungsbro. But later in the trip?"

"I think that I spoke with her again on some other occasion, in passing."

"When?"

"I don't actually remember."

"Did you see her during the latter part of the trip?"

"Not that I can remember."

"Did you know where her cabin was?"

No answer.

"Did you hear the question? Where was her cabin?"

"I'm really trying to remember. No, I don't think I ever knew."

"You were never inside her cabin?"

"No. The cabins are usually terribly small and anyway, they are double cabins."

"Always?"

"Well, there are a few singles. But not many. They are quite expensive."

"Do you know if Roseanna McGraw was traveling alone?"

"I haven't thought about it. She didn't say anything about it, as far as I can remember."

"And you never went with her to her cabin?"

"No, actually not."

"At Ljungsbro, what did you talk about there?"

"I remember that I asked her if she wanted to see the church at the Vreta monastery, which is right near there. But she didn't want to. And anyway, I'm not sure that she understood what I meant."

"What else did you talk about?"

"I don't actually remember. Nothing in particular. I don't think we spoke that much. We walked part of the way along the canal. A lot of other people did too."

"Did you see her with anyone else?"

The man sat quietly. He looked toward the window expressionlessly.

"This is a very important question."

"I understand that. I'm trying to remember. She must have spoken with other people while I stood next to her, some other American or Englishman. I don't remember anyone in particular."

Martin Beck got up and walked over to the water pitcher.

"Do you want something to drink?"

"No thank you. I'm not thirsty."

Martin Beck drank a glass of water and walked back, pressed a button under the desk, stopped the tape recorder and took off the tape.

A minute later Melander came in and went to his desk.

"Will you take care of this, please," he said.

Melander took the tape and left.

The man called Folke Bengtsson sat completely straight in his chair and looked at Martin Beck with blue, expressionless eyes.

"As I said before, you are the only person we know who remembers, or will admit that he has talked to her."

"I understand."

"It wasn't possibly you that killed her?"

"No, as a matter of fact it wasn't. Do you believe that?"

"Someone must have done it."

"I didn't even know that she was dead. And not even what her name was. You surely don't believe that . . ."

"If I had thought that you would admit it, I wouldn't have asked the question in that tone of voice," said Martin Beck.

"I understand . . . I think. Were you fooling?"

"No."

The man sat quietly.

"If I told you that we know for a fact that you were inside that woman's cabin, what would you say?"

He didn't answer for about ten seconds.

"That you must be wrong. But you wouldn't say that if you weren't certain, isn't that right?"

Martin Beck said nothing.

"In that case I must have been there without knowing what I was doing."

"Do you usually know what you are doing?"

The man lifted his eyebrow slightly.

"Yes, I usually do," he said.

Then he said, positively:

"I wasn't there."

"You understand," said Martin Beck. "This case is highly confusing."

"Thank God that isn't going on the tape," he thought.

"I understand."

Martin Beck stuck a cigarette in his mouth and lit it.

"Are you married?"

"No."

"Have you a steady relationship with any woman?"

"No. I'm a confirmed bachelor, I'm used to living alone."

"Have you any brothers or sisters?"

"No, I was an only child."

"And grew up with your parents?"

"With my mother. My father died when I was six. I hardly remember him."

"Have you no relationships with women?"

"Naturally, I'm not totally inexperienced. I am going on forty."

Martin Beck looked steadily at him.

"When you need female company do you usually turn to prostitutes?"

"No, never."

"Can you name some woman who you have been with for either a longer or shorter period of time?"

"Maybe I can, but I don't choose to."

Martin Beck pulled out the desk drawer a little bit and looked down into it. He rubbed his index finger along his lower lip.

"It would be best if you named someone," he said haltingly.

"The person who I'm thinking of at the moment, with whom my relationship was . . . most lasting, she . . . Yes, she's married now and we aren't in contact with one another any more. It would be painful for her."

"It would still be best," said Martin Beck without looking up.

"I don't want to bring her any unpleasantness."

"It won't be unpleasant for her. What's her name?"

"If you can guarantee . . . her married name is Siv Lindberg. But I ask you really . . ."

"Where does she live?"

"Lidingö. Her husband is an engineer. I don't know the address. Somewhere in Bodal I think."

Martin Beck took a last glance at the picture of the woman from Lincoln. Then he closed the drawer again and said:

"Thank you. I am sorry that I have to ask these kinds of questions. But, unfortunately, it's part of my job."

Melander came in and sat down at his desk.

"Would you mind waiting a few minutes," Martin Beck said.

In the room one flight below, the tape recorder played back the last replies. Martin Beck stood with his back against the wall and listened.

"Do you want something to drink?"

"No thank you. I'm not thirsty."

The Public Prosecutor was the first person to say something.

"Well?"

"Let him go."

The Public Prosecutor looked at the ceiling, Kollberg at the floor, and Ahlberg at Martin Beck.

"You didn't press him very hard," said the Prosecutor. "That wasn't a very long examination."

"No."

"And if we hold him?" asked the Prosecutor.

"Then we have to let him go by this time on Thursday," Hammar replied.

"We don't know anything about that."

"No," said Hammar.

"All right," said the Prosecutor.

Martin Beck nodded. He walked out of the room and up the stairs and he still felt ill and had some discomfort in the left part of his chest.

Melander and the man called Folke Bengtsson seemed as if they hadn't moved at all since he had left them.

"I am sorry that it was necessary to bother you. Can I offer you transportation home?"

"I'll take the subway, thank you."

"Maybe that's faster."

"Yes, actually."

Martin Beck walked with him to the ground floor out of routine.

"Goodbye then."

"Goodbye."

An ordinary handshake.

Kollberg and Ahlberg were still sitting and looking at the tape recorder.

"Shall we continue to tail him?" asked Kollberg.

"No."

"Do you think he did it?" asked Kollberg.

Martin Beck stood in the middle of the floor and looked at his right hand.

"Yes," he said. "I'm sure he did."

24

The apartment house reminded him, in a basic way, of his own in the southern part of Stockholm. It had narrow flights of stairs, standardized nameplates on the doors and incinerator doors between each floor. The house was on Fredgat Road in Bodal and he took the Lidingö train to get there.

He had chosen the time carefully. At a quarter past one, Swedish office workers are sitting at their desks and small children are having their afternoon naps. Housewives have turned on some music on the radio and sit down to have a cup of coffee with saccharin tablets.

The woman who opened the door was small, blond, and blue-eyed. Just under thirty and rather pretty. She held on to the doorknob anxiously, as if prepared to close the door immediately.

"The police? Has anything happened? My husband. . . ."

Her face was frightened and confused. It was also fetching, Martin Beck thought. He showed her his identification, which seemed to calm her.

"I don't understand how I can help you but, by all means, come in."

The furniture arrangement was nondescript, gloomy and neat. But the view was marvelous. Just below lay Lilla Värtan and two tugboats were in the process of bringing a freighter to the pier. He would have given a lot to have traded apartments with her.

"Do you have children?" he asked as a diversion.

"Yes, a little girl ten months old. I've just put her in her crib."

He took out the photographs.

"Do you know this man?"

She blushed immediately, looked away, and nodded uncertainly.

"Yes, I knew him. But—but it was several years ago. What has he done?"

Martin Beck didn't answer at once.

"You understand, this is very unpleasant. My husband . . ."

She was searching for the right words.

"Why don't we sit down," said Martin Beck. "Forgive me for suggesting it."

"Yes. Yes, of course."

She sat down on the sofa, tense and straight.

"You have no reason to be afraid or worried. The situation is this: we are interested in this man, for several reasons, as a witness. They have nothing to do with you, however. But it is important that we get some general information about his character from someone who has, in one way or another, been together with him."

This statement didn't seem to calm her particularly.

"This is terribly unpleasant," she said. "My husband, you understand, we have been married for nearly two years now, and he doesn't know anything . . . about Folke. I haven't told him, about that man . . . but, yes, naturally, as you can understand, he must surely have known that I had been with someone else . . . before. . . ."

She was even more confused and blushed profusely.

"We never speak about such things," she said.

"You can be completely calm. I am only going to ask you to answer some questions. Your husband will not know what you say, or anyone else for that matter. In any case, no one that you know."

She nodded but continued to look stubbornly to the side.

"You knew Folke Bengtsson?"

"Yes."

"When and where did you know him?"

"I . . . we met more than four years ago, at a place, a company where we both worked."

"Eriksson's Moving Company?"

"Yes, I worked there as a cashier."

"And you had a relationship with him?"

She nodded with her head turned away from him.

"For how long?"

"One year," she said, very quietly.

"Were you happy together?"

She turned and looked at him uncertainly and raised her arms in a helpless gesture.

Martin Beck looked over her shoulder and out the window toward a dismal, gray winter sky.

"How did it begin?"

"Well, we . . . saw each other every day and then we began to take our coffee breaks together and then lunches. And . . . yes, he took me home several times."

"Where did you live?"

"On Uppland Street."

"Alone?"

"Oh no. I was still living with my parents then."

"Did he ever come upstairs with you?"

She shook her head, energetically, still without looking at him.

"What else happened then?"

"He invited me to the movies a few times. And then . . . yes, he asked me to dinner."

"At his house?"

"No, not at first."

"When?"

"In October."

"How long had you been going out with him by then?"

"Several months."

"And then you began a real relationship?"

She sat quietly for a long while. Finally she said: "Do I have to answer that question?"

"Yes, it is important. It would be better if you answer here and now. It would save a great deal of unpleasantness."

"What do you want to know? What is it that you want me to say?"

"You had intimate relations with one another, didn't you?"

She nodded.

"When did it begin? The first time you were there?"

She looked at him helplessly.

"How often?"

"Not particularly often, I think."

"But every time you were there?"

"Oh, no. Not at all."

"What did you usually do when you were together?"

"Well . . . oh, everything, have something to eat, talk, look at TV and the fish."

"Fish?"

"He had a large aquarium."

Martin Beck took a deep breath.

"Did he make you happy?"

"I . . ."

"Try to answer."

"You . . . you are asking such difficult questions. Yes, I think so."

"Was he brutal to you?"

"I don't understand."

"I mean when you were together. Did he hit you?"

"Oh, no."

"Did he hurt you in any other way?"

"No."

"Never?"

"No, he never did. Why should he have?"

"Did you ever talk about getting married and living together?"

"No."

"Why not?"

"He never said anything about it, never a word."

"Weren't you afraid of becoming pregnant?"

"Yes. But we were always so careful."

Martin Beck managed to make himself look at her. She still sat completely straight on the edge of the sofa, with her knees tightly together and the muscles in her legs strained. She was not only red in the face but even her neck was red, and there were small, fine drops of perspiration along her hairline.

He started again.

"What kind of a man was he? Sexually?"

The question came as a total surprise to her. She moved her hands worriedly. Finally she said:

"Nice."

"What do you mean by nice?"

"He . . . I mean that I think he needed a lot of tenderness. And I, I am, I was the same."

Even though he was sitting less than five feet from her he had to strain to hear what she had said.

"Did you love him?"

"I think so."

"Did he satisfy you?"

"I don't know."

"Why did you stop seeing each other?"

"I don't know. It just ended."

"There is one more thing I must ask you to answer. When you had intimate relations, was it always he who took the initiative?"

"Well . . . what do you want me to say . . . I suspect that it was so, but it usually is that way. And I always agreed."

"How many times would you say it happened?"

"Five," she whispered.

Martin Beck sat quietly and looked at her. He should have asked: Was he the first man you slept with? Did you usually take all your clothes off? Did you have the lights on? Did he ever . . .

"Goodbye," he said, and got up. "Forgive me for having bothered you."

He closed the door after himself. The last thing he heard her say was:

"Forgive me, I'm a little shy."

Martin Beck walked back and forth in the slush on the platform while he waited for the train. He kept his hands in his coat pockets and hunched his shoulders, whistled absentmindedly and off key.

Finally, he knew what he was going to do.

25

Hammar was doodling old men on a piece of scratch paper while he listened. This was supposed to be a good sign. Then he said:

"Where will you get the woman from?"

"There must be someone on the force."

"You had better find her first."

Two minutes later Kollberg said: "Where are you going to get the girl from?"

"Is it you or I who has spent eighteen years with his rear end on the edge of other people's desks?"

"It won't do to get just anybody."

"No one knows the force better than you do."

"Well, I can always look around."

"Right."

Melander appeared totally uninterested. Without turning around or taking his pipe out of his mouth, he said: "Vibeke Amdal lives on Toldebod Street, is fifty-nine years old and the widow of a brewer. She can't remember having seen Roseanna McGraw other than on the picture she took at Riddarholm. Karin Larsson ran away from her boat in Rotterdam, but the police say that she isn't there. Presumably, she took another boat with false papers."

"Foreign ones, of course," said Kollberg. "She knows all about that. It can take a year before we find her. Or five. And then she might not say anything. Has Kafka answered?"

"Not yet."

Martin Beck went upstairs and called Motala.

"Yes," said Ahlberg calmly. "I guess it is the only way. But where are you going to get the girl from?"

"From the police force. Yours, for example."

"No, she doesn't fit."

Martin Beck hung up. The telephone rang. It was a man from the regular patrol force at the Klara Station.

"We did exactly as you said."

"And?"

"The man seems sure enough, but believe me, he's on the alert. He's watchful, turns around, stops often. It would be hard to tail him without his noticing it."

"Could he have recognized any of you?"

"No, there were three of us and we didn't follow him. We just stood still and let him walk by. Anyway, it's our job not to be recognized. Is there anything else we can do for you?"

"Not for the moment."

The next telephone call came from Adolf Fredrik's Station.

"This is Hansson in the fifth. I watched him at Bråvalla Street both this morning and now when he came home."

"How did he act?"

"Calm, but I have an idea that he was being careful."

"Did he notice anything?"

"Not a chance. This morning I was sitting in the car, and the second time there was a real crowd. The only time I was near him was just now at the newspaper stand on St. Erik's Square. I stood two places behind him in the line."

"What did he buy?"

"Newspapers."

"Which ones?"

"A whole bunch. All four morning papers and both of the evening rags."

Melander tapped on the door and stuck his head in.

"I think I'll go home now. Is that all right? I have to buy some Christmas presents," he explained.

Martin Beck nodded and hung up the phone and thought, "Oh God, Christmas presents," and immediately forgot what he had been thinking.

He went home late but even so he didn't manage to avoid the crowd. The Christmas rush was on and all the stores were open later than usual.

At home his wife said that he seemed absentminded, but he didn't hear her and didn't reply.

At breakfast she said: "Will you be off between the holi-days?"

Nothing happened before a quarter after four when Koll-berg thundered in and said: "I think I have one who will do."

"On the force?"

"Works at Berg Street. She's coming here at nine-thirty to-morrow morning. If she seems right, Hammar can fix it so that we can borrow her."

"What does she look like?"

"I think that she looks like Roseanna McGraw in some way. She's taller, a little prettier, and presumably shrewder."

"Does she know anything?"

"She's been with the police force for several years. A calm and good girl. Healthy and strong."

"How well do you know her?"

"Hardly at all."

"And she isn't married?"

Kollberg took a piece of paper out of his pocket.

"Here's everything you need to know about her. I'm leav-ing now. I have to go Christmas shopping."

"Christmas presents," thought Martin Beck and looked at the clock. Four-thirty, and struck by a thought, he grabbed the telephone and called the woman in Bodal.

"Oh, is it you. Yes, Mr. . . ."

"Am I calling at a bad time?"

"No, it's not . . . my husband doesn't get home before a quarter of six."

"Just one simple question. Did the man we spoke about yesterday ever get anything from you? I mean any present, a souvenir or something like that?"

"No, no presents. We never gave each other any. You un-derstand. . . ."

"Was he tight?"

"Economical, I would rather say. I am too. The only . . ."

Silence. He could almost hear her blushing.

"What did you give him?"

"A . . . a little amulet . . . or trinket . . . just an inexpensive little thing. . . ."

"When did you give it to him?"

"When we parted. . . . He wanted to have it . . . I always used to have it with me."

"He took it from you?"

"Well, I was glad to give it to him. One always wants a souvenir . . . even if . . . above all, I mean. . . ."

"Thank you very much. Goodbye."

He telephoned Ahlberg.

"I've talked to Larsson and the Commissioner. The Public Prosecutor is sick."

"What did they say?"

"Okay. They realized that there isn't any other way. It's certainly unorthodox, but . . ."

"It's been done many times before, even in Sweden. What I plan to suggest to you now is a great deal more unorthodox."

"That sounds good."

"Give out the news to the press that the murder is almost cleared up."

"Now?"

"Yes, immediately. Today. You understand what I mean?"

"Yes, a foreigner."

"Right. Like this, for example: 'According to the latest announcement a person, who has been searched for by Interpol for a long time for the murder of Roseanna McGraw, has finally been arrested by the American police.'"

"And we have known all along the murderer was not in Sweden?"

"That's only an example. The main thing is to get it out fast."

"I understand."

"Then I think you'd better come up here."

"Immediately?"

"Just about."

A messenger came into the room. Martin Beck gripped the telephone tightly with his left shoulder and ripped open the cable. It was from Kafka.

"What does he say?" asked Ahlberg.

"Only three words: 'Set a trap.'"

26

Policewoman Sonja Hansson was actually not unlike Roseanna McGraw. Kollberg had been right.

She sat in Martin Beck's office with her hands crossed lightly in her lap and looked at him with calm gray eyes. Her dark hair was combed into a page-boy and her bangs fell softly over her left eyebrow. Her face was healthy and her expression was open. She didn't seem to use make-up. She looked no more than twenty years old but Martin Beck knew that she was twenty-five.

"First of all I want you to understand that this is voluntary," he said. "You can say no if you want to. We have decided to ask you to take on this assignment because you have the best qualifications to handle it, mainly because of your looks."

The girl in the chair pushed the hair off her forehead and looked questioningly at him.

"Then too," Martin Beck continued, "you live in the middle of the city and you're not married or living with anyone, as it's so nicely put these days. Is that right?"

Sonja Hansson shook her head.

"I hope I can help you," she said. "But what's wrong with my looks?"

"Do you remember Roseanna McGraw, the girl from America, who was murdered on the Göta Canal last summer?"

"Do I? I'm in the Missing Persons Bureau and worked on the case for a while."

"We know who did it and we know that he's here in the

city. I've examined him. He admits that he was on the boat when it happened and that he had met her, but says he doesn't even know about the murder."

"Isn't that a rather improbable statement? I mean there was so much about it in the papers."

"He says that he doesn't read newspapers. We couldn't get anything out of him. He acted totally forthright and seemed to answer all our questions honestly. We couldn't hold him and we have stopped tailing him. Our only chance is that he will do it again and that's where you come in. If you are willing, and think you can handle it, of course, you shall be his next victim."

"How nice," said Sonja Hansson and reached for a cigarette from her purse.

"You are rather like Roseanna and we want you to act as a decoy. It would be like this: he works as an office manager for a moving company on Småland Street. You go there and say that you want to have something moved, flirt with him and see that he gets your address and telephone number. You must get him interested in you. Then, we have to wait and hope."

"You say that you've already examined him? Won't he be on his guard?"

"We have leaked some information that ought to have quieted him."

"Am I also supposed to vamp him? How the devil will that be? And if I succeed?"

"You don't need to be afraid. We will always be in the vicinity. But you have to learn everything about the case first. Read all the material we have. You must be Roseanna McGraw. Be like her, I mean."

"Of course I acted in school plays but mostly as angels or mushrooms."

"Well, then. You'll manage."

Martin Beck sat quietly for a few seconds. Then he said:

"This is our only chance. He only needs an impulse and we must provide it for him."

"Okay, I'll try. I hope I can handle it. It isn't going to be easy."

"You'd better start going through everything, reports, films, the examination reports, letters, photographs. After that we can talk about it again."

"Now?"

"Yes, today. Commissioner Hammar will arrange for you to be relieved of your other work until this is settled. And one more thing. We have to go to your apartment and see what it looks like. We have to arrange for duplicate keys as well. We'll get to the rest later."

Ten minutes later he left her in the room next to Kollberg's and Melander's office. She sat with her elbows on the table reading the first report.

Ahlberg arrived that afternoon. He had hardly sat down when Kollberg stormed in and thumped him on the back so hard that he almost fell out of the visitor's chair.

"Gunnar's going home tomorrow," said Martin Beck. "He ought to get a look at Bengtsson before he goes."

"It had better be a pretty careful look," said Kollberg. "But then we had better get going immediately. Every person in town plus half the population in general is running around buying Christmas presents."

Ahlberg snapped his fingers and struck his forehead with the palm of his hand.

"Christmas presents. I had completely forgotten."

"Me too," said Martin Beck. "That is to say I think of it from time to time but that's all that ever gets done about it."

The traffic was terrible. Two minutes before five they dropped Ahlberg at Norrmalms Square and watched him disappear into the crowds.

Kollberg and Martin Beck sat in the car and waited. After twenty-five minutes Ahlberg returned and climbed into the back seat. He said:

"It sure is the guy on the film. He took the number 56 bus."

"To St. Erik's Square. Then he'll buy milk, bread and butter and go home. Eat, look at the boob tube, go to bed and fall asleep," said Kollberg. "Where shall I drop you?"

"Here. Now we have our big chance to go Christmas shopping," Martin Beck said.

One hour later in the toy department, Ahlberg said: "Kollberg was wrong. The other half of the population is here too."

It took them nearly three hours to finish their shopping and another hour to get to Martin Beck's home.

The next day Ahlberg saw the woman who was to be their

decoy for the first time. She had still only managed to get through a small part of the case material.

That evening Ahlberg went home to Motala for Christmas. They had agreed to start the plan working right after the new year.

27

It was a gray Christmas. The man called Folke Bengtsson spent it quietly at his mother's house in Södertälje. Martin Beck thought unendingly about him, even during the Christmas service in church and in a bath of perspiration under his Santa Claus mask. Kollberg ate too much and had to spend three days in the hospital.

Ahlberg called the day after Christmas and was not sober.

The newspapers contained several differing and unengaging articles which pointed to the fact that the Canal Murder was almost cleared up and that the Swedish police no longer had any reason to bother with the case.

There was the traditional new year's murder in Gothenburg which was solved within twenty-four hours. Kafka sent a tremendously large repulsive postcard, which was lilac colored and portrayed a deer against a sunset.

January 7 arrived and looked like January 7. The streets were full of gray, frozen people without money. The sales had begun but even so, the stores were nearly empty. In addition, the weather was hazy and freezing cold.

January 7 was D-Day.

In the morning Hammar inspected the troops. Then he said:

"How long are we going to carry on with this experiment?"

"Until it succeeds," said Ahlberg.

"So *you* say."

Hammar thought about all the situations which might possibly arise. Martin Beck and Kollberg would be needed for other tasks. Melander and Stenström should, at least part of the time, be working on other cases. Soon, the Third District would begin to complain because the borrowed girl never came back.

"Good luck, children," he said.

A little later, only Sonja Hansson was there. She had a cold and sat in the visitor's chair and sniffled. Martin Beck looked at her. She was dressed in boots, a gray dress and long black tights.

"Do you plan to look like that?" he said sourly.

"No, I'll go home and change first. But I want to point out one thing. On July 3 last year, it was summertime and now it's winter. It might look a bit odd if I ran into a moving company office just now in sunglasses and a thin dress and asked if they could move a bureau for me."

"Do the best you can. The important thing is that you understand the main point."

He sat quietly for a while.

"If, indeed, *I* have understood it," he said.

The woman looked thoughtfully at him.

"I think I understand," she said, finally. "I have read every word that has been written about her, over and over again. I've seen the film at least twenty times. I have chosen clothing that would seem to fit and I have practiced in front of the mirror for hours. But I'm not starting off with much. My personality and hers are completely different. Her habits were different too. I haven't lived as she did and I'm not going to either. But I'll do the best I can."

"That's fine," said Martin Beck.

She seemed unapproachable and it wasn't easy to get through to her. The only thing he knew about her private life was that she had a daughter who was five years old and lived in the country with her grandparents. It seemed that she had never been married. But in spite of the fact that he didn't know her very well, he thought a great deal of her. She was shrewd, and down to earth, and dedicated to her job. That was a lot to say about someone.

It was four o'clock in the afternoon before he heard from her again.

"I've just been there. I went directly home afterwards."

"Well, he isn't going to come and break down the door right away. How did it go?"

"I think it went well. As well as one could wish. The bureau will be delivered tomorrow."

"What did he think of you?"

"I don't know. I got a feeling that he lit up a little bit. It's hard to say when I don't really know how he acts."

"Was it difficult?"

"To be honest, it wasn't very hard. I thought he seemed rather nice. He's attractive, too, in some way. Are you sure that he's the right guy? That's not to say that I have had a great deal of experience with murderers, but I find it difficult to think of him as the man who murdered Roseanna McGraw."

"Yes, I'm sure. What did he say? Did he get your telephone number?"

"Yes, he wrote the address and telephone number down on a loose sheet of paper. And I told him that I have a house phone but that I don't answer it if I am not expecting someone so that it's best to telephone ahead. In general, he didn't say very much."

"Were you alone in the room with him?"

"Yes. There was a fat, old lady on the other side of the glass partition but she couldn't hear us. She was talking on the telephone and I couldn't hear her."

"Did you get a chance to talk with him about anything other than the bureau?"

"Yes, I said that the weather was miserable and he said, it certainly was. Then I said that I was glad that Christmas was over and then he said that he was too. I added that when one was alone as I was, Christmas could be sad."

"What did he say then?"

"That he, too, was alone and thought that it was rather dismal at Christmas, even though he usually spent it with his mother."

"That sounds fine," said Martin Beck. "Did you talk about anything else?"

"No, I don't think so."

It was silent on the other end of the telephone for a while. Then she added: "Yes, I asked him to write down the address and telephone number of the company for me so that I wouldn't have to look it up in the telephone book. He gave me a printed business card."

"And then you left?"

"Yes, I couldn't stand around and chatter any longer but I

took my time leaving. I had opened my coat and so forth. To show my tight sweater. Yes, by the way, I said that if they didn't get there with the bureau during the day, it didn't make any difference to me since I was almost always home at night waiting for someone to call. But he thought that the bureau would get there during the morning."

"That's fine. Listen, we thought we'd have a rehearsal this evening. We are going to be at the Klara Police Station. Stenström will play Bengtsson and telephone you. You answer, call me at Klara, and we'll come to your house and wait for Stenström. Do you follow me?"

"Yes, I understand. I'll telephone you as soon as Stenström has called. About what time?"

"I'm not going to tell you. You won't know what time Bengtsson will call."

"No, you are right. And, Martin."

"Yes."

"He was actually charming in some way. Not at all unpleasant or snappy. Although it's certain that Roseanna McGraw must have thought so too."

The day room in the Fourth District Station House at Regering Street was neat and proper although it offered very few possibilities for entertainment.

It was a quarter past eight and Martin Beck had read the evening paper twice, just about everything except the sport pages and the classified advertisements. For the past two hours Ahlberg and Kollberg had been playing chess, which obviously took away any desire they might have had to talk. Stenström was sleeping in a chair near the door with his mouth open. He could be excused because he had been working on another case the night before. Anyway, he was there to play the villain and didn't need to be on the alert.

At twenty minutes past eight Martin Beck went over to Stenström and poked him.

"Let's start now."

Stenström got up, went over to the telephone, and dialed a number.

"Hi," he said. "Can I come over? Yes? Fine."

Then he went back to his chair and fell asleep.

Martin Beck looked at the clock. Fifty seconds later the telephone rang. It was tied into a direct line and reserved for their use. No one else could use it.

"This is Beck."

"It's Sonja, hi. He just called. He's coming in a half an hour."

"I got it."

He put down the phone.

"Now let's get started, boys."

"You can just as well give up," said Ahlberg across the chess board.

"Okay," said Kollberg. "One to nothing, in your favor."

Stenström opened one eye.

"Which way shall I come from?"

"Any way you want to."

They went down to the car which was parked in the police station's driveway. It was Kollberg's own car and he drove. When he swung out onto Regering Street he said: "Can I be the one to stand in the closet?"

"Oh, no. That's Ahlberg's job."

"Why?"

"Because he's the only one who can go into the house without the risk of being recognized."

Sonja Hansson lived on Runeberg Street, three flights up in the house on the corner facing Eriksberg Square.

Kollberg parked between the Little Theater and Tegner Street. They separated. Martin Beck crossed the street, went into the shrubbery and hid himself in the shadow of Karl Staaff's statue. From there he had a fine view of her house and also of Eriksberg Square as well as of the most important parts of the surrounding streets. He saw Kollberg walk casually down the south side of Runeberg Street with exquisite nonchalance. Ahlberg determinedly held his course toward the front door, opened it, and went in, as if he were a tenant on his way home. Forty-five seconds from now Ahlberg would be in the apartment and Kollberg in his place in the arch under Eriksberg Street. Martin Beck pushed his stop watch and looked at the time. It had been exactly five minutes and ten seconds since he had hung up the telephone after his conversation with Sonja Hansson.

It was raw and he turned up his coat collar and mumbled threateningly at a drunk who tried to bum a cigarette from him.

Stenström had really done his best.

He arrived twelve minutes early and from a completely un-expected direction. He sneaked around the corner from the

Eriksberg Park stairs and walked with a group of moviegoers. Martin Beck didn't see him until he slunk into the house.

Kollberg had also functioned satisfactorily because he and Martin Beck met in front of the door.

They went in together, unlocked the inner glass doors, and neither of them said anything.

Kollberg took the stairs. He was supposed to stand a half a flight below the apartment and not advance before he received the signal. Martin Beck tried to get the elevator down by pressing the button but it didn't come. He ran up the stairs and passed the surprised Kollberg on the second floor. The elevator was up on the third floor. Stenström had put it out of commission by not closing the inside door. Thus he had succeeded in ruining that part of the plan which had Martin Beck taking the elevator to the floor above the apartment and arriving at it from above.

It was still quiet in the apartment but Stenström must have depended upon speed, because after only thirty seconds they heard a muffled shriek and some noise. Martin Beck had his key ready and ten seconds later he was in Sonja Hansson's bedroom.

The girl sat on the bed. Stenström stood in the middle of the floor and yawned while Ahlberg held his right arm loosely against his back.

Martin Beck whistled and Kollberg thundered into the apartment like an express train. In his haste he knocked over the table in the hall. He hadn't had any doors to open.

Martin Beck rubbed his nose and looked at the girl.

"Good," he said.

She had chosen the realistic style he had hoped for. She was barefoot and bare-legged and had on a thin, short-sleeved cotton robe which stopped just above her knees. He was sure that she didn't have anything on underneath.

"I'll put something else on and make some coffee," she said.

They went into the other room. She came in almost immediately, dressed in sandals, jeans and a brown sweater. Ten minutes later the coffee was ready.

"My door key sticks," said Ahlberg. "I have to wiggle it like the devil."

"That doesn't matter so much," said Martin Beck. "You won't ever be in as much of a hurry as we are."

"I heard you on the stairs," said Stenström. "Just as she opened the door."

"Rubber soles," said Kollberg.

"Open it faster," said Martin Beck.

"The key hole in the closet is great," said Ahlberg. "I saw you almost the entire time."

"Take the key out next time," said Stenström. "I really wanted to lock you in."

The telephone rang. They all stiffened.

The girl picked up the receiver.

"Yes, hello . . . hi . . . no, not tonight . . . well, I'm going to be busy for a while . . . have I met a man? . . . yes, you could say that."

She hung up and met their glances.

"That was nothing," she said.

28

Sonja Hansson stood in the bathroom rinsing out her washing. When she turned off the water she heard the telephone ringing in the living room. She ran in and picked up the receiver without even taking time to dry her hands.

It was Bengtsson.

"Your bureau is on the way," he said. "The truck ought to be there in about fifteen minutes."

"Thanks. It was very nice of you to call. Otherwise, I wouldn't open the door, as I told you. I didn't think you would get it here so early. Shall I come down to your office and pay the bill or . . ."

"You can pay the driver. He has the invoice with him."

"Fine. I'll do that, Mr. . . . ?"

"The name's Bengtsson. I hope you'll be satisfied with our service. The truck will be there in fifteen minutes, as I said."

"Thank you. Goodbye."

When he hung up she dialed Martin Beck's number.

"The bureau will be here in fifteen minutes. He just telephoned. I almost missed the call. It was just luck that I heard the phone. I didn't think of it before, but when the water's running in the bathtub I can't hear the phone."

"You had better not bathe for a while," Martin Beck replied. "Seriously, though, you have to be near the telephone all the time. You can't go up to the attic or down to the laundry or anything like that."

"No. I know. Shall I go down to his office as soon as the bureau has come?"

"Yes, I think so. Then call me."

Martin Beck sat in the same room with Ahlberg. As he hung up the phone, Ahlberg looked at him questioningly.

"She's going there in about a half an hour," Martin Beck told him.

"We'll just have to wait then. She's a great gal. I like her."

When they had waited for over two hours Ahlberg said: "Surely nothing could have happened to her now . . ."

"Keep calm," Martin Beck answered. "She'll call."

She called after they had waited another half hour.

"Have you been waiting long?"

Martin Beck grimaced:

"What happened?" he said, and cleared his throat.

"I'll start at the beginning. Two drivers came with the bureau twenty minutes after I talked with you. I hardly glanced at it and told the men where it should go. After they left I noticed it was the wrong bureau and I went down to the office to complain."

"You were there quite a long time."

"Yes. He had a customer when I arrived. I waited outside the counter and he looked at me several times. It seemed as if he was trying to hurry the customer. He was very distressed about the bureau and I said that the mistake was mine, not the firm's. We almost got into an argument about whose fault it was. Then he went to find out if someone could bring the right bureau this evening."

"Yes?"

"But he couldn't arrange it. He promised to see that it would be delivered tomorrow morning, though. He said that he would have liked to bring it himself, and I said that was too much to ask although it certainly would have been pleasant."

"Okay. Did you leave then?"

"No. Of course I stayed on."

"Was he hard to talk to?"

"Not particularly. He seemed a little shy."

"What did you talk about?"

"Oh, about how terrible the traffic is and how much better Stockholm was before. And then I said that it was no city to be alone in, and he agreed, although he said he rather liked to be alone."

"Did he seem pleased to talk to you?"

"I think so. But I couldn't hang around forever. He

mentioned that he liked to go to the movies but other than that he didn't go out very much. Then, there wasn't much more to say. So I left. He walked out to the door with me and was very polite. What do we do now?"

"Nothing. Wait."

Two days later Sonja Hansson went back to the moving company again.

"I wanted to thank you for your help and tell you that I received the bureau. I'm sorry to have caused so much trouble."

"It was no trouble at all," Folke Bengtsson said. "Welcome back. What can I do for you?"

A man walked into the room and interrupted. He was clearly the head of the firm.

When she left the office she knew Bengtsson was looking at her over the counter and before she reached the outer door, she turned and met his glance.

A week went by before the experiment was repeated. Once again the pretext was a transportation problem. She hadn't been in her apartment on Runeberg Street very long and she was still in the process of gathering some furniture from the attics of various relatives.

After still another five days she stood in his office again. It was just before five o'clock and because she was passing by, she thought she'd drop in.

Sonja Hansson sounded annoyed when she telephoned in.

"He still isn't reacting?" Martin Beck asked.

"Only moderately. You know, I don't believe it's him."

"Why not?"

"He seems so shy. And rather disinterested. I've pressed hard these last few times, practically given him an open invitation. Seven out of ten men would have been sitting outside my door howling like wolves by now. I guess I just don't have any sex appeal. What should I do?"

"Keep on."

"You ought to get someone else."

"Keep on."

Continue. But how long? Hammar's look became more questioning each day that passed. And each time Martin Beck looked in the mirror the face that he met was more and more haggard.

The electric clock on the wall at the Klara Police Station

ticked away another three uneventful nights. Three weeks had passed since the dress rehearsal. The plan was well conceived but it didn't seem as if they would ever have the chance to put it into effect. Absolutely nothing had happened. The man called Folke Bengtsson lived a quiet, routine life. He drank his buttermilk, went to work, and slept nine hours each night. But they were almost losing contact with their normal environments and the outer world. The hounds chased themselves to death without the fox even noticing it, Martin Beck thought.

He stared angrily at the black telephone which hadn't rung for three weeks. The girl in the apartment on Runeberg Street knew that she should only use it for one specific situation. They called her twice each evening to check. Once at six o'clock and again at midnight. That was the only thing that happened.

The atmosphere in Martin Beck's home was strained. His wife didn't say anything but the doubting look in her eyes was more and more unmistakable each time he looked at her. She had given up faith in this project a long time ago. It had not produced results and kept him away from home night after night. And he neither could nor would explain.

It was somewhat better for Kollberg. At least Melander and Stenström relieved him every third night. Ahlberg kept occupied by playing chess by himself. That was called solving problems! All topics of conversation had long since been pre-empted.

Martin Beck had lost the train of thought in the newspaper article he was pretending to read. He yawned and looked at his exemplary colleagues who, eternally silent, sat directly opposite each other, their heads heavy with profound thoughts.

He looked at the clock. Five to ten. Yawning again, he got up stiffly and went out to the toilet. He washed his hands, rinsed his face with cold water, and went back.

Three steps from the door he heard the telephone ring.

Kollberg had already finished the conversation and hung up.

"Has he . . . ?"

"No," said Kollberg. "But he's standing outside on the street."

This was unexpected, but actually, it changed nothing. During the next three minutes Martin Beck analyzed the plan in detail. Bengtsson couldn't force the downstairs door and even if he managed to, he would hardly have time to get upstairs before they got there.

"We had better be careful."

"Yes," said Kollberg.

They drove to a fast stop in front of the Little Theater. They separated.

Martin Beck stood, watched Ahlberg go through the door, and looked at his watch. It was exactly four minutes since she had called. He thought about the woman alone in the apartment two flights above. Folke Bengtsson was not in sight.

Thirty seconds later a light was turned on in a window on the third floor. Someone came to the window and seemed to look out, but disappeared almost immediately. The light went off. Ahlberg was in his place. They waited in silence by the bedroom window. The room was dark but a narrow stream of light came through the door. The lamp in the living room was lit to show that she was home. The living room window looked out on the street and from the bedroom they could see several of the cross streets leading to the intersection.

Bengtsson stood by the bus stop directly across the street. He looked up at her window. He was the only person there and after he had stood for a while he looked up and down the block. Then he walked slowly to the island that separated the street's traffic. He disappeared in back of a telephone booth.

"Here it comes," said Ahlberg and motioned in the dark.

But the telephone didn't ring and after several minutes Bengtsson could be seen walking up the street.

Along the sidewalk there was a low, stone wall which ran all the way to the building below her window. In back of it was an area planted with grass and low shrubbery which led to the house.

Once again, the man stopped on the sidewalk and looked up toward her house. Then he began to walk toward her door slowly.

He disappeared out of sight and Ahlberg stared out over the square until he caught sight of Martin Beck who stood completely still by a tree in the planted area. A trolley on Birger Jarls Street hid him for several seconds and after it had passed, he was gone.

Five minutes later they saw Bengtsson again.

He had been walking so close to the wall that they hadn't

seen him until he stepped out into the street and began to walk toward the trolley stop. At a kiosk, he stopped and bought a frankfurter. While he ate it, he leaned against the kiosk and stared up at her window constantly. Then he began to pace back and forth with his hands in his pockets. Now and then he looked up at her window.

Fifteen minutes later Martin Beck was behind the same tree again.

The traffic was heavier now and a stream of people crowded the streets. The movie had ended.

They lost sight of Bengtsson for a few minutes but then saw him in the midst of a group of moviegoers on the way home. He walked toward the telephone booth but stopped again a few feet from it. Then suddenly, he walked briskly toward the planted area. Martin Beck turned his back and slowly moved away.

Bengtsson passed the little park, crossed the street toward the restaurant and disappeared down Tegner Street. After a few minutes he appeared again on the opposite sidewalk and began to walk around Eriksberg Square.

"Do you think that he's been here before?" asked the woman in the cotton dressing gown. "I mean, it's only pure chance that I saw him tonight."

Ahlberg stood with his back against the wall near the window and smoked a cigarette. He looked at the girl beside him who was turned toward the window. She stood with her feet apart and had her hands in her pockets. In the weak light reflected from the street, her eyes looked like dark holes in her pale face.

"Maybe he's been here every night," she said.

When the man below had completed his fourth swing around the square, she said: "If he's going to tramp around like this the whole night I'll go crazy and Lennart and Martin will freeze to death."

At 12:25 he had gone around the square eight times, each time moving faster. He stopped below the steps leading to the park, looked up at the house, and half-ran across the street to the trolley stop.

A bus drove in to the bus stop, and when it moved on, Bengtsson was no longer there.

"Look. There's Martin," Sonja Hansson said.

Ahlberg jumped at the sound of her voice. They had been

whispering to one another all along and now she spoke in her normal voice for the first time in two hours.

He saw Martin Beck hurry across the street and jump into a car which had been waiting in front of the theater. The car started even before he managed to close the door and drove off in the same direction as the bus.

"Well, thanks for your company tonight," Sonja Hansson said. "I think I'll go to sleep now."

"Do that," said Ahlberg.

He would have liked some sleep too. But ten minutes later he walked through the door at the Klara Police Station. Kollberg arrived shortly after.

They had made five moves in their chess game when Martin Beck came in.

"He took the bus to St. Erik's Square and went home. He put out the light almost immediately. He's probably asleep by now."

"It was mere chance that she caught sight of him," said Ahlberg. "He could have been there several times before."

Kollberg studied the chess board.

"And if he was? That wouldn't prove anything."

"What do you mean?"

"Kollberg's right," Martin Beck answered.

"Sure," said Kollberg. "What would it prove? Even I have roamed around like an alley cat outside of the houses of willing girls."

Ahlberg shrugged his shoulders.

"Although I was younger, a lot younger."

Martin Beck said nothing. The others made a half-hearted attempt to concentrate on their game. After a while, Kollberg repeated a move which caused a draw, in spite of the fact that he had been winning.

"Damn," he said. "That chatter makes me lose my train of thought. How much are you leading by?"

"Four points," said Ahlberg. "Twelve and a half to eight and a half."

Kollberg got up and paced around the room.

"We'll bring him in again, make a thorough search of his house, and rough him up as much as we can," he said.

No one answered.

"We ought to tail him again, with new guys."

"No," said Ahlberg.

Martin Beck continued biting on his index finger knuckle. After a while he said: "Is she getting frightened?"

"It doesn't seem so," Ahlberg answered. "That girl doesn't get nervous easily."

"Neither did Roseanna McGraw," Martin Beck thought.

They didn't say much more to one another but were still wide awake when the noise of the morning traffic on Regering Street indicated that although their work day had ended, it was just beginning for others.

Something had happened, but Martin Beck didn't know exactly what.

Another twenty-four hours passed. Ahlberg increased his lead by another point. That was all.

The following day was a Friday. Three days were left before the end of the month and the weather was still mild. It had been rainy and misty most of the time and at twilight the fog had rolled in.

At ten minutes after nine the sound of the telephone broke the silence. Martin Beck picked up the receiver.

"He's here again. He's standing by the bus stop."

They got there fifteen seconds faster than the last time in spite of the fact that Kollberg had parked on the street. After another thirty seconds they saw the signal indicating that Ahlberg was in his place.

The repetition was almost frightening. The man named Folke Bengtsson wandered around Eriksberg Square for four hours. Four or five times, he hesitated outside of the telephone booth. Once he stopped and ate a frankfurter. Then he rode home. Kollberg followed him.

Martin Beck had been very cold. He walked quickly back to the police station with his hands in his pockets and his eyes on the ground.

Kollberg arrived a half hour later.

"Everything's quiet."

"Did he see you?"

"He was like a sleepwalker. I don't think he would have seen a hippopotamus three feet in front of him."

Martin Beck dialed Policewoman Sonja Hansson's number. He felt that he must think about her in terms of her job and her rank. Otherwise, he couldn't stand it.

"Hello. It's Saturday tomorrow, or more correctly, today. He works until noon. Be there when he finishes work. Rush past him as if you were on your way somewhere. Take hold of his arm and say: 'Hi, I've been waiting for you. Why haven't I heard from you?' or something like that. Don't say any more. Then take off. Leave your coat open too."

He paused briefly.

"You have to do your very best this time."

He hung up. The others stared at him.

"Which one of you is the best tail?" he said absently.

"Stenström."

"Okay. From the minute he leaves his house early tomorrow morning I want him followed. Stenström can do it. Report all his movements. Here. On the other telephone. Two of us must be here all the time."

Ahlberg and Kollberg were still staring at him but he didn't notice.

At twenty-two minutes to eight Bengtsson walked out of his front door and Stenström's assignment had begun.

He stayed near the moving company's office on Småland Street until a quarter after eleven when he went into a cafe and sat down by the window waiting.

At five minutes of twelve he saw Sonja Hansson on the corner.

She was dressed in a thin, blue tweed coat which was open. He could see that her belt was drawn tightly around her waist. Under the coat she had on a black turtleneck sweater. She was bare-headed and carried gloves but no pocketbook. Her stockings and black pumps seemed much too thin for the weather.

She continued across the street and disappeared out of his sight.

The moving company's employees began to leave the office and finally the man named Bengtsson came out and locked the door. He ambled along the sidewalk and when he had moved a few feet, Sonja Hansson came running toward him. She greeted him, took hold of his arm, and said something to him as she looked in his eyes. She let go of his arm almost immediately and continued talking while she took a few steps away from him. Then she turned on her heels and ran on.

Stenström had seen her face. It had expressed eagerness, pleasure and appeal. Silently he applauded her performance.

The man remained where he was and watched her run down the street. He moved slightly, as if to follow her, but changed his mind, put his hands in his pockets and walked off slowly with his head lowered.

Stenström got his hat, paid the cashier, and looked out the door carefully. When Bengtsson had turned the corner, Stenström left and followed him.

At the Klara Police Station Martin Beck stared dismally at the telephone. Ahlberg and Kollberg had temporarily given up their chess game and sat silently behind their newspapers. Kollberg was working on a crossword puzzle and chewing frantically on a pencil.

When the telephone finally rang, he bit so hard on the pencil that it broke in two.

Martin Beck had the receiver at his ear before the first ring ended.

"Hi. It's Sonja. I think it went well. I did exactly as you said."

"Good. Did you see Stenström?"

"No, but I guess he was there someplace. I didn't dare turn around so I just kept on going for several blocks."

"Are you nervous?"

"No. Not at all."

It was a quarter after one before the telephone rang again.

"I'm in a tobacco shop on Järn Square," said Stenström. "Sonja was great. She must have put a few bees in his bonnet. We've walked through the center of town, over the main bridge and now he's wandering around in the Old City."

"Be careful."

"No problem. He's walking like a zombie. He doesn't see or hear anything around him. I've got to take off now so that I don't lose him."

Ahlberg got up and walked back and forth on the floor.

"It's not exactly a pleasant job we've given her," he said.

"She'll do fine," said Kollberg. "She'll take care of the rest of it well too. I hope Stenström doesn't scare him off though."

"Stenström's okay," he said, after a while.

Martin Beck said nothing.

It was a few minutes after three when they heard from Stenström again.

"Now we're on Folkung Street. He just keeps going up and down the streets. He never stops and never looks around. He seems apathetic in some way."

"Just keep on," Martin Beck replied.

Normally, it would take a lot to break down Martin Beck's

calm exterior. But after he had looked from the clock to the telephone for forty-five minutes and no one in the room had uttered a word, he suddenly got up and went out.

Ahlberg and Kollberg looked at one another. Kollberg shrugged his shoulders and began to set up the chess board.

Out in the washroom Martin Beck rinsed his hands and face with cold water and dried himself carefully. When he walked out into the corridor, a policeman in shirtsleeves told him that he had a telephone call.

It was his wife.

"I haven't seen hide nor hair of you for an eternity and now I'm not even supposed to call you. What are you doing? When are you coming home?"

"I don't know," he said tiredly.

She continued to talk and her voice became harsh and shrill. He broke in and interrupted her in the middle of a sentence.

"I don't have time now," he said irritably. "Goodbye. Don't call any more."

He regretted his tone even before he put down the receiver but shrugged his shoulders and went back to his chess-playing colleagues.

Stenström's third call came from Skepps Bridge. By then it was twenty minutes to five.

"He went into a restaurant for a while. He's sitting alone in a corner drinking a beer. We've walked around the entire southern part of the city. He still seems strange."

Martin Beck realized that he hadn't eaten anything all day. He sent out for some food from the cafeteria across the street. After they had eaten, Kollberg fell asleep in his chair and began to snore.

When the telephone rang he woke up with a start. It was seven o'clock.

"He's been sitting here until now and he's had four beers. He's just left and is on his way toward the center of the city again. He's walking faster now. I'll call in as soon as I can. So long."

Stenström sounded out of breath as if he had been running and he hung up the phone before Martin Beck had a chance to say anything.

"He's on his way there," said Kollberg.

The next call came at half past seven and was even shorter and just as one-sided.

"I'm at Englebrekts Square. He's walking on Birger Jarls Street at a pretty fast pace."

They waited. They watched the clock and the telephone in turn.

Five after eight. Martin Beck picked up the receiver in the middle of the ring. Stenström sounded disappointed.

"He's swung onto Eriksberg Street and crossed the viaduct. We're on Oden Street now. I guess he's going home. He's walking slowly again."

"Damn it! Call me when he's home."

A half hour went by before Stenström called again.

"He didn't go home. He turned onto Uppland Street. He doesn't seem to realize that he has feet. He just walks and walks. Mine won't hold up much longer."

"Where are you now?"

"North Ban Square. He's passing the City Theater now."

Martin Beck thought about the man who had just passed the City Theater. What was he thinking about? Was he really thinking at all; or was he just walking around unconscious of his surroundings, withdrawn and with one thought or possibly one decision ripening within him?

During the next three hours Stenström telephoned four times from different places. The man stayed on the streets near Eriksberg Square but never went really close to her house.

At 2:30 a.m. Stenström reported that Bengtsson had finally gone home and that the light in his room had just gone out.

Martin Beck sent Kollberg as a replacement.

At eight o'clock on Sunday morning Kollberg came back, awakened Ahlberg who was sleeping on a sofa, threw himself down on it and slept.

Ahlberg went over to Martin Beck who sat brooding by the telephone.

"Has Kollberg arrived?" he asked and looked up with bloodshot eyes.

"He's sleeping. Out like a light. Stenström's on watch."

They only had to wait two hours for the first telephone call of the day.

"He's gone out again," Stenström reported. "He's walking toward the bridge to Kungsholm."

"How does he look?"

"Just the same. Even the same clothes. God knows if he even took them off."

"Is he walking fast?"

"No, rather slowly."

"Have you slept?"

"Yes, a little. But I don't exactly feel like a man of steel."

Between ten in the morning and four in the afternoon Stenström called in approximately every hour. Except for two short breaks in a coffee shop, Folke Bengtsson had been walking for six hours. He had wandered around Kungsholm, the old part of the city, and southern Stockholm. He hadn't gone anywhere near Sonja Hansson's apartment.

At five-thirty Martin Beck fell asleep in his chair by the telephone. Fifteen minutes later Stenström's call awakened him.

"I'm at Norrmalms Square. He's walking toward her part of the city. He seems different now."

"In what way?"

"It's as if he's come to life. He seems compelled in some way."

Eight-fifteen.

"I have to be more careful now. He's just swung onto Sveavägen still headed in her direction. He's looking at girls now."

Nine-thirty.

"Sture Street. He's going slowly toward Sture Square. He seems calmer and is still looking at the girls."

"Take it easy," Martin Beck said.

Suddenly he felt fresh and rested in spite of the fact that he hadn't really slept for forty-eight hours.

He stood and looked at the map on which Kollberg was trying to follow Bengtsson's wandering with a red pen. The phone rang again.

"That's the tenth time he's called today," said Kollberg.

Martin Beck picked up the receiver and looked at the clock. One minute to eleven.

It was Sonja Hansson. Her voice was hoarse and quivered a little.

"Martin! He's here again."

"We'll be right there," he said.

* * *

Sonja Hansson pushed the telephone away and looked at the clock. One minute after eleven. In four minutes Ahlberg would come through the door and relieve her of that helpless, creeping feeling of unpleasantness she had at the thought of being alone. She wiped her perspiring palms on her cotton dressing gown. The cloth clung to her hips with the dampness.

She walked softly into the dark bedroom and over to the window. The parquet floor felt cold and hard under her bare feet. She stood on her toes, supported herself with her right hand against the window frame, and peeked carefully through the thin curtains. A number of people were on the street, several of them in front of the restaurant across the way but she didn't see Bengtsson for at least a minute and a half. He turned off of Runeberg Street and continued straight out onto Birger Jarls Street. Right in the middle of the trolley tracks he turned sharply to the right. After about half a minute, he disappeared from her sight. He had moved very fast, with long, gliding steps. He looked directly in front of him as if he didn't see anything around him or was concentrating on something in particular.

She went back into the living room which seemed welcoming with its light and warmth and the familiar accessories she liked. She lit a cigarette and inhaled deeply. In spite of the fact that she was fully conscious of what she had taken on, she was also a little relieved when he walked by and didn't stop at the telephone booth. She had already waited too long for that clanging telephone ring which would smash her peace of mind into splinters and bring an irrational and unpleasant element into her home. Now she hoped that it would never come, that everything was wrong, that she could go back to her regular work routine and never have to think about that man again.

She picked up the sweater she had been knitting for the last three weeks, walked over to the mirror and held it to her shoulders. It would soon be finished. She looked at the clock again. Ahlberg was now about ten seconds late. He wouldn't break any records today. She smiled because she knew that would irritate him. She met her own calm smile in the mirror and saw the small beads of perspiration that glittered along her hairline.

Sonja Hansson walked through the hall and into the bathroom. She stood with her feet spread apart on the cool tile floor, bent forward and washed her face and hands with cold water.

When she turned off the tap she heard Ahlberg clattering with his key in the front door. He was already more than a minute late.

With the towel still in her hand she stepped out into the hall, stretched out her other hand, unlocked the safety latch, and threw open the door.

"Thank God. I'm so glad that you're here," she said.

It wasn't Ahlberg.

With a smile still on her lips she backed slowly into the apartment. The man called Folke Bengtsson didn't let go of her with his eyes as he locked the door behind him and put on the safety chain.

29

Martin Beck was the last man out and already through the door when the telephone rang again. He ran back and grabbed the receiver.

"I'm in the lobby of the Ambassador Hotel," said Stenström. "I've lost him. Somewhere outside here in the crowd. It can't have been more than four or five minutes ago."

"He's already on Runeberg Street. Get there as fast as you can."

Martin Beck threw the phone down and rushed out to the stairs after the others. He climbed in the car past the back of Ahlberg's front seat. They always sat in the same places. It was important that Ahlberg got out first.

Kollberg put the car in gear but had to release the clutch immediately and swerve to avoid a gray police truck which was coming in. Then he got underway and turned up Regering Street between a green Volvo and a beige Volkswagen. Martin Beck supported his arms on his knees and stared out at the cold gray drizzle. He was excited and alert both mentally and physically but felt collected and well prepared like a well trained athlete before a try for a new record.

Two seconds later the green Volvo ahead of them collided with a small delivery truck which came out of a one-way street, the wrong way. The Volvo swung sharply to the left one second before the collision and Kollberg, who had already started to pass, was also forced to turn to the left. He reacted quickly and didn't even touch the car in front of him but the other cars came to a stop right across the intersection and very close to each other. Kollberg had already put his car in reverse when the beige Volkswagen smashed into their left front door. The driver had stopped suddenly, which was a grave error in terms of the congestion at the intersection.

It was not a serious accident. In ten minutes several traffic policemen would be there with their tape measures. They would write down the names and the license numbers, ask to see drivers' licenses, identity cards and radio licenses. Then they would write "body damage" in their official books, shrug their shoulders and go away. If none of the drivers who were now yelling and shaking their fists at one another smelled of whisky, they would then get back into their cars and drive off in their own directions.

Ahlberg swore. It took ten seconds for Martin Beck to understand why. They couldn't get out. Both doors were blocked as effectively as if they had been soldered together.

In the same second that Kollberg took the desperate decision to back out of the confusion, a number 55 bus stopped in back of them. With that, the only way of retreat was cut off. The man in the beige Volkswagen had come out into the rain, clearly furious and loaded with arguments. He was out of sight and was probably somewhere behind the other two cars.

Ahlberg pressed both of his feet against the door and pushed until he groaned, but the beige colored car was still in gear and couldn't be budged.

Three or four nightmare-like minutes followed. Ahlberg yelled and waved his arms. The rain lay like a frozen gray membrane over the back window. Outside a shadowy policeman could be seen in a shining dark raincoat.

Finally several observers seemed to understand the situation and began to push the beige Volkswagen away. Their movements were fumbling and slow. A policeman tried to stop them. Then, after a minute he tried to help them. Now there was a distance of three feet between the cars but the hinge had stuck and the door wouldn't move. Ahlberg swore and pushed. Martin Beck felt the perspiration run from his neck, down under his collar, and collect in a cold runnel between his shoulder blades.

The door opened, slowly and creakingly.

Ahlberg tumbled out. Martin Beck and Kollberg tried to get out of the door at the same time and somehow managed to do so.

The policeman stood ready with his pad in his out-stretched hand.

"What happened here?"

"Shut up," Kollberg screamed.

Fortunately he was recognized.

"Run," yelled Ahlberg, who was already fifteen feet ahead of them.

Groping hands tried to stop them. Kollberg ran into an old man selling frankfurters from a box resting on his stomach.

Four hundred and fifty yards, Martin Beck thought. That would take a trained sportsman only a minute. But they weren't trained sportsmen. And they weren't running on a cinder track, but on an asphalt street in below freezing rain. Ahlberg was still fifteen feet ahead of them at the next corner when he tripped and nearly fell. That cost him his lead and they continued, side by side down the slope. Martin Beck was beginning to see stars. He heard Kollberg's heavy panting right behind him.

They turned the corner, crashed through the low shrubbery, and saw it, all three of them at the same time. Two flights up in the apartment house on Runeberg Street the weak, light rectangle which showed that the lamp in the bedroom was on and the shades were drawn.

The red stars before his eyes had disappeared and the pain in his chest was gone. When Martin Beck crossed the street he knew that he was running faster than he had ever run in his life even though Ahlberg was nine feet ahead of him and Kollberg by his side. When he got to the house, Ahlberg already had the downstairs door open.

The elevator was not on the ground floor. They hadn't thought about using it anyway. On the first flight landing he noted two things: he no longer was getting air in his lungs and Kollberg was not at his side. The plan worked, the damned perfect plan, he thought as he climbed the last stairs with the key already in his hand.

The key turned once in the lock and he pushed against the door which opened a few inches. He saw the safety chain stretched across the crevice and from inside the apartment heard no human sound, only a continuous, peculiarly metallic telephone signal. Time had stopped. He saw the pattern on the rug in the hall, a towel and a shoe.

"Move away," said Ahlberg hoarsely but surprisingly calmly.

It sounded as if the whole world had cracked into pieces

when Ahlberg shot through the safety chain. He was still pushing against the door and fell, rather than rushed, through the hall and the living room.

The scene was as unreal and as static as a tableau in Madame Tussaud's Chamber of Horrors. It seemed as immutable as an overexposed photograph, drowned in flooding white light, and he took in every one of its morbid details.

The man still had his overcoat on. His brown hat lay on the floor, partly hidden by the torn, blue and white dressing gown.

This was the man who had killed Roseanna McGraw. He stood bent forward over the bed with his left foot on the floor and his right knee on the bed, pressed heavily against the woman's left thigh, just above her knee. His large, sunburned hand lay over her chin and mouth with two fingers pressed around her nose. That was his left hand. His right hand rested somewhat lower down. It sought her throat and had just found it.

The woman lay on her back. Her wide-open eyes could be seen through his outstretched fingers. A thin stream of blood ran along her cheek. She had brought up her right leg and was pressing against his chest with the sole of her foot. She was naked. Every muscle in her body was straining. The tendons in her body stood out as clearly as on an anatomical model.

A hundredth of a second, but long enough for each detail to become etched into his consciousness and remain there always. Then the man in the overcoat let go his grip, jumped to his feet, balanced himself and turned around, all in a single, lightning quick movement.

Martin Beck saw, for the first time, the person he had hunted for six months and nineteen days. A person called Folke Bengtsson who only slightly reminded him of the man he had examined in Kollberg's office one afternoon shortly before Christmas.

His face was stiff and naked; his pupils contracted; his eyes flew back and forth like those of a trapped animal. He stood leaning forward with his knees bent and his body swaying rhythmically.

But once again—only a tenth of a second—he cast himself forward with a choked, gurgling sob. At the same moment Martin Beck hit him on the collarbone with the back side of his right hand and Ahlberg threw himself over him from behind and tried to grab his arms.

Ahlberg was hindered by his own pistol and Martin Beck was caught unawares by the strength of the attack, partly because the only thing he could think about was the woman on the bed who didn't move and just lay there, stretched out and limp, with her mouth open and her eyes half-closed.

The man's head hit him in the diaphragm with an amazing force and he was thrown backwards against the wall at the same time as the madman broke out of Ahlberg's incomplete grip and rushed for the door, still crouching and with a speed in his long stride that was just as unbelievable as everything else in this absurd situation.

The entire time the unceasing telephone signal continued.

Martin Beck was never nearer to him than a half a flight of stairs and the distance kept increasing.

Martin Beck heard the fleeing man below him but didn't see him at all until he reached the ground floor. By that time the man had already gone through the glass door near the entry and was very close to the relative freedom of the street.

But Kollberg was there. He took two steps away from the wall and the man in the overcoat aimed a powerful blow at his face.

One second later Martin Beck knew that the end was finally here. He heard very clearly the short, wild scream of pain when Kollberg grabbed the man's arm and bent it all the way up to his shoulder with a fast, merciless twist. The man in the overcoat lay powerless on the marble floor.

Martin Beck stood leaning against the wall and listened to the police sirens which seemed to be coming from several directions at the same time. A picket had already been set up and out on the sidewalk several uniformed policemen were warding off the stubborn group of curious bystanders.

He looked at the man called Folke Bengtsson who was half lying where he had fallen with his face against the wall and the tears streaming down his cheeks.

"The ambulance is here," said Stenström.

Martin Beck took the elevator up. She sat in one of the easy chairs dressed in corduroy slacks and a woolen sweater. He looked at her unhappily.

"The ambulance is here. They'll be right up."

"I can walk myself," she said, tonelessly.

In the elevator she said, "Don't look so miserable. It wasn't your fault. And there's nothing seriously wrong with me."

He wasn't able to look her in the eye.

"Had he tried to rape me I might have been able to cope with him. But it wasn't a question of that. I had no chance, none at all."

She shook her head.

"Ten or fifteen seconds more and ... Or if he hadn't started to think about the downstairs telephone, that disturbed him. Broke the isolation in some way. Ugh! God, it's awful."

When they went out to the ambulance she said: "Poor man."

"Who?"

"Him."

Fifteen minutes later only Kollberg and Stenström were left outside the house on Runeberg Street.

"I came just in time to see how you fixed him. Stood on the other side of the street. Where did you learn to do that?"

"I was a parachute jumper. I don't use it very often."

"That's the best I've ever seen. You can take anyone with that."

> *"In August was the jackal born,*
> *The rains fell in September.*
> *'Now such a fearful flood as this,'*
> *Says he, 'I can't remember!'"*

"What is that?"

"A quote," said Kollberg. "Someone named Kipling."

30

Martin Beck looked at the man who sat slouched before him with one arm in a sling. He kept his head bowed and didn't look up.

This was the moment he had waited for for six and a half months. He leaned over and turned on the tape recorder.

"Your name is Folke Lennart Bengtsson, born in Gustaf Vasa's parish on the sixth of August, 1926, now living at Rörstand Street in Stockholm. Is that correct?"

The man nodded almost imperceptibly.

"You must answer out loud," Martin Beck said.

"Yes," said the man called Folke Bengtsson. "Yes that's correct."

"Do you admit that you are guilty of murder and sexual assault of the American citizen Roseanna McGraw on the night of July 4–5 last year?"

"I haven't murdered anyone," Folke Bengtsson said.

"Speak up."

"No, I didn't do it."

"Earlier you have admitted that you met Roseanna McGraw on July 4 last year on board the passenger ship *Diana*. Is that correct?"

"I don't know. I didn't know what her name was."

"We have evidence that you were with her on July 4. That night you killed her in her cabin and threw her body overboard."

"No, that's not true!"

"Killed her the same way you tried to kill the woman on Runeberg Street?"

"I didn't want to kill her."

"Who didn't you want to kill?"

"That girl. She came to me several times. She asked me to come to her apartment. She didn't mean it seriously. She only wanted to humiliate me."

"Did Roseanna McGraw also want to humiliate you? Was that why you killed her?"

"I don't know."

"Were you inside her cabin?"

"I don't remember. Maybe I was. I don't know."

Martin Beck sat quietly and studied the man. Finally he said: "Are you very tired?"

"Not really."

"Does your arm hurt?"

"Not any more. They gave me a shot at the hospital."

"When you saw that woman last night, didn't she remind you of the woman last summer, the woman on the boat?"

"They aren't women."

"What do you mean? Of course they're women."

"Yes but . . . like animals."

"I don't understand what you mean."

"They are like animals, completely given over to . . ."

"Given over to what? To you?"

"For God's sake don't mock me. They were given over to their lust. To their shamelessness."

Thirty seconds of silence.

"Do you really think so?"

"All true human beings must think so, except for the most decadent and depraved."

"Didn't you like those women? Roseanna McGraw and the girl on Runeberg Street, whatever her name was. . . ."

"Sonja Hansson."

He spat out the name.

"Yes, that's right. Didn't you like her?"

"I hate her. I hated the other one too. I don't remember very well. Don't you see how they act? Don't you understand what it means to be a man?"

He spoke quickly and eagerly.

"No. What do you mean?"

"Ugh! They're disgusting. They sparkle and exult with their decadence, and later they're insolent and offensive."

"Do you visit prostitutes?"

"They aren't as disgusting, not as shameless. And then they take money. At least there's a certain honor and honesty about them."

"Do you remember what you answered when I asked you the same question the last time?"

The man seemed confused and anxious.

"No. . . ."

"Do you remember that I asked you if you went to prostitutes?"

"No, did you do that?"

Martin Beck sat quietly for a moment again. He rubbed his nose.

"I want to help you," he said finally.

"With what? Help me? How can you help me? Now, after this?"

"I want to help you to remember."

"Yes."

"But you must try, too."

"Yes."

"Try to remember what happened after you went on board the *Diana* in Söderköping. You had your motor bike and fishing things with you and the boat was a lot behind schedule."

"Yes, I remember. The weather was beautiful."

"What did you do when you went on board?"

"I think I ate breakfast. I hadn't eaten earlier because I remember that I planned to eat on board."

"Did you talk with the people at your table?"

"No, I think I was alone. The others had already eaten."

"And then? After you had eaten?"

"I suspect I went out on the deck. Yes, that's what I did. The weather was good."

"Did you talk to anyone?"

"No, I stood by myself up in the bow. Then it was time for lunch."

"Did you eat alone then too?"

"No, there were others at the table, but I didn't talk to anyone."

"Was Roseanna McGraw at your table?"

"I don't remember. I didn't think much about who sat there."

"Do you remember how you met her?"

"No, actually not."

"Last time you said that she asked you about something and that you began to have a conversation."

"Yes, that's right. Now I remember. She asked me what was the name of the place we were passing."

"What was it called?"

"Norsholm, I think."

"And then she stayed there and talked to you?"

"Yes. I don't remember much of what she said."

"Did you think badly of her immediately?"

"Yes."

"Why did you talk with her then?"

"She forced herself on me. She stayed there and talked and laughed. She was like all the others. Shameless."

"What did you do then?"

"Then?"

"Yes, didn't you go on land together?"

"She followed me when I left the boat for a while."

"What did you talk about?"

"I don't remember. Everything and anything. Nothing in particular. I remember thinking that it was good practice for my English."

"When you went back on board, what did you do then?"

"I don't know. I really don't remember. Maybe we ate dinner later."

"Did you meet her later that evening?"

"I remember that I stood in the bow for a while after it got dark. But I was alone then."

"Didn't you meet her that evening? Try to remember."

"I think so. I don't really know, but I think that we sat on a bench in the stern and talked. I really wanted to be left in peace but she forced herself on me."

"Didn't she invite you into her cabin?"

"No."

"Later that evening you killed her, isn't that so?"

"No, I didn't do anything like that."

"Do you really not remember that you killed her?"

"Why are you plaguing me? Stop repeating that word all the time. I didn't do anything."

"I don't want to plague you."

Was that the truth? Martin Beck didn't know. Anyway he suspected that the man was on the defensive again, that his barriers against the outer world were on the point of functioning again, and that it would be more difficult to breach them the more he tried to break them down.

"Well, it's not so important."

The look in the man's eyes once again lost its sharpness and became frightened and roaming.

"You don't understand me," he said thickly.

"I'm trying to. I understand that you don't like a number of people. That you find them repulsive."

"Don't you understand that? People can be disgusting."

"Yes, I understand. You think particularly badly of a certain category, especially the women who you call shameless. Is that right?"

The man didn't say anything.

"Are you religious?"

"No."

"Why not?"

He shrugged his shoulders confusedly.

"Do you read religious books or magazines?"

"I've read the Bible."

"Do you believe in it?"

"No, there's too much in it that can't be explained and is passed over."

"What, for example?"

"All the dirtiness."

"Do you think that women like Roseanna McGraw and Miss Hansson are dirty?"

"Yes. Don't you agree? Look at all the disgusting things that happen all around us. I read the newspapers for a few weeks at the end of the year and they were full of disgusting things every day. Why do you think that is?"

"And you don't want to have anything to do with these dirty people?"

"No, I don't."

He held his breath for a second and added: "Absolutely not."

"Okay, so you don't like them. But don't women like Roseanna McGraw and Sonja Hansson have a great deal of attraction for you? Don't you want to look at them and touch them? Feel their bodies?"

"You don't have the right to say such things to me."

"Don't you want to look at their legs and arms? To feel their skin?"

"Why are you saying these things?"

"Don't you want to feel them? Take off their clothes? See them naked?"

"No, no, that's not so."

"Don't you want to feel their hands on your body? Don't you want them to touch you?"

"Be quiet," screamed the man, and started to get out of his chair.

His sudden movement caused him to pant and he grimaced badly. Probably it had hurt his wounded arm.

"Oh well, there's nothing unusual about that. Actually it is really very normal. I have the same thoughts when I see certain women."

The man stared at him.

"Are you saying that I am not normal?"

Martin Beck said nothing.

"Are you stating that I would be abnormal just because I had a few shameful feelings in my body?"

No answer.

"I have a right to my own life."

"Yes, but not to the lives of others. Last night I saw with my own eyes how you nearly killed another human being."

"You did not. I didn't do anything."

"I never say anything I'm not sure of. You tried to kill her. If we hadn't gotten there in time, you would have had a human life on your conscience now. You would have been a murderer."

Strangely enough this made a strong impression on him. He moved his lips for a long time. Finally he said, almost inaudibly:

"She deserved it. It was her fault, not mine."

"Sorry, I didn't hear you."

Silence.

"Will you please repeat what you said."

The man looked sulkily at the floor.

Suddenly Martin Beck said: "You're lying to me."

The man shook his head.

"You say that you only buy magazines about sports and fishing. But you also buy magazines with pictures of naked women in them."

"That's not true."

"You forget that *I* never lie."

Silence.

"There are over one hundred such magazines stuffed in the back of your closet."

His reaction was very strong.

"How do you know that?"

"We've had men searching your apartment. They found the magazines in the back of your closet. They found a lot of other things also, for example, a pair of sunglasses that actually belonged to Roseanna McGraw."

"You break into my home and violate my private life. What's the reason for that?"

After a few seconds he repeated his last sentence and added: "I don't want to have anything to do with you. You're detestable."

"Well, it isn't forbidden to look at pictures," said Martin Beck. "Not at all. There's nothing wrong with that. The women in these magazines look like any other women. There's no great difference. If the pictures had shown, for example, Roseanna McGraw or Sonja Hansson or Siv Lindberg. . . ."

"Be quiet," the man screamed. "You shouldn't say that. You have no right to mention that name."

"Why not? What would you do if I told you that Siv Lindberg has been photographed in magazines like that?"

"You lying devil."

"Remember what I said before. What would you do?"

"I would punish . . . I would kill you also because you had said it. . . ."

"You can't kill me. But what would you do with that woman, what is her name now, oh yes, Siv. . . ."

"Punish, I would, I would . . ."

"Yes?"

The man opened and closed his hands time after time.

"Yes, that's what I would do," he said.

"Kill her?"

"Yes."

"Why?"

Silence.

"You shouldn't say that," the man said.

A tear ran down his left cheek.

"You destroyed many of the pictures," said Martin Beck quietly. "Cut them with a knife. Why did you do that?"

"In my home . . . you have been inside my home. Searched and snooped. . . ."

"Why did you cut up the pictures?" Martin Beck said very loudly.

"That's none of your business," said the man hysterically. "You devil! You debauched swine!"

"Why?"

"To punish. And I'll punish you too."

Two minutes of silence followed. Then Martin Beck said in a friendly tone: "You killed the woman on the boat. You don't remember it yourself but I shall help you remember. The cabin was small and narrow. It was poorly lit inside. The boat was going through a lake, isn't that right?"

"It was at Boren," said the man.

"And you were in her cabin and you took off her clothes."

"No. She did that herself. She began to undress. She wanted to infect me with her dirtiness. She was disgusting."

"Did you punish her?" said Martin Beck calmly.

"Yes. I punished her. Don't you understand? She had to be punished. She was debauched and shameless."

"How did you punish her? You killed her, didn't you?"

"She deserved to die. She wanted to make me dirty too. She gloried in her shamelessness. Don't you understand," he screamed. "I had to kill her. I had to kill her dirty body."

"Weren't you afraid that someone would see you through the ventilator?"

"There wasn't any ventilator. I wasn't afraid. I knew that I was doing the right thing, she was guilty. She deserved it."

"After you had killed her? What did you do then?"

The man sank into his chair and mumbled.

"Don't plague me any more. Why do you have to talk about it all the time. I don't remember."

"Did you leave the cabin when she was dead?"

Martin Beck's voice was soft and calm.

"No. Yes. I don't remember."

"She lay naked on the bunk, didn't she? And you had killed her. Did you remain in the cabin?"

"No, I went out. I don't remember."

"Where on the boat was the cabin located?"

"I don't remember."

"Was it far below decks?"

"No, but it was quite far back . . . farthest back . . . the last one toward the stern on the deck."

"What did you do with her after she was dead?"

"Don't ask me about that all the time," he said, whining like a little child. "It wasn't my fault. It was her fault."

"I know that you killed her and you have said that you did it. What did you do with her afterwards?" asked Martin Beck in a friendly voice.

"I threw her in the lake. I couldn't stand to look at her," the man screamed loudly.

Martin Beck looked at him calmly.

"Where?" he said. "Where was the boat then?"

"I don't know. I only threw her in the lake."

He collapsed in his chair and began to cry.

"I couldn't stand to look at her. I couldn't stand looking at her," he said in a monotone with the tears running down his cheeks.

Martin Beck turned off the tape recorder, picked up the telephone and called for a police constable.

When the man who had killed Roseanna McGraw was taken away, Martin Beck lit a cigarette. He sat completely still and stared in front of him.

Things looked crooked in front of his eyes and he rubbed them with his thumb and index finger.

He reached for a pencil in the holder on the desk and wrote:

GOT HIM. CONFESSED ALMOST EMMEDIATELY, IMIDI-
AEMED. . . .

He put the pencil back, crumpled up the paper and threw it in the wastebasket. He decided to telephone Kafka when he had gotten some sleep and was rested.

Martin Beck put on his hat and coat and left. It had begun to snow at two o'clock and by now the ground was covered with a blanket of snow several inches thick. The flakes were large and wet. They dipped down in long, listless swirls, tight and abundant, dampening all sound and making the surroundings remote and unattainable. The real winter had arrived.

Roseanna McGraw had come to Europe. At a place called Norsholm she had met a man who was travelling to Bohus-län to fish. She wouldn't have met him if the boat hadn't had an engine breakdown or if the waitress hadn't moved her to another table in the dining room. Later, he had happened to kill her. She could just as easily have been run over on King Street in Stockholm or fallen down her hotel stairs and broken her neck. A woman named Sonja Hansson might possibly never again feel completely calm or sleep soundly and dream-less with her hands between her knees as she did when she was a little girl. Even so, she had actually not had anything to do with all this. They had all sat in their offices in Motala and Stockholm and Lincoln, Nebraska, and solved this case by means that could never be made public. They would always re-member it, but hardly with pride.

Round-shouldered and whistling Martin Beck walked through the pulsing, white mist to the subway station. People looking at him would probably have been surprised if they knew what he was thinking.

Here comes Martin Beck and it's snowing on his hat. He walks with a song; he walks with a sway! Hello friends and brothers; it squeaks underfoot. It is a winter night. Hello to you all; just give a call and we'll go home to southern Stockholm! By subway. To my part of town.

He was on the way home.

THE MAN
WHO WENT UP
IN SMOKE

INTRODUCTION

I first went to America in 1979. I had to buy another holdall to bring home the books. Discovering dedicated mystery book-sellers was a bit like going to heaven without having to die first. There were so many crime writers whose books were available in the U.S. only—ironically, some of them British—and in those pre-Internet days, the only apparent way to acquire them was to physically go there and buy them. Which I did. In industrial quantities.

Among the books in the holdall were ten paperbacks in the black livery of Vintage Press. They comprised a decalogue of crime novels written by the Swedish husband-and-wife team Maj Sjöwall and Per Wahlöö. They'd been on my must-read list since I'd read about them in Julian Symonds's definitive overview of the genre, *Bloody Murder*. He said, "They might come under the heading of 'Police Novels' except that the authors are more interested in the philosophical implications of crime than in straightforward police routine . . . [They] are markedly individual and very good." I suppose it was a bit of a gamble to buy all ten on the recommendation alone. But it's a gamble I've never regretted.

Reading the Martin Beck series with twenty-first-century eyes, it's almost impossible to grasp how revolutionary they felt when they first appeared almost forty years ago. So many of the elements that have become integral to the point of cliché in the police procedural subgenre started life in these ten novels. So many of the features we take for granted and sigh over in a world-weary way have their roots in the work of a couple of journalists turned crime writers.

In the mid-sixties, when Sjöwall and Wahlöö started writing, there were plenty of examples of the police procedural novel around. Going back to the golden age of the 1930s, Ngaio Marsh's Inspector Alleyn and Freeman Wills Crofts's Inspector French were among those who led the way, but they were followed in a steady stream by the likes of J. J. Marric's Gideon and, on the other side of the Atlantic, Ed McBain.

What these examples of *roman policier* have in common is that they are wedded to the status quo. Their world is divided into black and white, good and evil, right and wrong, with no uncomfortable intervening gray area. Bad men—and very occasionally bad women—do bad things and thus are bound to come to a bad end. Their police officers are honorable, upstanding family men who believe in the rule of law and the delivery of justice by their own hands. A bent cop is almost unthinkable; an incompetent one only a little less so.

And while the star of the series may have a sidekick, invariably less gifted and often more brawny, little more than lip service is paid to the rest of the squad, whose legwork goes mostly unrecognized. (McBain later became an exception to this, but in the earlier 87th Precinct novels Steve Carella is invariably center-stage.) The police procedural was home to a singular hero. There was no room to share the limelight.

The books of Sjöwall and Wahlöö are different. Although they are generally referred to as the Martin Beck novels, they're not really about an individual. They're ensemble pieces.

Beck is not some solo maverick who operates with flagrant disregard for the rules and thinly disguised contempt for the lesser mortals who surround him. Nor is he a phenomenal genius blessed with so extraordinary a talent that mere mortals can only stand back in amazement as he leads them unerringly to the solution to the baffling mystery. He's not glamorous either. Not the scion of some high-society family, not the husband of an acclaimed portrait painter, nor the flamboyant solver of baffling mysteries with an upward flick of a single eyebrow.

No, Martin Beck is none of these things. He's a driven, middle-aged dyspeptic whose marriage slowly disintegrates during the series. Not because of some cataclysmic infidelity or clash of belief systems, but rather because of the quiet desperation that builds between two people who once loved each other but now have nothing in common but their children and their address.

He's also something of an idealist whose job forces him to confront the gulf between what should exist in an ideal world and what exists in actuality. His awareness of that gap colors his life, making him depressed and sometimes fatalistic about whether what he does can ever make a difference.

But more than this, he is part of a team, each member of which is a fully realized character. His strengths and weaknesses are balanced by those of his colleagues. He relies on them as they rely on him. This is a world where ideas are kicked around, where no individual has the monopoly on shafts of brilliant insight. Nor are the repetitive tedious tasks carried out offstage by minor minions. Both action and routine are shared between Beck and his underlings. Friendships and enmities are equally tested in the course of the ten books, and everyone is portrayed as an individual who has virtues and vices in distinct measure.

Of itself, that would be enough to mark these books out as different from the run of the mill. But Sjöwall and Wahlöö add other elements to the mix which demonstrate the uniqueness of their vision.

Their plots, for example, are second to none, both in terms of structure and subject. Sometimes it's the starting point which is surprising, a seemingly eccentric moment that leads cunningly to the heart of something much darker. Sometimes it's the choice of the underlying issue which confounds us; lulled into thinking we're getting one kind of story, we suddenly find ourselves in a very different place. Wherever their stories take us, Sjöwall and Wahlöö find ways to catch the reader on the back foot, making us reassess our take on the world.

Then there is that aspect that Julian Symonds picked on so astutely—their interest in the philosophical aspects of crime. These days, it is a given that the crime novel is capable of shining a light on society, of illuminating us to ourselves. At its best, the contemporary crime novel tells us how our society works, revealing its social strata and its patterns. It can strip away the surfaces, leaving the malign and the benign exposed, and it can use both characters and story lines to excoriate us for our sins.

But back when Sjöwall and Wahlöö started writing, those jobs were left to literary novelists. Crime writers were only supposed to entertain. The Swedish duo demonstrated that there was a different way to write about murder. Through the eyes of Martin Beck and his colleagues, they held a mirror up to Swedish society at a time when the ideals of the welfare state were beginning to buckle under the realities of everyday life. They write unsparingly and unswervingly about social ills and problems, but they never forget that they are writing novels, not polemics. They dress up their social concerns in fast-moving storytelling, never losing sight of the need to keep their readers engaged.

The end product, though serious in intent, is far from gloomy. Sjöwall and Wahlöö are blessed with the gift of humor. It manifests itself in the sly, dark wit of Beck, but also in the knock-about farce that erupts from time to time, generally through the characters of Kristiansson and Kvant, a pair of patrol cops who are as stupid as they are unlucky. Their slapstick interludes are as funny to the reader as they are frustrating to the detectives. Before Sjöwall and Wahlöö, such a pair of Keystone Kops would have been unthinkable, undermining as they do the seriousness of police investigation and bringing it squarely into the realm of normal human behavior.

In many respects, however, *The Man Who Went Up in Smoke* is an exception to the rest of the novels. It takes place mostly outside Sweden, in Budapest, at a time when the cold war was still an unnerving backdrop to everyday life. For much of the book, Beck is on his own in a strange land, without back-up and without any visceral understanding of the society he's trying to operate in. His investigation into the disappearance of a Swedish journalist seems to run into brick walls at every turn, growing more and more baffling with each successive revelation.

Soon we come to understand that Beck can't crack the case on his own. He has to draw on help from both his colleagues at home and from unexpected sources in Budapest before the pieces can finally fall into place, revealing a truth that manages to be both banal and original.

Sjöwall and Wahlöö won the Mystery Writers of America's Edgar Award for Best Novel in 1971 with *The Laughing Policeman*. It remains the only novel in translation ever to have won the award. To me, that's not particularly surprising. I guarantee if you read their books, you'll end up agreeing with me. And with all the other crime writers who know only too well how much we owe to that pair of Swedish journalists turned novelists.

—*Val McDermid*

1

The room was small and shabby. There were no curtains and the view outside consisted of a gray fire wall, a few rusty armatures and a faded advertisement for margarine. The center pane of glass in the left half of the window was gone and had been replaced by a roughly cut piece of cardboard. The wallpaper was floral, but so discolored by soot and seeping moisture that the pattern was scarcely visible. Here and there it had come away from the crumbling plaster, and in several places there had been attempts to repair it with adhesive strips and wrapping paper.

There were a heating stove, six pieces of furniture and a picture in the room. In front of the stove stood a cardboard box of ashes and a dented aluminum coffee pot. The end of the bed faced the stove and the bedclothes consisted of a thick layer of old newspapers, a ragged quilt and a striped pillow. The picture was of a naked blonde standing beside a marble balustrade, and it was hanging to the right of the stove so that the person lying in the bed could see it before he fell asleep and immediately when he woke up. Someone appeared to have enlarged the woman's nipples and genitals with a pencil.

In the other part of the room, nearest to the window, stood a round table and two wooden chairs, of which one had lost its back. On the table were three empty vermouth bottles, a soft-drink bottle and two coffee cups, among other things. The ash tray had been turned upside down and among the cigarette butts, bottle tops and dead matches lay a few dirty sugar lumps, a small penknife with its blades open, and a piece of sausage. A third coffee cup had fallen to the floor and had broken. Face down on the worn linoleum, between the table and the bed, lay a dead body.

In all probability this was the same person who had improved upon the picture and tried to mend the wallpaper with strips of adhesive and wrapping paper. It was a man and he was lying with his legs close together, his elbows pressed against his ribs and his hands drawn up toward his head, as if in an effort to protect himself. The man was wearing a woolen vest and frayed trousers. On his feet were ragged woolen socks. A large sideboard had been tipped over him, obscuring his head and half the top part of his body. The third wooden chair had been thrown down beside the corpse. Its seat was bloodstained and on the top of the back handprints were clearly visible. The floor was covered with pieces of glass. Some of them had come from the glass doors of the sideboard, others from a half-shattered wine bottle which had been thrown onto a heap of dirty underclothes by the wall. What was left of the bottle was covered with a thin skin of dried blood. Someone had drawn a white circle around it.

Of its kind, the picture was almost perfect, taken by the best wide-angle lens the police possessed and in an artificial light that gave an etched sharpness to every detail.

Martin Beck put down the photograph and magnifying glass, got up and went across to the window. Outside it was full Swedish summer. And more than that. It was hot. On the grass of Kristineberg Park a couple of girls were sunbathing in bikinis. They were lying flat on their backs with their legs apart and their arms stretched outward away from their bodies. They were young and thin, or slim as they say, and they could do this with a certain grace. When he focused sharply, he even recognized them as two office girls from his own department. So it was already past twelve. In the morning they put on their bathing suits, cotton dresses and sandals and went to work. In the lunch hour they took off their dresses and went out and lay in the park. Practical.

Dejectedly, he recalled that soon he would have to leave all this and move over to the south police headquarters in the rowdy neighborhood around Västberga Allé.

Behind him he heard someone fling open the door and come into the room. He did not need to turn around to know who it was. Stenström. Stenström was still the youngest in the department and after him there would presumably be a whole generation of detectives who did not knock on doors.

"How's it going?" he said.

"Not so well," said Stenström. "When I was there fifteen minutes ago he was still flatly denying everything."

Martin Beck turned around, went back to his desk and once again looked at the photo of the scene of the crime. On the ceiling above the newspaper mattress, the ragged quilt and the striped pillow, there was an old patch of dampness. It looked like a sea horse. With a little good will it could have been a mermaid. He wondered if the man on the floor had had that much imagination.

"It doesn't matter," said Stenström officiously. "We'll get him on the technical evidence."

Martin Beck made no reply. Instead he pointed at the thick report Stenström had put down on his desk and said, "What's that?"

"The record of the interrogation from Sundbyberg."

"Take the miserable thing away. Starting tomorrow I'm on my holiday. Give it to Kollberg. Or to anybody you damn please."

Martin Beck took the photograph and went up one flight of stairs, opened a door and found himself with Kollberg and Melander.

It was much warmer in there than in his room, presumably because the windows were closed and the curtains drawn. Kollberg and the suspect were sitting opposite each other at the table, quite still. Melander, a tall man, was standing by the window, his pipe in his mouth and his arms folded. He was looking steadily at the suspect. On a chair by the door sat a police guard in uniform trousers and a light-blue shirt. He was balancing his cap on his right knee. No one said anything and the only moving thing was the reel of the tape recorder. Martin Beck situated himself to one side and just behind Kollberg and joined in the general silence. A wasp could be heard bouncing against the window behind the curtains. Kollberg had taken off his jacket and unbuttoned his shirt, but even so, his shirt was soaked with sweat between his plump shoulder blades. The wet patch slowly changed shape and spread downward in a line along his spine.

The man on the other side of the table was small, with thinning hair. He was slovenly dressed and the fingers gripping the arms of his chair were uncared-for, with bitten, dirty nails. His face was thin and sickly, with weak evasive lines around his mouth. His chin was trembling slightly and his eyes seemed cloudy and watery. The man hunched up and two tears fell down his cheeks.

"Uh-huh," said Kollberg gloomily. "You hit him on the head with the bottle, then, until it broke?"

The man nodded.

"Then you went on hitting him with the chair as he lay on the floor. How many times?"

"Don't know. Not many. Quite a lot though."

"I can imagine. And then you tipped the sideboard over him and left the room. What did the third one of you do in the meantime? This Ragnar Larsson? Didn't he try to interfere; I mean, stop you?"

"No, he didn't do anything. He just let it go on."

"Don't start lying again now."

"He was asleep. He'd passed out."

"Try to speak a little louder, all right?"

"He was lying on the bed, asleep. He didn't notice anything."

"No, not until he came to and then he went to the police. Well, so far it's clear. But there's one thing I still don't really understand. Why did it turn out this way? You'd never even seen each other before you met in that beer hall."

"He called me a damned nazi."

"Every policeman gets called a damned nazi several times a week. Hundreds of people have called me a nazi and gestapo man and even worse things, but I've never killed anyone for it."

"He sat there and said it over and over again, damned nazi, damned nazi, damned nazi . . . It was the only thing he said. And he sang."

"Sang?"

"Yes, to get my goat. Annoy me. About Hitler."

"Uh-huh. Well, had you given him any cause to talk like that?"

"I'd told him my old lady was German. That was before."

"Before you began drinking?"

"Yes. Then he just said it didn't matter what kind of mother a guy had."

"And when he was about to go out into the kitchen, you took the bottle and hit him from behind?"

"Yes."

"Did he fall?"

"He sort of fell to his knees. And began bleeding. And then he said, 'You bloody little nazi runt, you, now you're in for it.'"

"And so you went on hitting him?"

"I was . . . afraid. He was bigger than me and . . . you don't know what it feels like . . . everything just goes round and round and goes red . . . I didn't seem to know what I was doing."

The man's shoulders were shaking violently.

"That's enough," said Kollberg, switching off the tape recorder. "Give him something to eat and ask the doctor if he can have a sedative."

The policeman by the door rose, put his cap on and led the murderer out, holding him loosely by the arm.

"Bye for now. See you tomorrow," said Kollberg absently. At the same time he was writing mechanically on the paper in front of him, "Confessed in tears."

"Quite a character," he said.

"Five previous convictions for assault," said Melander. "In spite of his denying it every time. I remember him very well."

"Said the walking card file," Kollberg commented.

He rose heavily and stared at Martin Beck.

"What are *you* doing here?" he said. "Go take your holiday and let us look after the criminal ways of the lower classes. Where are you going, by the way? To the islands?"

Martin Beck nodded.

"Smart," said Kollberg. "I went to Rumania first and got fried—in Mamaia. Then I come home and get boiled. Great. And you don't have any telephone out there?"

"No."

"Excellent. I'm going to take a shower now anyhow. Come on. Run along now."

Martin Beck thought it over. The suggestion had its advantages. Among other things, he would get away a day earlier. He shrugged his shoulders.

"I'm leaving. Bye, boys. See you in a month."

2

Most people's holidays were already over and Stockholm's August-hot streets had begun to fill with people who had spent a few rainy July weeks in tents and trailers and country boardinghouses. During the last few days, the subway had once again become crowded, but it was now the middle of the working day and Martin Beck was almost alone in the car. He sat looking at the dusty greenery outside and was glad that his eagerly awaited holiday had at last begun.

His family had already been out in the archipelago for a month. This summer they had had the good fortune to rent a cottage from a distant relative of his wife's, a cottage situated all by itself on a little island in the central part of the archipelago. The relative had gone abroad and the cottage was theirs until the children went back to school.

Martin Beck let himself into his empty flat, went straight into the kitchen and took a beer out of the refrigerator. He took a few gulps standing by the sink, then carried the bottle with him into the bedroom. He undressed and walked out onto the balcony in nothing but his shorts. He sat for a while in the sun, his feet on the balcony rail as he finished off the beer. The heat out there was almost intolerable and when the bottle was empty, he got up and went back into the relative cool of the flat.

He looked at his watch. The boat would be leaving in two hours. The island was located in an area of the archipelago where transportation to and from the city was still maintained by one of the few remaining old steamers. This, thought

Martin Beck, was just about the best part of their summer holiday find.

He went out into the kitchen and put the empty bottle down on the pantry floor. The pantry had already been cleared of everything that might spoil, but for safety's sake he looked around to see if he had forgotten anything before he shut the pantry door. Then he pulled the refrigerator plug out of the wall, put the ice trays in the sink and looked around the kitchen before shutting the door and going into the bedroom to pack.

Most of what he needed for himself he had already taken out to the island on the weekend he had already spent there. His wife had given him a list of things which she and the children wanted brought out, and by the time he had included everything, he had two bags full. As he also had to pick up a carton of food from the supermarket, he decided to take a taxi to the boat.

There was plenty of room on board and when Martin Beck had put his bags down, he went up on deck and sat down.

The heat was trembling over the city and it was almost dead calm. The foliage in Karl XII Square had lost its freshness and the flags on the Grand Hotel were drooping. Martin Beck looked at his watch and waited impatiently for the men down there to pull in the gangplank.

When he felt the first vibrations from the engine, he got up and walked to the stern. The boat backed away from the quay and he leaned over the railing, watching the propellers whipping up the water into a whitish-green foam. The steam whistle sounded hoarsely, and as the boat began to turn toward Saltsjön, its hull shuddering, Martin Beck stood by the railing and turned his face toward the cool breeze. He suddenly felt free and untroubled; for a brief moment he seemed to relive the feeling he had had as a boy on the first day of the summer holidays.

He had dinner in the dining saloon, then went out and sat on deck again. Before approaching the jetty where he was to land, the boat passed his island, and he saw the cottage and some gaily colored garden chairs and his wife down on the shore. She was crouching at the water's edge, and he guessed she was scrubbing potatoes. She rose and waved, but he was not certain she could see him at such a distance with the afternoon sun in her eyes.

The children came out to meet him in the rowboat. Martin Beck liked rowing, and ignoring his son's protests, he took the oars and rowed across the bay between the steamer jetty and the island. His daughter—whose name was Ingrid, but who was called Baby although she would be fifteen in a few days—sat in the stern telling about a barn dance. Rolf, who was thirteen and despised girls, was talking about a pike he had landed. Martin listened absently, enjoying the rowing.

After he had taken off his city clothes, he took a brief swim by the rock before pulling on his blue trousers and sweater. After dinner he sat chatting with his wife outside the cottage, watching the sun go down behind the islands on the other side of the mirror-smooth bay. He went to bed early, after setting out some nets with his son.

For the first time in a very long time, he fell asleep immediately.

When he woke, the sun was still low and there was dew on the grass as he padded out and sat down on a rock outside the cottage. It looked as if the day would be as fine as the previous one, but the sun had not yet begun to grow warm, and he was cold in his pajamas. After a while he went in again and sat down on the veranda with a cup of coffee. When it was seven, he dressed and woke his son, who got up reluctantly. They rowed out and hauled in the nets, which contained nothing but a mass of seaweed and water plants. When they got back, the other two were up and breakfast was on the table.

After breakfast Martin Beck went down to the shed and began to hang up and clean the nets. It was work that tried his patience and he decided that in the future he ought to make his son responsible for providing fish for the family.

He had almost finished the last net when he heard the stutter of a motorboat behind him, and a small fishing boat rounded the point, heading straight for him. At once he recognized the man in the boat. It was Nygren, the owner of a small boatyard on the next island, and their nearest neighbor. As there was no water on the Becks' island, they fetched their drinking water from him. Nygren also had a telephone.

Nygren turned off the motor and shouted:

"Telephone. They want you to call back as soon as possible. I wrote the number down on a slip of paper by the telephone."

"Didn't he say who he was?" said Martin Beck, although he in fact already knew.

"I wrote that down too. I've got to go out to Skärholmen now, and Elsa's in the strawberry patch, but the kitchen door's open."

Nygren started up the motor again and, standing in the stern, headed out toward the bay. Before he vanished around the point, he raised his hand in farewell.

Martin Beck watched him for a short while. Then he went down to the jetty, untied the rowboat and began to row toward Nygren's boathouse. As he rowed he thought: Hell. To hell with Kollberg, just when I'd almost forgotten he existed!

On the pad below the wall telephone in Nygren's kitchen was written, almost illegibly: Hammar 54 10 60.

Martin Beck dialed the number and not until he was waiting for the exchange to put him through did he begin to feel real alarm.

"Hammar speaking," said Hammar.

"Well, what's happened?"

"I'm really sorry, Martin, but I've got to ask you to come in as soon as possible. You may have to sacrifice the rest of your holiday. Well, postpone it, that is."

Hammar was silent for a few seconds. Then he said, "If you will."

"The rest of my holiday? I haven't even had a day of it yet."

"Awfully sorry, Martin, but I wouldn't ask you if it wasn't necessary. Can you get in today?"

"Today? What's happened?"

"If you can get in today, it'd be a good thing. It's really important. I'll tell you more about it when you're here."

"There's a boat in an hour," said Martin Beck, looking out through the fly-specked window at the glittering, sunlit bay. "What's so important about it? Couldn't Kollberg or Melander—"

"No. You'll have to handle this. Someone seems to have disappeared."

3

When Martin Beck opened the door to his chief's room it was ten to one and he had been on holiday for exactly twenty-four hours.

Chief Inspector Hammar was a heavily built man with a bullneck and bushy gray hair. He sat quite still in his swivel chair, his forearms resting on the top of his desk, completely absorbed in what malicious tongues maintained was his favorite occupation: namely, doing nothing whatsoever.

"Oh, you've arrived," he said sourly. "Just in time too. You're due at the F.O. in half an hour."

"The Foreign Office?"

"Precisely. You're to see this man."

Hammar was holding a calling card by one corner, between his thumb and forefinger, as if it were a piece of lettuce with a caterpillar on it. Martin Beck looked at the name. It meant nothing to him.

"A higher-up," said Hammar. "Considers himself very close to the Minister." He paused slightly, then said, "I've never heard of the fellow either."

Hammar was fifty-nine and had been a policeman since 1927. He did not like politicians.

"You don't look so angry as you ought to," said Hammar.

Martin Beck puzzled on this for a moment. He decided that he was much too confused to be angry.

"What is this actually all about?"

"We'll talk about it later. When you've met this nitwit here."

"You said something about a disappearance."

Hammar stared in torment out through the window, then shrugged his shoulders and said, "The whole thing's quite idiotic. To tell you the truth, I've had . . . instructions not to give you any so-called further information until you've been to the F.O."

"Have we started taking orders from them too?"

"As you know, there are several departments," said Hammar dreamily.

His look became lost somewhere in the summer foliage. He said, "Since I began here we have had a whole regiment of Ministers. The overwhelming majority of them have known just about as much about the police as I know about the orange-shell louse. Namely, that it exists.

"G'bye," he said abruptly.

"Bye," said Martin Beck.

When Martin Beck reached the door, Hammar returned to the present and said, "Martin."

"Yes."

"One thing I can tell you, anyhow. You needn't take this on if you don't want to."

The man who was close to the Minister was large, angular and red-haired. He stared at Martin Beck with watery blue eyes, rose swiftly and expansively and rushed around his desk with his arm outstretched.

"Splendid," he said. "Splendid of you to come."

They shook hands with great enthusiasm. Martin Beck said nothing.

The man returned to his swivel chair, grabbed his cold pipe and bit on the stem of it with his large yellow horse teeth. Then he heaved himself backward in his chair, jammed a thumb into the bowl of his pipe, lit a match and fixed his visitor with a cold, appraising look through the cloud of smoke.

"No ceremony," he said. "I always begin a serious conversation this way. Spit in each other's faces. Things seem to go along more easily afterward. My name's Martin."

"So's mine," said Martin Beck gloomily.

A moment later, he added, "That's unfortunate. Perhaps it complicates the issue."

This seemed to confound the man. He looked sharply at Martin Beck, as if sensing some treachery ahead. Then he laughed uproariously.

"Of course. Funny. Ha ha ha."

Suddenly he fell silent and threw himself at the intercom. Pressing the buttons nervously, he mumbled, "Yes, yes. Really damned funny."

There was not a spark of humor in his voice.

"May I have the Alf Matsson file," he called.

A middle-aged woman came in with a file and put it down on the desk in front of him. He did not even condescend to glance at her. When she had closed the door behind her, he turned his cold, impersonal fisheyes on Martin Beck, slowly opening the file at the same time. It contained one single sheet of paper, covered with scrawled pencil notes.

"This is a tricky and damned unpleasant story," he said.

"Oh," said Martin Beck. "In what way?"

"Do you know Matsson?"

Martin Beck shook his head.

"No? He's quite well known, actually. Journalist. Mainly in the weeklies. Television too. A clever writer. Here."

He opened a drawer and rummaged around in it, then in another, finally lifting up his blotter and finding the object of his search.

"I hate carelessness," he said, throwing a spiteful look in the direction of the door.

Martin Beck studied the object, which turned out to be a neatly typed index card containing certain information about a person by the name of Alf Matsson. The man did indeed appear to be a journalist, employed by one of the larger weeklies, one which Martin Beck himself never read but sometimes saw—with unspoken anxiety and distrust—in the hands of his children. In addition, Alf Sixten Matsson was said to have been born in Gothenburg in 1934. Clipped to the card was also an ordinary passport photograph. Martin Beck cocked his head and looked at a fairly young man with a mustache, a short neat beard and round steel-rimmed glasses. His face was so utterly expressionless that the picture must have come from one of those photo booths around town. Martin Beck put the card down and looked questioningly at the red-haired man.

"Alf Matsson has disappeared," said the man with great emphasis.

"Oh, yes? And your inquiries haven't produced any results?"

"No inquiries have been made. And none are going to be made either," said the man, staring like a maniac.

Martin Beck, who did not realize at first that that watery look testified to a steely determination, frowned slightly.

"How long has he been gone?"

"Ten days."

The reply did not especially surprise him. If the man had said ten minutes or ten years, it would not have moved him particularly either. The only thing that surprised Martin Beck at that moment was the fact that he was sitting here and not in a rowboat out at the island. He looked at his watch. He would probably have time to catch the evening boat back.

"Ten days isn't very long," he said mildly.

Another official came in from a nearby room and entered into the conversation so directly that he must have been listening at the door. Apparently some kind of caretaker, thought Martin Beck.

"In this particular case, it's more than enough," said the new arrival. "The circumstances are highly exceptional. Alf Matsson flew to Budapest on the twenty-second of July, sent there by his magazine to write some articles. On the next Monday, he was to call the office here in Stockholm and read the text of a kind of regular column he writes every week. He didn't. It's relevant that Alf Matsson always delivered on time, as newspaper people say. In other words, he doesn't miss a deadline when it comes to turning in manuscripts. Two days later, the office phoned his hotel in Budapest, where they said that he *was* staying there, but he didn't seem to be in at that moment. The office left a message to say that Matsson should immediately inform Stockholm the moment he came in. They waited for two more days. Nothing was heard. They checked with his wife here in Stockholm. She hadn't heard anything either. That in itself wouldn't necessarily mean anything, as they're getting a divorce. Last Saturday the editor called us up here. By then they had contacted the hotel again and been told that no one there had seen Matsson since they called last, but that his things were still in his room and his passport was still at the reception desk. Last Monday, the first of August, we communicated with our people down there. They knew nothing about Matsson, but put out a feeler, as they called it, to the Hungarian police, who appeared 'not interested.' Last Tuesday we had a visit from the editor in chief of the magazine. It was a very unpleasant meeting."

The redheaded man had definitely been upstaged. He bit on the stem of his pipe in annoyance and said, "Yes, exactly. Damned unpleasant."

A moment later he added by way of explanation: "This is my secretary."

"Well," said his secretary, "anyhow, the result of that conversation was that yesterday we made unofficial contact with the police at top level, which in turn led to your coming here today. Pleased to have you here, by the way."

They shook hands. Martin Beck could not yet see the pattern. He massaged the bridge of his nose thoughtfully.

"I'm afraid I don't really understand," he said. "Why didn't the editors report the matter in the ordinary way?"

"You'll see why in a moment. The editor in chief and responsible publisher of the magazine—the same person, in fact—did not want to report the matter to the police or demand an official investigation because then the case would become known at once and would get into the rest of the press. Matsson is the magazine's own correspondent, and he has disappeared on a reporting trip abroad, so—rightly or wrongly— the magazine regards this as its own news. The editor in chief did seem rather worried about Matsson, but on the other hand, he made no bones about the fact that he smelled a scoop, as they say, news of the caliber that increases a publication's circulation by perhaps a hundred thousand copies just like that. If you know anything about the general line this magazine takes, then you ought to know . . . Well, anyhow, one of its correspondents has disappeared and the fact that he's done it in Hungary, of all places, doesn't make it any worse news."

"Behind the Iron Curtain," said the red-haired man gravely.

"We don't use expressions like that," said the other man. "Well, I hope you realize what all this means. If the case is reported and gets into the papers, that's bad enough—even if the story retained some kind of reasonable proportions and did get a relatively factual treatment. But if the magazine keeps everything to itself and uses it for its own, opinion-leading purpose, then heaven only knows what . . . Well, anyhow it would damage important relations, which both we and other people have spent a long time and a good deal of effort building up. The magazine's editor had a copy of a completed article with him when he was here on Monday. We had the dubious pleasure of reading it. If it's published, it would mean absolute disaster in some respects. And they were actually intending to publish it in this week's issue. We had to use all our powers of persuasion and appeal to every conceivable ethical standard to put a stop to its publication. The whole thing ended with the editor in chief delivering an ultimatum. If Matsson has not made his presence known of his own accord or if we haven't found him before the end of next week . . . well, then sparks are going to fly."

Martin Beck massaged the roots of his hair.

"I suppose the magazine is making its own investigations," he said.

The official looked absently at his superior, who was now puffing away furiously on his pipe.

"I got the impression that the magazine's efforts in that direction were somewhat modest. That their activities in this particular respect had been put on ice until further notice. For that matter, they haven't the slightest idea as to where Matsson is."

"The man does undoubtedly seem to have disappeared," said Martin Beck.

"Yes, exactly. It's very worrisome."

"But he can't have just gone up in smoke," said the red-haired man.

Martin Beck rested one elbow on the edge of the table, clenched his fist and pressed his knuckles against the bridge of his nose. The steamer and the island and the jetty became more and more distant and diffuse in his mind.

"Where do I come into the picture?" he said.

"That was our idea, but naturally we didn't know it would be you personally. We can't investigate all this, least of all in ten days. Whatever's happened, if the man for some reason is keeping under cover, if he's committed suicide, if he's had an accident or . . . something else, then it's a police matter. I mean, insofar as the job can be done only by a professional. So, quite unofficially, we contacted the police at top level. Someone seems to have recommended you. Now it's largely a matter of whether you will take on the case. The fact that you've come here at all indicates that you can be released from your other duties, I suppose."

Martin Beck suppressed a laugh. Both officials looked at him sternly. Presumably they found his behavior inappropriate.

"Yes, I can probably be released," he said, thinking about his nets and the rowboat. "But exactly what do you think I'd be able to do?"

The official shrugged his shoulders.

"Go down there, I suppose. Find him. You can go tomorrow morning if you like. Everything is arranged, by way of our channels. You'll be temporarily transferred to our payroll, but you've no official assignment. Naturally we'll help you in every possible way. For example, if you want to you can make contact with the police down there—or otherwise not. And as I said, you can leave tomorrow."

Martin Beck thought about it.

"The day after tomorrow, in that case."

"That's all right too."

"I'll let you know this afternoon."

"Don't think about it too long, though."

"I'll phone in about an hour. Good-bye."

The red-haired man rushed up and round his desk. He thumped Martin Beck on the back with his left hand and shook hands with his right.

"Well, good-bye then. Good-bye, Martin. And do what you can. This is important."

"It really is," said the other man.

"Yes," said the redhead, "we might have another Wallenberg affair on our hands."

"That was the word we were told not to mention," said the other man in weary despair.

Martin Beck nodded and left.

4

"Are you going out there?" said Hammar.

"Don't know yet. I don't even know the language."

"Neither does anyone else on the force. You can be quite sure we checked. Anyhow, they say you can get by with German and English."

"Odd story."

"Stupid story," said Hammar. "But I know something that those people at the F.O. don't know. We've got a dossier on him."

"Alf Matsson?"

"Yes. The Third Section had it. In the secret files."

"Counter-Espionage?"

"Exactly. The Security Division. An investigation was made on this guy three months ago."

There was a deafening thumping on the door and Kollberg thrust his head in. He stared at Martin Beck in astonishment.

"What are you doing here?"

"Having my holiday."

"What's all this hush-hush you're up to? Shall I go away? As quietly as I came, without anybody noticing?"

"Yes," said Hammar. "No, don't. I'm tired of hush-hush. Come in and shut the door."

He pulled a file out of a desk drawer.

"This was a routine investigation," he said, "and it gave rise to no particular action. But parts of it might interest anyone who is thinking of looking into the case."

"What the hell are you up to?" said Kollberg. "Have you opened a secret agency or something?"

"If you don't pipe down, you can go," said Martin Beck. "Why was Counter-Espionage interested in Matsson?"

"The passport people have their own little eccentricities. At Arlanda airport, for instance, they write down the names of people who travel to those European countries that require visas. Some bright boy who looked in their books got it into his head that this Matsson traveled all too often. To Warsaw, Prague, Budapest, Sofia, Bucharest, Constanta, Belgrade. He was great for using his passport."

"And?"

"So Security did a little hush-hush investigation. They went, for instance, to the magazine he works for and asked."

"And what did they reply?"

"Perfectly correct, said the magazine. Alf Matsson *is* a great one for using his passport. Why shouldn't he be? He's our expert on Eastern European affairs. The results are no more remarkable than that. But there are one or two things. Take this rubbish and read it for yourself. You can sit here. Because now I'm going to go home. And this evening I'm going to go to a James Bond film. Bye!"

Martin Beck picked up the report and began to read. When he had finished the first page, he pushed it over to Kollberg, who picked it up between the tips of his fingers and placed it down in front of him. Martin Beck looked questioningly at him.

"I sweat so much," said Kollberg. "Don't want to mess up their secret documents."

Martin Beck nodded. He himself never sweated except when he had a cold.

They said nothing for the following half hour.

The dossier did not offer much of immediate interest, but it was very thoroughly compiled. Alf Matsson was not born in Gothenburg in 1934, but in Mölndal in 1933. He had begun as a journalist in the provinces in 1952 and been a reporter on several daily papers before going to Stockholm as a sports writer in 1955. As a sports reporter, he had made several trips abroad, among others to the Olympic Games, in Melbourne in 1956 and in Rome in 1960. A number of editors vouchsafed that he was a skillful journalist: ". . . adroit, with a speedy pen." He had left the daily press in 1961, when he was taken on by the weekly for which he still worked. During the last four years he had devoted more and more of his time to overseas reporting on a very wide variety of subjects, from politics and economics to sport and pop stars. He had taken his university entrance exam and spoke fluent English and German, passable Spanish and some French and Russian. He earned over 40,000 kronor a year and had been married twice. His first marriage took place in 1954 and was dissolved the following year. He had married again in 1961 and had two children, a daughter by his first marriage and a son by his second.

With praiseworthy diligence, the investigator now went over to the man's less admirable points. On several occasions he had neglected to pay maintenance for his elder child. His first wife described him as a "drunkard and a brutal beast." Parenthetically, it was pointed out that this witness appeared to be not entirely reliable. There were, however, several indications that Alf Matsson drank, among others a remark in a statement by an ex-colleague who said that he was "all right, but a bastard when he got drunk," but only one of these statements was supported by evidence. On the eve of Twelfth Day in 1966, a radio patrol in Malmö had taken him to the emergency room of General Hospital after he had been stabbed in the hand during a brawl at the home of a certain Bengt Jönsson, whom he had happened to be visiting. The case was investigated by the police but was not taken to court, as Matsson had not wished to press a charge. However, two policemen by the names of Kristiansson and Kvant described both Matsson and Jönsson as under the influence, so the case was registered at the Commission on Alcoholism.

The tone of the statement by his present boss, an editor called Eriksson, was snooty. Matsson was the magazine's "expert on Eastern Europe" (whatever use a publication of this kind could possibly have for such a person) and the editorial board found no cause to give the police any further information about his journalistic activities. Matsson was, they went on to say, very interested in and well-informed on Eastern European matters, often produced projects of his own, and had on several occasions proved himself ambitious by giving up holidays and days off without extra pay to be able to carry out certain reporting assignments that especially interested him.

Some previous reader had in turn appeared ambitious by

underlining this sentence in red. It could hardly have been Hammar, who did not mess up other people's reports.

A detailed account of Matsson's published articles showed that they consisted almost exclusively of interviews with famous athletes and reportage on sports, film stars and other figures from the entertainment world.

The dossier contained several items in the same style. When he had finished reading, Kollberg said, "Singularly uninteresting person."

"There's one peculiar detail."

"That he's disappeared, you mean?"

"Exactly," said Martin Beck.

A minute later, he dialed the Foreign Office number and Kollberg, much to his surprise, heard him say, " 'Is that Martin? Yes, hi Martin—this is Martin."

Martin Beck seemed to listen for a moment, a tortured expression on his face. Then he said, "Yes, I'm going."

5

The building was old and had no elevator. Matsson was the top name on the list of tenants down in the entrance hall. When Martin Beck had climbed the five steep flights of stairs, he was out of breath and his heart was thumping. He waited for a moment before ringing the doorbell.

The woman who opened the door was small and fair. She was wearing slacks and a cotton-knit top and had hard lines around her mouth. Martin Beck guessed she was about thirty.

"Come in," she said, holding open the door.

He recognized her voice from the telephone conversation they had had an hour earlier.

The hall of the flat was large and unfurnished except for an unpainted stool along one wall. A small boy of about two or three came out of the kitchen. He had a half-eaten roll in his hand and went straight up to Martin Beck, stood in front of him and stretched up a sticky fist.

"Hi," he said.

Then he turned around and ran into the living room. The woman followed him and lifted up the boy, who with a satisfied gurgle had sat down in the room's only comfortable armchair. The boy yelled as she carried him into a neighboring room and closed the door. She came back, sat down on the sofa and lit a cigarette.

"You want to ask me about Alf. Has something happened to him?"

After a moment's hesitation, Martin Beck sat down on the armchair.

"Not so far as we know. It's just that he doesn't seem to have been heard from for a couple of weeks. Neither by the magazine, nor, so far as I can make out, by you, either. You don't know where he might be?"

"No idea. And the fact that he's not let me know anything isn't very strange in itself. He's not been here for four weeks, and before that I didn't hear from him for a month."

Martin Beck looked toward the closed door.

"But the boy? Doesn't he usually . . ."

"He hasn't seemed especially interested in his son since we've separated," she said, with some bitterness. "He sends money to us every month. But that's only right, don't you think?"

"Does he earn a lot on the magazine?"

"Yes. I don't know how much, but he always had plenty of money. And he wasn't mean. I never had to go without, although he spent a lot of money on himself. In restaurants and on taxis and so on. Now I've got a job, so I earn a little myself."

"How long have you been divorced?"

"We're not divorced. It's not been granted yet. But he moved out of here almost eight months ago now. He got hold of a flat then. But even before that, he was away from home so much that it hardly made any difference."

"But I suppose you're familiar with his habits—who he sees and where he usually goes?"

"Not any longer. To be quite frank, I don't know what he's up to. Before, he used to hang around mostly with people from work. Journalists and the like. They used to sit around in a restaurant called the Tankard. But I don't know now. Maybe he's found some other place. Anyhow, that restaurant's moved or has been torn down, hasn't it?"

She put out her cigarette and went over to the door to listen. Then she opened it cautiously and went in. A moment later she came out and shut the door just as carefully behind her.

"He's asleep," she said.

"Nice little boy," said Martin Beck.

"Yes, he's nice."

They sat silent for a moment, and then she said, "But Alf was on an assignment in Budapest, wasn't he? At least, I heard that somewhere. Mightn't he have stayed there? Or have gone somewhere else?"

"Did he used to do that? When he was away on assignments?"

"No," she said hesitantly. "No, actually he didn't. He's not especially conscientious and he drinks a lot, but while we were together he certainly didn't neglect his work. For instance, he was awfully particular about getting his manuscripts in at the time he'd promised. When he lived here, he often sat up late at night writing to get things finished in time."

She looked at Martin Beck. For the first time during their conversation he noticed a vague anxiety in her eyes.

"It does seem peculiar, doesn't it? That he's never got in touch with the magazine. Supposing something really has happened to him."

"Have you any idea what might have happened to him?"

She shook her head.

"No, none at all."

"You said before that he drinks. Does he drink a lot?"

"Yes—sometimes, at least. Toward the end, when he lived here, he often came home drunk. If he generally ever came home at all."

The bitter lines around her mouth had returned.

"But didn't that affect his work?"

"No, it didn't really. Anyhow not much. When he began working for this weekly magazine, he often got special assignments. Abroad and that kind of thing. In between, he didn't have much to do and was often free. He didn't have to be at the office much. That was when he drank. Sometimes he sat around that café for days on end."

"I see," said Martin Beck. "Can you give me the names of anyone he used to go around with?"

She gave Martin Beck the names of three journalists who were unknown to him, and he wrote them down on a taxi receipt he found in his inside pocket. She looked at him and said:

"I thought the police always had little notebooks with black covers that they wrote everything down in. But maybe that's just in books and at the movies."

Martin Beck got up.

"If you hear anything from him, perhaps you'd be good enough to call me," she said. "Would you?"

"Naturally," said Martin Beck.

In the hall, he asked, "Where did you say he was living now?"

"On Fleminggatan. Number 34. But I didn't say."

"Have you got a key to the apartment?"

"Oh, no. I haven't even been there."

6

On the door was a piece of cardboard with MATSSON lettered on it in India ink. The lock was an ordinary one and caused Martin Beck no difficulties. Aware that he was overstepping his authority, he made his way into the flat. On the doormat was some mail—a few advertisements, a postcard from Madrid signed by someone called Bibban, a sports car magazine in English and an electricity bill amounting to 28:45 kronor.

The flat consisted of two large rooms, a kitchen, hall and toilet. There was no washroom, but two large wardrobes. The air in the flat was heavy and musty.

In the largest room, facing the street, were a bed, a night table, bookshelves, a low circular table with a glass top, a desk and two chairs. On the night table stood a record player and on the shelf below, a pile of long-playing records. Martin Beck read in English on the top sleeve: *Blue Monk*. It meant nothing to him. On the desk were a sheaf of typing paper, a daily paper dated July twentieth, a taxi receipt for 6:50 kronor dated the eighteenth, a German dictionary, a magnifying glass and a stenciled information sheet from a youth club. There was a telephone too, and telephone directories and two ash trays. The drawers contained old magazines, magazine photographs, receipts, a few letters and postcards, and a number of carbon copies of manuscripts.

In the back room there was no furniture at all except a narrow divan with a faded red cover, a chair and a stool that served as a night table. There were no curtains.

Martin Beck opened the doors of both wardrobes. One of

them contained an almost empty laundry bag and on the shelves lay shirts, sweaters and underclothes, some of them with the laundry's paper bands still unbroken around them. In the other hung two tweed jackets, a dark-brown flannel suit, three pairs of trousers and a winter overcoat. Three hangers were empty. On the floor stood a pair of heavy brown shoes with rubber soles, a pair of thinner black ones, a pair of boots and a pair of galoshes. There was a large suitcase in the cupboard above the one wardrobe, but the other cupboard was empty.

Martin Beck went out into the kitchen. There were no dirty dishes in the sink, but on the drainboard were two glasses and a mug. The pantry was empty except for a few empty wine bottles and two cans. Martin Beck thought about his own pantry, which he had quite unnecessarily cleaned out so thoroughly.

He walked through the flat one more time. The bed was made, the ash trays were empty, and there were neither passport, money, bankbooks nor anything else of value in the drawers of the desk. All in all, there was nothing to indicate that Alf Matsson had been home since he had left the flat and gone to Budapest two weeks previously.

Martin Beck left Alf Matsson's flat and stood for a moment by the deserted taxi stand down on Fleminggatan, but as usual at lunch time there were no taxis available and he took a trolley instead.

It was past one when he went into the dining room of the Tankard. All the tables were taken and the harassed waitresses took no notice of him. There was no headwaiter to be seen. He crossed over to the bar on the other side of the entrance hall. At that moment a fat man in a corduroy jacket gathered up his papers and rose from a round table in the corner next to the door. Martin Beck took his place. Here too, all the tables were full, but some of the customers were just paying their bills.

He ordered a sandwich and beer from the headwaiter and asked if any of the three journalists was there.

"Mr. Molin is sitting over there, but I haven't seen the others today. They'll probably be in later."

Martin Beck followed the headwaiter's glance toward a table where five men were sitting talking with large steins of beer in front of them.

"Which of the gentlemen is Mr. Molin?"

"The gentleman with the beard," said the headwaiter, and went away.

Confused, Martin Beck looked at the five men. Three of them had beards.

The waitress came with his sandwich and beer and gave him the chance to say, "Do you happen to know which of the gentlemen over there is Mr. Molin?"

"Of course, the one with the beard."

She followed his somewhat desperate look and added, "Nearest the window."

Martin Beck ate his sandwich very slowly. The man named Molin ordered another stein of beer. Martin Beck waited. The place began to empty. After a while Molin emptied his stein and was given another. Martin Beck finished eating his sandwich, ordered coffee, and waited.

Finally the man with the beard got up from his place by the window and walked toward the entrance hall. Just as he was passing, Martin Beck said, "Mr. Molin?"

The man stopped. "Just a moment," he said, and went on out.

A short while later, he returned, breathed heavily all over Martin Beck, and said, "Do we know each other?"

"No, not yet. But perhaps you'd like to sit down a moment and have a beer with me. There's something I'd like to ask you about."

He himself could hear that it didn't sound especially good. Smelled of police business a mile away. But it worked anyhow. Molin sat down. He had fair, rather thin hair, combed forward onto his forehead. His beard was reddish and neat. He looked about thirty-five and was quite plump. He waved a waitress over to him.

"Say Stina, get me a round, will you?"

The waitress nodded and looked at Martin Beck.

"The same," he said.

A "round" turned out to be a bulbous and considerably larger stein than the cylindrical though quite large one he himself had drunk with his sandwich.

Molin took a large gulp and wiped his mustache with his handkerchief.

"Uh-huh," he said. "What was it you wanted to talk to me about? Hangovers?"

"About Alf Matsson," said Martin Beck. "You're good friends, aren't you?"

It still didn't sound quite right and he tried to improve on it by saying, "Buddies, aren't you?"

"Of course. What's up with him? Does he owe you money?"

Molin looked suspiciously and haughtily at Martin Beck.

"Well then, I'd first like to point out that I'm not any kind of collection agency."

Clearly, he would have to watch his tongue. Moreover, the man was a journalist.

"No, nothing like that at all," said Martin Beck.

"Then what do you want Alfie for?"

"Alfie and I've known each other for a long time. We worked on the same . . . well, we were on the same job together a number of years ago. I met him quite by chance a few weeks ago and he promised to do a job for me, and then I never heard another word from him. He talked about you quite a bit, so I thought perhaps you'd know where he was."

Somewhat exhausted by this strenuous oratorical effort, Martin Beck took a deep gulp of his beer. The other man followed suit.

"Oh, hell. You're an old pal of Alfie's, are you? The fact is that I've been wondering where he was too. But I suppose he's stayed on in Hungary. He's not in town, anyhow. Or we'd have seen him here."

"In Hungary? What's he doing there?"

"On some trip for that gossip sheet he works for. But he should really be home by now. When he left, he said he was only going to be away for two or three days."

"Did you see him before he left?"

"Yes indeed. The night before. We were here in the daytime and then went to a couple of other places in the evening."

"You and him?"

"Yes, and some of the others. I don't really remember who. Per Kronkvist and Stig Lund were there, I think. We got really stoned. Yes, Åke and Pia were there too. Don't you know Åke, by the way?"

Martin Beck thought. It seemed somewhat pointless.

"Åke? I don't know. Which Åke?"

"Åke Gunnarsson," said Molin, turning around toward the table where he had been sitting before. Two of the men had left during their conversation. The two remaining were sitting silently over their beers.

"He's sitting over there," said Molin. "The guy with the beard."

One of the beards had gone, so there was no doubt which of them was Gunnarsson. The man looked quite pleasant.

"No," said Martin Beck. "I don't think I know him. Where does he work?"

Molin gave the name of a publication that Martin Beck had never heard of, but it sounded like some kind of auto magazine.

"Åke's all right. He got pretty high that night too, if I remember rightly. Otherwise, he doesn't get really drunk very often. No matter how much he pours into himself."

"Haven't you seen Alfie since then?"

"That's a hell of a lot of questions you're asking. Aren't you going to ask me how I am too?"

"Of course. How are you?"

"Absolutely god-damned awful. Hangover. Damned bad one, too."

Molin's fat face grew gloomy. As if to obliterate the last shreds of the pleasures of living, he drank the remains of his beer in one huge gulp. He took out his handkerchief, and with a brooding look in his eyes, mopped his foamy mustache.

"They ought to serve beer in mustache cups," he said. "There isn't much service left these days."

After a brief pause he said, "No, I haven't seen Alfie since he left. The last I saw of him was when he was pouring his drink over some gal in the Opera House bar. Then he went to Budapest the next morning. Poor devil, having to sit up flying right across half of Europe with a hangover like that. Hope he didn't fly Scandinavian Airlines anyhow."

"And you've not heard anything from him since then?"

"We don't usually write letters when we're on overseas trips," said Molin haughtily. "What the hell kind of a rag do you work for, anyhow? The *Kiddy Krib*? Well, what about another round?"

Half an hour and two more rounds later, Martin Beck managed to escape from Mr. Molin, after having first lent him ten kronor. As he left, he heard the man's voice behind him, "Fia, old thing, get me a round, will you?"

7

The plane was an Ilyushin 18 turboprop from Czechoslovak Airlines. It rose in a steep are over Copenhagen and Saltholm, and an Öresund that glittered in the sun.

Martin Beck sat by the window and looked down at Ven Island below, with Backafall Cliffs, the church and the little harbor. He had just had time to see a tugboat rounding the harbor pier before the plane turned south.

He liked traveling, but this time disappointment over his spoiled holiday overshadowed most of his pleasure. Moreover, his wife had not seemed to understand at all that his own choice in the matter had not been very great. He had called the evening before and tried to explain, but had not been particularly successful.

"You don't care a bit about me or the children," she had said.

And a moment later:

"There must be *other* policemen besides you. Do you have to take on *every* assignment?"

He had tried to convince her that he would in fact have preferred to go out to the island, but she had gone on being unreasonable. In addition, she had demonstrated various evidence of faulty logic.

"So you're going to Budapest to enjoy yourself while the children and I are stuck by ourselves out on this island."

"I am not going for fun."

"Hmm-mph."

In the end she had put down the receiver in the middle of

a sentence. He knew she would calm down eventually, but he had not attempted to call again.

Now, at an altitude of 16,000 feet, he tipped his seat back, lit a cigarette and let his thoughts of the island and his family sink into the back of his mind.

During their stopover at Schönefeld airport in East Berlin, he drank a beer in the transit lounge. He noted that the beer was called Radeberger. It was excellent beer, but he didn't think he would have cause to remember the name. The waiter entertained him in Berlin German. He did not understand very much of it and wondered gloomily how he was going to manage in the future.

In a basket by the entrance lay a few pamphlets in German and he took one out at random to have something to read while he waited. Clearly he needed to practice his German.

The leaflet was published by the German journalist's union and dealt with the Springer concern, one of the most powerful newspaper and magazine publishers in West Germany, and its chief, Axel Springer. It gave examples of the company's menacing fascist politics and quoted several of its more prominent contributors.

When his flight was called, Martin Beck noted that he had read almost the whole pamphlet without difficulty. He put the pamphlet into his pocket and boarded the plane.

After an hour in the air, the plane again came down to land, this time in Prague, a city that Martin Beck had always wanted to visit. Now he had to be content with a brief glimpse, from the air, of its many towers and bridges and of the Moldau; the stopover was too short to give him time to get into the city from the airport.

His red-haired namesake in the Foreign Office had apologized for the connections between Stockholm and Budapest which were not the world's best, but Martin Beck had no objections to the delays, although he was not able to see more of Berlin and Prague than their transit lounges.

Martin Beck had never been to Budapest and when the plane had taken off again, he read through a couple of leaflets he had received from the redhead's secretary. In one dealing with the geography of Hungary, he read that Budapest had two million inhabitants. He wondered how he was going to find Alf Matsson if the man had decided to disappear in this metropolis.

In his mind he reviewed what he knew about Alf Matsson. It was not a great deal, but he wondered whether there was really anything else to know. He thought of Kollberg's comment: "Singularly uninteresting person." Why should a man like Alf Matsson want to disappear? That is, if he had disappeared of his own free will? A woman? It seemed hardly credible that he should sacrifice a well-paid position—one that he seemed to be happy with, moreover—for that reason. He was still married, of course, but perfectly free to do as he wished. He had a home, work, money and friends. It was hard to think of any plausible reason why he should voluntarily leave all that.

Martin Beck took out the copy of the personal file from the Security Division. Alf Matsson had become an object of interest to the police simply because of his many and frequent trips to places in Eastern Europe. "Behind the Iron Curtain," the redhead had said. Well, the man was a reporter, and if he preferred to undertake assignments in Eastern Europe, then that in itself wasn't so peculiar. And if he had anything on his conscience now, why should he disappear? The Security Division had consigned the case to oblivion after a routine investigation. "A new Wallenberg affair," the man at the F.O. had said, thinking of the famous case of a well-known Swede last seen in Budapest in 1945: "Spirited away by the Communists." "You see too many James Bond movies," Kollberg would have said if he had been there.

Martin Beck folded up the copy and put it into his briefcase. He looked out the window. It was completely dark now but the stars were out, and way down there he could see small dots of light from villages and communities and pearl strings of light where the street lamps were on.

Perhaps Matsson had started to drink, abandoning the magazine and everything else. When he sobered up again he would be broke and full of remorse and would have to make his presence known. But that didn't sound likely either. True, he drank occasionally, but not to that degree, and normally he never neglected his job.

Perhaps he had committed suicide, had an accident, fallen into the Danube and drowned or been robbed and killed. Was this more likely? Hardly. Somewhere or other, Martin Beck had read that, of all the capitals in the world, Budapest had the lowest crime rate.

Perhaps he was sitting in the hotel dining room right now,

having his dinner, and Martin Beck would be able to take the plane back the next day and continue his holiday.

The signs lit up. No smoking. Please fasten your seatbelts. And then they repeated the same thing in Russian.

When the plane stopped taxiing, Martin Beck picked up his briefcase and walked the short stretch toward the airport buildings. The air was soft and warm although it was late in the evening.

He had to wait quite a long time for his only suitcase, but the passport and customs formalities were dispensed with swiftly. He went through a huge lounge, its walls lined with shops, and then out onto the steps outside the building. The airport appeared to be far outside the city. He saw no other lights except those within the area of the airport itself. As he stood there, two elderly ladies climbed into the only taxi there was on the turn-around drive in front of the steps.

Some time elapsed before the next taxi drove up, and as it took him through suburbs and dark industrial areas, Martin Beck realized he was hungry. He knew nothing about the hotel he was going to stay at—other than its name and the fact that Alf Matsson had stayed there before he had disappeared—but he hoped he would be able to get something to eat there.

The taxi drove along broad streets and around large open squares into what appeared to be the center of the city. There were not many people about and most of the streets were empty and rather dark. For a while they went down a wide street with brightly lit store windows before continuing into narrower and darker side streets. Martin Beck had no idea whatsoever where he was in the city, but all the while he kept an eye out for the river.

The taxi stopped outside the lighted entrance of the hotel. Martin Beck leaned over and read the figure on the red meter before paying the driver. It seemed expensive, more than a hundred forints. He had forgotten what a forint was worth in his own money, but he realized that it couldn't be very much.

An elderly man, with a gray mustache, a green uniform and visored cap, opened the taxi door and took his bag. Martin Beck walked through the revolving doors behind him. The entrance hall was large and very lofty, the reception desk running at an angle across the left-hand corner of the hall. The night porter spoke English. Martin Beck gave him his passport and asked if he could have dinner. The porter indicated a glass door farther down the hall and explained that the dining room was open until midnight. Then he gave the key to the waiting elevator man who took Martin Beck's bag and preceded him into the elevator. The car creaked its way up to the first floor. The elevator man appeared to be at least as old as the elevator, and Martin Beck tried in vain to relieve him of the bag. They walked down a long corridor, turned to the left twice, and then the old man unlocked some enormous double doors and put the bag inside.

The room was over twelve feet high and very large. The mahogany furniture was dark and huge. Martin Beck opened the door to the bathroom. The bathtub was spacious with large, old-fashioned taps and a shower.

The windows were high and had shutters on the inside, and in front of the window alcove hung heavy white lace curtains. He opened the shutters on one side and looked out. Immediately below was a gas lamp, throwing out a yellowish-green light. Far away he could see lights, but quite a time elapsed before he realized that the river was flowing between him and the lights over there.

He opened the window and leaned out. Below, a stone balustrade and large flower urns encompassed tables and chairs. Light was streaming out onto them, and he could hear a little orchestra playing a Strauss waltz. Between the hotel and the river ran a road with trees and gas lamps, a trolley line and a broad quay, on which there were benches and big flower pots. Two bridges, one to his right and the other to the left, spanned the river.

He left the window open and went down to eat. Opening the glass doors from the hall, he came into a lobby with deep armchairs, low tables and mirrors along one wall. Two steps led up to the dining room and at the far end sat the little orchestra he had heard up in his room.

The dining room was colossal, with two huge mahogany pillars and a balcony running along three of the walls, high up under the roof. Three waiters wearing reddish-brown jackets with black lapels were standing inside the door. They bowed and greeted him in chorus, while a fourth rushed forward and directed him to a table near the window and the orchestra.

Martin Beck stared at the menu for a long time before he found the column written in German and began to read. After a while the waiter, a gray-haired man with the physiognomy of a friendly boxer, leaned over toward him and said:

"Very gut Fischsuppe, gentleman."

Martin Beck at once decided upon fish soup.

"*Barack?*" said the waiter.

"What's that?" said Martin Beck, first in German, then in English.

"Very gut apéritif," said the waiter.

Martin Beck drank the apéritif called *barack*. *Barack palinka*, explained the waiter, was Hungarian apricot brandy.

He ate the fish soup, which was red and strongly spiced with paprika and was indeed very good.

He ate fillet of veal with potatoes in strong paprika sauce and he drank Czechoslovakian beer.

When he had finished his coffee, which was strong, and an additional *barack*, he felt very sleepy and went straight up to his room.

He shut the window and the shutters and crept into bed. It creaked. It creaked in a friendly way, he thought, and fell asleep.

8

Martin Beck was waked by a hoarse, long-drawn-out toot. As he tried to orient himself, blinking in the half-light, the toot was repeated twice. He turned over on his side and picked his wristwatch up off the night table. It was already ten to nine. The great bed creaked ceremoniously. Perhaps, he thought, it had once creaked as majestically beneath Field Marshal Conrad von Hötzendorf. The daylight was trickling through the shutters. It was already very warm in the room.

He got up, went out into the bathroom and coughed for a while, as he usually did in the mornings. After drinking a gulp of mineral water, he pulled on his dressing gown and opened the shutters and the window. The contrast between the dusky light of the room and the clear, sharp sunlight outside was almost overwhelming. So was the view.

The Danube was flowing past him on its calm, even course from north to south, not especially blue, but wide and majestic and indubitably very beautiful. On the other side of the river rose two softly curved hills crowned by a monument and a walled fortress. Houses clambered only hesitantly along the sides of the hills, but farther away were other hills strewn with villas. That was the famous Buda side, then, and there you were very close to the heart of central European culture. Martin Beck let his glance roam over the panoramic view, absently listening to the wingbeats of history. There the Romans had founded their mighty settlement Aquincum, from there the Hapsburg artillery had shot Pest into ruins during the War of Liberation of 1849, and there Szalasis' fascists and

Lieutenant General Pfeffer-Wildenbruch's SS troops had stayed for a whole month during the spring of 1945, with a meaningless heroism that invited annihilation (old fascists he had met in Sweden still spoke of it with pride).

Immediately below lay a white paddle steamer tied up to the quay, with its red, white and blue Czechoslovak flag hanging limply in the heat and tourists sunbathing in deckchairs on board. What had waked him was a Yugoslavian paddle-wheel tugboat that was slowly struggling upstream. It was big and old, with two tall funnels tilting asymmetrically, and it was pulling six heavily loaded barges. On the last barge a line had been strung between the wheelhouse and the low loading crane between the hatches. A young woman in a head scarf and blue work garb was tranquilly picking washing out of a basket and carefully hanging up baby clothes, unmoved by the beauty of the shores. To the left, arching over the river, was a long, airy, slender bridge. It seemed to lead directly to the mountain with the monument—a tall, slim bronze woman with a palm leaf raised above her head. Across the bridge thronged cars, buses, trolleys and pedestrians. To the right, northward, the tugboat had reached the next bridge. Again it let out three hoarse toots to announce the number of barges it was pulling, let down its funnels fore and aft and slid in under the low arch of the bridge. Just in front of the window a very small steamer swung in toward the shore, slid over fifty yards athwartship with the current and smartly completed the maneuver, putting in with hardly an inch to spare at a pontoon jetty. A preposterous number of people went ashore from the steamer and an equally preposterous number then boarded it.

The air was dry and warm. The sun was high. Martin Beck leaned out of the window, letting his eyes sweep from north to south as he considered a few facts he had gleaned from the brochures he had read on the plane.

"Budapest is the capital of the Hungarian People's Republic. It is considered to have been founded in 1873, when the three towns Buda, Pest and Óbuda were united into one, but excavations have revealed settlements several thousand years old, and Aquincum, the capital of the Roman province of Lower Pannonia, was situated on this spot. Today the city has nearly two million inhabitants and is divided into twenty-three districts."

It was certainly a very large city. He remembered the

legendary Gustaf Lidberg's almost classic reflection on landing in New York in 1899, on his search for the counterfeiter
Skog: "In this ant-heap is Mr. Who, address: Where?"

Well, New York was certainly larger than this, even at that
time, but on the other hand, Chief Detective Lidberg had had
unlimited time at his disposal. He himself had only a week.

Martin Beck left history and the river traffic to their re-
spective fates and went and took a shower. He put on his sandals and his light-gray Dacron slacks and wore his shirt outside.
As he critically observed his unconventional attire in the
mirror in the huge wardrobe, the mahogany doors suddenly
opened by themselves, slowly and fatefully, with an unnerving
creak, as in early thriller films. He still hadn't got his pulse under control when the telephone began to ring with short, urgent little signals.

"There's a gentleman to see you. He's waiting in the foyer.
A Swedish gentleman."

"Is it Mr. Matsson?"

"Yes, I'm sure it is," said the receptionist happily.

Of course it is, thought Martin Beck as he went down the
stairs. In that case there would be a thoroughly honorable
end to this odd assignment.

It was not Alf Matsson, but a young man from the Embassy,
extremely correctly dressed in a dark suit, black shoes, white
shirt and a pale-gray silk tie. The man's eyes ran over Martin
Beck, a glint of wonder in them, but only a glint.

"As you will understand, we are aware of the nature of your
assignment. Perhaps we should discuss the matter."

They sat down in the lobby and discussed the matter.

"There are better hotels than this one," said the man
from the Embassy.

"Really?"

"Yes. More modern. Tip-top. Swimming pool."

"Oh yes."

"The night club here isn't much good either."

"Oh yes."

"With regard to this Alf Matsson."

The man lowered his voice and looked around the lobby,
which was empty except for an African sleeping in the farthest corner.

"Yes. Have you heard from him?"

"No. Nothing at all. The only thing we know for certain is

that he checked in at Ferihegyi, that's the airport here, on the evening of the twenty-second. He spent the night at some kind of youth hotel called Ifjuság up on the Buda side. The next morning he moved in here. About half an hour later, he went out and took his room key with him. Since then, no one has seen him."

"What do the police say?"

"Nothing."

"Nothing?"

"The ones I've spoken with don't seem interested. Officially speaking, that attitude is defensible. Matsson had a valid visa and he has registered as a resident at this hotel. The police have no reason to concern themselves with him until he leaves the country, so long as he doesn't overstay the period of his residence permit."

"Couldn't he have left the country?"

"Quite unthinkable. And even if he had succeeded in getting over the border illegally, where would he go then? Without a passport. Anyhow, we've made some inquiries at the embassies in Prague, Belgrade, Bucharest and Vienna. Even in Moscow, for safety's sake. No one knows anything."

"His employer seemed to think that he had two things to do here. An interview with Laszlo Papp, the boxer, and an article on the Jewish museum."

"He hasn't been to either place. We've done a little investigating. He had written a letter from Sweden to the curator of the museum, a Dr. Sos, but did not look him up. We've also talked to Papp's mother. She had never heard of Matsson's name and Papp himself is not even in town."

"Is his luggage still in his hotel room?"

"His possessions are at the hotel. Not in his room. He had reserved a room for three nights only. The hotel management retained it at our request, then moved his luggage into the office. Out here. Behind the reception desk. In fact, it wasn't even unpacked. We paid the bill."

The man sat in silence for a while, as if he were thinking something over. Then he said solemnly, "Naturally we're going to demand the amount back from his employers."

"Or his estate," said Martin Beck.

"Yes, if things turn out to be as bad as that."

"Where's his passport?"

"I have it here," said the man from the Embassy.

He unzipped his flat briefcase, took out the passport and handed it over, simultaneously taking his fountain pen out of his inside pocket.

"Here you are. Would you sign for it, please?"

Martin Beck signed. The man put away his pen and the receipt.

"Well, then. Is there anything else? Yes, of course, the hotel bill. You needn't worry about that. We've had instructions to cover your expenses. Rather unorthodox, I feel. Naturally you should have had daily expenses in the usual fashion. Well, if you need any cash, you can collect it at the Embassy."

"Thank you."

"Then I don't think there's anything else, is there? You can go through his possessions whenever you like. I've let them know."

The man got up.

"In fact you're occupying the same room that Matsson had," he said in passing. "It's 105, isn't it? If we hadn't insisted on the room remaining in Matsson's name, you would probably have had to stay at some other hotel. It's the height of the season."

Before they parted, Martin Beck said, "What do you personally think about this? Where's he gone?"

The man from the Embassy looked at him expressionlessly.

"If I think anything at all, I prefer to keep it to myself."

A moment later he added, "This thing is very unpleasant."

Martin Beck went up to his room. It had already been cleaned. He looked around. So Alf Matsson had stayed here, had he? For an hour, at the most. To expect any clues from his activities during that brief period would be demanding too much.

What had Alf Matsson done during that hour? Had he stood by the window like this, looking out at the boats? Perhaps. Had he seen somebody or something that made him leave the hotel so quickly he'd forgotten to hand in his key? Possibly. What would it have been, then? Impossible to say. If he'd been run over in the street, it would have been reported at once. If he had planned to jump into the river, he would have had to wait until dark. If he had tried to nurse his hangover with apricot brandy and had plunged into another drinking bout as a result, then he'd had sixteen days in which to sober up. That was a bit much. Anyway, he had not been in the habit of drinking while on an assignment. He was the modern type of journalist, it had said someplace in the report from the Third Division: quick, efficient and direct. He was the type who did the job first and relaxed afterward.

Unpleasant. Very unpleasant. Singularly unpleasant. Damned unpleasant. Blasted unpleasant. Almost painfully so.

Martin Beck lay down on the bed. It creaked magnificently. Gone were thoughts of Baron Conrad von Hötzendorf. Had it scrunched beneath Alf Matsson? Presumably. Was there anybody who didn't test the bed as soon as he stepped into a hotel room? So Matsson had lain here and looked up at the ceiling over twelve feet above. Then, without unpacking and without handing in his key, he had gone out . . . and disappeared. Had the telephone rung? With some startling news?

Martin Beck unfolded his map of Budapest and studied it at length. Then he was seized with an urge to perform some kind of duty, so he rose, put the map and his passport into his hip pocket and went down to inspect the luggage.

The porter was a somewhat stout, elderly man, friendly, dignified and admirably intelligible.

No, no one had phoned Mr. Matsson while Mr. Matsson was still in the hotel. Later, when Mr. Matsson had left, there had been several calls. They had been repeated the following days. Was it the same person who had phoned? No, several different people—the operator at the board was sure of that. Men? Both men and women, at least one woman. Had the people who had phoned left any messages or telephone numbers? No, they had left no messages. They hadn't given their telephone numbers either. Later there had been calls from Stockholm and from the Swedish Embassy. Then, however, both messages and telephone numbers had been left. They were still here. Would Mr. Beck like to see them? No, Mr. Beck would not like to see them.

The luggage was indeed to be found in a room behind the reception desk. It was very easily inspected. A portable typewriter of the standard make Erika and a yellowish-brown pigskin suitcase with a strap around it. A calling card was fitted into the leather label dangling from the handle. Alf Matsson, Reporter, Fleminggatan 34, Stockholm K. The key was in the lock.

Martin Beck took the typewriter out of its case and studied

it for a long time. Having come to the conclusion that it was a portable typewriter of the Erika make, he went over to the suitcase.

The bag appeared neatly and carefully packed, but all the same he had a feeling that someone with a practiced hand had been through it and put everything back into place. The contents consisted of a checked shirt, a brown sport shirt, a white poplin shirt with the laundry band still around it, a pair of freshly pressed light-blue trousers, a kind of blue cardigan, three handkerchiefs, four pairs of socks, two pairs of colored shorts, a fishnet undershirt and a pair of light-brown suede shoes. Everything was clean. In addition, a shaving kit, a sheaf of typing paper, a typewriter eraser, an electric razor, a novel and a dark-blue plastic wallet of the kind that travel agencies usually give away free and that aren't big enough for the tickets. In the shaving kit were shaving lotion, talcum powder, a cake of soap still in its wrapper, a tube of toothpaste that had been opened, a toothbrush, a bottle of mouthwash, a box of aspirin and a pack of contraceptives. In the dark-blue plastic wallet were $1500 in $20 bills and six Swedish 100-kronor notes. An astonishingly large sum for traveling money, but Alf Matsson seemed to be accustomed to doing things in a grand manner.

Martin Beck put everything back as nicely and neatly as possible and returned to the reception desk. It was noon and high time to go out. As he still didn't know what he should do, he might at least do it out in the fresh air—for instance, in the sun on the quay. He took his room key out of his pocket and looked at it. It looked just as old, as venerable and as solid as the hotel itself. He put it down on the desk. The porter at once reached out his hand for the key.

"That's a spare key, isn't it?"

"I don't understand," said the porter.

"I thought that the previous guest took the key with him."

"Yes, that's right. But we got the key back the next day."

"Got it back? Who from?"

"From the police, sir."

"From the police? Which police?"

The porter shrugged his shoulders in bewilderment.

"From the ordinary police, of course. Who else? A policeman handed in the key to the doorman. Mr. Matsson must have dropped it somewhere."

"Where?"

"I'm afraid I don't know, sir."

Martin Beck asked one more question.

"Has anyone else besides me gone through Mr. Matsson's luggage?"

The porter hesitated for a moment before answering.

"I don't think so, sir."

Martin Beck went through the revolving door. The man with the gray mustache and a visored cap was standing in the shade beneath the balcony, perfectly still with his hands behind his back, a living memorial to Emil Jannings.

"Do you remember receiving a room key from a policeman two weeks ago?"

The old man looked at him questioningly.

"Of course."

"Was it a uniformed policeman?"

"Yes, yes . . . A patrol car stopped here and one of the policemen got out and turned in the key."

"What did he say?"

The man thought.

"He said: 'Lost property.' Nothing else, I believe."

Martin Beck turned around and walked away. After three steps, he remembered that he had forgotten to leave a tip. He went back and placed a number of the unfamiliar light-metal coins into the man's hand. The doorman touched the visor of his cap with the fingertips of his right hand and said, "Thank you, but it isn't necessary."

"You speak excellent German," said Martin Beck.

And he thought: Hell of a lot better than I do, anyway.

"I learned it at the Isonzo front in 1916."

As Martin Beck turned the corner of the block, he took out the map and looked at it. Then he walked, map still in hand, down toward the quay. A big white paddle steamer with two funnels was forging its way upriver. He looked at it joylessly.

There was something fundamentally wrong with all this. Something was quite definitely not as it should be. What it was he did not know.

9

It was Sunday and very warm. A light haze of heat trembled over the mountain slopes. The quay was crowded with people walking back and forth or sitting sunning themselves on the steps down to the river. On the small steamers and motor launches shuttling up and down the river people clad in summer clothes crowded together on their way to bathing sites and holiday spots. Long lines were waiting at the ticket offices.

Martin Beck had forgotten that it was Sunday and was at first surprised by the crowds. He followed the stream of strollers and walked along the quay, watching the lively boat traffic. He had thought of starting the day with a walk across the next bridge to Margaret Island, out in the middle of the river, but changed his mind when he imagined the crowds of Budapest citizens spending their Sunday out there.

He was slightly irritated by the crush, and the sight of all these people, happy on their free Sunday, filled him with an urge for activity. He would visit the hotel at which Alf Matsson spent his first and perhaps only night in Budapest—a young people's hotel on the Buda side, the Embassy man had said.

Martin Beck broke out of the stream of people and went up to the street above the quay. He stood in the shade of the gable of a house and studied the map. He hunted for a long time, but could not find a hotel called Ifjuság, and finally he folded up the map and began to walk toward the bridge over to the island and onto the Buda side. He looked around for a police patrolman but did not succeed in finding one. At the end of the bridge there was a taxi stand and a taxi was waiting there. It looked free.

The driver could speak only Hungarian and did not understand a word until Martin Beck showed him the piece of paper with the hotel's name written on it.

They drove across the bridge, past the green island, where he caught sight of a high-flung surge of water between the trees, then on along a shopping street, up steep narrow streets and in onto an open square with lawns and a modernistic bronze group representing a man and a woman sitting staring at each other.

The taxi stopped there and Martin Beck paid—probably much too much, for the driver thanked him profusely in his incomprehensible language.

The hotel was low and spread out along the square, which was more like a widening of the street, with flower beds and parking places. The building appeared to be built just recently, in contrast to the other houses that surrounded the square. The architecture was modern and the entire façade was covered with balconies. The steps leading up to the entrance were wide and few.

Inside the glass doors was a long, light foyer, containing a souvenir stand (which was closed), elevator doors, a couple of groups of chairs and a reception desk. The reception desk was empty and there was not a soul in the foyer.

Adjoining the foyer was a big lounge with armchairs and low tables and large windows all along the far wall. This room was empty too.

Martin Beck went across to the wall with the windows and looked out.

A few young people were lying on the lawn outside, sunning themselves in bathing suits.

The hotel was situated on a hill with a view across to the Pest side. The houses on the slope between the hotel and the river appeared old and shabby. From the taxi Martin Beck had seen bullet holes in most of the façades, and on a number of houses the plastering had been almost entirely shot away.

He looked out into the foyer, which was still just as deserted, and sat down in one of the armchairs in the lounge. He did not expect much from his visit to the Ifjuság. Alf Matsson had stayed here one night, there was a shortage of hotel rooms in Budapest in the summer, and the fact that this particular hotel had a room free was probably sheer chance. It was hardly plausible that anyone would remember a guest who had come late in the evening and left the next morning, at the height of the summer season.

He extinguished his last Florida cigarette and looked gloomily at the sunburned youngsters out on the lawn. It suddenly seemed to him quite ridiculous that he should be gadding about Budapest trying to find a person to whom he was completely indifferent. He could not remember ever being given such a hopeless, meaningless assignment.

Steps could be heard out in the foyer, and Martin Beck got up and went out after them. A young man was standing behind the reception desk with a telephone receiver in his hand, staring up at the ceiling and biting his thumbnail as he listened. Then he began to speak and at first Martin Beck thought the man was speaking Finnish, but then remembered that Finnish and Hungarian stemmed from the same linguistic stock.

The young man put down the receiver and looked inquiringly at Martin Beck, who hesitated while trying to decide which language he should begin with.

"What can I do for you?" said the youth in perfect English, to Martin Beck's relief.

"It's about a guest who stayed at this hotel the night of July twenty-second. Have you any idea who was on duty here that night?"

The young man looked at a wall calendar.

"I really don't remember," he said. "It's more than two weeks ago. One moment, and I'll have a look."

He hunted around for a while on a shelf under the desk, retrieved a little black book and leafed through it. Then he said, "It was me, in fact. Friday night, yes . . . What kind of person? Did he stay just one night?"

"Yes, as far as I know," said Martin Beck. "He might have stayed here later, of course. A Swedish journalist named Alf Matsson."

The youth stared at the ceiling and chewed his nail. Then he shook his head.

"I can't remember any Swede. We get very few Swedes here. What did he look like?"

Martin Beck showed him Alf Matsson's passport photograph. The youth looked at it for a moment and said hesitantly, "I don't know. Perhaps I've seen him before. I can't really remember."

"Do you have a ledger? A guest register?"

The young man pulled out a card-file drawer and began to search. Martin Beck waited. He felt an urge to smoke and hunted through his pockets, but his cigarettes were irrevocably at an end.

"Here it is," said the youth, taking a card out of the drawer. "Alf Matsson. Swedish, yes. He stayed here the night of July twenty-second, just as you say."

"And he didn't stay here after that night?"

"No, not afterward. But he did stay here for a few days at the end of May. But that was before I came here. I was taking my exams then."

Martin Beck took the card and looked at it. Alf Matsson had stayed at the hotel from the twenty-fifth to the twenty-eighth of May.

"Who was on duty here then?"

The youth thought about it. Then he said, "It must have been Stefi. Or else the man who was here before me. I really can't remember what his name is."

"Stefi," said Martin Beck. "Does he still work here?"

"She," said the young man. "It's a girl—Stefania. Yes, she and I work in shifts."

"When is she coming in?"

"She's bound to be here already. I mean in her room. She lives here at the hotel, you see. But she has the night shift this week, so she's probably asleep."

"Could you find out?" asked Martin Beck. "If she's awake, I'd like to speak to her."

The youth lifted the receiver and dialed a number. After a while he replaced the receiver.

"No answer."

He lifted the flap door in the desk and came out.

"I'll see if she's in," he said. "Just a moment."

He got into one of the elevators and Martin Beck saw from the signal light that he had stopped at the second floor. After a while he came down again.

"Her roommate says she's out sunbathing. Wait a moment and I'll go get her."

He disappeared into the lounge and returned a moment later with a girl. She was small and chubby, wearing sandals on her feet and a checkered cotton robe over her bikini. She was buttoning up the robe as she came toward Martin Beck.

"I'm sorry to bother you," he said.

"It doesn't matter," said the girl called Stefi. "Can I help you with anything?"

Martin Beck asked her if she had been on duty during the particular days in May. She went behind the desk, looked in the black book and nodded.

"Yes," she said. "But only in the daytime."

Martin Beck showed her Alf Matsson's passport.

"Swedish?" she asked without looking up.

"Yes," said Martin Beck. "A journalist."

He looked at her and waited. She looked at the passport photograph and cocked her head.

"Ye-es," she said hesitantly. "Yes, I think I remember him. He was alone at first in a room with three beds, and then we had a Russian party, so I needed the room and had to move him. He was awfully angry that he didn't get a telephone in the new room. We haven't got telephones in all the rooms. He made such a fuss about not having one, I was forced to let him exchange rooms with someone who didn't need a telephone."

She closed the passport and put it down on the desk.

"If it was him," she said, "that photo's not very good."

"Do you remember if he had any visitors?" said Martin Beck.

"No," she said. "I don't think so. Not so far as I can remember, anyhow."

"Did he use the phone a lot? Or did he receive any calls which you can remember?"

"It seems to me that a lady rang several times, but I'm not certain," said Stefi.

Martin Beck pondered awhile and then said, "Do you remember anything else about him?"

The girl shook her head.

"He had a typewriter with him, I'm sure. And I remember that he was well dressed. Otherwise I can't remember anything special about him."

Martin Beck put the passport back in his pocket and recalled that he had run out of cigarettes.

"May I buy a pack of cigarettes here?" he said.

The girl bent forward and looked in a drawer.

"Certainly," she said. "But I've only got Tervs."

"That's fine," said Martin Beck, taking the pack made of gray paper, with a picture of a factory with tall smokestacks on it. He paid with a note and told her to keep the change. Then he took a pen and a pad from the desk, wrote down his own name and that of his hotel, tore off the sheet and handed it to Stefi.

"If you can think of anything else, perhaps you'd call me, would you?"

Stefi looked at the piece of paper with a frown.

"I've just remembered something else when you were writing that note," she said. "I think it was that Swede who asked how you got to an address in Újpest. It might not have been him, I'm not certain. Perhaps it was a different guest. I drew a little map for him."

She fell silent and Martin Beck waited.

"I remember the street he was asking about, but not the number. My aunt lives on that street, so that's why I remembered it."

Martin Beck pushed the pad toward her.

"Would you be good enough to write down the name of the street for me?"

As Martin Beck came out of the hotel, he looked at the slip of paper. Venetianer út.

He put the paper into his pocket, lit a Terv and began strolling down toward the river.

10

It was Monday the eighth of August and Martin Beck was waked by the telephone. He propped himself sleepily up on his elbow, fumbled with the receiver a moment and heard the telephone operator say something he did not understand. Then a familiar voice said:

"Hullo."

Out of sheer astonishment, Martin Beck forgot to reply.

"Hulloo-o-o, is anyone there?"

Kollberg could be heard as clearly as if he had been in the room next door.

"Where are you?"

"At the office, of course. It's already quarter past nine. Don't tell me you're still lying snoring in bed."

"What's the weather like up your way?" said Martin Beck, then falling silent, paralyzed himself by the idiocy of the remark.

"It's raining," said Kollberg suspiciously, "but that wasn't why I called. Are you sick or something?"

Martin Beck managed to sit up on the edge of the bed and light one of those unfamiliar Hungarian cigarettes from the pack with the factory on it.

"No. What d'you want?"

"I've been digging around a bit up here. Alf Matsson doesn't seem to be a very nice guy."

"How so?"

"Well. Mostly just an impression I've got. He just seems to be one big all-round ass."

"Did you call to tell me that?"

"No, actually, I didn't. But there was one thing I thought you ought to know. I didn't have anything to do on Saturday so I went and sat around in that bar place. The Tankard."

"Listen, don't go poking your nose in too much. Officially you've never even heard about this case. And you don't know I'm here."

Kollberg sounded clearly offended.

"D'you think I'm a moron?"

"Only occasionally," said Martin Beck, amiably.

"I didn't speak to anyone. Just sat at the table next to that gang and listened to them shoot the breeze. For five hours. They sure put away the liquor."

The telephone operator broke in and said something incomprehensible.

"You're bankrupting the government," said Martin Beck. "What's up? Get it off your chest."

"Well, the guys were shooting the bull back and forth, one thing and another about Alfie, as they call him. They're just the type to let off a lot of hot air behind each other's backs. As soon as one of them goes to the head, then the others all get started on him."

"Don't be so long-winded."

"That Molin seems to be the worst. He was the one who started talking about the thing I'm calling about, too. Nasty, but it might not be *all* lies."

"Come on now, look sharp, Lennart."

"And *you* tell me that! Anyhow it turned out that Matsson makes off like a shot for Hungary because he's got a gal down there. Some sort of small-time athlete he met while he was a sports reporter here in Stockholm—at some international sports meet or other. While he was still living with his wife."

"Uh-huh."

"They also said it was very likely that he arranged his trips to other places—Prague and Berlin and so forth—so he could meet her when she was competing there."

"Doesn't sound likely to me. Girl athletes are usually kept under lock and key."

"Take it for what it's worth."

"Thanks," said Martin Beck, without a trace of enthusiasm. "So long."

"Wait a second. I haven't finished yet. They never men-tioned her name—I don't think they even knew it. But they gave enough details for me to be able to . . . It rained yester-day too."

"Lennart," said Martin Beck desperately.

"I managed to force my way into the Royal Library and sat all day yesterday looking through back numbers. As far as I can make out, it can only be a gal named—I'll spell it."

Martin Beck switched on the bedside lamp and wrote the letters on the edge of the map of Budapest, A-R-I B-Ö-K-K.

"Got it?" said Kollberg.

"Of course."

"She's German actually, but a Hungarian citizen. Don't know where she lives, nor that the spelling's quite right. Not very famous. I couldn't think of any name that reminded me of hers in any connection since May of last year. Apparently she was some kind of substitute. On the second team."

"Have you finished now?"

"One more thing. His car is where it ought to be. In the airport parking place here at Arlanda. An Opel Rekord. Noth-ing special about it."

"Really. Have you finished now?"

"Yes."

"G'bye, then."

"Bye."

Martin Beck stared listlessly at the letters he had written down. Ari Bökk. It did not even look like the name of a hu-man being. Probably the particulars were wrong and the in-formation completely useless.

He got up, opened the shutters and let in the summer. The view over the river and the Buda side was just as fascinating as it had been twenty-four hours ago. The Czech paddle steamer had left, making way for a propeller-driven motor vessel with two low funnels. It was Czechoslovakian too and was called *Druzba.* People dressed for summer were sitting eating break-fast at the tables in front of the hotel. It was already half past nine. He felt useless and negligent of his duties, so he swiftly washed and dressed, put the map in his pocket and hurried downstairs to the vestibule. Having hurried all the way down, he then remained standing absolutely motionless. To hurry seemed pointless when you didn't know what to do when you got there anyway. He meditated on this for a moment, then went into the dining room, sat down by one of the open windows and had breakfast served to him. Boats of every size were passing by. A large Soviet tugboat towing three oil barges worked its way upstream. Presumably it came from Batum. That was a long way away. The captain was wearing a white cap. The waiters swarmed around Martin Beck's table as if he were Rockefeller. Small boys were kicking a ball on the street. A big dog wanted to join in and almost knocked over the well-dressed lady holding its leash. She had to grab hold of one of the stone pillars of the balustrade to keep from falling. After a while she let go of the pillar but retained her hold on the leash, running, at a sharp backward tilt behind the dog, in among the ballplayers. It was already very warm. The river sparkled.

His lack of constructive ideas was conspicuous. Martin Beck turned his head and saw a person staring at him: a sunburned man of his own age, with graying hair, straight nose, brown eyes, gray suit, black shoes, white shirt and gray tie. He had a large signet ring on the little finger of his right hand and beside him on the table lay a speckled green hat with a narrow brim and a fluffy little feather in the band. The man returned to his double espresso.

Martin Beck moved his eyes and saw a woman staring at him. She was African and young and very beautiful, with clean features, large brilliant eyes, white teeth, long slim legs and high insteps. Silver sandals and a tight-fitting light-blue dress of some shiny material.

Presumably they were both staring at Martin Beck—the man with envy, the woman with ill-concealed desire—because he was so handsome.

Martin Beck sneezed and three waiters blessed him. He thanked them, went out into the vestibule, took the map out of his pocket and showed the letters he had written on it to the porter.

"Do you know of anybody by this name?"

"No sir."

"It's supposed to be some kind of sports star."

"Really?"

The porter looked politely sympathetic. Naturally, a guest was always right.

"Perhaps not so well known, sir."

"Is it a man's or a woman's name?"

"Ari is a woman's name—almost a nickname. A different version of Aranka, for children."

The porter cocked his head and looked at the words.

"But the last name, sir. Is it really a name?"

"May I borrow a telephone directory?"

Naturally there was no one called Bökk, anyhow no human being. But he didn't give up that easily. (A cheap virtue when a person still doesn't know what to do.) He tried several other possibilities. The result was as follows: BOECK ESZTER penzió XII Venetianer út 6 292–173.

Struck by his first thought of the day, he took out the slip of paper he had received from the girl at the young people's hotel. Venetianer út. It could hardly be a coincidence.

At the reception desk a young lady had taken the august old porter's place.

"What does this mean?"

"*Penzió.* Pension—boarding house. Shall I call the number for you?"

He shook his head.

"Where is this street?"

"The Fourth District. In Újpest."

"How do you get there?"

"It's quickest by taxi, of course. Otherwise, Trolley Line Three from Marx Square. But it's more comfortable to take one of the boats that tie up outside here. Heading north."

11

The boat was called *Úttörő* and was a joy to the eye. A little coal-fired steamer with a tall, straight funnel and open decks. As it calmly and comfortably chugged up the river past the Parliament building and green Margaret Island, Martin Beck stood at the railing philosophizing about the accursed cult of the combustion engine. He walked over to the engine room and peered down. The heat came out like a column from the boiler room. The fireman was dressed in bathing trunks, and his muscular back was shiny with sweat. The coal shovel rattled. What was this man thinking about down in that infernal heat? In all probability, about the blessing of the combustion engine: he no doubt saw himself sitting reading the newspaper beside a diesel engine, cotton waste and an oil can within easy reach. Martin Beck returned to studying the boat, but the fireman had spoiled his enjoyment. It was the same with most things. You couldn't have your cake and eat it too.

The boat slid past spacious, open-air parks and bathing places, edged its way through a swarm of canoes and pleasure boats, passed two bridges and continued through a narrow sound into quite a small tributary of the river. It gave a short hoarse toot of triumph and tied up in Újpest.

After Martin Beck had gone ashore, he turned around and looked at the steamer, so exquisite in form and so functional—in its day. The fireman came up on deck, laughed at the sun and leaped straight into the water.

This part of the city was of a different character from the

sections of Budapest he had seen previously. He walked diagonally across the large, bare square and made a few feeble attempts to ask his way, but could not make himself understood. Despite the map, he went astray and wound up in a yard behind a synagogue, evidently a home for elderly Jews. Frail survivors from the days of great evil nodded cheerfully at him from their wicker chairs in the narrow strip of shade along the walls.

Five minutes later he was standing outside the building Venetianer út Number 6. It was built in two stories and nothing about its exterior gave the impression that it was a boarding house, but out on the street stood two cars with foreign license plates. He met the landlady as soon as he got into the hall.

"Frau Boeck?"

"Yes—we're full up I'm afraid."

She was a stout woman of fifty years. Her German sounded extraordinarily fluent.

"I am looking for a lady named Ari Boeck."

"That's my niece. One flight up. Second door to the right."

With that, she went away. Simple as that. Martin Beck stood for a moment outside the white-painted door and heard someone moving about inside. Then he knocked quite lightly. The door was opened at once.

"Fräulein Boeck?"

The woman seemed surprised. Very likely, she had been expecting someone. She was wearing a dark-blue, two-piece bathing suit and in her right hand she was carrying a green rubber diving mask and a snorkel. She was standing with her feet wide apart and her left hand still on the lock, quite still, as if paralyzed in the middle of a movement. Her hair was dark and short, and her features were strong. She had thick black eyebrows, a broad straight nose and full lips. Her teeth were good but somewhat uneven. Her mouth was half-open and the tip of her tongue was resting against her lower teeth, as if she was just about to say something. She was hardly taller than five foot one, but strongly and harmoniously built, with well-developed shoulders, broad hips and quite a narrow waist. Her legs were muscular and her feet short and broad, with straight toes. She had a very deep suntan and her skin appeared soft and elastic, especially across her diaphragm and stomach. Shaved armpits. Large breasts and curved stomach with thick down that seemed very light against her tanned skin. Here and there, long and curly black hairs had made their way out from under the elastic at her loins. She might have been twenty-two or twenty-three years old, at the most. Not beautiful in the conventional sense of the word, but a highly functional specimen of the human race.

A questioning look in large, dark-brown eyes. Finally she said, "Yes, that's me. Were you looking for me?"

Not quite such fluent German as her aunt's, but almost.

"I'm looking for Alf Matsson."

"Who is that?"

Her general attitude was that of a child in a state of shock. It made him incapable of discerning any definite reaction to the name. Quite possibly it was completely new to her.

"A Swedish journalist. From Stockholm."

"Is he supposed to be living here? There's no Swede here at the moment. You must have made a mistake."

She thought for a moment, frowning.

"But how did you know my name?"

The room behind her was an ordinary boarding-house room. Clothes lay carelessly strewn about on the furniture. Only women's clothing, as far as he could see.

"He gave me this address himself. Matsson is a friend of mine."

She looked suspiciously at him and said: "How odd."

He took the passport out of his pocket and turned to the page with Matsson's photo on it. She looked at it carefully.

"No. I've never seen him before."

After a while she said, "Have you lost each other?"

Before Martin Beck had time to reply, he heard a padding sound behind him and took a step to one side. A man in his thirties went past him into the room. Wearing bathing trunks, below average height, blond, very strongly built, with the same formidable tan as the woman. The man took a position behind her and to one side and peered inquisitively at the passport.

"Who's that?" he said in German.

"I don't know. This gentleman has lost him. Thought he'd moved here."

"Lost," said the blond man. "That's not good. And without his passport too. I know what a bother that can be. I'm in that line myself."

Playfully, he pulled the elastic of the woman's bathing suit as far as he could and let it go with a smack. She gave him a quick look of annoyance.

"Aren't we going out for a swim?" said the man.

"Yes, I'm ready."

"Ari Boeck," said Martin Beck. "I recognize the name. Aren't you the swimmer?"

For the first time, the girl's eyes wavered.

"I don't compete any longer."

"Haven't you done some swimming in Sweden?"

"Yes, once. Two years ago. I was last. Funny that he gave you my address."

The blond man looked inquiringly at her. No one said anything. Martin Beck put the passport away.

"Well, good-bye, then. Sorry to have troubled you."

"Good-bye," said the woman, smiling for the first time.

"Hope you find your friend," said the blond man. "Have you tried the camping site by the Roman Baths? It's up here, on the other side of the river. A huge number of people there. You can take a boat over."

"You're German, aren't you?"

"Yes, from Hamburg."

The man rumpled the girl's short dark hair. Lightly she brushed his chest with the back of her left hand. Martin Beck turned around and went away.

The entrance hall was empty. On a shelf behind the table that served as a reception desk lay a little stack of passports. The top one was Finnish, but underneath it lay two in that familiar moss-green color. As if in passing, he stretched out his hand and took one of them. He opened it and the man he had met in Ari Boeck's doorway stared glassily up at him. Tetz Radeberger, Travel Agency Official, Hamburg, born in 1935. Evidently no one had taken the trouble to lie to him.

He had bad luck on his journey home and ended up on a modern fast-moving ferryboat with roofed decks and growling diesel engines. There were only a few passengers on board— nearest to him sat two old women in gaudily colored shawls and bright dresses. They were carrying large white bundles and presumably had come from the country. Farther away in the saloon sat a serious, middle-aged man in a brown felt hat who was carrying a briefcase and wearing the facial expression of a civil servant. A tall man in a blue suit was whittling listlessly at a stick. By the landing stage stood a uniformed police officer, eating figure-eight-shaped cookies out of a paper cornet and talking sporadically to a small, well-dressed man with a bald head and a black mustache. A young couple with two doll-like children completed the assemblage.

Martin Beck inspected his fellow passengers gloomily. His expedition had been a failure. There was nothing to indicate that Ari Boeck had not been telling the truth.

Inwardly he cursed the strange impulse that had made him take on this pointless assignment. The possibilities of his solving the case became more and more remote. He was alone and without an idea in his head. And if, on the other hand, he had had any ideas, he would have lacked resources to implement them.

The worst of it was that, deep down within himself, he knew that he had not been guided by any kind of impulse at all. It was just his policeman's soul—or whatever it might be called—that had started to function. It was the same instinct that made Kollberg sacrifice his time off—a kind of occupational disease that forced him to take on all assignments and do his best to solve them.

When he got back to the hotel it was a quarter past four and the dining room was closed. He had missed lunch. He went up to his room, showered and put on his dressing gown. Taking a pull of whisky from the bottle he had bought on the plane, he found the taste raw and unpleasant and went out to the bathroom to brush his teeth. Then he leaned out the window, his elbows resting on the wide window sill, and watched the boats. Not even that managed to amuse him very much. Directly below him, at one of the outdoor tables, sat one of the passengers on the boat: the man in the blue suit. He had a glass of beer on the table and was still whittling at his stick.

Martin Beck frowned and lay down on the creaking bed. Again he thought the situation over. Sooner or later he would be forced to contact the police. It was a doubtful measure and no one would like it—at this stage not even he himself.

He whiled away the time remaining before dinner by sitting idling in an armchair in the lobby. On the other side of the room a gray-haired man wearing a signet ring was reading a Hungarian newspaper. It was the same man who had stared at him at breakfast. Martin Beck looked at him for a long time, but the man tranquilly went on drinking his coffee and seemed quite unconscious of his surroundings.

Martin Beck dined on mushroom soup and a perch-like fish from Lake Balaton, washed down felicitously with white wine. The little orchestra played Liszt and Strauss and other composers of that elevated school. It was a superb dinner, but it did not gladden him, and the waiters swarmed around their lugubrious guest like medical experts around a dictator's sickbed.

He had his coffee and brandy in the lobby. The man with the signet ring was still reading his newspaper on the other side of the room. Once again a glass of coffee was standing in front of him. After a few minutes, the man looked at his watch, glanced across at Martin Beck, folded up his paper and walked across the room.

Martin Beck was to be spared the problem of contacting the police. The police had taken that initiative. Twenty-three years' experience had taught him to recognize a policeman from his walk.

1 2

The man in the gray suit took a calling card out of his top pocket and placed it on the edge of the table. Martin Beck glanced down at it as he rose to his feet. Only a name. Vilmos Szluka.

"May I sit down?"

The man spoke English. Martin Beck nodded.

"I'm from the police."

"So am I," said Martin Beck.

"I realized that. Coffee?"

Martin Beck nodded. The man from the police held up two fingers and almost immediately a waiter hurried forward with two glasses. This was clearly a coffee-drinking nation.

"I also realize that you are here to make certain investigations."

Martin Beck did not reply immediately. He rubbed his nose and thought. Obviously this was the right moment to say, "Not at all—I'm here as a tourist, but I'm trying to get hold of a friend I'd like to see." That was presumably what was expected of him.

Szluka did not seem to be in any special hurry. With obvious pleasure he sipped at his double espresso, however many that made now. Martin Beck had seen him drink at least three earlier in the day. The man was behaving politely but formally. His eyes were friendly, but very professional.

Martin Beck went on pondering. This man was indeed a policeman, but so far as he knew there was no law in the whole world that said that individual citizens should tell the police the truth. Unfortunately.

"Yes," said Martin Beck. "That's correct."

"Then wouldn't the most logical thing to do have been to turn to us first?"

Martin Beck preferred not to reply to that one. After a pause of a few seconds, the other man developed the train of thought himself.

"In the event something that demands an investigation really should have happened," he said.

"I have no official assignment."

"And we have not been notified of any charge. Only an inquiry in very vague terms. In other words, it appears that nothing has happened."

Martin Beck gulped down his coffee, which was extremely strong. The conversation was growing more unpleasant than he had expected. But under any circumstances, there was no reason for him to allow himself to be lectured to in a hotel foyer by a policeman who did not even take the trouble to identify himself.

"Nonetheless, the police here have considered that they had cause to go through Alf Matsson's belongings," he said.

It was a random comment but it struck home.

"I don't know anything about that," said Szluka stiffly. "Can you identify yourself, by the way?"

"Can you?"

He caught a swift change in those brown eyes. The man was by no means harmless.

Szluka put his hand into his inside pocket, withdrew his wallet and opened it, swiftly and casually. Martin Beck did not bother to look, but showed his service badge clipped to his key ring.

"That's not valid identification," said Szluka. "In our country you can buy emblems of different kinds in the toyshops."

This point of view was not entirely without justification and Martin Beck did not consider the matter worth further argument. He took out his identification card.

"My passport is at the reception desk."

The other man studied the card thoroughly and at length. As he returned it, he said, "How long are you planning to stay?"

"My visa is good until the end of the month."

Szluka smiled for the first time during their conversation. The smile hardly came from the heart and it was not difficult to figure out what it meant. The Hungarian sipped up the last drop of coffee, buttoned up his jacket and said:

"I do not wish to stop you although, naturally, I could do it. As far as I can see, your activities are more or less of a private nature. I assume that they will remain so and that they will not harm the interests of the general public or any individual citizen."

"You can always go on tailing me, of course."

Szluka did not reply. His eyes were cold and hostile.

"What do you really think you're doing?" he said.

"What do *you* think?"

"I don't know. Nothing has happened."

"Only that a person has disappeared."

"Who says so?"

"I do."

"In that case you should go to the authorities and demand that the case be investigated in the ordinary way," said Szluka stiffly.

Martin Beck drummed on the table with his fingers.

"The man is missing—there's no doubt about it."

The other man was evidently just about to leave. He was sitting absolutely upright in the easychair, with his right hand on the arm.

"By that statement you actually mean—as far as I can make out—that the person in question has not been seen here at this hotel during the last two weeks. He has a valid residence permit and can travel freely within the country's borders. At present there are a couple hundred thousand tourists here, many of them spending their nights in tents or sleeping in their cars. This man might be in Szeged or Debrecen. He might have gone to Lake Balaton to spend his holiday bathing."

"Alf Matsson did not come here to swim."

"Is that so? In any case, he has a tourist visa. Why should he disappear, as you call it? Had he, for instance, booked his return ticket?"

The last question was worthy of some thought. The manner in which it was put indicated that the man already knew the answer. Szluka rose to his feet.

"Just a moment," said Martin Beck. "I'd like to ask you about one thing."

"Please go ahead. What do you want to know?"

"When Alf Matsson left the hotel, he took his room key with him. The next day, it was handed in here by a uniformed policeman. Where did the police get the key from?"

Szluka looked straight at him for at least fifteen seconds. Then he said, "Unfortunately, I cannot answer that question. Good-bye."

He walked swiftly through the lobby, stopped at the coat-check counter, received his gray-brown hat with a feather in it and stood with it in his hand, as if thinking about something. Then he turned around and went back to Martin Beck's table.

"Here is your passport."

"Thank you."

"It wasn't at the reception desk, as you thought. You were mistaken."

"Yes," said Martin Beck.

He found nothing amusing about the other man's behavior and did not bother to look up. Szluka remained standing there.

"What do you think of the food here?" he said.

"It's good."

"I'm delighted to hear it."

The Hungarian said this as if he really meant it, and Martin Beck raised his head.

"You see," explained Szluka, "nothing very dramatic or exciting happens here nowadays—it's not like in your country or in London or New York."

The combination was somewhat bewildering.

"We've had more than enough of that in the past," said Szluka solemnly. "Now we want peace and quiet, and we take an interest in other things. Food, for instance. I myself had four slices of fat bacon and two fried eggs for breakfast. And for lunch I had fish soup and fried, breaded carp. Apple strudel for dessert."

He paused. Then he said thoughtfully, "The children don't like fat bacon, of course. They usually have cocoa and buttered sweet rolls before they go to school."

"Uh-huh."

"Yes. And this evening I'm going to have veal schnitzel with rice and paprika sauce. Not bad. Have you tasted the fish soup here, by the way?"

"No."

Indeed, he had come across this fish soup on his first evening, but he could not see that this had anything to do with the Hungarian police.

"You definitely ought to try it. It's excellent. But it's even better at Matya's, a place quite near here. You ought to take the time to go there—like most of the other foreigners."

"Uh-huh."

"But I can assure you that I know a place where they have even better fish soup. The best fish soup in all Budapest. It's a little place up on Lajos út. Not many tourists find their way there. You have to go down to Szeged to find a soup like this."

"Uh-huh."

Szluka had become noticeably exhilarated during this report on culinary matters. He appeared to be collecting his thoughts now and looked at his watch. Presumably he was thinking about his veal schnitzel.

"Have you had time to see anything of Budapest?"

"A little. It's a beautiful city."

"Yes, it is, isn't it? Have you been to the Palatine Baths?"

"No."

"They're worth a visit. I'm planning to go there myself tomorrow. Perhaps we could go together."

"Why not?"

"Excellent. In that case I'll meet you at two o'clock outside the entrance."

"Good-bye."

Martin Beck remained seated awhile, thinking. The conversation had been unpleasant and disquieting. Szluka's last sudden change in attitude did not in any way alter that impression. More intensely than ever, he had a feeling that something did not fit, and at the same time, his own impotence seemed more and more apparent.

At about half past eleven, the foyer and the dining room began to empty and Martin Beck went up to his room. After he had undressed, he stood for a moment by the open window, inhaling the warm night air. A paddle steamer slid by on the river, brightly illuminated with green, red and yellow lights. People were dancing on the aft deck and the sound of the music came through intermittently across the water.

A few people were still sitting at the tables in front of the hotel, one of them a tall man in his thirties, with dark wavy hair. The man had a glass of beer in front of him and had obviously been home and exchanged his blue suit for a light-gray one.

He shut the window and went to bed. Then he lay in the dark thinking: the police may not be especially interested in Alf Matsson, but they're certainly interested in Martin Beck.

It was a long time before he fell asleep.

13

Martin Beck sat in the shade by the stone balustrade in front of the hotel, eating a late breakfast. It was his third day in Budapest and it promised to be just as warm and beautiful as the previous ones.

Breakfast was nearly over, and he and an elderly couple, who sat in silence a few tables away, were the only guests. There were a good many people moving about on the street and down on the quay, mostly mothers with children and low streamlined baby carriages like small white tanks.

The tall dark man with a stick was not visible, which in itself did not necessarily mean that he was no longer being watched. The police corps was large and there were no doubt replacements.

A waiter came over and cleared his table.

"Frühstück nicht gut?"

He looked unhappily at the untouched salami.

Martin Beck assured him that the breakfast had been very good. When the waiter had gone away, he took out a picture postcard he had bought in the hotel kiosk. It was of a paddle steamer on its way up the Danube, with one of the bridges in the background. The lady in the kiosk had stamped the card for him and he pondered for a moment over whom he should send it to. Then he addressed it to Gunnar Ahlberg, Police Station, Motala, wrote a few words of greetings on it, and put it back into his pocket.

He had met Ahlberg two summers ago, when the body of a woman had been found in the Göta Canal at Motala. They had become good friends during the six-month investigation and had kept in touch sporadically ever since. At the time the investigation and search for the murderer had become a personal affair for him. It had not been only the policeman in him that caused him to think of nothing else but the case for months on end.

And now, here in Budapest, it was only with the greatest effort that he could summon up any interest for his assignment.

Martin Beck felt stupidly useless as he sat there. He had several hours to dispose of before his meeting with Szluka, and the only constructive thing he could think of doing was putting the postcard to Ahlberg into the mailbox. It annoyed him that Szluka had asked him (before he had thought of it himself) whether he had checked to see if Matsson had booked a return flight. He took out his map and found one of the airline's branch offices near a square close to the hotel. Afterward he got up, walked through the dining room and the foyer, and put the postcard in the red mailbox outside the hotel entrance. Then he began walking in toward town.

The square was large, with shops and travel agencies and a great deal of traffic. Many people were already sitting at a sidewalk café, drinking coffee at the small tables. Outside this café he saw a stairway that led down underneath the street. "Földalatti" appeared on a sign and he supposed that the word meant W. C. He felt sticky and warm and decided to go down there and wash before he visited the airline office. He crossed the street diagonally and followed two gentlemen carrying briefcases down underground.

He descended into the smallest subway he had ever seen. On the platform was a little glassed-in wooden kiosk painted green and white, and the low roof was held up by decorative cast-iron pillars. The train, which was already standing there, looked more like a dwarf-sized train at an amusement park than an efficient means of transportation. He remembered that this subway was the oldest in Europe.

He paid the fare, and got a ticket at the kiosk and stepped into the little varnished wooden car—it could well have been the same one Emperor Frans Joseph had traveled in when he had opened the line some time at the end of the previous century. There was a pause before the doors closed, and the car was full as the train started.

On the small platform in the middle of the car stood three

men and a woman. They were deaf-mutes and were carrying on a lively conversation in sign language. When the train stopped for the third time, they got off, still eagerly gesticulating. Before the platform filled up again, Martin Beck had time to notice a man sitting at the other end of the car, half-turned away from him.

The man was dark and sunburned and Martin Beck recognized him at once. Instead of the gray jacket he was now wearing a green shirt, open at the neck. There was probably nothing left of the stick he had been whittling on all the previous day.

Suddenly the train plunged out of the tunnel and slowed down. It rode on into a green park with a big pool, shimmering in the sunlight. Then it stopped and the car emptied. This was evidently the end of the line.

The last to step out of the car, Martin Beck looked around for the dark man. He was nowhere to be seen.

A wide road led into the park, which looked cool and inviting, but Martin Beck decided against any further expeditions. He read the timetable on the platform and saw that the stretch between this park and the square where he had got on was the only line and that the train would be returning in a quarter of an hour.

It was half past eleven when he went into Malev's office. The five girls behind the counter were busy with customers, so Martin Beck sat down by the street window to wait.

He had not succeeded in spotting the man with the dark wavy hair on his return from the park, but he presumed that he was still somewhere in the vicinity. He wondered whether he would be tailing him during his meeting with Szluka too.

One of the chairs by the counter became free and Martin Beck went up to it and sat down. The girl behind the counter had her dark hair done in an elaborate set of curls on her forehead. She looked efficient and was smoking a cigarette with a scarlet filter tip.

Martin Beck carried out his errand. Had a Swedish journalist by the name of Alf Matsson booked a flight to Stockholm or anywhere else after the twenty-third of July?

The girl offered him a cigarette and began leafing through her papers. After a while she picked up the telephone and spoke to someone, shook her head and went over to speak to one of her colleagues.

After all five of them had leafed through their lists, it was past twelve o'clock and the girl with the curls informed him that no Alf Matsson had booked a flight on any plane leaving Budapest.

Martin Beck decided to skip lunch and went up to his room. He opened the window and looked down onto the lunch guests below. No tall man in a green shirt was visible.

At one of the tables sat six men in their thirties drinking beer. A thought struck him, and he went over to the telephone and set up a call to Stockholm. Then he lay down on the bed and waited.

A quarter of an hour later the phone rang and he heard Kollberg's voice.

"Hi! How's things?"

"Bad."

"Have you found that chick? Bökk?"

"Yes, but it was nothing. She didn't even know who he was. A musclebound blond boy was standing there feeling her up."

"So it was just a lot of big talk then. He was pretty much of a big mouth, according to his so-called buddies here."

"Have you got a lot to do?"

"Nothing at all. I can go on digging around if you like."

"You can do one thing for me. Find out the names of those guys at the Tankard and what sort of people they are, will you?"

"O.K. Anything else?"

"Be careful. Remember that they probably are journalists, all of them. So long. I'm going swimming now with somebody named Szluka."

"That's a hell of a name for a chick. Martin, listen, have you checked to see if he booked a return flight?"

"Bye," said Martin Beck, and put down the receiver.

He hunted up his bathing trunks from his bag, rolled them up in one of the hotel towels and went down to the boat station.

The boat was called *Óbuda* and one of the unpleasant roofed types. But he was late and it had the advantage of being faster than the coal-fired boats.

He stepped ashore below a large hotel on Margaret Island. Then he followed the road toward the interior of the island, walked swiftly beneath the shady trees along a lush green lawn, past a tennis court, and then he was there.

Szluka was standing waiting outside the entrance, his brief-case in hand. He was dressed as on the previous day.

"I'm sorry to have kept you waiting," said Martin Beck.

"I've just come," said Szluka.

They paid and went into the dressing room. A bald old man in a white undershirt greeted Szluka and unlocked two lockers. Szluka took a pair of black bathing trunks out of his briefcase, swiftly undressed and meticulously hung his clothes on a hanger. They pulled on their bathing trunks simultaneously, although Martin Beck had had considerably fewer garments to remove.

Szluka took his briefcase and went ahead out of the dressing room. Martin Beck followed behind with his towel rolled up in his hand.

The place was full of suntanned people. Immediately in front of the dressing room was a round pool with fountains spouting up tall streams of water. Shrieking children were running in and out under the waterfalls. On one side of the fountain pool was a smaller pool with steps sloping down into the water from one end. On the other was a large pool full of clear green water which darkened toward the middle. This pool was full of swimming and splashing people of all ages. The area between the pools and the lawns was covered with stone slabs.

Martin Beck followed Szluka along the edge of the large pool. In front of them and farther on they could see a semicircular arcade, for which Szluka was evidently heading.

A voice on the loudspeaker called out some information and a mob of people began to run toward the pool with the steps leading down into it. Martin Beck was almost knocked over and followed Szluka's example, stepping to one side until the rush was over. He looked inquiringly at Szluka, who said:

"Wave bathing."

Martin Beck watched the small pool swiftly filling with people, who finally stood packed like sardines. A pair of huge pumps began to swish water toward the high edges of the pool and the human shoal rocked on the high waves, amid cries of delight.

"Perhaps you'd like to go and ride the waves," said Szluka.

Martin Beck looked at him. He was quite serious.

"No, thank you," said Martin Beck.

"Personally, I usually bathe in the sulfur spring," said Szluka. "It is very relaxing."

The spring ran from a stone cairn in the middle of an oval pool—the water was knee-deep there and its far end was shaded by the arcade. The pool was built like a labyrinth, with walls that rose about ten inches above ground level. The walls formed back supports for molded armchairs in which one sat with the water up to one's chin.

Szluka stepped down into the pool and began to wade between the rows of seated people. He was still holding his briefcase in his hand. Martin Beck wondered if he was so used to carrying it that he had forgotten to put it down, but he said nothing and stepped down into the pool and began to wade along at Szluka's heels.

The water was quite warm and the steam smelled of sulfur. Szluka waded into the colonnade, put down his briefcase on the edge of the wall and sat down in the water. Martin Beck sat down beside him. It was very comfortable in the spacious stone armchair, which had broad arms about six inches below the surface of the water.

Szluka leaned his head against the back and closed his eyes. Martin Beck said nothing and looked at the bathers.

Nearly opposite him sat a small, pale, thin man, bouncing a fat blonde on his knee. They were both looking seriously and absent-mindedly at a little girl who was splashing about in front of them with a rubber ring around her stomach.

A pale, freckled boy in white bathing trunks came slowly wading by. Behind him he was towing a sturdy youth by a loose grip on his big toe. The youth was lying on his back, staring up at the sky, his hands clasped over his stomach.

On the edge of the pool stood a tall sunburned man with wavy dark hair. His bathing trunks were pale-blue with wide flapping legs, more like undershorts than trunks. Martin Beck suspected that this was in fact the case. Perhaps he should have warned him that he was going swimming, so that the man would have had time to go and get his trunks.

Suddenly, without opening his eyes, Szluka said, "The key was lying on the steps of the police station. A patrolman found it there."

Martin Beck looked in surprise at Szluka, who was lying utterly relaxed beside him. The hair on his sunburned chest was fluttering slowly about like white seaweed in the shimmering green water.

"How did it get there?"

Szluka turned his head and looked at him beneath half-closed lids.

"You won't believe me, of course, but the fact is, I don't know."

A long-drawn-out cry of disappointment, in unison, was heard coming from the smaller pool. The wave bathing was over for this time and the large pool filled up with people again.

"Yesterday you didn't want to tell me where you'd got the key from. Why did you tell me now?" said Martin Beck.

"As you seem to misinterpret most things anyway, and it was a piece of information you could have got hold of elsewhere, I considered it better to tell you myself."

After a while Martin Beck said, "Why are you having me tailed?"

"I don't understand what you're talking about," said Szluka.

"What did you have for lunch?"

"Fish soup and carp," said Szluka.

"And applestrudel?"

"No, wild strawberries and whipped cream and powdered sugar," said Szluka. "Delicious."

Martin Beck looked around. The man in the undershorts had gone.

"When was the key found?" he said.

"The day before it was handed in to the hotel. On the afternoon of the twenty-third of July."

"On the same day that Alf Matsson disappeared, in fact."

Szluka straightened up and looked at Martin Beck. Then he turned around, opened his briefcase, took out a towel and dried his hands. Then he pulled out a file and leafed through it.

"We have made some inquiries, actually" he said, "despite the fact that we have had no official request for an investigation."

He took a paper out of the file and went on, "You seem to be taking this matter more seriously than appears to be necessary. Is he an important person, this Alf Matsson?"

"Insofar as he has disappeared in a way that can't be explained, yes. We consider that sufficiently important grounds to find out what's happened to him."

"What is there to indicate that something has happened to him?"

"Nothing. But the fact is, he's gone."

Szluka looked at his paper.

"According to the passport and customs authorities, no Swedish citizen by the name Alf Matsson has left Hungary since the twenty-second of July. Anyway, he left his passport at the hotel, and he can hardly have left the country without it. No person—known or unknown—who might have been this Alf Matsson has been taken to a hospital or morgue here in this country during the period in question. Without his passport, Matsson cannot have been accepted at any other hotel in the country either. Consequently, everything indicates that for some reason or another your compatriot has made up his mind to stay in Hungary for an additional period."

Szluka put the paper back into the file and closed his briefcase.

"The man's been here before. Perhaps he's acquired some friends and is staying with them," he went on, settling himself down again.

"And yet there's no reasonable explanation for his leaving the hotel and not letting anyone know where he is," said Martin Beck a little later.

Szluka rose and picked up his briefcase.

"So long as he has a valid visa, I cannot—as I said—do anything more in the matter," he said.

Martin Beck also rose.

"Stay where you are," said Szluka. "Unfortunately I have to go. But perhaps we'll meet again. Good-bye."

They shook hands and Martin Beck watched him wading away with his briefcase. From his appearance, one would not think he ate four slices of fat bacon for breakfast.

When Szluka had disappeared, Martin Beck went over to the large pool. The warm water and sulfur fumes had made him drowsy, and he swam around for a while in the clear cooling water before sitting in the sun on the edge of the pool to dry. For a while he watched two deadly serious middle-aged men standing in the shallow end of the pool, tossing a red ball to each other.

Then he went in to change. He felt lost and confused. He was none the wiser for his meeting with Szluka.

14

After his bathe, the heat did not seem quite so oppressive any longer. Martin Beck found no reason to overtax his strength. He strolled slowly along the paths in the spacious park, often stopping to look around. He saw no sign of his shadow. Perhaps they had at last realized how harmless he was and had given up. On the other hand, the whole island was swarming with people and it was difficult to pick out anyone special in the crowd, especially when one had no idea what the person concerned looked like. He made his way down to the water on the eastern side of the island and followed the shoreline out to a landing stage where all the boats he had previously ridden on came in. He thought he could even remember the name of the station: Casino.

Along the edge of the shore above the landing stage stood a row of benches where a few people were waiting for the boats. On one of them sat one of the few people in Budapest familiar to him: the easily frightened girl from the house in Újpest. Ari Boeck was wearing sunglasses, sandals and a white dress with shoulder straps. She was reading a German paperback and beside her on the bench lay a nylon string bag. His first thought was to walk past, but then he regretted it, halted and said, "Good afternoon."

She raised her eyes and looked at him blankly. Then she appeared to recognize him and smiled.

"Oh, it's you, is it? Have you found your friend?"

"No, not yet."

"I thought about it after you'd gone yesterday. I can't understand how he came to give you my address."

"I don't understand it either."

"I thought about it last night too," she said frowning. "I could hardly sleep."

"Yes, it's peculiar."

(Not at all, my dear girl, there's an extremely simple explanation. For one thing, he didn't give me any address. For another, this is probably what happened: he saw you in Stockholm when you were swimming and thought there's a sweet piece, I'd like to—yes, exactly. And then when he came here six months later, he found out your address and the location of your street, but didn't have time to go there.)

"Won't you sit down? It's almost too hot to be standing upright today."

He sat down as she moved the nylon net. It held two things he recognized, namely the dark-blue bathing suit and the green rubber mask, as well as a rolled-up bath towel and a bottle of suntan oil.

(Martin Beck, the born detective and famous observer, constantly occupied making useless observations and storing them away for future use. Doesn't even have bats in his belfry—they couldn't get in for all the crap in the way.)

"Are you waiting for the boat too?"

"Yes," he said. "But we're probably going in different directions."

"I don't have anything special to do. I was thinking of going home, of course."

"Have you been swimming?"

(The art of deduction.)

"Yes, of course. Why do you ask that?"

(Well, that's a very good question.)

"What have you done with your boyfriend today?"

(What the hell has that got to do with me? Oh, it's just an interrogation technique.)

"Tetz? He's gone. Anyway, he's not my boyfriend."

"Oh, isn't he?"

(Extremely spiritual.)

"Just a boy I know. He stays at the boarding house now and again. He's a nice guy."

She shrugged her shoulders. He looked at her feet. They were still short and broad with straight toes.

(Martin Beck, the incorruptible, more interested in a woman's shoe size than the color of her nipples.)

"Uh-huh. And now you're going home, are you?"

(The wearing-them-down treatment.)

"Well, I thought I would. I don't have anything special to do around this time of the summer. What are you going to do yourself?"

"I don't know."

(At last a word of truth.)

"Have you been up to Gellért Hill to look at the view? From the Liberation Memorial?"

"No."

"You can see the whole city from there, as if it were on a tray."

"Mm-m."

"Shall we go there? Perhaps there'll even be a little breeze up there."

"Why not?" said Martin Beck.

(You can always keep your eyes open.)

"Then we'll take the boat that's coming in now. You would have taken that one anyway."

The boat was called Ifjugárda and had probably been built on the same design as the steamer he had been on the day before. The ventilators, however, were constructed differently and the funnel was slightly aft-braced.

They stood by the railing. The boat slid swiftly midstream toward Margaret Bridge. Just under the arch, she said, "What's your name, by the way."

"Martin."

"Mine's Ari. But you knew that before, didn't you—however that happened."

He gave no reply to that, but after a while said, "What does this name mean—Ifjugárda?"

"A member of the Youth Guard."

The view from the Liberation Memorial lived up to her promise and more so. There was even a little breeze up there, too. They had gone all the way on the boat to the last stop in front of the famous Gellért Hotel, then walked a bit along a street named after Béla Bártok and finally got on a bus which slowly and laboriously had taken them to the top of the hill.

Now they were standing on the parapet of the citadel above the monument. Beneath them lay the city, with hundreds of thousands of windows glowing in the late afternoon sun. They were standing so close to each other that he felt a light, brushing touch when she swung her body. For the first time in five days, he allowed himself to be caught thinking about something other than Alf Matsson.

"There's the museum I work in, over there," she said. "It's closed during the summer."

"Oh."

"Otherwise I go to the university."

"Uh-huh."

They went down on foot, along twisting paths traversing the bank down to the river. Then they walked across the new bridge and found themselves close to his hotel. The sun had rolled down below the hills in the northwest and a soft, warm dusk had fallen over the river.

"Well, what shall we do now?" said Ari Boeck.

She held him lightly by his arm and swung her body playfully as they walked along the quay.

"We could talk about Alf Matsson," said Martin Beck.

The woman gave him a swift look of reproach, but the next moment was smiling as she said, "Yes, why not? How is he? Are you great friends?"

"No, not at all. I only . . . know him."

At this stage he was almost convinced that she was telling the truth and that his vague idea that had taken him to the house in Újpest had been a false trail. But it's an ill wind that brings no one any good, he thought.

She was clinging to his arm a little now and zigzagging with her feet so that her body swung back and forth on a vertical axle.

"What kind of boat is that?" he said.

"It goes on moonlight cruises up the river, then around Margaret Island and back. It takes about an hour. Costs next to nothing. Shall we go along on it?"

They went on board and soon afterward the boat set out, peacefully splashing in the dark current. Of all the types of engine-driven vessels yet constructed, there is none that moves so pleasantly as the paddle steamer.

They stood above the wheelhouse and watched the shores gliding by. She leaned against him, quite lightly, and he now felt very clearly something he had noticed earlier: that she had no bra on under her dress.

A small ensemble was playing on the afterdeck and a number of people were dancing.

"Do you want to dance?" she said.

"No," said Martin Beck.

"Good. I don't think it's much fun either."

A moment later she said, "But I can, if necessary."

"So can I," said Martin Beck.

The boat passed Margaret Island and Újpest, before turning and soundlessly gliding back southward with the current. They stood behind the funnel for a moment and looked through the open hatches. The engine was beating with calm pulse beats, the copper pipes were shining and the warm oily current of air was flung upward in their direction.

"Have you been on this boat before?" he said.

"Yes, many a time. It's the best thing to do in this city on a really hot evening."

He did not really know who she was and what he thought of her, and this, above all else, irritated him.

The boat passed the colossal Parliament building—where nowadays a small red star shone discreetly above the central cupola—and then it slipped its lowered funnel under the bridge with large stone lions on it and hove to at the same place as where they started.

As they walked along the gangplank, Martin Beck let his eyes sweep over the quay. Under the lamp by the ticket office stood the tall man with dark hair brushed back on his head. He was again wearing his blue suit and was staring straight at them. A moment later the man turned around and vanished with swift steps behind the shelter. The woman followed Martin Beck's glance and put her left hand in his right one, suddenly but carefully.

"Did you see that man?" he said.

"Yes," she said.

"Do you know who he is?"

She shook her head.

"No. Do you?"

"No, not yet."

Martin Beck felt hungry for once. He had had no lunch and the dinner hour would soon be over.

"Would you like to come and have a meal with me?"

"Where?"

"At the hotel."

"Can I go there in these clothes?"

"Sure."

He almost added, "We're not in Sweden now."

Quite a number of people were still in the dining room and along the balustrade outside the open windows. Swarms of insects were dancing around the lamps.

"Little gnats," she said. "They don't sting. When they disappear, the summer's over. Did you know that?"

The food was excellent, as usual, and so was the wine. She was evidently hungry and ate with a healthy, youthful greed. Then she sat still and listened to the music. They smoked with their coffee and drank a kind of cherry-brandy liqueur which also tasted of chocolate. When she put out her cigarette in the ash tray, she brushed his right hand with her fingertips, as if by accident. A little later she repeated the maneuver and soon after that he felt her foot against his ankle under the table. Evidently she had kicked off her sandal.

After a while she moved her foot and her hand away and went off to the powder room.

Martin Beck thoughtfully massaged his hairline with the fingers of his right hand. Then he leaned over the table and picked up the nylon string bag that was lying on the chair beside him. He thrust his hand into it, unfolded the bathing suit and felt it. The material was completely dry, even in the seams and along the elastic. So dry that it could hardly have been in contact with water during the past twenty-four hours. He rolled up the bathing suit, put the net carefully back on the chair and bit his knuckle thoughtfully. Naturally it did not necessarily mean anything. In any case, he was still behaving like an idiot.

She came back and sat down, smiling at him. She crossed her legs, lit another cigarette and listened to the Viennese melody.

"How lovely it is," she said.

He nodded.

The dining room began to empty, the waiters gathering together in groups, talking. The musicians ended the evening's concert with "The Blue Danube." She looked at the clock.

"I must be going home."

He thought about this intensely. One floor up there was a small night-club-type bar with jazz music, but he loathed that kind of place so profoundly that only the most pressing assignment could make him go into them. Perhaps this was just what this was?

"How will you get home?" he said. "By boat?"

"No, the last one's gone. I'll go by trolley. It's quicker, in fact."

He went on thinking. In all its simplicity, the situation was somewhat complicated. Why, he did not know.

He chose to do nothing and say nothing. The musicians went away, bowing in exhaustion. She looked at the clock again.

"I'd better go now," she said.

The night porter bowed in the vestibule. The doorman whirled them respectfully out through the revolving doors.

They stood on the pavement, alone in the warm night air. She took a short step so that she was standing facing him, with her right leg between his. She stood on tiptoe and kissed him. Very clearly, he felt her breasts and stomach and loins and thighs through the material of her dress. She could hardly reach up to him.

"Oh my, how tall you are," she said.

She made a small supple movement and again stood firmly on the ground, an inch or so from him.

"Thank you for everything," she said. "See you again soon. Bye."

She walked away, turned her head and waved her right hand. The net with her bathing things in it swung against her left leg.

"Bye," said Martin Beck.

He went back into the vestibule, picked up his key and went up to his room. It was stuffy in there and he opened the window at once. He took off his shirt and shoes, went out to the bathroom and rinsed his face and chest with cold water. He felt a bigger idiot than ever.

"I must be completely nuts," he said. "What luck no one saw me."

At that moment there was a light tap on the door. The handle went down, and she came in.

"I crept past," she said. "No one saw me."

She closed the door behind her, quickly and quietly, took two steps into the room, dropped the net onto the floor and stepped out of her sandals. He stared at her. Her eyes had

changed and were cloudy, as if there were a veil over them. She
bent down with her arms crossed, took hold of the hem of her
dress with both hands and pulled off her dress in one swift
movement. She had nothing on underneath. This in itself was
not so surprising. Obviously she always sunbathed in the same
bathing suit, for across her breasts and hips ran sharply demarcated areas which looked chalk-white against the rest of her
dark-brown skin. Her breasts were smooth and white and
round, and her nipples were large and pink and cylindrical,
like anchored buoys. The jet-black hair growing up from her
loins was also sharply demarcated: an inscribed triangle that
filled a considerable part of the rectangular, white strip of skin.
The hair was curly and thick and stiff, as if electric. The areas
around her nipples was circular and light-brown. She looked
like a highly colored geometrical old man.

His depressing years with the Public Morals Squad had
made Martin Beck immune to provocations of this kind. And
even if this were perhaps not really provocation in the proper
sense of the term, he still found the situation far easier to deal
with than what had irritated him in the dining room half an
hour earlier. Before she even had time to get her dress over
her head, he put his hand on her shoulder and said:

"Just a minute."

She lowered the dress a little and looked at him over the
hem with glazed brown eyes, which neither reacted nor com-
prehended. She had got her left arm free from the dress. She
stretched it out, gripped hold of his right hand and slowly
drew it down between her legs. Her sex was swollen and open.
Vaginal secretion ran down his fingers.

"Feel it," she said, with a sort of helplessness, far beyond
good or evil.

Martin Beck freed himself, stretched out his arm, opened
the door to the hotel corridor and said in his schoolroom
German:

"Please dress yourself."

She stood still for a moment, quite nonplussed, just as
when he had knocked on the door in Újpest. Then she obeyed.

He put on his shirt and shoes, picked up her string bag and
led her down to the vestibule with a light grip on her arm.

"Call for a taxi," he said to the night porter.

The taxi came almost at once. He opened the door, but as
he was going to help her in, she freed herself vehemently.

"I'll pay the driver," he said.

She cast a look at him. The cloudy veil had gone. The patient had recovered. Her eyes were clear and dark and full of loathing.

"Like hell you will," she said. "Drive on."

She slammed the door and the taxi rolled away.

Martin Beck looked around. It was already long past midnight. He walked a bit south, up onto the new bridge, which was also deserted except for a few night trolleys. He stopped in the middle of the bridge and leaned against the railing, looking down into the silently running water. It was warm and empty and silent. An ideal place to think—if a man only knew what to think. After a while he went back to the hotel. Ari Boeck had dropped a cigarette with a red filter tip on the floor. He picked it up and lit it. It tasted unpleasant and he threw it out the window.

15

Martin Beck was lying in the bathtub when the telephone rang.

He had slept past breakfast and taken a walk on the quay before lunch. The sun was hotter than ever, and even down by the river, the air was not moving at all. When he returned to the hotel, he had felt a greater need for a quick bath than for food, and had decided to let lunch wait. Now he was lying in the lukewarm water and heard the telephone ring with short quick signals.

He climbed out of the tub, swept a large bath towel around him and lifted the receiver.

"Mr. Beck?"

"Yes?"

"Please forgive me for not using your title. As you will understand, it is purely—well, let's say a, well . . . precautionary measure."

It was the young man from the Embassy. Martin Beck wondered whom this precautionary measure was against, as both the hotel people and Szluka knew he was a policeman, but he said, "Of course."

"How are things going? Have you made any progress?"

Martin Beck let the bath towel fall and sat down on the bed.

"No," he said.

"Haven't you got any clues?"

"No," said Martin Beck.

There was a brief silence, and then he added, "I've spoken to the police here."

"I think that was a singularly unwise move," said the man from the Embassy.

"Possibly," said Martin Beck. "I could hardly avoid it. I was visited by a gentleman called Vilmos Szluka."

"Major Szluka. What did he want?"

"Nothing. He probably said more or less the same thing to me as he already said to you. That he had no reason to take up the case."

"I see. What are you thinking of doing now?"

"Having some lunch," said Martin Beck.

"I mean about the matter we were discussing."

"I don't know."

There was another silence. Then the young man said, "Well, you know where to phone if there's anything."

"Yes."

"Good-bye, then."

"Good-bye."

Martin Beck put down the receiver and went out and pulled the plug out of the bathtub. Then he dressed and went down and sat under the awning outside the dining room and ordered lunch.

It was uncomfortably hot even in the shade of the awning. He ate slowly, taking large gulps of the cold beer. He had an unpleasant feeling of being watched. He had not seen the tall, dark-haired man, but all the same he continually felt he was under surveillance.

He looked at the people around him. They were the usual gathering of lunch guests—mostly foreigners like himself and most of them staying at the hotel. He heard scattered fragments of conversation, mainly in German and Hungarian, but also English and some language he could not identify.

Suddenly he heard someone behind him say quite clearly in Swedish: "Crispbread." He turned around and saw two ladies, undeniably Swedish, sitting by the window in the dining room.

He heard one of them say, "Yes, I always take some with me. And toilet paper. It's always so bad abroad. If there is any at all."

"Yes," said the other. "I remember once in Spain . . ."

Martin Beck gave up listening to this typically Swedish conversation, and devoted himself to trying to decide which of those sitting around him was his shadow. For a long time he suspected a man who was past middle age—he was sitting some way away with his back to him and kept glancing over his shoulder in his direction. But then the man got up and lifted down a fluffy little dog that had been sitting, concealed, on his lap and vanished with the dog around the corner of the hotel.

When Martin Beck had finished eating and had drunk a cup of that strong coffee, much of the afternoon was already gone. It was exhaustingly hot, but he walked up into town for a bit, trying to keep in the shade all the time. He had discovered that the police station was only a few blocks away from the hotel and had no difficulty in finding it. On the steps—where the key had been found, according to Szluka—there was a patrolman in blue-gray uniform standing wiping the sweat from his forehead.

Martin Beck circled the police station and took another route home, all the time with an unpleasant feeling he was being watched. This was something quite new to him. During his twenty-three years with the police, he had many times been involved in keeping a watch on suspected persons and shadowing them. Only now did he understand to the full what it felt like to be shadowed. To know that all the while one was being observed and watched, that every movement one made was being registered, that all the time someone was keeping himself hidden somewhere in the vicinity, following every step one took.

Martin Beck went up to his room and stayed there in the relative cool for the rest of the day. He sat at the table with a piece of paper in front of him and a pen in hand, trying to make some kind of summary of what he knew about the Alf Matsson case.

In the end he tore up the paper into little pieces and flushed them down the toilet. What he knew was so infinitesimal that it seemed simply foolish to write it down. He would not have to strain himself to keep it all in mind. Actually, thought Martin Beck, he knew no more than what could be contained in a shrimp's brain.

The sun went down and colored the river red, the brief dusk passed unnoticeably into a velvet darkness, and with the dark came the first cool breezes from the hills down across the river.

Martin Beck stood by his window and watched the surface of the water being rippled by the light evening breeze. A man was standing by a tree just below his window. A cigarette glowed and Martin Beck thought he recognized the tall dark man. In some way it was a relief to see him there, to escape that vague, creeping sense of his presence in the vicinity.

He put on a suit, went down to the dining room and had dinner. He ate as slowly as possible and drank two *barack palinkas* before going up to his room again.

The evening breeze had gone, the river lay black and shiny, and the heat was just as suffocating outside as inside in the room.

Martin Beck left the windows and shutters open and drew back the curtains. Then he undressed and got into the creaking bed.

16

Heat that is really intense almost always becomes harder to tolerate when the sun has gone down. Anyone who is used to heat knows the routine and closes the window and shutters and draws the curtains. Like most Scandinavians, Martin Beck lacked these instincts. He had drawn back the curtains and opened the windows wide and was lying on his back in the dark, waiting for the cool air. It never came. He switched on the bedside lamp and tried to read. That did not work very well either. He did have a box of sleeping tablets in the bathroom, but was not very willing to take that way out. The past day had gone by without any positive achievements on his part and consequently there was every reason for him to try to remain on the alert and somehow produce results tomorrow. If he took the sleeping tablets, he would be walking around as if in a trance the next morning: he knew this of old.

He got up and sat down by the open window. The difference was infinitesimal: there was not the slightest draft, nor even a hot breeze from the Hungarian steppes, wherever they were. The city seemed almost as if it, too, had difficulty breathing, had fallen into a coma and become unconscious from the heat. After a while a lone yellow trolley appeared on the other side of the river. It drove slowly across Elisabeth Bridge, and the sound of the wheels' friction against the rails echoed and grew louder under the arch of the bridge before it rolled away across the water. Despite the distance, he could see that it was empty. Twenty-three hours earlier, he had been standing up there on the bridge, puzzling over his strange meeting with the woman from Ujpest. It had not been a bad place.

He pulled on his trousers and shirt and went out. The porter's desk was empty. On the street, a green Skoda started up and drove slowly and reluctantly around the corner. Pairs of lovers in cars are the same the world over. He walked along the edge of the quay—past some sleeping boats—went by the statue of the Hungarian poet Petőfi and then came up onto the bridge. It was quite silent and deserted, as on the preceding night, and was clearly lit up, in contrast to many of the city streets. Again he stopped on the middle of the bridge, his elbows on the parapet, and stared down into the water. A tugboat passed beneath him. Far behind it came its load, four long barges tied together in pairs. Soundlessly gliding with all their lights extinguished, only a shade darker than the night.

As he moved on a few yards, he heard his own footsteps give a faint echo somewhere on the silent bridge. He walked on a bit farther and again heard the echo. It seemed as if the sound could be heard a trifle too long. He stood still listening for a long time, but heard nothing. Then he walked quickly on for about twenty yards and stopped suddenly. The sound came again, and this time, too, he thought it came too late to be truly an echo. He walked as quietly as he could across to the other side of the bridge and looked back. It was quite silent now. Nothing moved. A trolley from the Pest side came up onto the bridge and made any further observations impossible. Martin Beck continued his promenade across the bridge. Evidently he was suffering from persecution mania. If someone had the energy and resources to watch him at this time of night, then it could hardly be anyone else but the police. And with that the problem was largely solved. So long as . . .

Martin Beck was almost over the bridge below Gellért Hill when the trolley rattled past. A lone passenger was sleeping with his mouth open, leaning against one of the windows.

He reached the steps leading down to the quay from the south side of the bridge and began to walk down them. Through the retreating rattle of the trolley, he thought he heard the sound of a car, which stopped somewhere in the vicinity, but he could not decide how far away or in which direction from him.

Martin Beck had reached the quay. Swiftly and silently he

walked south, away from the bridge, and stopped where the darkness was thickest. He turned around, stood quite still and listened. Nothing could be heard or seen. In all probability there was no one on the bridge, but this in itself was not certain. If someone had followed him from the other side, he could easily also have got to the end of the bridge and gone down to the quay from the north side of the bridge. He was sure that no one other than himself had gone down the south steps.

The slight sounds which could be heard now came from traffic very far away. There was complete silence in the immediate vicinity. Martin Beck smiled in the darkness. He was now almost convinced that no one had followed him, but the game amused him, and in his innermost self he wished that there were some confused fellow creature over there in the dark on the other side of the bridge. He himself knew the routine backward and forward and knew that whoever might have gone down on the other side could not take the risk of returning the same way, crossing the bridge and going down the steps on the south side. Under the bridge two parallel streets ran along the quay, the inner one nearly six feet higher than the quay itself, which in its turn sloped down toward the river in steps. The two streets were separated by a low wall. Farther up, there was also a tunnel through the actual foundations of the bridge. But none of these ways was accessible to anyone shadowing him, provided that person knew his job. Every attempt to pass under the bridge would mean that the man would have the light behind him and thus risk immediate discovery. Consequently only one alternative remained: to go around the entire abutment of the bridge in a wide semicircle, cross several approach ramps and make his way down onto the quay as far south as possible. But this would take some time, even if the man took the risk of running, and during that time the person being shadowed—in this case Inspector Martin Beck from Stockholm—would have time to vanish in practically any direction he chose.

Now it was unlikely, however, that there was anyone shadowing him at all, and in addition Martin Beck had intended to walk north along the river and return to the hotel via the next bridge. Consequently, he left his observation post in the sheltering darkness and walked north at an easy pace. He chose the inner of the two streets, passed under the bridge and continued along the stone wall, six feet above the quay. On the opposite shore the hotel was dark except for two narrow perpendicular rectangles of light. The windows of his own room. He sat down on the low stone wall and lit a cigarette. Large houses of the kind built at the turn of the century lined the street. In front of them stood parked cars. All the windows were shuttered and dark. Martin Beck sat still and listened to the silence. He was still on guard, but without being conscious of the fact himself.

On the other side of the street a car engine started up. He let his eyes sweep along the row of parked vehicles but could not locate the noise. The engine was turning over slowly, purring. This continued for about thirty seconds. Then he heard the car being put into gear. A pair of parking lights went on. More than fifty yards ahead a car came out of the shadows and moved away from the edge of the pavement. It came in his direction, but on the other side of the street, and extremely slowly. A dark-green Skoda, and he had a feeling he had seen it before. The car came nearer. Martin Beck sat still on the stone wall and followed it with his eyes. Almost level with him, it began to turn to the left, as if the driver were going to turn around in the street. But the turn was not completed: the car was moving almost more slowly than before, straight at him. Obviously someone wanted to meet him, but his way of going about it was astounding. The idea could hardly be to run him down—not at that speed—and, besides, he could get to safety behind the wall in a second, if necessary. Provided no one was hiding in the back seat, there was only one person in the car.

Martin Beck put out his cigarette. He was in no way afraid, but very curious to know what was going to happen.

The green Skoda had stopped with its engine running and its right front wheel against the curb, only nine feet away from him. The driver switched on the headlights and everything was drowned in a flood of light. But only for a few seconds, then all the lights went out. The car door opened and a man stepped out onto the pavement.

Martin Beck had seen him often enough to be able to recognize him at once, despite the blinding effect of the light. The tall man with dark hair brushed back on his head. The man was empty-handed. He took a step nearer. The engine of the car purred slowly.

He sensed something. Not a shadow, nor even a sound,

only a small movement in the air, just behind him. So faint that only the stillness of the night made it perceptible.

Martin Beck knew that he was no longer alone on the wall, that the car was only meant to distract his attention while someone silently approached down on the quay and heaved himself up onto the stone wall behind him.

And in the same second he also realized clearly and pene-tratingly that this was not shadowing, not a game, but deadly serious. And more than that. It was death: this time out for *him,* and not by chance, but in a cold, calculated, premeditated fashion.

Martin Beck was a bad fighter, but his reflex actions were remarkable. At the exact moment he felt the slight draft, he ducked his head down between his shoulders, put his right foot upon the edge of the wall, kicked away, twisted his body and threw himself backward, all in one lightning movement. The arm that had been on its way around his throat was pressed hard against the ridge of his nose and eyebrows be-fore it slid away over his forehead. He felt a hot, astonished breath against his cheek and caught the swift glint of a knife blade, which had already missed its mark and was on its way away from him. He fell backward down onto the quay, hit his left shoulder hard on the stone paving and rolled around to give himself time, if possible, to get his balance and get onto his feet. On the wall he saw two figures, silhouetted against the starry sky. Then there was only one and while he still had one knee on the stone paving, the man with the knife was on him again. His left arm was temporarily paralyzed after his fall against the quay, but for a second or two the light was in his favor: he himself was low in the dark and the other man was etched against the background. His attacker missed and a sec-ond later Martin Beck managed to seize hold of the man's right wrist. It was not a good grip and the wrist was unusually large, but he held on, very conscious of the fact that it was his only chance. For a tenth of a second or so, they stood up and he noted that the other man was shorter than himself, but considerably broader. Mechanically, he applied one of the hoary old method holds learned at police college and suc-ceeded in getting his opponent onto the ground. The only thing wrong was that he did not dare let go of the hand with the knife and was himself drawn down in the fall. They rolled around once and were now extremely close to the edge of the quay, where the steps down to the water began. The paralysis in his left arm had let up and he got a hold on the man's other wrist. But his opponent was stronger and slowly broke away. A hard kick in the head reminded him that he was not only physically but also numerically inferior. He was now lying on his back so close to the stairs that he felt the first step with his foot. The man with the knife was panting heavily in his face, smelling of sweat, shaving water and throat pastilles. His opponent began slowly but relentlessly to free his right hand.

Martin Beck felt it was all over—at least very nearly. Lightning bolts clashed in the throbbing haze, his heart seemed to swell more and more and more, like a purple tumor about to burst. His head was thumping like a pile driver. He thought he heard terrible roars, shots, piercing shrieks, and he saw the world drowned in a flood of blinding white light that obliterated all shapes and all life. His last conscious thought was that he was going to die here on a quay in a foreign city, just as Alf Matsson had presumably done, and without knowing why.

With a last reflex-like effort, Martin Beck gripped the other man's right wrist with both hands as he kicked with his foot and tipped both himself and his opponent over the edge of the quay. He hit his head on the second step and lost consciousness.

Martin Beck opened his eyes after an epoch of time that seemed boundless, and that in any case must have been very long. Everything was bathed in a white light. He was lying on his back with his head to one side and his right ear against the stone paving. The first thing he saw was a pair of well-polished black shoes, which almost filled his field of vision. He turned his head and looked up.

Szluka, in a gray suit and with that silly hunting hat still on his head, bent down over him and said:

"Good evening."

Martin Beck propped himself up on his elbow. The flood of light was coming from two police cars, one on the quay and the other driven up to the stone wall on the street above. About ten feet away from Szluka stood a policeman in a visored cap, black leather boots and a light-gray-blue uniform. He was holding a black night stick in his right hand and looking thoughtfully at a person lying at his feet. It was Tetz Radeberger, the man who had played with Ari Boeck's bathing suit in the house in Újpest. He was now on his back, deeply unconscious, with blood on his forehead and in his blond hair.

"The other one," said Martin Beck. "Where is he?"

"Shot," said Szluka. "Carefully, of course. In the leg."

A number of windows had been thrown open in the houses along the street and people were peering inquisitively down toward the quay.

"Lie still," said Szluka. "The ambulance will be here soon."

"No need," said Martin Beck, beginning to get up.

Exactly three minutes and fifteen seconds had passed since he had been sitting on the stone wall and had felt that draft at the back of his neck.

17

The car was a blue-and-white 1962 model Warsvawa. It had a flashing blue light on the roof and the siren sounded in a subdued, melancholy wail along the empty night streets. The word RENDŐRSÉG was painted in block capitals in the white band across the front door. It meant police.

Martin Beck was sitting in the back seat. At his side sat a uniformed officer. Szluka was sitting in the front seat, to the right of the driver.

"You did well," said Szluka. "Rather dangerous young men, those two."

"Who put Radeberger out of action?"

"He's sitting beside you," said Szluka. Martin Beck turned his head. The policeman had a narrow black mustache and brown eyes with a sympathetic look in them.

"He speaks only Hungarian," said Szluka.

"What's his name?"

"Foti."

Martin Beck put out his hand.

"Thanks, Foti," he said.

"He had to give it to them pretty hard," said Szluka. "Hadn't much time."

"Lucky he was around," said Martin Beck.

"We're usually around," said Szluka. "Except in the cartoons."

"They have their hangout in Újpest," said Martin Beck. "A boarding house on Venetianer út."

"We know that."

Szluka sat quietly a moment. Then he asked, "How did you come into contact with them?"

"Through a woman named Boeck. Matsson had asked for her address. And she had been in Stockholm. Competing as a swimmer. There could be a connection. That's why I looked her up."

"And what did she say?"

"That she was studying at the university and working at a museum. And that she had never heard of Matsson."

They had reached the police station at Deák Ferenc Tér. The car swung into a concrete yard and stopped. Martin Beck followed Szluka up to his office. It was very spacious and the wall was covered with a large map of Budapest, but to all intents and purposes it reminded him of his own office back in Stockholm. Szluka hung up his hunting hat and pointed to a chair. He opened his mouth, but before he had time to say anything, the telephone rang. He went over to his desk and answered. Martin Beck thought he could make out a torrent of words. It went on for a long time. Now and again Szluka replied in monosyllables. After a while he looked at his watch, exploded in a rapid, irritated harangue and put down the receiver.

"My wife," he said.

He went over to the map and studied the northern part of the city, with his back to his visitor.

"Being a policeman," said Szluka, "is not a profession. And it's certainly not a vocation either. It's a curse."

A little later he turned around and said:

"Of course, I don't mean that. Only think it sometimes. Are you married?"

"Yes."

"Then you know."

A policeman in uniform came in and put down a tray with two cups of coffee on it. They drank. Szluka looked at his watch.

"We're searching the place up there at the moment. The report should soon be here."

"How did you manage to be around?" said Martin Beck.

Szluka replied with exactly the same sentence as in the car.

"We're usually around."

Then he smiled and said, "It was what you said about being shadowed. Naturally it wasn't us watching you. Why should we do that?"

Martin Beck poked his nose, a little conscience-stricken.

"People imagine so many things," said Szluka. "But of course you're a policeman, and policemen seldom do. So we began to watch the man who was tailing you. Backtailing as the Americans call it, if I remember rightly. This afternoon our man saw that there were two men watching you. He thought it looked peculiar and sounded the alarm. It's as simple as that."

Martin Beck nodded. Szluka looked at him thoughtfully.

"And yet it was all so quick we just barely got there in time."

He finished his coffee and carefully put his cup down.

"Backtailing," he said, as if savoring the word. "Have you ever been to America?"

"No."

"Neither have I."

"I worked with them on a case, two years ago. With someone called Kafka."

"Sounds Czech."

"It was an American tourist who got murdered in Sweden. Ugly story. Complicated investigation."

Szluka sat silent for a moment. Then he said abruptly, "How did it go?"

"O.K.," said Martin Beck.

"I've only read about the American police. They have a peculiar organization. Difficult to understand."

Martin Beck nodded.

"And a lot to do," said Szluka. "They have as many murders in New York in a week as we have in the whole country in a year."

A uniformed police officer with two stars on his shoulder straps came into the room. He discussed something with Szluka, saluted Martin Beck and left. While the door was standing open, Ari Boeck walked along the corridor outside, with a woman guard. She was wearing the same white dress and the same sandals as the day before, but had a shawl over her shoulders. She threw a flat, vacant look at Martin Beck.

"Nothing of importance in Újpest," said Szluka. "We're taking the car apart now. When Radeberger comes around and the other one has been patched up, we'll tackle them. There's quite a bit I still don't understand."

He fell silent, hesitantly.

"But things will clear up soon."

The telephone rang and he was occupied for a while. Martin Beck understood nothing of the conversation except now and again the word *"Svéd"* and *"Svédország"* which he knew meant Swede or Swedish and Sweden. Szluka put down the receiver and said, "This must have something to do with your compatriot, Matsson."

"Yes, of course."

"The girl lied to you, by the way. She's not studied at the university and doesn't work at a museum. She doesn't really seem to do anything. Got suspended from competitive swimming because she didn't behave herself."

"There must be some connection."

"Yes, but where? Oh well, we'll see."

Szluka shrugged his shoulders. Martin Beck turned and twisted his mangled body. It ached in his shoulders and arms, and his head was far from what it ought to be. He felt very tired and found it difficult to think, and yet did not want to go home to bed at the hotel, all the same.

The telephone rang again. Szluka listened with a frown, and then his eyes cleared.

"Things are beginning to move," he said. "We've found something. And one of them is all right now, the tall one. His name's Fröbe, by the way. Now we'll see. Are you coming along?"

Martin Beck began to get up.

"Or perhaps you'd rather rest for a while."

"No, thank you," said Martin Beck.

18

Szluka sat down behind the desk with his hands clasped loosely in front of him, a passport with a green cover at his right elbow.

The tall man in the chair opposite Szluka had dark shadows under his eyes. Martin Beck knew that he had not had much sleep during the last twenty-four hours. The man was sitting up straight in the chair, looking down at his hands.

Szluka nodded at the stenographer and began.

The man raised his eyes and looked at Szluka.

"Your name?"

"Theodor Fröbe."

SZLUKA: When were you born?

FRÖBE: Twenty-first of April, 1936, in Hanover.

SZ: And you are a West German citizen. Living where?

F: In Hamburg. Hermannstrasse 12.

SZ: What is your occupation?

F: Travel guide. Or to be more correct, travel-agency official.

SZ: Where are you employed?

F: At a travel agency called Winkler's.

SZ: Where do you live in Budapest?

F: At a boarding house in Újpest. Venetianer út 6.

SZ: And why are you in Budapest?

F: I represent the travel agency and look after parties traveling to and from Budapest.

SZ: Earlier tonight you and a man called Tetz Radeberger were caught in the act of attacking a man on Groza Peter

Rakpart. You were both armed and your intention to injure or kill the man was obvious. Do you know this man?

F: No.

SZ: Have you seen him before?

F: . . .

SZ: Answer me!

F: No.

SZ: Do you know who he is?

F: No.

SZ: You don't know him, you've never seen him before and don't know who he is. Why did you attack him?

F: . . . . .

SZ: Explain why you attacked him!

F: We . . . needed money and . . .

SZ: And?

F: And then we saw him down there on the quay and—

SZ: You're lying. Please don't lie to me. It's no good. The attack was planned and you were armed. In addition, it is a lie that you've not seen him before. You have been following him for two days. Why? Answer me!

F: We thought he was someone else.

SZ: That he was who?

F: Someone who . . . who . . .

SZ: Who?

F: Who owed us money.

SZ: And so you followed him and attacked him?

F: Yes.

SZ: I've already warned you once. It is extremely unwise of you to lie. I know exactly when you are lying. Do you know a Swede called Alf Matsson?

F: No.

SZ: Your friends Radeberger and Boeck have already said that you know him.

F: I know him only slightly. I didn't remember that that was his name.

SZ: When did you last see Alf Matsson?

F: In May, I think it was.

SZ: Where did you meet him?

F: Here in Budapest.

SZ: And you haven't seen him since then?

F: No.

SZ: Three days ago this man was at your boarding house asking for Alf Matsson. Since then you have followed him and tonight you tried to kill him. Why?

F: Not kill him!

SZ: Why?

F: We didn't try to kill him!

SZ: But you attacked him, didn't you? And you were armed with a knife.

F: Yes, but it was a mistake. Nothing happened to him, did it? He wasn't injured, was he? You've no right to question me like this.

SZ: How long have you known Alf Matsson?

F: About a year. I don't remember exactly.

SZ: How did you meet?

F: At a mutual friend's place here in Budapest.

SZ: What's your friend's name?

F: Ari Boeck.

SZ: Have you met him several times since then?

F: A few times. Not very many.

SZ: Did you always meet here in Budapest?

F: We've met in Prague too. And in Warsaw.

SZ: And in Bratislava.

F: Yes.

SZ: And in Constanta?

F: . . . . .

SZ: Didn't you?

F: Yes.

SZ: How did it happen? That you met in all those cities where none of you lived?

F: I travel a lot. It's my job. And he traveled a lot too. It turned out that we met there.

SZ: Why did you meet?

F: We just met. We were good friends.

SZ: Now you are saying that you've been meeting him over a year in at least five different cities because you are good friends. A moment ago you were saying that you knew him only slightly. Why didn't you want to admit that you knew him?

F: I was nervous from sitting here being questioned. And I'm awfully tired. And my leg hurts, too.

SZ: Oh yes. So you're very tired. Was Tetz Radeberger also with you when you met Alf Matsson at all these different places?

F: Yes, we work for the same agency and travel together.

sz: How did it happen, do you think, that Radeberger didn't want to admit at once to knowing Alf Matsson either? Was he awfully tired, too, perhaps?

f: I don't know anything about that.

sz: Do you know where Alf Matsson is right now?

f: No, I have no idea.

sz: Do you want me to tell you?

f: Yes.

sz: I'm not going to do it, however. How long have you been employed at this Winkler's travel agency?

f: For six years.

sz: Is it a well-paid job?

f: Not especially. But I get everything free when I'm traveling. Food, keep and fares.

sz: But the salary isn't high?

f: No. But I manage.

sz: It seems so. You have enough so that you manage.

f: What do you mean by that?

sz: You have in fact fifteen hundred dollars, eight hundred and thirty pounds and ten thousand marks. That's a lot of money. Where did you get it from?

f: That's nothing to do with you.

sz: Answer my question and don't use that tone of voice.

f: It's not your business where I get my money from.

sz: It's possible and also very likely that you haven't half the sense I thought you had, but even with the very slightest intelligence, you ought to be able to see that you would be wiser to answer my questions. Well, where did you get the money from?

f: I did extra jobs and earned it all over a long period.

sz: What sort of jobs?

f: Different things.

Szluka looked at Fröbe and opened a drawer in his desk. Out of the drawer he took a package wrapped up in plastic. The package was about eight inches long and four inches wide and fastened with adhesive tape. Szluka put the package down on the desk between himself and Fröbe. All the while he was looking at Fröbe, whose eyes wavered, trying to avoid looking at the package. Szluka looked straight at him and Fröbe wiped away the sweat that had appeared in little beads around his nose. Then Szluka added, "Uh-huh. Different things. As for example, smuggling and selling hashish. A profitable occupation, but not in the long run, Herr Fröbe."

F: I don't understand what you're talking about.

SZ: No? And you don't recognize this little package either?

F: No, I don't. Why should I?

SZ: And not the fifteen similar packages that were found hidden in the doors and upholstery of Radeberger's car, either?

F: . . . . .

SZ: There's quite a lot of hashish in just one little package like this. We're not accustomed to such things here, so I in fact don't know what price it would bring in today. By how much would you have increased your capital when you'd sold your little supply?

F: I still don't understand what you're talking about.

SZ: I see in your passport here that you often travel to Turkey. You've been there seven times this year alone.

F: Winkler's arrange tours to Turkey. As a group guide I have to travel there quite often.

SZ: Yes, and it suits you very well, doesn't it? In Turkey hashish is fairly cheap and quite easy to get hold of. Isn't it, Mr. Fröbe?

F: . . . . .

SZ: If you prefer to say nothing it will be the worse for you. We already have enough evidence, and in addition to that a witness.

F: The dirty skunk squealed after all!

SZ: Exactly.

F: That god-damned bastard Swede!

SZ: Perhaps you realize that it is serving no useful purpose to keep this up any longer. Start talking now, Fröbe! I want to hear the whole thing, with all the facts you can remember, names, dates and figures. You can begin by telling me when you began smuggling narcotics.

Fröbe closed his eyes and fell to one side off the chair. Martin Beck saw him put his hand out before he actually fell prostrate onto the floor.

Szluka rose and nodded to the stenographer, who closed the notebook and vanished out the door.

Szluka looked down at the man lying on the floor.

"He's bluffing," said Martin Beck. "He didn't faint."

"I know," said Szluka. "But I'll let him rest for a while before I go on."

He went up to Fröbe and poked him with the tip of his shoe.

"Get up, Fröbe."

Fröbe did not move, but his eyelids quivered. Szluka went over to the door, opened it and called out something into the corridor. A policeman came in and Szluka said something to him. The policeman took Fröbe by the arm and Szluka said, "Don't lie there cluttering up the place, Fröbe. We'll get a bunk for you to lie on. It's much more comfortable."

Fröbe got up and looked offendedly at Szluka. Then he limped out behind the policeman. Martin Beck watched him go.

"How is his leg?"

"No danger," said Szluka. "Only a flesh wound. We don't often need to shoot, but when it's necessary, we shoot accurately."

"So that's what he was up to. Hashish smuggling," said Martin Beck. "I wonder what they've done with him."

"Alf Matsson? I expect we'll get it out of them. But it's best to wait until they've had a bit of rest. You must be tired yourself," said Szluka, sitting down behind his desk.

Martin Beck felt very tired indeed. It was already morning. He felt bruised and battered.

"Go back to the hotel and sleep for a few hours," said Szluka. "I'll phone you later. Go down to the entrance and I'll get a car sent around for you."

Martin Beck had no objections. He shook hands with Szluka and left him. As he closed the door behind him, he heard Szluka speaking into the telephone.

The car was already waiting for him when he got down to the street.

19

The cleaning woman had been into his room and switched off the light and closed the shutters. He did not bother to open them again. Now he knew that there would be no tall, dark man outside looking up at his window.

Martin Beck switched on the overhead light and undressed. His head and left arm ached. He looked in the long mirror in the wardrobe. He had a large bruise above his right knee, and his left shoulder was swollen and black and blue. He ran his hand over his head and felt a large bump at the back of it. He could not find any more injuries.

The bed looked soft and cool and inviting. He switched off the light and crept down between the sheets. He lay on his back for a while and tried to think as he stared out into the half-light. Then he turned over on his side and fell asleep.

It was nearly two o'clock when he woke to the sound of the telephone ringing. It was Szluka.

"Have you slept?"

"Yes."

"Good. Can you come over?"

"Yes. Now?"

"I'll send a car. It'll be there in half an hour. Is that all right?"

"Yes. I'll be down in half an hour."

He showered and dressed and opened the shutters. The sun was blazing and the sharp light stung his eyes. He looked toward the quay on the other side of the river. The past night seemed unreal and remote to him.

The car, with the same driver as before, was waiting. He found his way to Szluka's room by himself and knocked before opening the door and going in.

Szluka was alone. He was sitting behind his desk with a sheaf of papers and the indispensable coffee cup in front of him. He nodded and motioned toward the chair Fröbe had sat in. Then he lifted the receiver, said something and put it back again.

"How are you feeling?" he said, looking at Martin Beck.

"Fine. I've slept. And you? How's it going?"

A policeman came in and placed two cups of coffee on the table. Then he took Szluka's empty cup and left.

"It's all finished now. I've got everything here," said Szluka, picking up the sheaf of papers.

"And Alf Matsson?" said Martin Beck.

"Well," said Szluka. "That's the only point that's not clear yet. I haven't managed to get anything there. They insist that they don't know where he is."

"But he was one of the gang?"

"Yes, in a way. He was their middleman. The whole thing was organised by Fröbe and Radeberger. The girl was just used as a sort of clearinghouse for the whole business. Boeck, whatever her first name is."

Szluka fumbled in his papers.

"Ari," said Martin Beck. "Aranka."

"Yes, Ari Boeck. Fröbe and Radeberger had already been smuggling hashish from Turkey some time before they met her. Both of them seem to have had relations with her. After a while, they realized they could use her in another way and told her about the narcotics smuggling. She had no objections to joining in on it. Then they both lived with her when she moved to Újpest. She seems to be a fairly loose sort of creature."

"Yes," said Martin Beck. "I suppose so."

"Radeberger and Fröbe went to Turkey as travel guides. In Turkey they got hold of the hashish, which is quite cheap and easily obtainable there, and then smuggled it into Hungary. It was fairly easy, especially since they were group guides and had to deal with all the luggage belonging to the party. Ari Boeck made contact with the middlemen and helped sell the drugs here in Budapest. Radeberger and Fröbe also traveled to other countries such as Poland, Czechoslovakia, Rumania and Bulgaria with hashish for their pushers."

"And Alf Matsson was one of them?" said Martin Beck.

"Alf Matsson was one of the pushers," said Szluka. "They had some others who came from England, Germany and Holland, either here or to some other East European country where they met Radeberger and Fröbe. They paid in Western currencies—pounds, dollars or marks—and got their hashish, which they then took back home with them and sold there."

"So everyone profited a good deal from the business, except the people who in the end bought the junk to use," said Martin Beck. "It's odd that they've managed to get away with this for so long without being discovered."

Szluka rose and went across to the window. He stood there for a while, his hands behind his back, looking out onto the street. Then he went back and sat down again.

"No," he said. "It's not really that strange. So long as none of the stuff was sold here or in any other socialist country, except to the middlemen, then they had every chance of getting away with it. In the capitalist countries concerned, they don't think there's anything worth smuggling out of Eastern Bloc countries, so customs control hardly exists for travelers from these countries. On the other hand, if they'd tried to find a market for their goods here, they'd have soon been caught. But that wouldn't have been worth their while, either. It's Western currencies they want."

"They must have made a good deal of money," said Martin Beck.

"Yes," said Szluka. "But the pushers made a lot out of it too. The whole thing was quite cleverly organized, actually. If you hadn't come out here looking for Alf Matsson, it might have been a long time before we'd found all this out."

"What do they say about Alf Matsson?"

"They've admitted he was their pusher in Sweden. Over a period of a year he'd bought quite a lot of hashish from them. But they maintain they haven't seen him since May, when he was here to pick up a consignment. He didn't get as much as he wanted at that time, so he'd communicated with Ari Boeck again fairly soon. They say that they'd agreed to meet him here in Budapest almost three weeks ago, but he never turned up. They claim that the stuff hidden in the car was put aside for him."

Martin Beck sat in silence for a moment. Then he said:

"He might have quarreled with them for one reason or

another and threatened to report them. Then they might have got scared and done away with him. The way they tried to get rid of me last night."

Szluka sat in silence. After a while Martin Beck went on, quietly, as if talking to himself, "That's what must have happened."

Szluka got up and paced the floor for a bit. Then he said, "That's what I thought had happened too."

He fell silent again and stopped in front of the map.

"What do you think now?" said Martin Beck.

Szluka turned and looked at him.

"I don't know," he said. "I thought perhaps you'd like to talk to one of them yourself. This Radeberger. The one you fought with last night. He's talkative and I have an impression that he's too stupid to be able to lie well. Would you like to question him? Perhaps you'd do better than I did."

"Yes, please," said Martin Beck. "I'd very much like to question him."

20

Tetz Radeberger came into the room. He was dressed as he had been the previous night, in a snug pullover, thin Dacron trousers with elastic at the waist and light, rubber-soled cloth shoes. Dressed to kill. He stopped inside the door and bowed. The policeman escorting him prodded him lightly in the back.

Martin Beck gestured toward the chair on the other side of the desk, and the German sat down. There was an expectant and uncertain look in his deep-blue eyes. He had a bandage on his forehead and there was a blue swelling at his hairline. Otherwise he looked well and strong and fairly intact.

"We're going to talk about Alf Matsson," said Martin Beck.

"I don't know where he is," said Radeberger immediately.

"Possibly. But we're going to talk about him all the same."

Szluka had got out a tape recorder. It was standing on the right of the desk and Martin Beck stretched out his hand and switched it on. The German kept a close watch on his movements.

"When did you meet Alf Matsson for the first time?"

"Two years ago."

"Where?"

"Here in Budapest. At a place called the Ifjuság. A sort of young people's hotel."

"How did you meet him?"

"Through Ari Boeck. She worked there. That was long before she moved to Újpest."

"What happened then?"

"Nothing special. Theo and I had just come back from

Turkey. We arranged trips there for tourists. From resorts in Rumania and Bulgaria. We brought a little stuff back with us from Istanbul."

"Had you already begun to smuggle drugs then?"

"Only a little. For our own use, so to speak. But we didn't use it all that often. We never use it now." He paused briefly, and then said, "It's not good for you."

"What did you want it for then?"

"Well, for broads and all that. It's good for broads. They get . . . more . . . inclined . . ."

"Matsson, then? Where does he come into the picture?"

"We offered him some to smoke. He wasn't all that interested either. Drank liquor mostly."

He thought for a moment, and then said foolishly, "That's not good for your body either."

"Did you sell narcotics to Matsson that time?"

"No, but he got a little. We hadn't got all that much. He grew interested when he heard how easy it was to buy in Istanbul."

"Had you yourselves already thought about smuggling on a large scale at that time?"

"We'd talked about it. The difficulty was getting the stuff into the countries where it paid you to sell it."

"Where, for instance?"

"Scandinavia, Holland, at home in Germany. The customs and the police are on the alert there, especially when they know you come from countries like Turkey. Or North Africa and Spain too, for that matter."

"Did Matsson offer to become a pusher?"

"Yes. He said that when you traveled from Eastern Europe, the customs people were hardly ever interested in your luggage, especially if you were flying. It wasn't difficult for us to get the stuff out of Turkey, to here, for instance. We were travel guides, after all. But then we couldn't get much farther with it. The risks were too great. And you can't sell it here. You'd get caught, and anyhow, it isn't worth it."

He thought about this for a moment.

"We didn't want to get caught," he said.

"I can see that. Did you make an agreement with Matsson then?"

"Yes. He had a good idea. We were to meet at different places—ones that suited Theo and me. We let him know and then he went there for his magazine. It was a good cover-up. Looked innocent."

"How did he pay you?"

"In dollars—cash. It was a fine plan, and we built up our organization that summer. Got hold of more pushers—a Dutchman we met in Prague and—"

This was Szluka's department. Martin Beck said, "Where did you and Matsson meet next time?"

"In Constanta, in Rumania, three weeks later. Everything went very smoothly."

"Was Miss Boeck in on it then too?"

"Ari? No, what use would she have been?"

"But she knew what you were doing?"

"Yes, part of it anyhow."

"How many times did you and Matsson meet altogether?"

"Ten, maybe fifteen. It worked beautifully. He always paid what we asked and must have earned a lot himself."

"How much, do you think?"

"Don't know, but he always had plenty of money."

"Where is he now?"

"I don't know."

"Really?"

"Yes, it's true. We met here in May, when Ari had moved to Újpest. He stayed at that young people's hotel. He got a shipment at that point. He said he had a big market, and we decided that we should meet here again on the twenty-third of July."

"And?"

"We came here on the twenty-first. That was a Thursday. But he never turned up."

"He was here in Budapest. He came on the twenty-second in the evening. He left his hotel on the twenty-third, in the morning. Where were you going to meet?"

"In Újpest. At Ari's place."

"So he went there on the twenty-third in the morning."

"No, I tell you. He never turned up. We waited, but he didn't come. Then we phoned the hotel, but he wasn't there."

"Who called?"

"Theo and I did, and Ari. We took turns."

"Did you call from Újpest?"

"No. From different places. He didn't come, I tell you. We sat there waiting."

"You claim you haven't seen him since he came here, in other words?"

"Yes."

"Let's pretend that I believe you. You haven't met Matsson. But that doesn't stop Fröbe or Miss Boeck from having contacted him, does it?"

"No, I know they haven't."

"How do you know that?"

Radeberger's expression began to grow slightly desperate. He was sweating freely. It was very hot in the room.

"Now listen," he said. "I don't know what you think, but that other man seems to believe we got rid of him. But why should we do that? We made money off him, a lot of money."

"Did you give Miss Boeck money too?"

"Oh, yes. She helped and got her share. Enough so that she didn't have to work."

Martin Beck stared at the man for a long time. Finally he said, "Did you kill him?"

"No, I keep telling you. Would we have stayed on here for three weeks with nearly that whole supply of stuff if we'd done that?"

His voice had grown shrill and tense.

"Did you like Alf Matsson?"

The man's eyes flickered.

"Please answer when I ask you something," said Martin Beck seriously.

"Of course."

"Miss Boeck appears to have said at her interrogation that neither you nor Theo Fröbe liked Matsson."

"He was nasty when he drank. He . . . despised us because we were Germans."

He turned an appealing blue look upon Martin Beck and said, "And that's not fair, is it?"

There was a silent pause. Tetz Radeberger did not like it. He fidgeted and pulled nervously at the joints of his fingers.

"We haven't killed anyone," he said. "We're not that kind."

"You tried to kill me last night."

"That was different."

The man said this in such a low voice that his words were almost inaudible.

"In what way?"

"It was our only chance."

"Chance to what? To be hanged? Or to get a life sentence in prison?"

The German gave him a shattered look.

"You'll probably get that anyway," said Martin Beck, in a friendly way. "Have you been to prison before?"

"Yes. At home."

"Well, what did you mean by your only chance being to try to kill me?"

"Don't you see? When you came to Újpest and had his— Matsson's—passport with you, we thought at first that he hadn't been able to come and had sent you instead. But you didn't say anything, and besides you weren't the right type. So Matsson must have been caught and spilled the beans. But we didn't know who you were. We'd already been here twenty days, and we had the whole consignment lying around, and we were getting nervous about it. And after three weeks we'd have to get our visas extended. So Theo followed you when you went and . . ."

"Yes, go on."

"And I took the car apart and hid the stuff. Theo couldn't figure out who you were, so we agreed that Ari should find out. The next day, Theo followed you to those baths. He phoned Ari from there and she went and watched for you outside. Then Theo saw you together with that guy in the pool. Afterward he followed the other guy and saw him go into the police station. So it was obvious. All that afternoon and evening we waited and nothing happened. We figured you hadn't said anything yet or else the police would already have been there. Then Ari came back during the night."

"What had she found out?"

"I don't know, but it was something. She just said, 'Fix that bastard, and quick.' She was in a bad mood. Then she went into her room and slammed the door behind her."

"Oh?"

"Next day we watched you all the time. We were in a hell of a situation. We had to keep you quiet before you went to the police. We didn't get a chance and had almost given up hope when you went out in the night. Theo followed you across the bridge and I drove around with the car across the other bridge, Lanc-híd. Then we changed over. Theo didn't dare do it. And I'm the strongest. I've always looked after my body."

He fell silent for a moment then said appealingly, as if this were some excuse, "We didn't know you were the police."

Martin Beck did not reply.

"Are you a policeman?"

"Yes, I'm a policeman. Let's go back to Alf Matsson. You said that you met him through Miss Boeck. Had they known each other long?"

"Awhile. Ari had been on some athletic team in Sweden, swimming, and she met him there. Then she wasn't allowed to swim any more, but he looked her up when he came here."

"Are Matsson and Miss Boeck good friends?"

"Fairly."

"Do they often have intimate relations with each other?"

"Do you mean do they sleep together? Of course."

"Do you sleep with Miss Boeck too?"

"Of course. When I feel like it. Theo too. Ari is a nymphomaniac. There's not much you can do about it. Obviously Matsson slept with her when he was here. Once we all three had a go at her, in the same room. Ari does anything in that line. Otherwise she's a good girl."

"Good?"

"Yes, she does what you tell her. As long as you fuck her now and then. I don't do it so much now. It's not really very good for you to do it too much. But Theo is always at it. So he's got no energy for anything."

"Have you never quarreled with Matsson?"

"About Ari? She's nothing to fight over."

"But about other things?"

"Not about business. He was good at the business."

"Otherwise then?"

"Once he kicked up such a fuss I had to smack him. He was drunk at the time, of course. Then Ari took him in hand and calmed him down. That was a long time ago."

"Where do you think Matsson is now?"

Radeberger shook his head helplessly.

"I don't know. Here somewhere."

"Didn't he associate with other people here?"

"He just came, collected his consignment and paid. And then he did some kind of magazine article to make it all watertight. Three or four days later he went back."

Martin Beck sat silently for a while, looking at the man who had tried to kill him.

"I think that'll do now," he said, switching off the tape recorder.

Evidently the German still had something on his mind.

"Say, that business yesterday . . . Can you forgive me?"

"No. I can't. Good-bye."

He made a sign to the policeman, who rose, took Radeberger by the arm and led him toward the door. Martin Beck watched the blond Teuton thoughtfully. Then he said, "One moment, Herr Radeberger. This is nothing to do with me personally. Yesterday you tried to murder a person to save your own skin. You had planned the murder as best you could and it was no thanks to you that it didn't succeed. That's not only illegal, but it's also a breach of a basic rule of life and an important principle. That's why it's unforgivable. That's all. Think about it."

Martin Beck rewound the tape, put it into the cassette and returned to Szluka.

"I think you're probably right. Perhaps they haven't killed him."

"No," said Szluka. "It doesn't seem like it. We've got all the stops out now, looking for him."

"So have we."

"Has your assignment become official yet?"

"Not so far as I know."

Szluka scratched the back of his neck.

"Peculiar," he said.

"What?"

"That we can't locate him."

Half an hour later, Martin Beck returned to his hotel. It was already time for dinner. Dusk fell over the Danube, and on the other side of the river he saw the quay and the stone wall and the steps.

21

Martin Beck had just finished dressing and was on his way to the dining room when the telephone rang.

"From Stockholm," said the telephone operator. "A Mr. Eriksson."

The name was familiar to him: it was Alf Matsson's boss, the editor in chief of the aggressive weekly.

A pompous voice came over the line.

"That's Beck, is it? This is Eriksson, the editor in chief here."

"This is Inspector Beck."

The man ignored this and went on. "Well, as you are probably aware, I know all about your assignment. I was the one to put you on the track. And I've good connections with the Foreign Office, too."

So his hideous namesake had not been able to keep his mouth shut either.

"Are you still there?"

"Yes."

"Perhaps we'd better be a little careful what we say, if you know what I mean. But first I must ask: have you found the man you're looking for?"

"Matsson? No, not yet."

"No clue at all?"

"No."

"It's absolutely unheard-of."

"Yes."

"Well, how can I put it now . . . How's the atmosphere down there?"

"It's hot. A little misty in the mornings."

"What d'you say? Misty in the mornings? Yes, I think I understand. Yes, exactly. Now, however, I think the time has come when in all good conscience we can't keep this thing under wraps any longer. Why, what's happened is perfectly incredible—it could lead to dreadful things. We have a great responsibility for Matsson personally too. He's one of our best people, an excellent man, thoroughly honest and loyal. I've had him on my general staff for a couple of years now, and I know what I'm talking about."

"Where?"

"What?"

"Where have you had him?"

"Oh, that. On my general staff. We say that, you know. Editorial general staff. I know what I'm talking about. I'd stake my life on that man and that makes my responsibility even greater."

Martin Beck stood thinking about something else. He was trying to imagine what Eriksson looked like. Probably a fat, bumptious little man with pig eyes and a red beard.

"So today I've decided to publish our first article on the Alf Matsson case in next week's issue. This coming Monday, without further delay. The moment has come to focus public attention on this story. I just wanted to know whether you'd found any trace of him, as I said."

"I think you should take your article and—"

Martin Beck stopped himself just in time and said, ". . . throw it into the wastebasket."

"What? What did you say? I don't understand."

"Read the papers in the morning," said Martin Beck and put down the receiver.

His appetite had vanished during the conversation. He took out his bottle and poured himself a stiff whisky. Then he sat down and thought. He was in a bad temper and had a headache, and on top of that he had been discourteous. But that was not what he was thinking about.

Alf Matsson had come to Budapest on the twenty-second of July. He had been seen at the passport control. He had taken a taxi to the Hotel Ifjuság and stayed there for one night. Someone at the reception desk must have dealt with him. The following morning, Saturday the twenty-third, he had, again by taxi, moved to the Hotel Duna and stayed there for half an hour. At about ten o'clock in the morning he had gone out. The people at the reception desk had noticed him.

After that, as far as was known, no one had seen or spoken to Alf Matsson. He had left one single clue behind him: the key to his hotel room, which, according to Szluka, had been found on the steps outside the police station.

Assuming that Fröbe and Radeberger were telling the truth, he had not turned up at the meeting place in Újpest and, consequently, they had not been able either to kidnap or kill him.

So for some unknown reason, Alf Matsson had gone up in smoke.

The existing material was extremely thin but, nevertheless, it was all there was to work on.

Five people, it was established, had had contact with Alf Matsson on Hungarian soil and could be regarded as witnesses.

A passport officer, two taxi drivers and two hotel receptionists.

If something wholly unexpected had happened to him—if, for instance, he had been attacked, kidnapped or killed in an accident or gone insane—then their testimonies were useless. But, on the other hand, if he had made himself invisible of his own free will, then those people might have observed some detail in his appearance or behavior which might be important to the investigation.

Martin Beck had personally been in contact with two of these hypothetical witnesses. Considering the language difficulties, however, it was uncertain whether he had been able to exploit them fully. Neither the taxi drivers nor the passport official could be located, and even if he found them, he would presumably not be able to speak to them.

The only substantial material he had to go on was Matsson's passport and luggage. Neither told him anything.

This was his summary of the Alf Matsson case. Extremely depressing insofar as it showed that, as far as he was concerned, the investigation had ended in complete deadlock. If, despite everything, Matsson's disappearance was connected with the gang of smugglers—and it was difficult to believe that it was *not*—then Szluka would sooner or later clear the matter up. In that case, the best support he could give the Hungarian police would be to go home, bring in the Narcotics Squad and help wind up the Swedish end of the case.

Martin Beck came to a decision and converted it immediately into action by means of two telephone calls.

First, the well-dressed young man from the Swedish Embassy.

"Have you managed to find him?"

"No."

"Nothing new, in other words."

"Matsson was a narcotics smuggler. The Hungarian police are looking for him. For our part, we'll put out a description through Interpol."

"How very unpleasant."

"Yes."

"And what is this going to mean for you?"

"That I go home. Tomorrow, if it can be arranged. I'd like some help with that little matter."

"It may be difficult, but I'll do my best."

"Yes, do that. It's very important."

"I'll phone early tomorrow morning."

"Thank you."

"Good-bye. I hope you've had a nice time these few days, all the same."

"Yes, very nice. Good-bye."

After that, Szluka. He was at police headquarters.

"I'm going back to Sweden tomorrow."

"Oh, yes. Have a good trip."

"You'll get our report eventually."

"And you'll get ours. We've still not found Matsson."

"Are you surprised?"

"Very. Frankly, I've never seen anything like it. But we'll get him soon."

"Have you checked the camping sites?"

"We're doing that. Takes a little time. Fröbe's tried to kill himself, by the way."

"And?"

"Didn't succeed, of course. He threw himself at the wall head first. Got a bump on his skull. I've had him transferred to the psychiatric department. The doctor says he's a manic-depressive. The question is whether we'll have to let the girl go the same way."

"And Radeberger?"

"All right. Asking whether there's a gymnasium in the prison. There is."

"Could I ask you something?"

"Go ahead."

"We know that Matsson had contact with five people here in Budapest from Friday evening until Saturday morning."

"Two hotel receptionists and two taxi drivers. Where do we get the fifth from?"

"The passport control officer."

"My only excuse is that I haven't been home for thirty-six hours. So you want him questioned?"

"Yes. Everything he can remember. What he said, how he behaved, what he was wearing."

"I see."

"Can you get the report done in German or English and airmail it to Stockholm?"

"Telex is better. Anyhow, perhaps there'll be time to get it to you before you leave."

"Hardly. I'll probably be going about eleven."

"We're famous for our speed. The wife of the Minister of Trade had her bag snatched at Nep Stadium last autumn. She took a taxi here to report it. When she got here, she was handed back her bag at the desk downstairs. That kept us in good shape for a long time. Well, we'll see."

"Thanks then. And good-bye."

"Good-bye. Pity there wasn't time to meet a little more informally."

Martin Beck paused briefly to think. Then he set up a call to Stockholm. The call came through in ten minutes.

"Lennart's away," said Kollberg's wife. "As usual, he didn't say where he was going. 'Duty calls, be back on Sunday, take care of yourself.' He took the car with him. To hell with policemen."

Melander next. This time it took only five minutes.

"Hi! Did I disturb you?"

"I'd just gone to bed."

Melander was famous for his memory, his ten hours' sleep a night and a singular capacity for constantly being in the W. C.

"Are you in on the Matsson case?"

"Yeah."

"Find out what he did the night before he left. In detail. How he behaved, what he said, what he was wearing."

"Tonight?"

"Tomorrow will do."

"Uh-huh."

"Bye, then."

"Bye."

Martin Beck had finished with the telephone. He took pen and paper and went downstairs.

Alf Matsson's luggage was still standing in the room behind the reception desk.

He took the cover off the typewriter, placed it on the table, inserted a piece of paper in the machine and typed:

Portable typewriter, Erika, with case
Yellowish-brown pigskin suitcase with strap, fairly new

He opened the case and set its contents out on the table. He then went on typing.

Gray-and-black checked shirt
Sport shirt, brown
White poplin shirt, fresh-laundered, Metro Laundry,
    Stockholm
Light-gray gabardine trousers, well-pressed
Three handkerchiefs, white
Four pairs socks, brown, dark-blue, light-gray, wine-red
Two pairs colored undershorts, green-and-white check
One fishnet undershirt
One pair light-brown suede shoes

He looked gloomily at the cardigan-like garment, picked it up and went out to the girl at the reception desk. She was very pretty, in a sweet, ordinary way. Rather small, well built, long fingers, pretty calves, fine ankles, a few dark hairs on her shins, long thighs under her skirt. No rings. He stared at her with his thoughts far away.

"What's this kind of thing called?" he said.

"A jersey blazer," she said.

He remained standing there, thinking about something. The girl blushed. She moved to the other end of the reception desk, adjusting her skirt and pulling at her bra and girdle. He could not understand why. He went back, sat down at the table and typed:

> Dark blue jersey blazer
> 58 sheets typing paper, legal size
> One typewriter eraser
> Electric shaver, Remington
> *The Night Wanderer* by Kurt Salomonson
> Shaving kit
> Shaving lotion, Tabac
> Tube of toothpaste, Squibb, opened
> Toothbrush
> Mouthwash, Vademecum
> Aspirin with codeine, box unopened
> Dark-blue plastic wallet
> $1500 in $20 bills
> Skr 600 in hundred-kronor notes, new type
> Typed on Alf Matsson's typewriter

He repacked all the things, folded the list and left. The girl at the reception desk looked at him in confusion. Now she appeared prettier than ever.

Martin Beck went into the dining room and ate a late dinner, with an absent-minded expression still on his face.

The waiter put a Swedish flag in front of him. The maestro came up to his table and played a patriotic Swedish melody in his left ear. He did not seem to notice it.

He drank his coffee in one gulp, put a red hundred-forint note on the table without even waiting for the bill and went upstairs to bed.

22

It was just a few minutes past nine o'clock when the young man from the Embassy telephoned.

"You're in luck," he said. "I've managed to get a seat on the plane that leaves Budapest at twelve o'clock. You get to Prague at ten to two and you have five minutes to wait before the SAS plane to Copenhagen leaves."

"Thanks," said Martin Beck.

"It wasn't easy to arrange at such short notice. Can you pick up the tickets yourself at Malev's? I've arranged for the payment of them, so they can just be collected."

"Naturally," said Martin Beck. "Thanks very much indeed."

"Have a nice flight then, Mr. Beck. It's been very pleasant having you here."

"Thank you," said Martin Beck. "Good-bye."

As predicted the tickets were waiting for him, with the dark curly-haired beauty he had spoken to three days earlier.

He returned to his hotel room, packed his bag and sat at the window for a while, smoking and looking out over the river. Then he left the room (in which he had stayed for five days and Alf Matsson had stayed for half an hour), went down to reception and ordered a taxi. As he came outside onto the steps, he saw a blue-and-white police car approaching at great speed. It braked in front of the hotel, and a uniformed policeman whom he had not seen before leaped out and hurried through the revolving doors. Martin had time to see that he had an envelope in his hand.

His taxi swung around and stopped behind the police car,
and the doorman with the gray mustache opened the back
door. Martin Beck asked him to wait and went back into the
revolving doors just as the policeman went into them from
the other direction, closely followed by the receptionist. When
the receptionist caught sight of Martin Beck, he waved and
pointed to the policeman. After having whirled around a couple of times in the revolving doors, they all three succeeded in
meeting up on the hotel steps and Martin Beck was given his
envelope. He stepped into the taxi after having given out his
last aluminum coins to the receptionist and the doorman.

On the plane, he was seated beside a boastful, loud-voiced
Englishman, who hung over him, spraying saliva into his face
as he related stories about his totally uninteresting activities as
some kind of commercial traveler.

In Prague, Martin Beck just had time to rush through the
transit hall into the next plane, before it took off. To his relief
the expectorating Englishman was nowhere to be seen, and
when they were up in the air, he opened the envelope.

Szluka and his men had done their best to live up to their
reputation for speed. They had questioned six witnesses and
done the report in English. Martin Beck read:

Summary of interrogation of those persons known by
the police to have had contact with the Swedish citizen Alf Sixten Matsson from the time of his arrival at
Ferihegyi Airport in Budapest at 10:15 P.M. on July 22,
1966, until his disappearance from Hotel Duna in Budapest at unknown time between 10:00 A.M. and
11:00 A.M. on July 23 of the same year.

Ferenc Havas, passport control officer who was on
duty alone at the passport control point at Ferihegyi
on the night between July 22 and July 23, 1966, says
that he does not remember seeing Alf Matsson.

János Lucacs, taxi driver, says that he remembers
that on the night between July 22 and 23 he took a passenger from Ferihegyi to Hotel Ifjúság. According to
Lucacs, the passenger was a man between 25 and 30
years of age, had a beard and spoke German. Lucacs,
who does not speak German, understood only that the

man wanted to be taken to Ifjuság. Lucacs thinks he remembers that the man had a suitcase, which he put down beside him on the back seat.

Léo Szabo, medical student, night porter at Hotel Ifjuság on July 22–23, remembers a man who came to the hotel late one evening between July 17–24. Everything indicates that this man was Alf Matsson although Szabo remembers neither the exact time of the man's arrival, nor his name or nationality. According to Szabo, the man was between 30 and 35 years old, spoke good English and had a beard. He was wearing light-colored trousers, blue jacket, probably a white shirt, and tie, and had light luggage—one or two bags. Szabo cannot remember having seen this man on any other occasion but this one.

Béla Péter, taxi driver, drove Alf Matsson from the Hotel Ifjuság to the Hotel Duna on the morning of July 23. He remembers a young man with a brown beard and glasses, whose luggage consisted of one large and one smaller bag, the smaller probably a typewriter.

Béla Kovacs, porter at the Hotel Duna, received Matsson's passport and gave him the key to Room 105 on the morning of July 23. According to Kovacs, Matsson was then wearing light, probably gray trousers, white shirt, blue jacket and a plain-colored tie. He was carrying a light-colored coat over his arm.

Eva Petrovich, receptionist at the same hotel, saw Matsson both when he arrived at the hotel shortly before 10:00 A.M. on July 23, and when he left the hotel about half an hour later. She has given the most extensive description of Matsson and maintains she is certain about all details, except the color of his tie. According to Miss Petrovich, Matsson was of medium height, had blue eyes, dark-brown hair, beard and mustache and steel-rimmed glasses. He was wearing light-gray trousers, dark-blue summer blazer, white shirt, blue or red tie, and beige shoes. Over his arm he had a light-beige poplin coat.

Szluka had added something:

As you see we have not found out much more than what we al-
ready knew. None of the witnesses can remember anything special that
Matsson did or said. I have added the description of his clothing at
his disappearance to the personal description we have sent all over the
country. Should any other facts come to light, I shall let you know im-
mediately. Have a good trip!

Vilmos Szluka

Martin Beck read through Szluka's summary again. He wondered whether Eva Petrovich was the same girl who had helped him identify the cardigan-like garment in Alf Matsson's suitcase. On the back of Szluka's letter, he wrote:

> Light-gray trousers
> White shirt
> Dark-blue blazer
> Red or blue tie
> Beige shoes
> Light-beige poplin coat

Then he took out the list he had made of the contents of Alf Matsson's bag and read through it before putting everything into his briefcase and closing it.

He leaned back in his seat and closed his eyes. He did not sleep, but sat like this until the plane began to go down through the thin cloud bank over Copenhagen.

Kastrup was as usual. He had to stand in a line before being sluiced into the transit hall, where people of all nationalities were crowding in front of the counters. He drank a Tuborg in the bar to gather his strength before tackling the trying task of collecting his luggage.

It was past three o'clock when he finally stood with his bag outside the airport building. A whole row of taxis was standing in the stand and he put his bag in the first one, got into the front seat and gave the driver the address of the harbor in Dragør.

The ferry, which was in and appeared ready to leave, was called *Drogden* and was an unusually ugly creation. Martin Beck put his bag and briefcase down in the cafeteria and went up on deck as the ferry eased its way out and headed for Sweden.

After the heat of the last few days in Budapest, the breeze in the Sound felt cold and after a while Martin Beck went in and sat down in the cafeteria. There were a great many people on board, mostly housewives who had been shopping over in Denmark.

The trip took scarcely an hour, and in Limhamn he at once got a taxi that would take him to Malmö. The taxi driver was talkative and spoke a southern Swedish dialect that sounded to Martin Beck almost as incomprehensible as Hungarian.

23

The taxi stopped outside the police station on David-hall Square. Martin Beck got out, walked up the wide steps and deposited his bag in the glass reception office. He had not been there for two years but was struck, as always, by the massiveness and majestic solemnity of the building and by its pompous halls and wide corridors. Two flights up, he stopped in front of a door marked INSPECTOR, knocked and slipped in. Someone had once said that Martin Beck knew the art of standing inside a room having already shut the door behind him at the same time as he knocked on it from the outside. There was a grain of truth in this.

"Hiya," he said.

There were two people in the room. One of them was standing leaning against the window, chewing a toothpick. He was very large. The other, who was sitting at the desk, was tall and thin, with his hair brushed straight back and his eyes lively. Both were in civilian clothes. The man at the desk looked critically at Martin Beck and said, "Quarter of an hour ago I read in the paper that you were abroad, breaking up international narcotics rings. And now you just walk in here saying hiya. Is that any way to behave? Do you want something?"

"Do you remember a stabbing case here on the eve of Twelfth Day? Guy called Matsson?"

"No. Should I?"

"I remember it," said the man by the window, apathetically.

"This is Månsson," said the Inspector. "He does . . . what are you doing, actually, Månsson?"

"Nothing. I was just thinking of going home."

"Exactly. He isn't doing anything and was thinking of going home. Well, what is it you remember?"

"I've forgotten."

"Is there any other way you can be of service?"

"Not until Monday. I'm off duty now."

"Must you munch like that?"

"I'm giving up smoking."

"What do you remember about that stabbing case?"

"Nothing."

"Nothing at all?"

"No. Backlund was in charge."

"What did he think, then?"

"Don't know. He worked hard on the preliminary investigation for several days. Was very secretive about it."

"You're very lucky," said the man at the desk to Martin Beck.

"Why?"

"Well, to be allowed to meet Backlund," said Månsson.

"Exactly. He's popular. Coming back in half an hour. Room 312. Take a ticket for the queue."

"Thanks."

"This Matsson, is he the same guy you're looking for?"

"Yes."

"Was he here in Malmö?"

"I don't think so."

"They're no fun," said Månsson mournfully.

"What aren't?"

"Toothpicks."

"Then for God's sake, smoke. No one asked you to eat toothpicks."

"They say there's a kind with taste to them," said Månsson.

Martin Beck recognized the lingo only too well. Something had probably wrecked their day. Their wives had no doubt called and pointed out that their food was spoiling and inquired whether there were no other policemen.

He left them to their troubles, went up to the canteen and had a cup of tea. He took out Szluka's paper from his inside pocket and read through the meager testimonies once again. Somewhere behind him there was an exchange of remarks.

"Excuse me for asking, but is this really a mazarine cupcake?"

"What else do you think it is?"

"Some kind of cultural monument, maybe. Seems a pity to eat it. The Bakery Museum ought to be interested."

"If you don't like it, you can go somewhere else."

"Yeah, two floors down for instance, and report you for harboring dangerous weapons. I order a mazarine cupcake and you go and give me a fossilized fetus that not even the Swedish State Railway would serve up without the locomotive blushing. I'm a sensitive person and—"

"Sensitive, eh? And by the way, you took it off the counter yourself."

Martin Beck turned around and looked at Kollberg.

"Hi," he said.

"Hi."

Neither of them seemed particularly surprised. Kollberg pushed away the objectionable cake and said, "When did you get back?"

"This moment. What are you doing here?"

"I thought I'd talk to someone named Backlund."

"Me too."

"Actually, I had something else to do here," said Kollberg apologetically.

Ten minutes later it was five o'clock. They went down together. Backlund turned out to be an elderly man with a friendly, ordinary face. He shook hands and said:

"Oh, yes. VIP's from Stockholm, eh?"

He put out two chairs for them and sat down, saying:

"Well, I am grateful. To what do I owe this honor?"

"You had a stabbing case on the eve of Twelfth Day," said Kollberg. "A guy called Matsson."

"Yes, that's quite correct. I remember the case. It's closed. No charge brought."

"What really happened?" said Martin Beck.

"Well, hm-m . . . Wait a minute and I'll get the file."

The man called Backlund went out and returned about ten minutes later with a typed report stapled together. It seemed remarkably detailed. He leafed through it for a moment, evidently renewing his acquaintance with it with both delight and pride. Finally he said, "We'd better take it from the beginning."

"We only want a general idea of what happened," said Kollberg.

"I see. At 1:23 A.M. on January 6 of this year a radio patrol

consisting of Patrolman Kristiansson and Patrolman Kvant—
who were patrolling in their car on Linnégatan here in town—
received orders to go to Sveagatan 26 in Limhamn, where
someone was said to have been stabbed. Patrolmen Kristiansson and Kvant at once went to this address, where they arrived
at about 1:29 A.M. They took charge of a person who stated that
he was a journalist: one Alf Sixten Matsson, residing in Stockholm at Fleminggatan 34. Matsson also stated that he had been
assaulted and stabbed by Bengt Eilert Jönsson, a journalist who
is a resident of Malmö and lives at Sveagatan 26 in Limhamn.
Matsson, who had a flesh wound approximately two inches
long on the outside of his left wrist, was taken to the emergency
ward of General Hospital by Patrolmen Kristiansson and Kvant
while Bengt Eilert Jönsson was held and taken to police headquarters in Malmö by Patrolmen Elofsson and Borglund, who
had been called in by Patrolmen Kristiansson and Kvant. Both
men were under the influence of alcohol."

"Kristiansson and Kvant?"

Backlund gave Kollberg a look of reproach and went on:

"After Matsson had been treated at the emergency ward
of General Hospital, he was also taken to testify at police
headquarters in Malmö. Matsson stated that he was born on
August 5, 1933, in Mölndal and was a resident of—"

"Just a minute," said Martin Beck. "We don't really need
all the details."

"Oh. But I must tell you, it isn't easy to get a clear picture
if you don't go through it all."

"Does that report give a clear picture?"

"I can answer both yes and no to that question. The stories differ considerably. Times too. The testimonies are very
vague. That's why there was no charge brought."

"Who questioned Matsson?"

"I did. I questioned him very thoroughly."

"Was he drunk?"

Backlund leafed through the report.

"One moment. Yes, here it is. He admitted to consuming
alcohol, but denied that he had done so in excess."

"How did he behave?"

"I didn't make a note of that. But Kristiansson said—here,
just a second—that his walk was unsteady and his voice was
calm but occasionally slurred."

Martin Beck gave up. Kollberg was more obstinate.

"What did he look like?"

"I didn't make any kind of note on that. But I remember that his apparel was neat and tidy."

"What happened when he was stabbed?"

"It can be said that it is difficult to get a clear picture of the actual course of events. Their stories differ. If I remember rightly—yes, that's right—Matsson stated that the injury was inflicted upon him at about midnight. On the other hand, Jönsson stated that the incident did not occur until after one o'clock. It was very difficult to get this point cleared up."

"Had he been assaulted?"

"I have Jönsson's statement here. Bengt Eilert Jönsson states that he and Matsson, whom he met through his profession, had been acquaintances for almost three years, and on the morning of January 5 he happened to meet Matsson, who was staying at the Savoy Hotel and was alone, so Jönsson invited him home to dinner, to commence at—"

"Yes, but what did he say about the assault itself?"

Backlund now began to appear a trifle irritated. He turned over a few more pages.

"Jönsson denies intentional assault, but admits that at one fifteen he gave Matsson a shove, at which the latter may have fallen over and cut himself on a glass which he had been holding in his hand."

"But had he been stabbed?"

"Well, that question is dealt with in an earlier section. I'll have a look. Here it is. Matsson states that some time before eleven P.M. he had a scuffle with Bengt Jönsson and thus, probably from a knife he had previously seen in Jönsson's home, he received an injury to his left arm. You can see for yourselves. Just before eleven P.M.! A quarter past one! A difference of two hours and twenty minutes! We also received a certificate from the doctor at the General Hospital. He describes the injury as a two-inch flesh wound, which was bleeding freely. The edges of the wound—"

Kollberg leaned forward and stared hard at the man with the report.

"We're not so interested in all that. What do you think yourself? Something happened, anyway. Why? And how did it come about?"

The other man could now conceal his irritation no longer. He removed his glasses and cleaned them feverishly.

"Oh now, please—please," he said. " 'Happened.' Hmmph. Everything is examined thoroughly here in these preliminary investigations. If I can't present an account of it all, then I don't see how I can clearly explain the case for you. You can go through the material for yourselves if you like."

He put the report down on the edge of the desk. Martin Beck leafed through it listlessly and looked at the photographs of the scene of the crime attached at the back. The photos showed a kitchen, a living room and some stone stairs. Everything was clean and tidy. On the stairs there were a few dark spots, hardly bigger than a one-öre piece. If they had not been marked with white arrows, they would have been scarcely visible. He handed the document over to Kollberg, drummed his fingers on the arm of the chair and said, "Was Matsson questioned here?"

"Yes, here in this room."

"You must have talked for a long time."

"Yes, he had to give a detailed statement."

"What sort of impression did he make—as a person, I mean?"

Backlund was now so irritated that he could not sit still. He kept moving the objects on the bare varnished surface of his desk and putting them back in exactly the same places.

"Impression!" he said. "Everything is covered thoroughly in the preliminary investigation. I've already told you that. Anyhow, the incident occurred on private property and when it came down to it, Matsson did not wish to bring a charge. I cannot understand what it is you want to know."

Kollberg put down the report without even having opened it. Then he made one last attempt.

"We want to know your personal opinion of Alf Matsson."

"I haven't got one," said the man.

When they left him, he was sitting at his desk reading the report of the preliminary investigation, his expression stiff and disapproving.

"Some people," said Kollberg in the elevator.

24

Bengt Jönsson's house was a rather small bungalow with an open veranda and a garden. The gate was open and on the gravel path inside was a blond, suntanned man, poised on his haunches in front of a tricycle. His hands were covered with grease and he was trying to repair the chain, which had come off. A boy of about five was standing watching him, a wrench in his hand.

When Kollberg and Martin Beck came through the gate, the man rose and wiped his hands on the back of his trousers. He was about thirty and wearing a checked shirt, dirty khaki trousers and wooden-soled shoes.

"Bengt Jönsson?" said Kollberg.

"Yes, that's me."

The man looked at them suspiciously.

"We're from the Stockholm police," said Martin Beck. "We've come to ask for some information about a friend of yours—Alf Matsson."

"Friend," said the man. "I'd hardly call him that. Is it about what happened last winter? I thought that was all dead and buried a long time ago."

"Yes, it is. The case is closed and won't be taken up again. It's not your part in the affair we're interested in, but Alf Matsson's," said Martin Beck.

"I saw in the papers that he's disappeared," said Bengt Jönsson. "He was in on some kind of narcotics ring, it said. I didn't know he used drugs."

"Perhaps he didn't, either. He sold them."

"Oh, Christ," said Bengt Jönsson. "What sort of information do you want? I don't know anything about that drug business."

"You can help us get a general picture of him," said Martin Beck.

"What do you want to know?" asked the fair-haired man.

"Everything you know about Alf Matsson," said Kollberg.

"That's not much," said Jönsson. "I hardly knew him, although we'd been acquainted for three years. I'd only met him a few times before that time last winter. I'm a journalist too, and we met when we were on a job together."

"Would you tell us what really happened last winter?" said Martin Beck.

"We might as well sit down," said Jönsson, going up onto the veranda. Martin Beck and Kollberg followed him. There were a table and four basket chairs, and Martin Beck sat down and offered Jönsson a cigarette. Kollberg looked at his chair suspiciously before cautiously sitting down in it. The chair creaked precariously beneath his weight.

"You'll understand that what you tell us is of no interest to us except as a testimony on Alf Matsson's character. Neither we nor the Malmö police have any reason to take up the case again," said Martin Beck. "What happened?"

"I met Alf Matsson by chance in the street. He was staying at a hotel in Malmö and I invited him home to dinner. I didn't really like him much, but he was on his own in town and wanted me to go out drinking with him, so I thought it'd be better if he came out to our place. He came in a taxi and I think he was sober then. Almost, anyhow. Then we ate and I offered him schnapps with the food and both of us drank quite a bit. After the meal we listened to records and drank whisky and sat talking. He got drunk pretty quickly and then he was unpleasant. My wife had a friend in at the same time and suddenly Alfie said to her, "Say, d'you mind if I fuck you?""

Bengt Jönsson fell silent, and Martin Beck nodded and said, "Go on."

"Well, that's what he said. My wife's friend was very upset, because she's not at all used to being spoken to like that. And my wife got angry and told Alfie he was a boor, and then he called my wife a whore and was damned rude. Then I got angry and told him to watch his mouth and the girls went into another room."

He fell silent again and Kollberg asked, "Was he usually unpleasant like that when he was drunk?"

"I don't know. I'd never seen him drunk before."

"What happened then?" said Martin Beck.

"Well, then we went on drinking. I didn't drink all that much myself, in fact, and didn't feel high at all. But Alfie got drunker and drunker, sitting there, hiccuping and belching and singing, and then suddenly he vomited all over the floor. I got him out to the bathroom and after a while he was all right again and appeared a bit more sober. When I said we should try to wipe up the mess, he said, 'That whore you're married to can do that.' That made me really mad and I told him he'd have to go, that I didn't want him in the house. But he just laughed and sat belching in the chair. When I said I was going to phone for a taxi for him, he said he was going to stay and sleep with my wife. Then I hit him and when he got up and said something dirty about my wife again, I hit him one more time so that he fell over the table and broke two glasses. Then I went on trying to get him out of the house, but he refused to go. Finally my wife called the police—it seemed the only way to get rid of him."

"He injured his hand, I understand," said Kollberg. "How did that happen?"

"I saw he was bleeding, but I didn't think it was serious. I was so angry, anyway, I didn't care. He cut himself on a glass when he fell. Then he claimed I'd stabbed him, which was a lie. I didn't have a knife. Then I was questioned at the police station for the rest of the night. A hellish business all around."

"Have you met Alf Matsson since that night?" said Kollberg.

"Oh, good God, no. Not since that morning at the police station. He was sitting in the corridor when I came out from seeing that cop—sorry, policeman—who was questioning me. And then that bastard had the nerve to say, "Hey, you've got a bit left. Let's go back to your place and finish it off later." I didn't even answer and thank God, I haven't seen him since."

Bengt Jönsson rose and went down to the boy, who was standing hitting the tricycle with the wrench. He crouched down and went on working on the chain.

"I've nothing else to tell you about it all. That was exactly what happened," he said over his shoulder.

Martin Beck and Kollberg got up, and he nodded to them as they went out through the gate.

On the way into Malmö, Kollberg said, "Nice guy, our friend Matsson. I don't think humanity has suffered any great loss if something really has happened to him. If so, then it's only your holiday that suffered."

25

Kollberg was staying at the St. Jörgen Hotel on Gustav Adolf's
Square, so after they had picked up Martin Beck's suitcase at
the police station, they went there. The hotel was full, but
Kollberg used his powers of persuasion and it was not long
before he had arranged for a room.

Martin Beck did not bother to unpack his suitcase. He
considered phoning his wife out on the island, but realized
that it was too late. She would hardly be pleased at having to
row across the sound in the dark in order to hear him tell her
that he did not know when he could get there.

He undressed and went into the bathroom. As he stood
under the shower, he heard Kollberg's characteristic thumping on the door to the corridor. As he had forgotten to take
the key out from the outside, a second or two elapsed before
Kollberg rushed into the room, calling out to him.

Martin Beck turned off the shower, swept a bath towel
around himself and went out to Kollberg.

"A dreadful thought suddenly occurred to me," said Kollberg. "It's five days since the opening of the crayfish season
and you probably haven't had a single one. Or do they have
crayfish in Hungary?"

"Not so far as I know," said Martin Beck. "I didn't see any."

"Get yourself dressed. I've ordered a table."

The dining room was crowded, but a corner table had
been reserved for them and laid for a crayfish dinner. On each
of their plates lay a paper hat and a bib, and each of the bibs
had a verse printed in red across it. They sat down and Martin

Beck looked dismally at his hat, made of blue crepe paper, with a shiny paper visor and POLICE in gold letters above the visor.

The crayfish were delicious, and the men did not talk much as they ate. When they had finished them, Kollberg was still hungry—an almost permanent state of affairs—so he ordered a steak fillet. While they waited for it, he said:

"There were four guys and a broad together with him that night before he left. I made a list for you. It's up in my room."

"Good," said Martin Beck. "Was it difficult?"

"Not especially. I got some help from Melander."

"Melander, yes. What's the time?"

"Half past nine."

Martin Beck got up and left Kollberg alone with his steak.

Of course, Melander had already gone to bed and Martin Beck waited patiently through several rings before the telephone was answered.

"Were you asleep in bed?"

"Yes, but it doesn't matter. Are you back?"

"In Malmö. How did things go with Alf Matsson?"

"I found out what you asked me to. Do you want to know now?"

"Yes, please."

"Wait a moment."

Melander went away, but returned very shortly.

"I wrote a report, but it's still at the office. Perhaps I can tell you from memory," he said.

"I'm sure you can," said Martin Beck.

"It deals with Thursday, the twenty-first of July. In the morning Alf Matsson first went up to the magazine, where he picked up his tickets from the office and four hundred kronor from the cash desk. Then he left almost at once and collected his passport and visa from the Hungarian Embassy. After that, he went back to Fleminggatan and, I imagine, packed his suitcase. Anyhow, he changed clothes. In the morning he had been wearing gray trousers, a gray jersey sweater, a blue machine-knit blazer with no lapels and beige suede shoes. In the afternoon and evening, he was wearing a lead-gray suit of thin flannel, a white shirt, black knit tie, black shoes and a gray-beige poplin coat."

It was warm in the phone booth. Martin Beck had got a piece of paper out of his pocket and was scribbling down some notes as Melander was talking.

"Yes, go on," he said.

"At quarter past twelve, he took a taxi from Fleminggatan to the Tankard, where he had lunch with Sven-Erik Molin, Per Kronkvist and Pia Bolt. Her name's Ingrid, but she's called Pia. He drank several steins of beer during and after the meal. At three o'clock, Pia Bolt left and the three men stayed on. About an hour later that is, about four o'clock—Stig Lund and Åke Gunnarsson came in and sat down at their table. They went over to drinking whisky then. Alf Matsson drank whisky and water. The conversation at the table was shop talk, but the waitress remembers that Alf Matsson said he was going away. Where to, she didn't hear."

"Was he drunk?" said Martin Beck.

"Must have been a little, but not noticeably. Not then. Can you hang on a moment?"

Melander went away again and Martin Beck opened the door of the telephone booth wide to let in a little air while he waited. Then Melander came back.

"Just getting my dressing gown on. Where was I? Yes, of course, at the Tankard. At six o'clock, they left—that's Kronkvist, Lund, Gunnarsson, Molin and Matsson—and took a taxi to the Golden Peace and had dinner and drinks. The conversation was mostly about various mutual acquaintances and liquor and girls. Alf Matsson was beginning to get very high and made loud comments about female guests there. Among other things, he's said to have shouted to a middle-aged woman artist, who was sitting at the other side of the room, something like, "Stunning pair of tits you've got there. Can I rest my head on them?" At half past nine they all moved on to the Opera House bar by taxi. There, they went on drinking whisky. Alf Matsson was drinking whisky and soda. Pia Bolt, who was already at the Opera House bar, joined Matsson and the other four men. At about midnight, Kronkvist and Lund left the restaurant, and shortly before one, Pia Bolt left with Molin. They were all drunk. Matsson and Gunnarsson stayed until the place closed and they were both very drunk. Matsson could not walk straight and accosted several women. I haven't managed to find out what happened after that, but presume he went home in a taxi."

"Didn't anyone notice when he left?"

"No, no one I talked to. Most of the guests leaving at that time were more or less drunk, and the staff were in a hurry to get home."

"Thanks a lot," said Martin Beck. "Will you do me another favor? Go up to Matsson's flat early tomorrow morning and see if you can find that lead-gray suit he was wearing that evening."

"Didn't you go there?" said Melander. "Before you went to Hungary?"

"Yes," said Martin Beck, "but I haven't got the memory of an elephant, like you. Go to bed and sleep now. I'll phone you tomorrow morning."

He returned to Kollberg, who had already polished off the steak and a dessert which had left sticky pink traces behind it on the plate in front of him.

"Had he found anything?"

"I don't know," said Martin Beck. "Perhaps."

They had coffee and Martin Beck told Kollberg about Budapest and Szluka and about Ari Boeck and her German friends. Then they took the elevator up and Martin Beck fetched Kollberg's typed report before going to bed.

He undressed, switched on the bed lamp and turned out the overhead light. Then he got into bed and began to read.

Ingrid (Pia) Bolt, born 1939 in Norrköping, unmarried, secretary, own flat at Strindbergsgatan 51.

Is included in the same gang as Matsson, but doesn't like M. much and has probably never had relations with him. Has gone around with Stig Lund for a year until quite recently. Nowadays seems to go around with Molin. Secretary at a fashion firm, Studio 45.

Per Kronkvist, born 1936 in Luleå, divorced, reporter on evening paper. Shares a flat with Lund, Sveavägen 88.

One of the gang, but no great friend of Matsson's. Divorced in 1936 in Luleå, since then a resident in Stockholm. Drinks quite a bit, nervous and restless. Appears stupid, but a nice guy. Found guilty of drunken driving in May 1965.

Stig Lund, born 1932 in Gothenburg, unmarried, photographer on the same magazine as Kronkvist. Flat on Sveavägen owned by the magazine.

Came to Stockholm in 1960 and has known Matsson since that time. They spent a lot of time together earlier, but during the last two years they have only met because they go to the same pubs. Quiet and gentle, drinks a lot and usually falls asleep at the table when he's drunk. Ex-athlete, took part in competitions with cross-country running his specialty, 1945–51.

Åke Gunnarsson, born 1932 in Jakobstad, Finland. Unmarried, journalist, writes about cars. Own flat, Svartensgatan 6.

Came to Sweden 1950. Journalist on various auto magazines and in the daily press since 1959. Earlier various jobs such as auto mechanic. Speaks Swedish almost without accent. Moved to flat on Svartensgatan July 1 of this year; before that he lived in Hagalund. Plans to marry at beginning of September, to a girl from Uppsala who is not one of the gang. No more friendly with Matsson than the aforementioned. Drinks quite a bit, but is known for not appearing drunk when he is. Seems quite a bright boy.

Sven-Erik Molin, born 1933 in Stockholm, divorced, journalist, house in Enskede.

Alf Matsson's "best friend," i.e. he maintains he is, but speaks ill of M. behind his back. Divorced in Stockholm four years ago, keeps up support payments and sees his children now and again. Conceited, overbearing and tough attitude, especially when drunk, which happens often. Charged with intoxication in Stockholm twice, 1963 and 1965. Relationship with Pia Bolt not very serious on his side.

There are some more in the group: Krister Sjöberg, commercial artist; Bror Forsgren, advertising representative; Lena Rosén, journalist; Bengtsfors, journalist; Jack Meredith, film cameraman, as well as a few more, more or less peripheral. None of these was actually present on the day or evening in question.

Martin Beck got up and fetched the piece of paper he had made notes on while talking to Melander.

He took the paper back to bed with him.

Before putting out the light, he read the whole lot through again—Kollberg's report and his own carelessly scribbled notes.

26

Saturday, the thirteenth of August, was gray and windy, and the plane to Stockholm took its time against the headwind.

The lingering taste of crayfish was anything but delicious at this time of day and the paper mug of bad coffee that the airline had to offer hardly improved matters. Martin Beck leaned his head against the vibrating window and watched the clouds.

After a while he tried smoking, but it tasted disgusting. Kollberg was reading a daily from southern Sweden, glancing critically at the cigarette. He probably did not feel too good either.

As far as Alf Matsson was concerned, it could now be said that he was probably seen for the last time exactly three weeks ago—in the foyer of the Hotel Duna in Budapest.

The pilot informed them that the weather was cloudy and that the temperature was fifteen degrees centigrade in Stockholm, and it was drizzling.

Martin Beck extinguished his cigarette in the ashtray and said, "That murder you were on ten days ago, is it cleared up?"

"Oh, yes."

"No difficulties?"

"No. Psychologically, it was utterly uninteresting, if that's what you mean. Drunk as pigs, both of them. The guy who lived in the flat sat there giving the other guy trouble until he got angry and hit him with a bottle. Then he got scared and hit him twenty times more. But you know all that."

"And afterward. Did he try to get away?"

"Oh, yes, of course. He went home and wrapped up his bloodstained clothes. Then he got a bottle of wood alcohol and went and sat under Skanstull Bridge. All we had to do was to go and pick him up. Then he flatly denied everything for a while and then began to bawl."

After a brief pause, he said, still without looking up, "He's got a screw or two missing. Skanstull Bridge! But he did his best."

Kollberg lowered his paper and looked at Martin Beck.

"Exactly," he said. "He did his best."

He returned to his paper.

Martin Beck frowned, picked up the list he had received the night before and read it through again. Time and time again, until they arrived. He put the paper in his pocket and fastened his safety belt. Then came the usual few minutes of unpleasantness as the plane waddled in the wind and slid down its invisible chute. Gardens and rooftops and two bounces on the concrete, and then he could let out his breath again.

They exchanged a few remarks in the domestic flight lounge while they were waiting for their luggage.

"Are you going out to the island tonight?"

"No, I'll wait a bit."

"There's something rotten about this Matsson story."

"Yes."

"Aggravating."

In the middle of Traneberg Bridge, Kollberg said, "And it's even more aggravating that we can't stop thinking about the miserable business. Matsson was a boor. If he's really disappeared, then that's a good deed done. If he's on the run, then someone'll get him one of these days. That's not our business. And if by any chance he's somehow died down there, then that's nothing to do with us either. Is it?"

"That's right."

"But supposing the man just goes on having disappeared. Then we'll be thinking about it for ten years. Christ!"

"You're not being particularly logical."

"No. Exactly," said Kollberg.

The police station seemed unusually quiet, but of course it was Saturday and, despite everything, still summer. On

Martin Beck's desk lay a number of uninteresting letters and a note from Melander:

"A pair of black shoes in the flat. Old. Not used for a long time. No dark-gray suit."

Outside the window, the wind tore at the treetops and the rain was driving against the windowpane. He thought of the Danube and the steamers and the breeze from the sunny hills. Viennese waltzes. The soft, warm night air. The bridge. The quay. Martin Beck gingerly felt the bump on the back of his head with his fingers, then went back to his desk and sat down.

Kollberg came in, looked at Melander's message, scratched his stomach and said, "It's probably our concern in any case."

"Yes, I think so."

Martin Beck thought for a moment.

"When you were in Rumania, did you turn in your passport?"

"Yes, the police collected your passport at the airport. Then you got it back at the hotel a week later. I saw mine standing in my pigeonhole for several days before they gave it to me. It was a big hotel. The police handed in whole bundles of passports every evening."

Martin Beck pulled the telephone toward him.

"Budapest 298–317, a person-to-person call to Major Vilmos Szluka. Yes, Major S-Z-L-U-K-A. No, it's in Hungary."

He returned to the window and stared out into the rain without saying anything. Kollberg sat in the visitor's chair and studied his nails. Neither of them moved or spoke until the telephone rang.

Someone said in very bad German, "Yes, Major Szluka will come in a minute."

Steps echoed through police headquarters in Deák Ferenc Tér. Then Szluka's voice came over: "Good morning. How are things in Stockholm?"

"It's raining and windy. Cold."

"Oh, it's over 85° Fahrenheit here. Almost too hot. I was just thinking of going to Palatino. Anything new?"

"Not yet."

"Same here. We haven't found him yet. Can I help you with anything?"

"Doesn't it sometimes happen that people lose their passports now during the tourist season?"

"Yes, unfortunately. It's always troublesome. Fortunately that's not one of my concerns."

"Could you find out whether any foreigner has reported the loss of his passport at the Ifjuság or the Duna since the twenty-first of July?"

"Of course. But it's not my department, as I said. Will it be all right if I get the answer back by five?"

"You can telephone whenever you like. And one more thing."

"Yes?"

"If someone has reported this, do you think you could find out what the person looked like? Just a brief description."

"I'll call you at five o'clock. Good-bye."

"Good-bye. Hope you don't miss going to the baths."

He put down the receiver. Kollberg looked at him suspiciously.

"What the hell is the business about baths?"

"A sulfur bath, where you sit in marble armchairs under water."

"Oh."

There was a brief silence. Kollberg scratched his head and said, "So in Budapest he was wearing a blue blazer and gray trousers and brown shoes."

"Yes, and the raincoat."

"And in his suitcase there was a blue blazer."

"Yes."

"And a pair of gray trousers."

"Yes."

"And a pair of brown shoes."

"Yes."

"And the night before he left he was wearing a dark suit and black shoes."

"Yes, and the raincoat."

"And neither the shoes nor the suit are in his flat."

"No."

"Christ!" said Kollberg simply.

"Yes."

The atmosphere in the room changed and seemed to become less tense. Martin Beck rummaged in his drawer, found a dry old Florida and lit it. Like the man in Malmö, he was trying to give up smoking, but much more halfheartedly.

Kollberg yawned and looked at his watch.

"Shall we go and eat somewhere?"

"Yes, why not?"

"The Tankard?"

"Sure."

27

The wind had dropped and in Vasa Park the light rain was falling peacefully down onto the double row of tombola stalls, a carousel and two policemen in black rain capes. The carousel was running and on one of the painted horses sat a lone child: a little girl in a red-plastic coat with a hood. She was riding round and round in the rain with a solemn expression on her face and her eyes focused straight ahead. Her parents were standing under an umbrella a little way away, regarding the amusement park with melancholy eyes. A fresh smell of greenery and wet leaves came from the park. It was Saturday afternoon and, despite everything, still summer.

The restaurant diagonally opposite the park was almost empty. The only audible sound in the place was a faint comforting rustle from the evening papers of two elderly regular customers and the muted sound of darts thudding into the board in the dart room. Martin Beck and Kollberg took a seat in the bar, six feet or so from the table that was the favorite refuge of Alf Matsson and his fellow journalists. There was no one there now, but in the middle of the table stood a glass containing a red reservation card. Presumably this was a fixture.

"The lunch hour is over now," said Kollberg. "In an hour or so people begin dropping in again, and in the evening it's so chock-full of people spilling beer all over each other that you can hardly get your foot inside."

The atmosphere did not make for extensive discussion. They ate a late lunch in silence. Outside the Swedish summer was pouring away. Kollberg drained a stein of beer, folded up his table napkin, wiped his mouth and said, "Is it difficult to get across the border down there? Without a passport?"

"Fairly. They say the borders are guarded well. A foreigner who didn't know his way around would hardly make it."

"And if you leave by the ordinary routes, then you have to have a visa in your passport?"

"Yes, and an exit permit besides. That's a loose piece of paper that you get on entry and keep in your passport until you leave the country. Then the passport control people take it. The police also stamp the date of departure beside the visa in your passport. Look."

Martin Beck took his passport out of his inside pocket and put it on the table. Kollberg studied the stamps. Then he said:

"And assuming that you've got both a visa and an exit permit, then you can cross any border you like?"

"Yes. You have five countries to choose from—Czechoslovakia, the Soviet Union, Rumania, Yugoslavia and Austria. And you can go any way you like—by air, train, car or boat."

"Boat? From Hungary?"

"Yes, on the Danube. From Budapest you can get to Vienna or Bratislava in a few hours by hydrofoil."

"And you can ride a bicycle, walk, swim, ride horseback or crawl?" said Kollberg.

"Yes, as long as you make your way to a border station."

"And you can go to Austria and Yugoslavia without a visa?"

"That depends on what kind of passport you've got. If it's Swedish for instance, or German or Italian, then you don't need one. On a Hungarian passport you can go to Czechoslovakia or Yugoslavia without a visa."

"But it's hardly likely that he did that?"

"No."

They went on to coffee. Kollberg was still looking at the stamps in the passport.

"The Danes didn't stamp it when you got to Kastrup," he said.

"No."

"Then in other words there's no evidence that you've returned to Sweden."

"No," said Martin Beck.

A moment later he added, "But on the other hand, I'm sitting here—right?"

A number of customers had dropped in during the last half hour, and there was already a shortage of tables. A man of about thirty-five came in and sat down at the table with the red reservation card on it, was given a stein of beer and sat leafing through the evening paper, seemingly bored. Now and again he looked anxiously toward the door, as if he were waiting for someone. He had a beard and was wearing thick-rimmed glasses, a brown checked tweed jacket, a white shirt, brown trousers and black shoes.

"Who's that?" said Martin Beck.

"Don't know. They all look alike. Besides, there are a number of marginal creatures who only show up now and then."

"It's not Molin, anyhow, because I'd recognize him."

Kollberg glanced at the man.

"Gunnarsson maybe."

Martin Beck thought.

"No, I've seen him too."

A woman came in. She had red hair and was quite young, dressed in a brick-red sweater, tweed skirt and green stockings. She moved easily, letting her eyes wander over the room as she fingered her nose. She sat down at the table with the red card and said, "Ciao, Per."

"Ciao, sweetheart."

"Per," said Kollberg. "That's Kronkvist. And that's Pia Bolt."

"Why have they all got beards?"

Martin Beck said it thoughtfully, as if he had pondered the problem for a long time.

"Perhaps they're false," said Kollberg solemnly.

He looked at his watch.

"Just to give us trouble," he said.

"We'd better get back," said Martin Beck. "Did you tell Stenström to come on up?"

Kollberg nodded. As they were leaving, they heard the man named Per Kronkvist call out to the waitress:

"More beer! Over here!"

It was very quiet at the police station. Stenström was sitting in the downstairs office playing patience.

Kollberg looked critically at him, and said, "Have you already started with that? What are you going to do when you get old?"

"Sit thinking the same thing I'm thinking now: why am I sitting here?"

"You're going to check some alibis," said Martin Beck. "Give him the list, Lennart."

Stenström was given the list. He glanced at it.

"Now?"

"Yes, this evening."

"Molin, Lund, Kronkvist, Gunnarsson, Bengtsfors, Pia Bolt. Who is Bengtsfors?"

"That's a mistake," said Kollberg gloomily. "Supposed to be Bengt Fors. The *t* on my typewriter sticks to the *s*."

"Shall I question the girl too?"

"Yes, if it amuses you," said Martin Beck. "She's at the Tankard."

"Can I talk to them direct?"

"Why not? Routine investigation in the Alf Matsson case. Everyone knows what it's all about now. How's things with the Narcotics boys, by the way?"

"I spoke to Jacobsson," said Stenström. "They'll soon have it all tied up. As soon as the heads here knew that Matsson had had it, they began to talk. I was thinking of something, by the way. Matsson sold the stuff directly to a few people who were really desperate and he made them pay through the nose."

"What were you thinking?"

"Couldn't it be one of the poor devils he skinned—that one of his customers got tired of him, so to speak?"

"Could be," said Martin Beck solemnly.

"Especially at the movies," said Kollberg. "In America."

Stenström put the piece of paper into his pocket and got up. At the door he stopped and said huffily, "Sometimes something different actually might happen here too."

"Possibly," said Kollberg. "But you've forgotten that Matsson disappeared in Hungary, on his way to pick up some more stuff for his poor customers. Now scram."

Stenström left.

"That was nasty of you," said Martin Beck.

"He might do a little thinking for himself too," said Kollberg.

"That's what he was doing."

"Huh!"

Martin Beck went out into the corridor. Stenström was just putting on his coat.

"Look at their passports."

Stenström nodded.

"Don't go alone."

"Are they dangerous?" said Stenström sarcastically.

"Routine," said Martin Beck.

He went back in to Kollberg. They sat in silence until the telephone rang. Martin picked up the receiver.

"Your call to Budapest will be coming through at seven o'clock instead of five," said the telephone operator.

They digested the message for a moment. Then Kollberg said, "God. This is no fun."

"No," said Martin Beck. "It's not much fun."

"Two hours," said Kollberg. "Shall we drive around a little and have a look-see?"

"Yes, why not?"

They drove over West Bridge. The Saturday traffic had thinned out and the bridge was practically deserted. On the crest they passed a German tourist coach that had slowed down. Martin Beck saw the passengers inside standing up and staring out across the silvery bay and at the misty silhouette of the city.

"Molin is the only one who lives outside the city," said Kollberg. "Let's take him first."

They went on over Liljeholm Bridge, and Kollberg swung in off the main road among the houses, twisting along the narrow roads for a while, before finding the right house. He let the car run slowly past the row of hedges and fences as he read the names on the gateposts.

"Here it is," he said. "Molin lives on the left. That's his porch you can see. The house must have been occupied once by a single family, but now it's divided. The other entrance is around the back."

"Who lives in the other part of the house?" said Martin Beck.

"A retired customs official and his wife."

The garden in front of the house was wild, with gnarled apple trees and overgrown berrybushes. But the hedges around it were well trimmed, and the white fencing looked recently painted.

"Big garden," said Kollberg. "And well sheltered. Do you want to see any more?"

"No. Drive on."

"Then we'll take Svartensgatan," said Kollberg. "Gunnars-son."

They drove back into the south side of the city, parking the car in Mosebacke Square.

Svartensgatan 6 was right by the square. It was an old building with a large paved courtyard. Gunnarsson lived three floors up, facing the street.

"He hasn't lived here all that long," said Martin Beck when they had got back to the car.

"Since the first of July."

"And before that he lived in Hagalund. Do you know where?"

Kollberg stopped at a red traffic light.

He nodded toward the large corner window of the Opera House bar.

"Perhaps they're all sitting together in there now," he said. "All of them except Matsson. In Hagalund? Yes, I've got the address."

"Then we'll go there later," said Martin Beck. "Go along Strandvägen. I'd like to look at the boats."

They drove along Strandvägen and Martin Beck looked at the boats. At one quay lay a large white ocean-going vessel with the American flag aft, and farther on, flanked by two Åland sailing-smacks, lay a Polish motor launch.

Outside the entrance of the building where Pia Bolt lived on Strindbergsgatan, a small boy in a checked sou'wester and poncho was pushing a plastic double-decker bus back and forth across the step as he imitated the sound of its motor with his lips. The sound grew muted and uneven as he braked the bus to allow Kollberg and Martin Beck to pass.

Inside the entrance, Stenström was standing gloomily looking at Kollberg's list.

"What are you hanging around here for?" said Kollberg.

"She's not home. And she wasn't at the Tankard. I was just wondering where to go next. But if you're thinking of taking over, then I can go home."

"Try the Opera House bar," said Kollberg.

"Why are you on your own, by the way," said Martin Beck.

"I've had Rönn with me. He'll be back in a minute. He's just gone home to his old lady with some flowers. It's her birthday and she lives right here on the corner."

"How's it going?" said Martin Beck.

"We've checked Lund and Kronkvist. They left the Opera House bar about midnight and went straight to the Hamburger Exchange. There they met two gals they knew, and at about three they went back home with one of them."

He looked at the list.

"Her name is Svensson and she lives in Lidingö. They stayed there until eight o'clock on Friday morning and then took a taxi together to work. At one o'clock, they went to the Tankard and sat there until five, when they went to Karlstad on a reporting job. I haven't got around to the others yet."

"I realize that," said Martin Beck. "Just carry on. We'll be at the station after seven. Phone if you've finished before too late."

The rain grew heavier as they drove toward Hagalund. When Kollberg stopped the car outside the low block of flats in which Gunnarsson had lived until two months ago, the water was pouring down the windowpanes and the drumming on the car roof was deafening.

They put up their coatcollars and ran across the pavement into the entrance. The building was three-storied and on one of the doors on the second floor there was a calling card fastened on with a thumbtack. The name on the calling card was also on the list of tenants in the entrance hall, and the white plastic letters looked newer and whiter than the others.

They walked back to the car and drove around the block, then stopped in front of the building. The flat where Gunnarsson had presumably lived had only two windows and appeared to consist of only one room.

"It must be a pretty small flat," said Kollberg. "He's going to get married now since he's got a bigger one."

Martin Beck looked out into the rain. He wanted to smoke and felt cold. There was a field and wooded slope on the other side of the street. At the far end of the field was a newly built highrise building and another one was in the process of being built beside it. The whole field was probably going to be built on with a row of identical highrises. From the dismal block where Gunnarsson had lived, one at least had an open, country-like view, but now that, too, would be spoiled.

In the middle of the field stood the charred remains of a burnt-out house.

"A fire?" he said, pointing.

Kollberg leaned forward and peered through the rain.

"That's an old farm," he said. "I remember seeing it last summer. A fine old wooden house, but no one lived there. I think the fire department burned it down. You know—to practice. They set it alight and then put the fire out, and then they set it alight again and put it out again, and they go on like that until there's nothing left. Pity with such a fine old place. But they probably need the land to build on."

He looked at his watch and started the engine.

"We'll have to step on it if we're going to get your call," he said.

The rain poured down the windshield and Kollberg had to drive carefully. They sat in silence all the way back. When they got out of the car it was five to seven and already dark.

The telephone rang so precisely on the dot of seven that it seemed almost unnatural. It was unnatural.

"Where the hell's Lennart?" said Kollberg's wife.

Martin Beck handed over the receiver and tried not to listen to Kollberg's replies in the dialogue that followed.

"Yes, I'm coming soon now. . . . Yes, in a little while, I said. . . . Tomorrow? That'll be hard, I expect. . . ."

Martin Beck retired to the bathroom and did not come back until he had heard the receiver being replaced

"We should have children," said Kollberg. "Poor thing, sitting out there on her own, waiting for me."

They had only been married six months, so things would probably work out all right.

A bit later the call came through.

"I'm sorry to have kept you waiting," said Szluka. "It's more difficult to get hold of people here on Saturday. However, you were right."

"About the passport?"

"Yes. A Belgian student lost his passport at Hotel Ifjuság."

"When?"

"That hasn't been determined at the moment. He came to the hotel on Friday the twenty-second of July in the afternoon. Alf Matsson came in the evening of the same day."

"So it fits."

"Yes, it does, doesn't it? The difficulty is this. This man, whose name is Roeder, is visiting Hungary for the first time and doesn't know the regulations here. He himself claims that he found it quite natural to hand in his passport and not get it back until he had left the hotel. As he was to stay for three weeks, he didn't give the matter a thought and did not ask for his passport before Monday, in other words the day we met for the first time. He needed it to apply for a visa to Bulgaria. All this is, of course, according to the man's own statement."

"It could be right."

"Yes, of course. At the hotel reception they at once said that Roeder had been given back his passport on the morning after he had arrived, that is, the twenty-third, or the same day Matsson moved to Hotel Duna—and disappeared. Roeder swears he was never given his passport, and the hotel staff are equally certain his passport was put in his pigeonhole on the Friday evening and that, consequently, he should have received it back when he came down on the Saturday morning. That's the routine."

"Does anyone remember that he actually received it?"

"No. But that would be too much to ask. At this time of year, it often happens that people at the reception desk receive up to fifty foreign passports a day and hand out the same number. Also, the people who sort the passports into the pigeonholes are not the same ones who hand them out the next morning.

"Have you seen this Roeder?"

"Yes, he's still staying at the hotel. His embassy is arranging for his journey home."

"And? I mean, does it fit?"

"He has a beard. Otherwise they aren't especially alike, judging from the pictures. But unfortunately people don't often look like their passport photos either. Someone could well have stolen the passport out of the pigeonhole during the night. Nothing could be simpler. The night porter is alone and naturally has to turn his back sometimes, or leave his place. And the officials who check passports haven't time to study faces when tourists are pouring back and forth across the border. If we work on the theory that your fellow countryman took Roeder's passport, then he might well have left the country with its help."

There was a short silence. Then Szluka said:

"Someone has done it, anyway."

Martin Beck sat up.

"Do you know that?"

"Yes. We heard about it twenty minutes ago. Roeder's exit

permit is in our files. It was handed in to the border police in Hegyeshalom on the afternoon of Saturday the twenty-third of July. One of the passengers on the Budapest-Vienna express. And that passenger can't have been Roeder as he's still here."

Szluka paused again. Then he said hesitantly, "I suppose this means that Matsson has left Hungary."

"No," said Martin Beck. "He's never been there at all."

28

Martin Beck slept badly and got up early. The flat in Bagar-mossen was dismal and lifeless and the familiar objects seemed irrelevant and dreary. He took a shower. Shaved. Took out his newly pressed gray suit. Dressed carefully and correctly. Then went out on to the balcony. It had stopped raining. He looked at the thermometer. It was 60° Fahrenheit. He got himself a lugubrious grass-widower's breakfast of tea and rusks. Then he sat down and waited.

Kollberg came at nine o'clock. He had Stenström with him in the car. They drove to the police station.

"How did it go?" said Martin Beck.

"So so," said Stenström.

He leafed through his notebook.

"Molin was working on that Saturday, that's clear. He was at the office from eight o'clock in the morning. On that Friday, he seems to have been at home sleeping off his hangover. We argued a bit over his being asleep. He said that he hadn't been sleeping, but had passed out. 'Don't you know what it is to pass out and have little demons sitting there on your pillow, copper? That's good. Then you're suited to being a policeman, because you don't understand a god damn about anything.' I wrote down that remark, word for word."

"Why did he have little demons?" said Kollberg.

"That didn't come out. Didn't seem to know himself, and what he'd done the night between Thursday and Friday, he couldn't remember. He said he was grateful for that. He was pretty darned insolent and awkward all around."

"Go on," said Martin Beck.

"Well, I'm afraid I was wrong yesterday when I said Lund and Kronkvist were clear. It turned out, in fact, that it wasn't Kronkvist but Fors who had gone with those girls to Lidingö. On the other hand, it was Kronkvist who went with Lund to Karlstad, not on Friday but on Saturday. It is a bit of a mix-up, all this, but I don't think Lund was lying when he made the first statement. He really didn't remember. He and Kronkvist seem to have been the most drunk of the lot of them. Lund got everything mixed up. Fors was brighter and when I got hold of him things became clearer. Lund collapsed as soon as they got to the girls' place, and they didn't get a sign of life out of him all that Friday. Then on Saturday morning, he rang up Fors, who went there and picked him up, and then they went to the pub, not to the Tankard, as Lund had thought, but to the Opera House bar. When Lund had had something to eat and a couple of beers, he revived and went home and picked up Kronkvist and all his photographic gear. Kronkvist was at home at that time."

"What had he done before that?"

"Lain at home feeling ill and lonely, he said. The only definite thing is that he was there at half past four on Saturday afternoon."

"Is that verified?"

"Yes, they got to the hotel in Karlstad in the evening. Kronkvist also had a fearful hangover, he said. Lund said he was too high to have anything. Lund hasn't got a beard, by the way. I made a note of that."

"Uh-huh."

"Then there was Gunnarsson. His memory was a little better. He sat at home writing on Friday. On Saturday he was at the office at first in the morning and then in the evening, turning in various articles."

"Are you certain?"

"I wouldn't say that. The office there is large and I couldn't find anyone who could remember anything special. On the other hand, it's true that he handed in an article, but that could just as well have been in the evening as in the morning."

"And passports?"

"Wait a minute. Pia Bolt was also quite explicit. She refused to say where she'd been on that Thursday night, however. I got the impression that she'd been sleeping with someone but didn't want to say who."

"Sounds possible," said Kollberg. "It was Thursday and all that."

"What do you mean by that?" said Stenström.

"Nothing. Perhaps that was a little below the belt."

"Go on," said Martin Beck.

"On Saturday, anyway, she was at home with her mother from eleven in the morning on. I checked that in a discreet way. It was true. Well, now there are the passports. Molin refused to show his. He didn't have to identify himself in his own home, he said. Lund had an almost new passport. The last stamp was from Arlanda on the sixteenth of June, when he returned from Israel. That seemed to be all right."

"Refused to show his passport!" said Kollberg. "And you let him."

"Pia Bolt had been to Majorca for a week two years ago, that is all. Kronkvist had an old passport. It looked a mess, covered with notes and scribbles. The last stamp from Gothenburg in May. Returning from England. Gunnarsson also had an old passport, almost full, but a bit cleaner. He has stamps from Arlanda, left the country on the seventh of May and reentered the tenth. Had been to the Renault factories in Billancourt, he said. Evidently they don't stamp passports in France."

"No, that's right," said Martin Beck.

"Then there were the others. I haven't had time to get around to them all. Krister Sjöberg was at home with his family in Älvsjö. That Meredith, he's an American—colored, by the way."

"We'll skip that," said Kollberg. "We couldn't take him in anyhow, or we'd be lynched by the Mods."

"Now you're being really stupid."

"I usually am. Anyhow, I don't think you need go on."

"No, I don't think so," said Martin Beck.

"Do you know who it is?" said Stenström.

"We think so at least."

"Who?"

Kollberg glared at Stenström.

"Think for yourself, man," he said. "In the first place, was it Alf Matsson who was in Budapest? Would Matsson take a small fortune to pay for drugs and then not bother about it and leave the money in his bag at the hotel? Would Matsson throw his key down outside the entrance of the police station? A man who ought to make a long detour around any policeman he ever saw down there? Why should Matsson disappear of his own free will, in such an improvised manner?"

"No, of course not."

"Why should Matsson travel to Hungary dressed in a blue blazer, gray trousers and suede shoes, when he had exactly the same kind of clothes packed in his bag? What happened to Matsson's dark suit? The one he had on the night before and which was not in his bag and is not in his flat?"

"O.K. It wasn't Matsson. Who was it then?"

"Someone who had Matsson's glasses and raincoat, someone with a beard. Who was last seen with Matsson? Who had no alibi whatsoever before Saturday evening, at the earliest? Who of all that lot was sufficiently sober and intelligent to be able to cook up this little story? Think it over."

Stenström looked very solemn.

"I've thought of something else," said Kollberg.

He spread the map of Budapest out on the table.

"Look here. There's the hotel and there's the central station, or whatever it's called."

"Budapest Nyugati."

"Maybe. If I was going to walk from the hotel to the station, I would walk this way and thus pass police headquarters."

"That's right, but in that case you'd go to the wrong station. The trains to Vienna go from down here, from the old Eastern Railway Station."

Kollberg said nothing. He went on staring at the map.

Martin Beck spread out a blueprint of the Solna area and nodded at Stenström.

"Go on out to the Solna police," he said. "Ask them to rope this area off. There's a burnt-out house there. We'll be there soon."

"Now, at once?"

"Yes."

Stenström left. Martin Beck hunted for a cigarette and lit it. He smoked in silence. And looked at Kollberg who was sitting quite still. Then he put out the cigarette and said, "Let's go, then."

Kollberg drove swiftly through the empty Sunday streets and then they crossed the bridge. The sun came out from behind driving clouds and a light breeze swept across the water.

Martin Beck looked absently at a group of small sailing boats which were just rounding a buoy in the bay.

They drove in silence and parked in the same place as the day before. Kollberg pointed at a black Lancia parked a little farther on.

"That's his car," he said. "Then he's probably at home."

They crossed Svartensgatan and pushed open the door. The air felt raw and damp. They walked in silence up the worn stairs to the fifth floor.

29

The door was opened immediately.

The man in the doorway was wearing a dressing gown and slippers, and looking extremely surprised.

"Sorry," he said. "I thought you were my fiancée."

Martin Beck recognized him at once. It was the same man Molin had pointed out to him at the Tankard, the day before his Budapest trip. An open, pleasant face. Calm blue eyes. Quite powerfully built. He had a beard and was of medium height, but this was—as in the case of the Belgian student, Roeder—the only resemblance to Matsson.

"We're from the police. My name is Beck. This is Inspector Kollberg."

The introductions were stiff and courteous.

"Kollberg."

"Gunnarsson."

"May we come in for a minute?" said Martin Beck.

"Of course. What's it about?"

"We would like to talk about Alf Matsson."

"A policeman came yesterday and asked me about the same thing."

"Yes, we know that."

As Martin Beck and Kollberg entered the flat, they underwent a change. It happened to them both at the same time and without either of them being aware of it. All that had been tense, uncertain and vigilant about them vanished and was replaced by a routine calm, a mechanical determination which showed that they knew what was going to happen and that they had been through the same thing before.

They walked through the flat without saying anything. It was light and spacious and furnished with care and consideration, but in some way gave the impression that it had not yet been lived in properly. Much of the furniture was new and still looked as if it were standing in a shop window.

Two of the rooms had windows facing the street and the bedroom and kitchen looked out over the courtyard. The door to the bathroom was open and the light was on inside. Evidently the man had just begun getting washed and dressed when they had rung the bell. In the bedroom there were two wide beds standing close together, and one had recently been slept in. On the bedside table by the unmade bed stood a half-empty bottle of mineral water, a glass, two pillboxes and a framed photograph. There was also a rocking chair in the room, two stools, and a dressing table with drawers and movable mirror. The photo was of a young woman. She had fair hair, clean, healthy features and very light-colored eyes. No makeup, but a silver chain around her neck, a so-called Bismarck chain. Martin Beck recognized the kind. Sixteen years ago he had given his wife an exact replica of it. They went back into the study. The tour was complete.

"Do please sit down," said Gunnarsson.

Martin Beck nodded and sat down in one of the basket chairs by the desk, which was clearly intended for two people. The man in the dressing gown remained standing and glanced at Kollberg, who was still moving round the flat.

Manuscripts, books and papers lay in neat piles on the table. A page already started was inserted into the typewriter, and beside the telephone stood yet another framed photograph. Martin Beck at once recognized the woman with the silver chain and light eyes. But this picture had been taken out-of-doors. Her head was thrown back and she was laughing at the photographer, the wind tugging at her ruffled fair hair.

"What can I do to help you," said the man in the dressing gown, politely.

Martin Beck looked straight at him. His eyes were still blue and calm and steady. It was quiet in the room. Kollberg could be heard doing something in another part of the flat, presumably in the washroom or the kitchen.

"Tell me what happened," said Martin Beck.

"When?"

"The eve of the twenty-second of July, when you and Matsson left the Opera House bar."

"I've already done that. We parted in the street. I took a taxi and came home. He wasn't going in the same direction and waited for the next one."

Martin Beck leaned his forearms on the desk and looked at the woman in the photograph.

"May I look at your passport?" he said.

The man walked around the desk, sat down and pulled out one of the drawers. The basket chair creaked amiably.

"Here you are," he said.

Martin Beck turned over the pages of the passport. It was old and worn and the last stamp was indeed an entry stamp from Arlanda on the tenth of May. On the next page—which was also the last one in the passport—there were a few notes, among others two telephone numbers and a short verse. The inside of the cover was also full of notes. Most of them seemed to be comments on cars or engines, made long ago and in great haste. The verse was written across on a slant, with a green ball-point pen. He twisted the passport and read:

> There was a young man of Dundee
> Who said "They can't do without me.
> No house is complete
> Without me and my seat.
> My initials are W.C."

The man on the other side of the table followed his glance and explained, "It's a limerick."

"So I see."

"It's about Winston Churchill. They say that he wrote it himself. I heard it on the plane from Paris and thought it was so good that I ought to write it down."

Martin Beck said nothing. He stared at the verse. Underneath the writing, the paper was a little lighter and there were several small green dots that should not have been there. They could have been some perforations from a green stamp on the other side of the page, but no such stamp existed. Stenström ought to have noticed that.

"If you had left the plane in Copenhagen and taken the ferry to Sweden, you'd have been saved the trouble," he said.

"I don't understand what you mean."

The telephone rang. Gunnarsson answered. Kollberg came into the room.

"It's for one of you," said the man in the dressing gown.

Kollberg took the receiver, listened and said, "Oh, yes. Get them going then. Yes, wait out there. We'll be there soon."

He put the receiver down.

"That was Stenström. The fire department burned the house down last Monday."

"We have people searching through the remains of that burnt-out house in Hagalund," said Martin Beck.

"Well, what about it?" said Kollberg.

"I still don't know what you mean."

The man's eyes were still just as steady and open. There was a brief silence, and then Martin Beck shrugged his shoulders and said, "Go in and get dressed."

Without a word, Gunnarsson walked toward the bedroom door. Kollberg followed him.

Martin Beck remained where he was, immobile. His eyes rested again on the photograph. Although actually it was unimportant, for some reason he was annoyed that the conversation should end like this. After having seen the passport, he felt utterly certain, but the idea about the fire department's practice site was a guess, which might very well prove to be wrong. In that case, and if the man managed to maintain his attitude, the investigation would be very troublesome. And yet this was not really the main reason for his dissatisfaction.

Gunnarsson came back five minutes later wearing a gray sweater and brown trousers. He looked at his watch and said, "Now we can go. I'll be having a visitor soon, and would be grateful if . . ."

He smiled and left the sentence unfinished. Martin Beck remained seated.

"We're in no special hurry," he said.

Kollberg came in from the bedroom.

"The trousers and the blue blazer are still hanging in the wardrobe," he said.

Martin Beck nodded. Gunnarsson walked back and forth across the room. He was moving more nervously now, but his expression was as unshakably calm as before.

"Perhaps it's not so bad as it seems," said Kollberg in a friendly way. "You don't have to be so resigned."

Martin Beck glanced at his colleague quickly, then looked at Gunnarsson again. Of course, Kollberg was right. The man had given up. He knew the game was up and he had known it the moment they'd stepped over the threshold. Presumably he was now enveloped in this feeling as if in a cocoon. But still not completely invulnerable. Nevertheless, what had to be done was very unpleasant.

Martin Beck leaned back in the basket chair and waited. Kollberg stood silent and immobile by the bedroom door. Gunnarsson had remained standing in the middle of the floor. He looked at his watch again but said nothing.

A minute went past. Two. Three. The man again looked at his wristwatch. Probably a purely reflex action, and it was clear that it annoyed him. After two minutes more he did it again, but this time tried to mask his maneuver by running the back of his left hand over his face as he glanced down at his wrist. The door of a car slammed somewhere down on the street.

He opened his mouth to say something. Only one word came out.

"If . . ."

Then he was sorry, took two quick steps toward the telephone and said, "Excuse me, I have to call someone."

Martin Beck nodded and looked stubbornly at the telephone. 018. The area code for Uppsala. Everything fitted in. Six figures. Answer on the third ring.

"Hello. This is Åke. Has Ann-Louise left?"

"Oh. When?"

Martin Beck thought he heard a woman's voice say, "About a quarter of an hour ago."

"Oh, yes. Thanks very much. Good-bye."

Gunnarsson replaced the receiver, looked at his watch and said in a light voice, "Well, shall we go now?"

No one replied. Ten long minutes went by. Then Martin Beck said, "Sit down."

The man obeyed very hesitantly. Although he seemed to be making an effort to sit still, the basket chair did not stop creaking. The next time he looked at his watch, Martin Beck saw that his hands were trembling.

Kollberg yawned, much too studiedly or else from nervousness. It was hard to determine which. Two minutes later, the man called Gunnarsson said, "What are we waiting for?"

For the first time there was a trace of uncertainty even in his voice.

Martin Beck looked at him. He said nothing. He wondered what would happen if the man on the other side of the desk suddenly realized that the silence was just as much of a strain on them as it was on him. It probably wouldn't be of much help to him. In some way they were all in the same boat now.

Gunnarsson looked at his watch, picked up a pen that was lying on the desk and at once put it down again in exactly the same place.

Martin Beck looked away and at the photograph, then glanced at his watch. Twenty minutes had gone by since the phone call. At worst, they had half an hour at their disposal.

He again looked at Gunnarsson and caught himself thinking about everything they had in common. The giant creaking bed. The view. The boats. The room key. The damp heat from the river.

He looked at his watch quite openly. Something about this seemed to irritate the other man considerably—perhaps the reminder that they did in fact have a common interest.

Martin Beck and Kollberg looked at each other for the first time in practically half an hour. If they were right, the end should be very near.

Disintegration came thirty seconds later. Gunnarsson looked from the one man to the other and said in a clear voice, "O.K. What do you want to know?"

No one answered.

"Yes, you're right, of course. It was me."

"What happened?"

"I don't want to talk about it," said the man thickly.

He was staring stubbornly down at the desk now. Kollberg looked at him with a frown, glanced over at Martin Beck and nodded.

Martin Beck drew a deep breath.

"You must realize that we'll find out everything anyhow," he said. "There are witnesses down there who can identify you. We'll find the taxi driver who drove you here that night. He'll remember whether you were alone or not. Your car and flat will be examined by experts. The burnt-out house in Hagalund as well. If a body has been lying there, there'll be enough left of it. That doesn't matter now. Whatever happened to Alf Matsson and wherever he went, we'll find him. You won't be able to hide very much—nothing important, anyway."

Gunnarsson looked straight at him and said, "In that case, I don't understand the point of all this."

Martin Beck knew that he would remember that remark for years, perhaps for the rest of his life.

It was Kollberg who saved the situation. He said tonelessly, "It is our duty to tell you that you are suspected of manslaughter, or possibly murder. Naturally you have the right to legal representation during the formal hearing."

"Alf came with me in the taxi. We came here. He knew I had a bottle of whisky at home and insisted that we should finish it off."

"And?"

"We had already drunk a good deal. We quarreled."

He fell silent. Shrugged his shoulders.

"I'd rather not talk about it."

"Why did you quarrel?" said Kollberg.

"He . . . he made me mad."

"In what way?"

A swift change in those blue eyes. Uncontrolled and anything but harmless.

"He behaved like a . . . well, he said certain things."

"About my fiancée. Just a moment—I can explain how it started. If you look in the top right-hand drawer . . . there are some photographs there."

Martin Beck pulled out the drawer and found the photographs. He held them carefully between his fingertips. They had been taken on a beach somewhere, and were just the sort of pictures people in love might take on a beach, provided they were quite undisturbed. He went through them swiftly, almost without looking at them. The bottom one was bent and damaged. The woman with the light-colored eyes smiled at the photographer.

"I had been in the bathroom. When I came back, he was standing there rummaging in my drawers. He'd found . . . those pictures. He tried to put one in his pocket. I was already angry with him, but then I became . . . furious."

The man paused briefly and then said apologetically, "Unfortunately I can't remember those particular details very clearly."

Martin Beck nodded.

"I took the photograph away from him, although he resisted. Then he began shouting filthy things about, well, about Ann-Louise. Of course, I knew that every last word was a lie, but I couldn't bear listening to him. He was talking very loudly. Almost yelling. I think I was afraid the neighbors would wake up too."

The man lowered his eyes again. He looked at his hands and said, "Well, that wasn't all that important. But it probably entered in, I don't know. Do I have to try to repeat . . ."

"Forget the details for the time being," said Kollberg. "What happened?"

Gunnarsson looked stubbornly at his hands.

"I strangled him," he said very quietly.

Martin Beck waited for ten seconds. Then he ran his forefinger down his nose and said, "And after that?"

"I suddenly turned completely sober, or at least I thought I had. He was lying there on the floor. Dead. It was about two o'clock. Naturally I should have called the police. It didn't seem so simple then."

He thought for a moment.

"Why, everything would have been ruined."

Martin Beck nodded and looked at his watch. This seemed to hurry the other man.

"Well, I sat here probably for a quarter of an hour, roughly, thinking what to do. In this chair. I refused to accept that the situation was hopeless. Everything that had happened was so . . . startling. It seemed so pointless. I wasn't really able to realize that it was me who had suddenly—oh, well, we can talk about that later."

"You knew that Matsson was going to Budapest," said Kollberg.

"Yes, of course. He had his passports and tickets on him. Had only had to go home and pick up his bag. I think it was his glasses that gave me the idea. They had fallen off and were lying here on the floor. They were rather special ones, changing his appearance in some way. Then I happened to think about that house out there. I had sat on the balcony watching the fire department practicing, how they set it alight and extinguished the fire again. Every Monday. They didn't investigate very carefully before setting fire to it. I knew they'd soon completely burn down the little that was left. It's no doubt cheaper than tearing things down in the ordinary way."

Gunnarsson threw a swift, desperate look at Martin Beck and said hastily:

"Then I took his passport, tickets, car keys and the keys to his flat. Then . . ."

He shuddered but collected himself at once.

"Then I carried him down to the car. That was the hardest part, but I was . . . well, I was just about to say I was lucky. I drove out to Hagalund."

"To the old farmhouse?"

"Yes. It was absolutely quiet out there. I carried . . . Alfie up to the attic. It was difficult because the stairs were half gone. And then I put him behind a loose wall, under a mass of rubbish so that no one would find him. He was dead, after all. It didn't matter all that much. I thought."

Martin Beck glanced anxiously at his watch.

"Go on," he said.

"It was beginning to get light. I went to Fleminggatan and collected his bag, which was already packed, and put it in Alfie's car. Then I came back here, cleaned up a bit and took the glasses and his coat, which was still hanging in the hall. I came back almost at once. I didn't dare stay and wait. So I took his car, drove to Arlanda and parked it there."

The man threw an appealing look at Martin Beck and said, "Everything went so easily, as if of its own accord. I put on the glasses, but the coat was too small. I carried it over my arm and went through the passport control. I don't remember much about the trip, but everything seemed just as simple."

"How had you planned to get away from there?"

"I just knew that it would work out somehow. I thought that the best way would be to take the train to the Austrian border and try to get over illegally. I had my own passport in my pocket and could return home from Vienna on that. I'd been there before, so I knew they didn't stamp the date of exit in your passport. But I was lucky again. I thought."

Martin Beck nodded.

"There was a shortage of rooms there and Alfie had been booked into two different hotels, just the first night at the one. I don't remember what it was called."

"The Ifjúság."

"Yes, maybe. Anyhow, I arrived there at the same time as a

party of people speaking French. I gathered that they had come earlier the same day. They looked like students—several of the fellows had beards. When I turned in Alfie's—Matsson's passport, the porter was just sorting other passports into the pigeonholes. People who had already registered. I stayed on a moment in the vestibule and then when the porter stepped away for a minute, I got the chance to take one of those passports. I only had to look at three of them before I found one I thought was suitable—it was Belgian. The fellow was named Roederer or something like that. Anyway, the name reminded me of some kind of champagne.

Martin Beck looked carefully at his watch.

"And the next morning?"

"Then I was given back Alfie's—Matsson's passport and went to the other hotel. It was large and grand. The Duna, it was called. I handed in the passport, still Alfie's, at the reception desk and put his bag up in the room. I didn't stay longer than half an hour. Then I left. I'd got hold of a map and made my way to the railway station. On the way, I discovered I still had the room key in my pocket. It was large and a nuisance, so I threw it down outside a police station as I was walking past. I thought it was a good idea."

"Not especially," said Kollberg.

Gunnarsson smiled faintly.

"I managed to catch the express to Vienna and it took only four hours. First I took off Alfie's glasses, of course, and rolled up the coat. At that point I used the Belgian passport and that worked just as well. The train was very crowded and the passport officer was in a hurry. It was a girl, by the way. In Vienna, I took a taxi from the Eastern Railway Station directly to the airport and got on the afternoon plane to Stockholm."

"What did you do with Roeder's passport?" said Martin Beck.

"Tore it up and flushed the pieces down a toilet at the Eastern Railway Station. The glasses too. I smashed the glass and broke up the frames."

"And his coat?"

"I hung that up on a hook in the cafeteria on the station."

"And by the evening you were back here again?"

"Yes, I went up to the office then and handed in two articles I'd written earlier."

It was silent in the room. Finally Martin Beck said, "Did you try the bed?"

"Where?"

"At the Duna?"

"Yes. It creaked."

Gunnarsson looked down at his hands again. Then he said quietly, "I was in a very difficult situation. Not only for myself."

He looked quickly at the photograph.

"If nothing untoward had happened, I would have got married on Sunday. And . . ."

"Yes?"

"Actually it was an accident. Can you understand . . ."

"Yes," said Martin Beck.

Kollberg had hardly moved during the last hour. Now he suddenly shrugged his shoulders and said irritably, "O.K. Come on, let's go."

The man who had killed Alf Matsson suddenly sagged.

"Yes, of course," he said thickly. "I'm sorry."

He rose quickly and went out to the bathroom. Neither of the other two men moved, but Martin Beck looked unhappily at the closed door. Kollberg followed his look and said, "There's nothing in there he can hurt himself with. I've even taken away the toothbrush glass."

"There was a box of sleeping pills on the night table. Twenty-five in it, at least."

Kollberg went into the bedroom and came back.

"It's gone," he said.

He looked at the bathroom door.

"Shall we—"

"No," said Martin Beck. "We'll wait."

They did not need to wait more than thirty seconds. Åke Gunnarsson came out unbidden. He smiled weakly and said, "Can we go now?"

No one answered him. Kollberg went into the bathroom, got up on the toilet, lifted the lid of the tank, thrust his hand down and pulled out the empty pillbox. He read the label on it as he walked back into the study.

"Vesperax," he said. "A dangerous sort."

Then he looked at Gunnarsson and said in a troubled voice, "That was rather unnecessary, wasn't it? Now we've got to take you to the hospital. They'll put a bib on you which reaches all the way down to your feet and then they stick a rubber tube down your throat. Tomorrow you won't be able to eat or talk."

Martin Beck phoned for a radio car.

They walked swiftly down the stairs, all driven by the same wish to get away quickly.

The radio car was already there.

"Stomach-pump case," said Kollberg. "It's quite urgent. We'll follow you."

When Gunnarsson was already seated in the car, Kollberg seemed to remember something. He held the door open for a moment and said, "When you went from the hotel to the train, did you go to the wrong station at first?"

The man who had killed Alf Matsson looked at him with eyes that had already begun to look glazed and unnatural.

"Yes. How did you know that?"

Kollberg shut the door. The car drove away. The policeman at the wheel switched on the siren at the first corner.

Policemen in gray overalls were moving carefully among heaps of ash and charred beams on the site of the burnt-out house. A small group of Sunday walkers with baby carriages and pastry cartons had gathered outside the roped-off area and were staring inquisitively. It was already past four o'clock.

As soon as Martin Beck and Kollberg got out of the car, Stenström detached himself from a group of policemen and came over to them.

"You were right," he said. "He's in there, but there isn't much left of him."

An hour later they were again on their way into the city. As they passed the old city limit Kollberg said, "In a week the firm that is building there would have driven over it all with a bulldozer."

Martin Beck nodded.

"He did his best," said Kollberg philosophically. "And it wasn't that bad. If he'd known a little more about Matsson, and gone to the trouble of looking to see what was in the bag, and left the plane in Copenhagen instead of taking the risk of rubbing things out in his passport . . ."

He left the sentence unfinished. Martin Beck looked at him sideways.

"Then what? Do you mean he might have got away with it?"

"No," said Kollberg. "Of course not."

Despite the debatable summer weather, there were crowds of people at Vanadis Baths. As they passed it, Kollberg cleared his throat and said, "I don't see why you should go on with this any longer. Why, you're supposed to be on holiday."

Martin Beck looked at his watch. He would not have time to get out to the island today.

"You can drop me at Odengatan," he said.

Kollberg stopped in front of a movie theater on the corner.

"G'by, then," he said.

"Bye."

They did not even shake hands. Martin Beck stood on the pavement watching the car drive away. Then he walked diagonally across the street, around the corner and into a restaurant there, the Metropole. The lighting in the bar was subdued and pleasant and at one of the corner tables a low-keyed conversation was going on.

He sat down at the bar.

"Whisky," he said.

The barman was a large man with calm eyes, swift movements and a snow-white jacket.

"Icewater?"

"Yes, why not?"

"Right," said the barman. "Great. Double whisky with icewater. Can't be beat."

Martin Beck stayed on the bar stool for four hours. He did not speak again, but now and again pointed at his glass. The man in the white jacket did not say anything either. It was better that way.

Martin Beck looked at his own face in the smoky mirror behind the row of bottles. When the image began to blur, he called for a taxi and went home. He began to undress while he was still in the hall.

30

Martin Beck woke up with a start from a deep and dreamless sleep. The blanket and sheet had fallen to the floor and he was cold. When he got up to shut the balcony door, he saw stars before his eyes. His head thumped and his mouth felt stiff and dry. He went out into the bathroom and with difficulty swallowed two anodyne tablets, which he rinsed down with a tumbler of water. Then he went back to bed, pulled the sheet and blanket over him and tried to go back to sleep. After a couple hours half-sleep filled with nightmares, he got up and stood under the shower for a long time before dressing slowly. Then he went out onto the balcony and stood there with his elbows on the balcony rail, his chin in his hands.

The sky was high and clear and the cool morning air held an omen of autumn. For a while, he watched a fat dachshund leisurely making its way through the tree trunks in the little green arc outside the building. It was called a grove, but hardly lived up to its name. The ground between the evergreens was covered with pine needles and trash, and the little grass that had been there in the early summer had long since been trampled away.

Martin Beck went back into the bedroom and made his bed. Then he walked restlessly through the rooms for a while, putting a few trifles and books into his briefcase before leaving the flat.

He took the subway to the quay. The boat was not due to leave for an hour, so he strolled slowly along the quay toward the bridge. His boat was in and the gangway down: a couple of the crew were piling boxes on the foredeck. Martin Beck did not go on board but continued walking and then stopped for a cup of tea, which immediately made him feel even worse.

A quarter of an hour before the time of departure, he boarded the island boat, which had now got up steam and was belching white smoke out of its funnel. He went up on deck and sat in the same place he had sat when he had begun his holiday, scarcely two weeks ago. Now nothing would stop him completing it, he thought, but he no longer felt any pleasure or enthusiasm at the thought of his holiday or the island.

The engine thumped, the boat backed out, the whistle sounded out and Martin Beck leaned over the railing, staring down into the foaming whirlpools of water. The sense of a summer holiday was gone and he felt nothing but misery.

After a while, he went into the saloon and drank a mineral water. When he came out on deck again, his place had been taken by a fat, red-faced gentleman in a sportsuit and a beret. Before Martin Beck had time to retreat, the fat man introduced himself and let loose a gushing stream of words on the beauty of the archipelago, which he knew intimately. Martin Beck listened apathetically while the man pointed out the islands they passed and gave their names. Finally managing to break off the one-sided conversation, Martin Beck fled to the aft saloon.

For the rest of the journey he lay in the half-light on one of the hard, plush-upholstered benches, looking at the dust swirling in the shaft of greenish light from the scuttle.

Nygren was sitting waiting in his motorboat at the steamer jetty. As they approached the island, he switched off the motor and let the boat glide past the little jetty so that Martin could jump ashore. Then he switched on the motor again, waved his hand and vanished around the point.

Martin Beck walked up to the cottage. His wife was lying in the lee behind the house, sunbathing naked on a blanket.

"Hi."

"Hi, I didn't hear you coming."

"Where are the kids?"

"Out with the boat."

"Oh."

"How was Budapest?"

"Very beautiful. Didn't you get the postcard I sent?"

"No."

"It'll come later, I suppose."

He went on into the cottage, drank a scoop of water and stood still, staring at the wall. He thought of the fair-haired woman with the chain necklace and wondered whether she had stood for a long time ringing the bell without anyone coming to open the door. Or whether she had come so late that the apartment had already been crawling with policemen with tweezers and cans of powder.

He heard his wife coming into the room.

"How are you, really?"

"Not well," said Martin Beck.

MAJ SJOWALL and
PER WAHLÖÖ

Maj Sjöwall and her husband, Per Wahlöö, wrote ten Martin Beck mysteries. Mr. Wahlöö, who died in 1975, was a reporter for several Swedish newspapers and magazines and wrote numerous radio and television plays, film scripts, short stories, and novels. Maj Sjöwall is a poet. The books, together known as "The Story of Crime," remain one of the greatest series of crime stories ever written.